W9-AXK-318

BLOOD RED ROSES

Other Avon Books by
Margaret Lawrence

HEARTS AND BONES

Coming Soon in Hardcover

THE BURNING BRIDE

MARGARET LAWRENCE

Blood Red Roses

AVON
TWILIGHT

AVON BOOKS, INC.
1350 Avenue of the Americas
New York, New York 10019

Copyright © 1997 by Margaret K. Lawrence
Excerpt from *The Burning Bride* copyright © 1998 by Margaret K. Lawrence
Visit our website at **http://www.AvonBooks.com/Twilight**
Library of Congress Catalog Card Nubmer: 97-15120
ISBN: 0-380-78880-2

First Avon Twilight Printing: October 1998
First Avon Books Hardcover Printing: October 1997

AVON TWILIGHT TRADEMARK REG. U.S. PAT. OFF. AND IN OTHER COUNTRIES, MARCA REGISTRADA, HECHO EN U.S.A.

Printed in the U.S.A.

WCD 10 9 8 7 6 5 4 3 2 1

To the silent roses who leave no histories behind them.
Homage is due to our ghosts.

✖   ✖

By the banks of red roses my love and I lay down,
And I took up my fiddle for to play her a tune.
In the midst of that tune, ah, my love
     sat down and cried,
"O Johnnie, lovely Johnnie, never leave me."

—English folk song

PROLOGUE:
HOW SHE MADE GOD WEEP

*O*n the morning she killed them, the woman woke sweat-soaked and gasping, the corner of his pillow stuffed into her mouth and her wolf's teeth tearing it. For a moment she lay still, uncertain where she was, in what bed and with what lost man beside her.

Then she slipped her thin legs from between the sheets and eased herself to the edge of the sodden featherbed. The man slept like the dead, his face set and waxen, his long hands clutching the frayed edge of the sheet.

He had wept like a child when he came, and stroked her hair in the dark and called her "dearest," though he could not bear to look at her for shame in the light of day.

Suddenly furious, she spat out the broken threads and the lint from the pillowcase and went to stand in the doorway where the wind would find her and wash her clean. The sun was just coming up over the river, touching the pale masts of ships and fishing boats, restoring color to the blue carpet of a field of flax on the far hillside, lighting the steeple of the whitewashed meetinghouse.

She took up the money the man had left for her on the table—two shillings, it was, and generous at that. For each small thing she did for him—cooking, candle dipping, emptying slops—he paid her promptly. With bedding, it was the same.

I will pay you a sum for each service you do me, and from that you shall take what is spent on my household accounts. So you shall learn economy.

She went to the bed where he was sleeping and drew back the sheet from his body, letting her fingers visit him lightly. The skin of his thigh was smooth and soft as a woman's, and she bent and kissed it, found his torpid sex and made it rise to her.

"I am," she whispered. "See me. What I am."

How I break. How I am broken. How my jagged halves tear at each other and grieve.

When she was done, she laid the two coins in his hand and closed his fingers tight around them. Then she washed herself and dressed, and taking a splint basket from the kitchen, she set out for the great dark woods.

The strawberries had finished a fortnight ago and the blueberries in Triler's Bog bore as yet only a faint hint of greyish blue. The sky was that same strange unripe color, a cold blue for a hot month.

By midmorning the others were all at the haying, but she had come out early to look for wild raspberries and needed not go back till she chose. Though it was near the middle of July in that year 1786, there were still a few fine berries left at the sunny edge of the woods, and the deaf child at Two Mills liked to string them for make-believe necklaces when they were dry.

There was nothing she would not do for the child they called Jennet.

My daughter, she thought, and paced her footsteps to the words. *My. Daughter. Mine.*

She could lay no claim to the little girl, of course. They would never believe her, they would only tell more lies. The air swirled thick with them, like dust-motes in the sunlight.

She hated the sun.

*   *   *

The woman crossed the open space of the sheep meadow and moved on, into the dark woods that loomed over the little Maine village of Rufford, its shops and cottages strung crazily along both banks of the wide, gleaming river they called the Manitac. Where Blackthorne Creek emptied into the stream, the great wooden wheel of the Markhams' double mill turned night and day, now, sawing the logs rafted downriver and grinding the first of the summer's barley into flour.

She was quieter when she could hear it—less frantic in the long days of the northern summer, less apt to seek out the silent woods to hide in. In daylight she never lost the feel of eyes upon her, nor the echo of the cool relentless voice that questioned her.

Where do you live now, pretty Mistress?
Why, sir, I sleep poor in Dog's Alley, where the rich men throw their bones.

Already the day was hot and her breath came short. Sweat soaked her blue bodice and her thin shift clung to her bare legs under the long skirt of heavy homespun. As she entered the first of the trees where the great ancient forest known as the Outward began to rise on a granite scarp to the north and west, clouds of blackflies flew up under the skirt and stung her. But she waded on through the tall ferns, barefoot to spare her shoes, treading un-flinching upon sharp stones and brambles.

She was wild at the bone and very strong, and she did not feel pain as other people did. On the day the men came to take her from her burnt house, she had fought them all, clawing and biting until her nails tore away.

Sometimes in the slow dusk she paced out the rooms of that lost house, stopping to raise invisible window sashes, to unlock and open doors that were not there. To refill the painted tin candlebox on its nail by the kitchen hearth. To put clean sheets on her marriage bed.

She had made her husband turn it towards the east window, because she wanted the sun on her face when she woke with him beside her.

She had loved the sun, then, as she loved him.

He had been sweet and fond and his passion amazed her, for she had not thought herself a thing that any man could want. But she knew he did not really see her, how the dark, silent birds of her rage dived and struck at her. Once he was gone, she focused all her hate upon him, and in her mind he was greater, more cruel than God Himself.

And yet for a single moment, alone in the great woods that July morning, she forgot the hate as she forgot the flies and the heat and the raspberries she had come for. She remembered only his warm, hard limbs and the peaceful weight of his sex inside her, clean as a scoured stone.

The woman stumbled a few steps, like a wild thing that treads the ground for the spoor of its lost mate, and when she looked up she saw him plainly, as if she had conjured him there. He stood no more than a hundred yards ahead of her among the trees—her own husband, Jacob Ramsay, who should have been six years dead.

He might not have been the same man at all. His body had been lithe and straight and slender, prideful even in repose, and that, too, had altered; now he moved stiffly and his shoulders hunched as though God's fist bore down upon him.

His shape was half hidden by waist-high ferns as he hacked hopelessly with an ax at some scrubs of birch in a thicket. They grew a few yards beyond a tumbledown cabin; in the dooryard a boy of ten hoed a straggling patch of cornstalks and cabbages. The woman—Grace, he called her, and sometimes "my dear"—was making soap, stirring a great black pot over coals; it smelled of rancid grease and wood-ash lye, a heavy sour smell.

Nearby, a dark-headed little boy of almost three toddled half-naked, red-faced and wailing, dragging a tattered hobbyhorse made of cornhusks tied to a stick.

"Betsy!" cried the woman Grace. A solemn little girl

of seven came out of the cabin and took the stirring stick from her mother. She began to stir the pot of soap carefully, her small tongue thrust out in concentration.

"Well, then. Come, Noah, my love," the woman crooned. She sat down on a fallen log and began to undo the laces of her gown; she gave him her breast and he cuddled against her, his small, eager hands pressing her belly greedily as he took her milk. "There, now," she said softly, and kissed his fine brown hair. As he suckled she began to sing tunelessly, the words of an old catch.

> *The hart, he loves the high wood,*
> *The hare, he loves the hill,*
> *The knight, he loves the lady,*
> *Who loves against her will.*

That child is my child, thought the watcher. *You have hidden him here all these years. You have taken all the children that should have been mine.*

She felt very light, weightless, and she looked from a great distance at them, through the long lens of her rage. Inside her, the muscle of her heart knotted itself hard and tore away from the cave of her chest and left her husked like a locust-pod from which the desperate insect is long gone.

She was no more a woman, nor anything human. She looked up at the ice-blue sky where God was laughing, and then at the woman called Grace, and at the children and the man.

"I should have eaten your heart on my wedding day," she said aloud.

But nobody heard her, and she did not know if she spoke to her husband or to God.

Then she left them and went deeper into the woods, higher, up a narrow path to the bluff above the cabin, where she had made her grave.

My dower, she called it. *My property.*

It was not far from the small patch of marshy ground where the wood ducks nested and the berries grew, at the foot of a lone sugar maple. In truth, it was more a shallow trench than a grave, for she had had only her hands to dig with.

Sometimes she took things from the houses she visited, and these she kept in the trench, wrapped in a fold of oilskin: a leatherbound book, though she could not read; a bird carved from birch wood; an embroidered lawn kerchief like her own mother's, black-edged for sorrow.

When she had picked a pint or two of the raspberries that grew in the sunniest parts of the clearing, she took a small penknife from her basket and cut new, soft-needled boughs of white pine, sweet-smelling and sticky with pitch. Then she lay down in the shallow cradle of her grave and pulled the boughs over her, over her milkless breasts and her face and over her wide eyes. From far away she heard a woman's voice again, clear as a flute, and did not know it was her own.

> *The cuckoo loves the summer,*
> *The wild goose loves the fall.*
> *The lady loves the blood red rose*
> *That climbs upon the wall.*

She did not remember afterward if she had slept, then, or only imagined sleeping, nor what she had done in that sleep.

When she came to herself, she was running, running, running, naked through the woods, down the steep path from the bluff. Wild things scuttled past her—squirrels and rabbits and foxes and nattering chickadees. She looked down and saw that she held the great ax in her hands.

Still, she made nothing of it. Even when she remembered their screaming she thought it must have been bird cries, for the children's voices were high and sweet like the music of birds.

Then suddenly the woods were gone and the sky was

gone and there was no sound but the wind rustling the long, spikey leaves of the corn plants in the kitchen garden. The crackling of the small fire that still burned under the pot of half-made soap.

She stood alone in the clearing, the ax gripped tight in her hands, its keen edge bright with blood. "Husband," she said aloud. "God! I am!"

But only the dead were there.

The woman called Grace lay sprawled on the doorstep as though she had tried to run into the house before the ax struck her. It had crashed against the back of her neck, almost severing her head from her spine. The second blow had smashed her skull.

The two little children had fallen together near the fire, a small bloody heap of tangled arms and legs. The stirring stick was still clutched in the girl's pale little fist and the baby's mouth and cheeks were sticky with his mother's milk.

The older boy had run, but that, too, had been useless. He lay on his face a few yards down the path, two fistfuls of dirt in his hands.

What else remained? The small bones scattered. The spilled blood that soaked the dust. The greyish-pink ooze that was brain.

She heard a great howl, then, come from the throat of God.

Ah, she thought, *I have hurt Him at last. I have made Him weep.*

The thought pleased her and she swallowed the guilt of it greedily.

She put down the ax onto the ground and left it there. Then she stepped lightly past the woman's dead body and entered the cabin. From the table on the far wall, she took up the razor her husband had laid there, still wet, with a faint cream of lather along the blade where he had neglected to wipe it. Carefully, touching nothing else that was theirs, she gathered the faded quilts from the pallet beds and took them out into the dooryard and covered the dead to keep the blackflies from them, weighting the corners with stones and pieces of firewood so the young foxes and the ravens could not pull them too easily away.

She barely noticed the chamois-skin bag lined with faded green silk, though she did see the gold pieces that spilled from it onto the ground. She took the bag from the dead woman's hand, then, and ran with it into the thicket, spilling gold coins as she went.

"Husband!" she cried again. "Jacob, I have killed them! I am free!"

But already memory was leaving her. Perhaps he had never been there.

After a time, she walked away into the woods, her naked body pale as the moon in the deep of the trees. Still she kept in her hand the chamois-skin pouch, empty now of all its gold pieces but one.

When she reached the lone maple tree, she found her skirt and bodice lying neatly folded by the grave near the blueberry bog and she put them on, then lay down in the cold hollow she had dug in the earth. She pulled the branches over her and slept. And did not dream, for once, the dispassionate and weary face of God, her inquisitor.

Where do you sleep now, pretty Mistress?
Why, sir, I lie cold in Dog's Alley, where the dead men leave their bones.

✳ ONE ✳

THE SECOND JOURNAL OF
HANNAH TREVOR, MIDWIFE

12 July, the year 1786

I *write upon the first day of Midsummer Fair, these*
pages which are mine own.

A clear morn, and very hot. No rain this fortnight, nor
none to promise. The heat favors the new hay in the great
water meadows, which we mow this day on shares. Major
Josselyn bids us to a haying-supper at the Grange when
it is done.

I have not spoke to Daniel Josselyn since the winter, when
my long purpose of separation from him ended. I find I
am no Sovereign Island as I had thought to be, for my
heart claims me to some Human Converse.
  Love maketh a Fool of Pride and a Liar of Resolve.
  And yet I would not sell my freedom for comfort in the
arms of any man. It remains to know if the one may re-
solve with the other in some just balance. For the freedom
of women falls like grass to the blade of custom and law.

I am not with child, yet tongues will wag. I am told he
has come twice to blows for my sake in the town, and

dismissed One who spoke ill of me, whose Name shall not come in these Pages.

I know not what he has spoke to my Love against me. Though my daughter I send near every day to see him, I have heard nothing privately from Daniel these five months, except nine shillings in payment for my attendance upon his wife in April.

Shall send Lady Josselyn my decoction of gold-thread and sumac berries, which may give her some addition of strength, for which I do pray. Though in truth I have little hope of her. Her monthly courses last now some three weeks instead of one, and I have much ado to halt them with parsley and burnet root.

Have gone these two days for nothing to wait upon the delivery of Molly Bacon, who is three weeks past her time. If I be summoned again to no purpose, the chit may have her babe with a mare for midwife, for I shall not come myself!

Am paid at length six shillings from the delivery of Mrs. Pitt, who does cleverly, and her son Jabez the same. As a gift, a fine mourning kerchief worked with black silk upon the border, my own name and my husband's in crosses.

Have folded the kerchief away till I may pick out the work and devise some other. I wear no blacks for him and I will not play the grieving widow, for in my heart I rejoice that James Trevor is dead.

Yesterday weeded some in my rue and lovage. Cut five pounds sage from the bed next the springhouse and thinned the onions. My Cousin Jonathan brought us in the forenoon a fine turtle of some twenty or twenty-five pound, which, it being well hanged overnight to settle the blood, I will clean and put to bake.

To dress a Turtle for Baking: When you have gutted your Turtle and scaled Him, and taken his Fins and his Shell

*from his Back and the yellow Skin from his Belly, and all
the meat else is white and clean and sweet, then cut it
into pieces and wash them. For every twelve pound of
meat, make three Spoonfuls of seasoning, as cayenne or
black pepper, nutmeg and mace, pounded fine and mixt
with sweet herbs of thyme, savory, rosemary, and marjo-
ram, rubbed fine and mixt with the meat. Lay this in a
common basin of brown ware to bake it, and a quarter
pound of butter at the bottom of each dish, and layer the
meat with the seasonings and more of the butter to an
inch and a half from the top. Boil the blood of your Turtle
and put atop the dish and lay on forcemeat of Veal sufficient to cover the meat. In each dish put a gill of Madeira
and as much water as it may hold. Then break on the top
five or half a dozen eggs to keep the meat from scorching
and bake in an Oven of the right heat for Bread, an hour
and half or two hours according to the size of the dish.*

*This day I rose with Daughter Jennet before daylight to
stone the last of the cherries from my Uncle Henry's trees.
Preserved ten pound in the small crock and boiled sixteen
bottles cordial, but sugar being now very dear and our
honey still in the skips, shall dry the rest for mincemeat.*

*Churned also, and set the butter in the new fluted molds
of my uncle's carving. Most fine and pleasing. A Beauty
in Small Things doth steady the Soul.*

*The old red cow Bluebell does not give above a half-
bucket. Dosed her with a poultice of sorrel, which may
assist.*

*The landing horn heard yesterday at Lamb's Inn Dock,
speaking another vessel come upriver. The bark* Intrepid
*from Halifax with passengers, among whom a fine old
lady, very grand, and a dignified gentleman.*

*Have put in the frame these two days since my quilt of
Red Roses, which I name for my living daughter and for
my first children, Susannah, Martha, and Benjamin Trevor,*

*who are dead fourteen years this same week of the world.
For the flower bunches, my aunt gives her second-best bed
curtains. Faded at the folds, but shall cut to advantage
and use what is sound.*

*Mrs. Pinch the Hunchback tarries here till the autumn to
labor, and will sew me a new winter gown of the rose-
colored wool. Some say she is crack-brained and whimsi-
cal. But she stitches very neat and true.*

*The loosestrife and the Queen Anne's lace blooms fine,
and I make hollyhock ladies for my girl Jennet, with blossoms for bonnets. Though she is mute, she is loving and
quick of wit. I thank God for her and for my scarce-
fledged freedom, both dearly-paid.*

*God pardon me and assist me. I wish for another child
to bear.*

*I grow old, and time creeps upon me. I found this morning
six grey hairs in the teeth of my comb.*

*I do not sleep well, and watch through the nights for
lightning.*

My soul aches for rain.

TWO

The Rightful Station of a Wife

On that first morning of Midsummer Fair, halfway through her thirty-eighth year and free at last of the lingering illness they had called her marriage, Hannah Trevor should have been happy to welcome any decent suitor. Or so, at any rate, the Reverend Matthew Gwynn considered as he sat in the workroom of Two Mills Farm watching her gather the pages of her journal and put them discreetly out of sight till he was gone.

Gwynn was new in the town—nearly fifty, pale and thin, with fine patrician features many women called handsome. Hannah found him placid and a trifle smug, and she wondered if he did not suffer from costiveness; he looked as if a rhubarb purge and a dose of senna would do him good.

She smothered a smile with her hand and put on her spectacles for the sake of self-discipline. ''How is your sister? I hope she is not much plagued with the heat and the flies?''

''Merriam is of a fine, robust constitution.'' The minister perched nervously on the settle, his wide-brimmed hat balanced on his knee and tilting precariously in the breeze from the open door. ''Robust. And I— I should call this excellent weather, should not you? For the last of the haying, that is. '*Diffugere nives redeunt iam gramina campis.*' ''

Hannah sniffed. "Are you apt to speak in tongues at all hours, sir, or have you held yourself back until now for my sake?"

Gwynn smiled. "I did not fancy you would know the Latin, ma'am. But you have an eager mind. Do you read?"

"When the wind is westerly," she told him coolly, "and I have the leisure to sit down."

Like her beloved Aunt Julia, Midwife Trevor had been educated somewhat above her station and could read and write and cipher. She had a well-thumbed copy of Mr. Shakespeare's *King Lear,* and Daniel had given her an old book of sonnets he treasured, but study was hard work and there was little time for it. In summer, there was the extra bother of the vegetable garden and the herb beds, of hoeing and weeding and pruning and carrying buckets of water uphill from the well when—as now—there was not enough rainfall. And there was always some fever making the rounds of the village children, so that she must traipse to her patients on Flash, the old mare, or row herself there in the skiff till her arms threatened to drop straight off into the river, and then nurse and sponge and stroke and comfort, and sit nodding by a sickbed till dawn.

Through the open door, the laughter and shouts of the mowers drifted in upon them. Hannah glanced again in their direction, hoping for a glimpse of Daniel Josselyn, but the sun on the river blinded her. Disappointed, she perched beside the quilting frame and began to stab her unthreaded needle up and down in the carefully pieced pattern of angular, squared-off red blossoms and latticelike strips.

At last Gwynn summoned his nerve, venturing so close that his breath made her short curls drift. He smelled heavily of clove oil; it meant his teeth were bad.

"My dear Mrs. Trevor," he said softly. "Dearest Hannah. I am a bachelor. You are a widow. Surely you can guess why I have come?"

He laid a hand on her shoulder and she felt it edge onto the sweat-dampened skin of her throat.

"Let me fetch you some cold buttermilk, sir," she said sharply. "I perceive you are somewhat too warm."

Matthew Gwynn stood with his eyes closed, in a positive ecstasy of passion. Hannah could not repress a smile, and he bowed slightly and let her go. When she had stepped into the stillroom for the buttermilk, he sank down on a joint-stool to recover himself and consider.

Mistress Trevor was no girl, but she was still handsome. Behind the austere wire spectacles, her brown eyes gazed unflinchingly at the world, and though they bore in their depths a dangerous proclivity to passion, surely it might be turned to the service of God once they were wed.

What the Siwalls would say to the match, he could not bear to think. He owed them his new pulpit, and Madam Siwall would not take kindly to any proposal made without her advice. She was a distant cousin on his mother's side, and but for her he would still be seeking a place.

Yet he *could* not forbear. His hopes were pinned upon Hannah Trevor, whatever his sober judgment said.

She had, he was told, no money of her own for dowry. But the Markhams were prosperous and generous folk. No doubt her uncle would settle a comfortable sum upon her, should she marry again.

Matthew Gwynn needed a woman desperate enough to marry even a penniless clergyman, and he needed money even more.

"Thank— Thank you," he stammered, taking the mug of buttermilk from her and sipping it gratefully. "The day is very warm. Very warm, indeed. Is your—your—"

"They are all gone to the haying," Hannah told him, a wicked half smile still lurking at the corners of her mouth and her dark eyes crinkled with amusement. "I should be there myself, but for finishing the cordial. My daughter, too, has gone with them."

She knew it was the chief disadvantage. Jennet, her daughter.

Hannah's husband, James, had been driven from Rufford for his Loyalist opinions in January of 1778, and Jenny was born a month at least beyond the proper time if Trevor had really been the father. The gossips and the tavern wags all said the child was Daniel Josselyn's bastard, and the rumors had taken a nasty edge after the pair had been caught in the woods to wait out a blizzard in the February past.

But it was foolish talk, Gwynn was sure of it. Josselyn seemed devoted to his ailing wife, and Hannah was perfectly modest. Had she not blushed when he ventured with her just now? Surely, surely there was nothing in it.

"I am told a vessel is come in yesterday from Halifax," she said suddenly, looking out the open door again as she stoppered the bottles of cordial. "With a lady passenger set on shore in a sedan chair and taken to Mapleton Grange."

The Grange. Daniel Josselyn's fine manor. A chill breeze struck Matthew Gwynn's ardor.

"She is Lady Sibylla Josselyn," he snapped. "The sister of Major Josselyn's grandfather, old Lord Bensbridge who is dead. Have you some particular interest in events at the Grange, Mrs. Trevor?"

"Oh, most particular," she replied, laughing. "For I have not seen a sedan chair since I lived with my husband in Boston, before the War. I expect hers is very fine. Were the bearers in livery?"

"I take no account of such vanities. I must go." Gwynn stood up abruptly, then paused again, reaching into his pocket. "But here. I had almost forgot your post, ma'am."

He laid two letters on the table, both folded and sealed at the edge. For a moment he stood in the doorway, undecided. Then he reached into his pocket again and took out a small parcel wrapped in brown paper and tied with string. He smiled awkwardly, and his face was suddenly boyish and soft, a lock of blond hair falling across his eyes. "I was walking through the fair this morning, and I hoped— Please accept it. A token of my regard."

Hannah cut the string and two small lengths of ribbon came tumbling out of the packet. It was poor stuff but of a handsome color, a clear rich claret red.

She looked up at him, smiling with pleasure this time. Midwife Trevor wore no widow's cap despite—or because of—all her aunt's pleadings, her thick ash-brown curls cut short as a boy's and bleached by the summer sun to a strange warm color that blended with the honey-brown of her tanned skin and made her seem all one thing, hair and flesh and bones all modeled from the same mellow piece of the secret world.

Suddenly Gwynn dropped to his knees on the floor, his arms clasping Hannah's calves and his lips on the hem of her gown.

"What comedy do you play, sir?" she said quietly. "Get up, before you soil your fine stockings on the floor."

She pulled away and stepped back, scarcely disarranging the folds of her skirt. This silly business had nothing to do with her; it was a scene he had read in some novel, poor thing. *Pamela,* or *Virtue Rewarded.*

Hannah went to the hearth and bent over a kettle simmering on the raked coals.

"I offer you the rightful station of a wife," Gwynn said in a chilly voice. He stood up, brushing the sand from his breeches. "It is more than you can hope from Daniel Josselyn."

"And what has he to do with me?" Hannah's face was calm as before, but her hand on the pot ladle shook slightly.

Gwynn noted it and felt encouraged. He struck harder this time.

"Perhaps the reports are untrue," he said. "But I shall not reproach you or the child once we are wed. The woman taken in adultery found forgiveness in the eyes of God."

Hannah put down the ladle on the dripping tray and wiped her hands on a towel.

"I do wonder that you should wish to marry at all, sir,"

she said pleasantly. "For you live so snug in God's vest-pocket, and surely there is not room enough for two."

Gwynn picked up his hat from the settle. "Only pray for His direction," he said. "I will speak to you again."

He was almost out the door when Hannah noticed the lengths of ribbon spilled across the tabletop.

"Here," she said suddenly. "Take these again. Frills never suit me, and the shade would not do for my daughter." She paused for a fraction of a second, and smiled. "Jennet has her father's coloring."

When he passed the mill pond, Matthew Gwynn held the soft, fraying lengths of satin ribbon out until the wind took them and sailed them onto the bright water. They floated for a moment there, red against pewter, before they soaked through and sank.

Daniel Josselyn's hair and Jennet's were the same soft shade of reddish brown. It was as good as a confession. But perhaps she had only been teasing him. Women in courtship were fond of such games.

THREE

The Man Who Could Not Mow

Nearly forty people had come to cut the last great field of hay, from a dozen small farms and cottages along the river as well as from the Grange itself. They had brought their hired men and girls and their wives and children and horses and dogs and baskets of new bread and cold ham and roasting ears and pickled onions and cherry pie and worn quilts to spread them on.

Jacob Bull had brought along his drum and Blind Patrick his tin whistle, and as they played the mowers' strokes paced themselves subtly to the old tunes—"Yankee Doodle," "The Maid in the Foggy Dew," "Let Simon's Beard Alone"—so that it was, after all, far more than a task to be finished before the dancing could begin.

Indeed, thought Daniel Josselyn as he leaned on his scythe at the top of the rise, the mowing itself was a strange sort of dance, partnerless except for sky and air and the sweet, high, secret grass.

Oxcarts lumbered up and down the two adjacent fields, come to collect each family's share of last month's cutting, which was already dried, ricked, and bundled for stacking in lofts and mows at home. The field might be Daniel's, but they owned the grass in common, as it owned them.

The day's cutting began at the top of the slope nearest the house and worked down to the river. The old men went first, wading in the long ripe hay almost to their armpits as they cut a wide swath with the big scythes. Strong old men, they were, with faces burnt by so many summers that the sun lived all winter in their bones. The younger fellows held back and followed them, timing themselves to the swinging blades that rocked like cradles as the old men's bodies swayed from side to side, cutting clean and laying the grass in perfect windrows.

Behind them came the women, raking the newmown hay into low ricks, then moving on. At the high end of the field, Daniel's own dry stacks were taking shape from the unloading carts—three great shaggy mounds, each laid tight and solid as a mason's wall.

The children—Hannah's Jennet among them—dived in and out of the ricks, covered with hay, darting and laughing like delighted scarecrows at tag. And their elders, too, felt the ebullient joy of the morning.

"You been too long a-minding that mill, Henry Markham!" cried a red-faced giant with white hair in a thick braid down his back. "You can't keep the pace of a proper mower no more! Past it, that's what you be!"

"That so, Enoch?" said Hannah's uncle, his grey eyes bright with mischief.

Henry paused to mop his bald head with a corner of his smock; the mouldering horsehair tie-wig he usually wore sat perched on the newel post at home till the weather cooled off in the fall. He had another, too, far grander and kept for Sundays, an ancient grizzle wig of massed curls that hung down over his shoulders like the flapping ears of some exotic breed of hound. He had worn it to his son Jonathan's wedding a year ago, and to one or two funerals since. If the mice didn't find it out and nest in it, he meant to be laid in his casket wearing it.

Younger men had already abandoned the fashion and wore their own hair tied back or softly cropped, as Daniel did. But to Henry's generation a wig was a mark of standing; it meant you were a good, solid citizen, deserving of respect.

"A wager, then, Luckett!" he shouted, rubbing his

hands together gleefully. "I'll show you who's past it, all right!"

"Husband!" came a peremptory honk from the nearest stack. Then the shrill voice fell lower, meant for Henry alone. "Have we not debts enough, my dear?" she murmured in his ear.

Even at past sixty, wooden hayfork in hand, her oldest gown hiked up over a faded red petticoat and her eternal white ruffled cap peering out from under a wide straw bonnet, Julia Markham was a woman to be reckoned with. She had the face of a supremely intelligent horse, the figure of a good plum pudding, and the bearing of a duchess, and for thirty years she had been Rufford's chief midwife. Now her favorite niece had taken on the task, but the old woman's authority was strong among them and her will was not to be ignored—especially by a husband of nearly fifty years.

Henry beamed with pride in spite of the rebuke, but it was a joyless smile, at that. He *was* worried about money, and well he might be.

For the tax collector, Gabriel Bent, was come from the county town of Salcombe and sat this very minute in the parlor of Lamb's Inn, and a tax was not to be paid with a fine fleece or a prize cabbage. The new paper dollars they called Continentals had no sterling behind them and the army muster-pay was worth no more than four or five dollars the thousand. Most men who had fought with the Rufford regiment had a mattress full of the stuff, but the taxman could take nothing but hard money, gold coin or silver. That was the law.

And hard money almost nobody had. Many whose need had outstripped their credit were broken by the want of it; the Debtors' Jail at Salcombe was so full that men were said to sleep there standing up.

They had begged the General Court in Boston for sound money and a closing of the debtors' courts. Hamilton Siwall, the local magistrate, had gone off to represent them in the legislature, but it was also Siwall who bought up at cutthroat prices nearly every farm foreclosed upon in the county and grew richer with every poor man's fall. Nobody liked him, and if they had a choice, they would sooner have sent Josh Lamb or Henry Markham.

But just as under the king, only men of great property could hold high office. Dan Josselyn wanted nothing to do with politics, and no other man was rich enough but Siwall.

Henry Markham drew a deep breath of the hay-scented air and closed his eyes. He had borrowed a hundred pound from Siwall two years since, to add another stone to the gristmill and replace the sawmill's sluice gate. They had managed the interest well enough so far, but if Bent should raise the taxes, they'd be in a fine pickle indeed.

"Well, Harry Markham? Fish, then, blast you, or cut your bait and drift!" cried Luckett. "Have we a wager, y'old fool, or have we not?"

Henry considered. Why, hang it! Wasn't there more than one way to skin a cat?

"Now then, Luckett, my old dear," he said at last, with a wicked sparkle in his eye. "We shall mow down side by side, and if you come to the river afore me, you shall have my old Sunday wig for a hen's nest!" He turned to his wife and laid a big square hand on her arm. "How do you say to that, now, Mother? Will it suit?"

Julia peered at him down her long, equine nose. That wig was his secret pride, as hers was the dresser of fine, bright pewter in her kitchen; it would cost him sore to lose it. But she drew a deep breath, and met his eye and smiled.

"Your old Sunday wig, sir?" she trumpeted. "Why, that lamentable object has been a *moth's* nest these fifteen years, and the sooner it infests this old rascal's hens and not my best wool stockings, the better I am pleased!"

A shout went up as the match began and the two old fellows swung their scythes with practiced skill. But Daniel Josselyn, watching from the top of the field, was in no form for a contest today; his own blade struck a rock and jerked out of his hands as if some devil took it.

He had been seventeen years a British officer and then—after the Siege of Montreal—an American, and when he drilled his militia on Training Day each quarter, nobody ever accused him of a lack of skill with sword or musket.

He was no mean hand at the anvil, either. When he first came up to Maine to lick his wounds after Saratoga, unwelcome in England and nearly penniless, he had worked for his keep at the Forge, shoeing horses and making sleigh runners and plowshares.

Now, these eight years later, with the help of his grandfather's legacy, he had a fine house and ten thousand acres of timberland as agent for the Bristol Company, besides the home farm and the dairies. He had a library of books and a harp and a spinet and a sloop to take him twice a year to Boston and a fine china dinner service and more maids and grooms than even his wife, Charlotte, could want.

And what was it all but such a box as boys kept tame crickets in? A handsome box. A fine box. But a box.

He shaded his eyes and tried to shut out the noise and the heat and the smell of grass. There was a reason for his clumsiness at mowing; he had been waiting all morning to follow the figure of Mrs. Hannah Trevor as she walked down the hill path on the opposite bank, and she had not come.

His life turned always upon the sight of her—even more intently since the winter, for now he knew her heart better. As she went upon her nursing visits, Hannah was a bright fleck of color—her hooded red cloak against the winter snow, and in summer, a plain linen bodice and a homespun skirt that might have been dyed in the same pot of cochineal as the cloak.

She had been wearing the red cloak when he first met her, at the Forge where he worked. She had come on some errand or other, the smoke and steam like a fog between them and the ivory oval of her face appearing suddenly through it, framed by the cardinal-colored hood.

Her body, too, had been ivory when he saw it less than a fortnight after, by flickering candlelight in his small cold room up the stair. How she had come in so silently, so invisibly, he never knew. She stood there in the soft half-darkness, undressed to her shift and stockings and waiting for him. It was her breath he had seen first, a pale smoke in the cold.

Daniel had hesitated beside the door. He was covered with soot from his work and had taken no time to wash, too weary to care for anything but rest. "You know I have a wife in England," he said. "I will not abandon Charlotte."

Hannah padded barefoot across the floor and stood very close, so that he could feel the tremors come from her and know she was afraid. "I am cold," she whispered, and leaned against him. "Warm me."

She took his hands, then, and put the palms to her lips and kissed them. On the left, he wore a stitched-down leather glove, for he had been wounded and had two fingers hacked off; Hannah pulled the glove away and kissed the raw stumps and the scars and did not waver.

She undressed him, eyes lowered, letting her head bend so that her short curls brushed against his chest or his shoulder or the livid scar on his back where a musket ball had caught him. She brought a pan of coals and heated water, then made him sit shivering while she washed the smoke and dirt from him.

For the first time since the War began, Daniel felt as she touched him that he was safe in some deep place, that he would live in spite of himself, and not drift away and die.

"You must not wait on me so," he said gently.

"I wanted to see you," she told him. "To know if you are true."

"Am I no more than what you see?"

But to this, Hannah did not reply.

When she had finished her work, she would have gone straight to the bed. But he would not have it.

"Sit down," he said.

Daniel poured clean water into the basin; he knelt down before her, naked as he was, and took off her stockings carefully, rough hands catching the fine knitting. Then he washed her feet and her long, smooth legs, letting the dripping cloth travel an inch or two beneath her shift to seek out the deep secret warmth that bore her towards him. At last he eased the loose shift down and let it fall to the floor and washed her shoulders and her breasts and her back. If he had done the same for his wife Charlotte, she would have submitted to his touch out of duty, secretly appalled.

And yet it was a simple thing, chaste and gentle, as he might have washed a child or a hurt beast.

"My heart," he said softly, and kissed her. But again Hannah did not reply.

Then he took the huckaback towel from the washstand and dried her, and she slipped under the quilts and lay waiting, watching him. Suddenly ashamed, he wrapped her red cloak around him and sat beside her. "Think what may become of you," he told her. "I'm not a man for one night only, and there's danger in that."

"My husband is gone now," she said, a low monotone he could barely hear, "and if he comes back, I will kill him. All my children are dead. They will take my house and what little is in it. I have not even shame left me. Only I'm cold. Please. I am cold."

She drew him towards her and the red cloak drifted to the floor. Daniel came shyly to her beneath the quilts and would have been delicate and slow, for it was his way. But Hannah would have no tenderness; her determined body rose to take him before he had time to think or delay, her still-damp legs tangled wildly with his own, her hands guiding him. Daniel tried to slip away from her unfinished, thinking again of the consequences if she fell pregnant. "No more," he said. "I won't risk you."

"God damn you," she said, a low growl through clenched teeth. "Please. Please. Please. Please. Please."

His coming swept over him and he was helpless, but suddenly complete and perfectly human and amazed, as though he had waked after sickness, surprised to find himself alive and in the same body as before. His hands stroked Hannah's face and her shape curved upwards to meet his own like the sweet bend of a longbow when the height of it took her, her hands clutching his back, her legs locked close around him.

"Christ," he said, and kissed her again. He felt a wetness on his face and thought she must be crying. But the tears were his own.

"You're not rocking the blade, sir," said the voice of John English, Daniel's steward and manager. He was big and rough-hewn, his grey-brown hair falling untied and shaggy to his shoulders. "Grip's wrong. Right hand higher up, like this. Now, then, you just try it again."

Bracing his feet wide apart, Daniel took a furious swipe through the long meadow grass. Then he took another, and another. It was no use. The cut blades fell in no clear row, and many were not cut at all, but only broken over.

"I reckon lordships wasn't made for mowing," said a voice from one of the moving lines of men. It was Isaiah Squeer, a sour, stringy laborer with a mop of greasy black hair in a queue. "But I heard tell of a rich lordship one time fucked a Tory's leavings, and he made a proper enough job planting *her*."

The men laughed; Squeer was a drifter, just returned to Rufford in spring, and he always had a pack of bully boys about him. It was not the first time he'd spoken ill of Hannah, and it had already cost him a job at the Grange and one of his front teeth. This time, he wouldn't get off so cheap.

Daniel's broad back straightened and the hooded hazel

eyes flashed. But John English laid a calming hand on his arm.

"I don't doubt you could lick him again, sir. But not here, eh?"

Daniel drew a breath and looked down the long row of women; Hannah was nowhere in the field and could not have heard the jibe. Julia and the hired girls, Parthenia and Kitty and Susan, were building a new rick nearby and did not seem to notice the menfolk at all.

Only hunchbacked Bertha Pinch, the traveling seamstress, looked up and her deep blue eyes found Daniel and knew him. "Good morrow, Shadow!" she cried. "I am glad to see you. For when you are crooked by daylight as I am, all shadows be welcome and kind!"

She laughed and turned back to her work, but little Jennet, floundering happily in the sweet-smelling hay, caught sight of Daniel just then and clambered out from among the ricks.

"Here, Childie!" cried Bertha, and tried to catch her. But Jennet was already running up the long line of mowers towards him, her soft reddish hair in its two long braids slapping her shoulders.

Suddenly she stopped. For a moment she studied him, wide-eyed and sober and secret. Then she raised her right hand slowly to the side of her head just above her ear. She cupped and spread the fingers and made a motion like combing her hair.

Since winter, he had been teaching her the Indian finger language, but he had thought the word too hard for her. Daniel smiled and held out his arms for her to come. *Daughter,* it meant.

Squeer put the cork in his rum bottle. "Aye, lads," he said loudly. "Lordships do seem better at plowing than reaping. And Tory whores breed little deaf monkeys that jabber with their hands."

Daniel let his scythe fall to the ground, then turned on his boot heel and strode the few paces down the field toward the bullies. He lifted Jennet onto his shoulders and walked on, straight past Squeer and his friends, the child's hands locked tight across his forehead and her small body warm and damp and sturdy against the back of his neck.

Jenny had his own broad face and regular features; the same wide, dark amber eyes that caught fire when she was crossed, even the same stubborn lock of reddish hair that fell across her forehead as she walked or ran. The sight of them together made it plain enough whose child she was.

The mowing-match broke off as Daniel passed. "Is the man mad?" murmured Julia Markham. But she smiled and slipped an arm around her husband's waist.

With Jennet riding high on his shoulders, Daniel moved on down the gauntlet of mowers. Some stared at their shoes as he passed, but many smiled, and one or two men—soldiers he had served with—saluted. It was a bold thing and a proud thing and it put strength in them to see it, for it was not a thing most would have done for a woman's sake, nor for a child's.

A gaggle of children and dogs followed them, laughing, and Daniel raced with them, winded and suddenly happy, almost forgetting what had begun it. Blind Patrick struck up "Green Broom," and the dogs howled and Bertha Pinch began to sing in a sweet high soprano.

> *Dear Johnny, said she, O can you fancy me,*
> *Will you marry a lady in bloom, in bloom?*
> *Will you marry a lady in bloom?*

At the river, Daniel turned and came back up the field again and stopped when he reached the bully a second time. He smiled, a flicker like the flash of gunpowder. "As you say, Mr. Squeer," he told the man calmly, "I cut a wide swath, but unsteady. So I'd advise you keep your distance from my fields henceforward. Lest I strike something you hold dearer than idle talk."

"Now there he has you, Ike, my lad! For there's nothing you're better at, you know, than being idle!" roared old Enoch Luckett.

He began to laugh, a giant's laugh that seemed to shake the ground and make the haystacks tremble. It echoed along the line of silent mowers, and they, too, began to laugh. Here and there at first, like scattered raindrops falling, then everywhere across the field—a downpour of laughter upon the sour pride of Isaiah Squeer.

He shouldered his scythe and marched angrily out of the field, a half dozen others with him—George Anson; the Penny brothers, Rufus and Simon; Freddy O'Neal; and old Ethan Longstaff, who'd had a grudge against the world since Noah was a common sailor.

It was said that one or two of them were Regulators, as they called themselves, and Daniel believed it of Rufus Penny at least, and of Ike Squeer too. They disappeared into the Outward for days and sometimes weeks, always near the time some fat shopkeeper's stores were broken into or a constable or sheriff hanged in effigy with TORY written across the straw man that dangled from the gibbet in the village square.

For what the king's officials and the loyalist burghers had been to them before the War, the new rich were now. It no longer had to do merely with a loyalty to England. Presumption, it meant. Money breeding money and protecting its own. *Tory, Tory!* The Regulators used it as a rallying cry, with a jaunty sprig of long-needled pine tucked into their hats for a badge. Some said a war or another rebellion was the only way to better things, and perhaps they were right. Daniel could feel it even here, a bitter edge on the hay-sweet air of the sunny field.

''By your leave, sir, I'll set a guard tonight,'' said John English, a worried frown on his brow. ''Dry weather like this, fire's a right scourge. And a sore temptation.''

''Arson? Has Squeer the bottle for it, do you think?''

''Got friends, don't he? Take on one, you take 'em all.''

''Then post your guards, John,'' said Daniel quietly. English nodded curtly and walked away toward the house.

Josselyn hid his face against Jennet's warm neck and kissed her, holding her so close that she began to squirm.

He swung her lightly to the ground and she scurried back to her game of tag. Hannah was still nowhere in sight, and the Markham women had returned to their raking— except for little Bertha Pinch.

"Where is the hunchbacked woman?" he asked one of the others.

Daniel had been born to privilege, but with it had come a relentless sense of responsibility. He felt, however absurdly, that he owed a debt to the likes of the little crooked seamstress.

"Where is Mrs. Pinch?" he repeated.

"Oh," replied Parthenia with a curtsy, "Bertha be up on the hill, by the cookfires. You see, sir? Just there, a-making of kindling." She smiled shyly and giggled. "Crooked or not, sir, she's a dab hand with an ax."

�֎ FOUR ✖

THE COMPASSIONATE NATURE
OF THE LAW

**Summons of Mrs. Lucy Hannah Trevor,
Relict of James Ramsay Trevor,
Esquire, Convicted Tory and Traitor
To Attend at the Orphanmasters'
Court, County of Sussex
Province of Maine, State of Massachusetts
Bartholomew Whinnet, Clerk**

*I*NASMUCH *as the Court of Equity of this County hath
received from the Royal Province of Upper Canada the
Certificate of Demise of James Ramsay Trevor, Esquire—*
AND INASMUCH *as the Lands, Accounts, Properties and
Moveables of the late James Ramsay Trevor were con-
fiscate upon his conviction in the year 1778, leaving
his Relict a Woman of no Property and his surviving
Issue without Inheritance—*
WE, THE COURT, *do hereby summon her to show before
us on the Thirtieth Day of July of this present Year
sound cause why her Daughter, Jennet Elizabeth, shall
not be Indentured hereafter to some willing Master of
Good Character until her Majority, in order that the
Burden of her Care fall not upon the People at Large.*

31

✖ FIVE ✖

A WOMAN OF NO PROPERTY

*U*pstairs, in the small, newly whitewashed chamber she shared with her daughter, Hannah read the summons from the Orphanmasters' Court a second time, then laid it on the pine table beneath the window.

The other letter the parson had brought remained unopened. It was a double fold of mushy, brownish paper clumsily sealed with a greasy puddle of beeswax. The writing was large and square, but not familiar.

To the Midwife Trevor at Two Mills Farm was all it said.

Hannah pushed it aside. It was more than likely a note of indebtedness from a certain Mr. Reuben Stark who had owed her money for some weeks, now. She had never met him, but she had tended his wife, Grace, and their children through an ague while he was off in the woods in early June. A very poor family, they were; in better times, she would have forgiven the debt altogether.

But she no longer had such a luxury now that the law had questioned her power to provide; the court wanted land and property as surety, and Hannah had none. She earned her fees from births and deaths and watchings, bought the few necessities she could not make, and paid the rest to her protesting uncle for their food and the use of the single room in which she now sat thinking.

It was cooler than most in summer and sparsely furnished at any time of year. Now, with the curtains and bed hangings removed to let in any hint of breeze and the few pictures draped with sheeting to keep the flies from specking them, the place had an air of transience. It might have been a room in some inn along the Boston road or even a ship's cabin, for all the permanence it implied.

But it suited her well enough, for Hannah wanted nothing she and Jennet could not pack in an hour and be gone, if need be. And surely, she thought, the need was now. She was not without skill, after all, and competent midwives could make a respectable living in cities like Philadelphia and New York, providing they advertised:

Mrs. Hannah Trevor has lately arrived in this city from Upper Massachusetts, where she studied and practiced midwifery for a number of years. Any Ladies choosing to employ her may send to her Lodgings at Mrs. ————'s, and may depend upon the utmost attention in the way of her business.

The summons from the Orphanmasters' Court was for the thirtieth, but the Boston packet boat came in at Lamb's Inn Dock on the fifteenth to take back mail and passengers. That was three days from now. In three days, she and Jennet might be gone.

Through the open window came the shouts of the haymakers across the river and the rumble of oxcarts down to the ferry. Hannah took off her spectacles and shaded her eyes to peer out.

A lone man stood at the top of the field, very still in the sunshine, leaning on his scythe. It was how she always knew him, by the deep and centered quiet of his bearing; even when his body thrashed and labored, he was still to the marrow of his bones.

Daniel. I am drowning. Can you not see?

Hannah seized Jennet's pillow from the bed and buried her face in it. She had washed the child's hair yesterday and the scent still clung to the linen. It smelled of the rose geranium leaves they used to store the soap, and of the vinegar rinse, and when she let her tongue rasp across the fabric she caught the faint salt of Jennet's sweat.

In Europe, Daniel Josselyn might have adopted his child to legitimize her and give her a fair claim to his property. He had no other heirs and would never have, for Charlotte could not even have him in her bed now, let alone bear him children. But here in free America, adoption of that sort was out of the question.

Passed off as James Trevor's daughter, Jennet was a Loyalist's penniless orphan; as an admitted bastard she would be nobody's child under the law. She would be owned by the township she was born in, and the Court could do with her as it liked.

Calmed by the fact of Daniel, Hannah let her reason begin to work. Had she not always known this dilemma might one day confront them? Ever since the notice of Trevor's death arrived, the demand for an accounting had been possible, if not inevitable; she had foolishly pushed it out of her mind and hoped it would not happen. Now it had, that was all, and she must deal with it.

The easiest way out would have been to accept Matthew Gwynn's marriage proposal; Jennet would have a guardian ready made, and the court would not quibble with a clergyman's providing.

But it was not only her daughter Hannah Trevor was thinking of. In the eight years since her husband's departure, she had lived through her own war of independence, and its secret battles haunted her yet.

Ah, how can I? she thought. *To be bricked up in marriage again. To be property under the law, and be used and ground down as he wishes. To say, Yes, husband. As you choose, husband. Forgive me, husband. Do with me, body and mind, as you like. And oh, if you wish to correct me, my dear, then pray let me fetch you the rod.*

Not all marriages were so. Her aunt and uncle, surely, were deep in each other's bones after almost fifty years. And Josh and Dolly Lamb the same.

But the law was the law. A woman surrendered her

name and took her husband's, and with her wedding her separate existence ended. As an independent thing, she was dead to the courts. If her husband wished, he could sell her into indenture and take her children and have them brought up by another woman or put out to work.

For Jennet's sake, Hannah would even have married Mr. Gwynn. But would he do well by the child? Merely to speak of her had made him crust over with righteousness.

And what of Daniel? She had already brought shame on him, so that he must battle daily for his own good name and hers. Would he not be better off if she were gone?

Hannah bent her face again to the sweet-scented pillow.

Oh Jennet, my flower. Find your voice now. Tell me what I must do.

But she had no more time to sit pondering.

"Mrs. Trevor, ma'am!" cried a voice from below stairs. "Mrs. Trevor, are you in the house? Oh, do come, ma'am! Molly Bacon's child is borning, and she's took terrible bad!"

While little Mercy Lewis, the Siwalls' servant, waited in the kitchen, Hannah gathered the tools of her trade— her timepiece and spectacles and instruments, the record of births and deaths she was obliged to keep for the Magistrate's Court, and a selection of herbal medicines. She took an ointment of feverfew, and a mixture of tansy, mugwort, camomile and hyssop, for soreness and strain. And against hemorrhages, the powdered roots of burnet dug from her own garden patch.

All these were in her basket as Hosea Sly, the one-eyed ferryman, poled the two women and the little riding mare, Flash, across to the dock below Burnt Hill Manor.

The house of Magistrate Hamilton Siwall was large and fine, with a long lane of pines leading up to the white portico and the double front doors, painted Indian red. But Hannah, as always when she was sent for, rode up to the back door and went straight into the stifling kitchen of Mrs. Margery Kemp, the Siwalls' housekeeper.

"Oh, Mrs. Trevor dear, I hope and pray you're not too late!" said the old woman. She dabbed at her red-rimmed raptor's eyes with a handkerchief that had—by the look of it—been doing dabbing service all day long. "Oh, you'll not let her expire, will you, ma'am? My poor nerves would scarcely abide it if she was so impertinent as to die just now!"

"Boil some water, Mrs. Kemp, if you please," Hannah said gently, "and steep these herbs for me." She laid the cloth bag of hyssop and tansy on the table. "Now, where is the chamber?"

"AAAAAaaaaaaooooooooow!!!!"

"My stars and hope!" sighed Mrs. Kemp, and dumped herself into a chair by the hearth.

"AAAAAAAAaaaaaaaaaaoooooooooooooowwwwww!!!!!!"

"Mercy, dear! The herbs, please. Quickly!" Hannah commanded, and marched off in the direction of the yowls.

At the end of a narrow passage, on a narrow rope bed in a narrow windowless room that smelled of stale mattress straw and piss-soaked linen after her long night's labor, Molly Bacon, the Siwalls' kitchen maid, lay sprawled on a blood-stained sheet. Her thick black hair was tangled and matted and spread across the uncased pillow, and her eyes were huge and dilated, her thin face so taut that blue veins showed on her temples and her throat.

The girl could not be more than seventeen, and she had been a servant, both free and indentured, since she was ten. This bastard would be her second. The first, she had had at fourteen.

On a low stool in the far corner of the room sat a blank-eyed young man who looked barely twenty, though he was surely thirty or more.

He was Jeremy Siwall, the spoiled apple of his mother's chilly, Puritanical eye and the pawn of his father's ambitions in politics. Intending him for a marriage that would consolidate old Siwall's power with the General Court in

Boston, his parents had bought Jem out of scrapes, paid his racing and gaming debts, hushed up his philanderings, bought off his whores. In the winter just past, he had been mixed up in a serious swindle that had gone wrong and cost several lives; it had ended Daniel's uneasy partnership with Jeremy's father. But no charges had ever been brought.

Still, perhaps it had sobered him. Just now he looked a frightened boy in old buff breeches and a shirt twice too big for his narrow shoulders, his brown hair soaked with sweat and great black smudges of weariness under his eyes.

"How long have you been here?" Hannah said to him gruffly, her attention on the girl upon the bed.

"Don't know. 'Twas yet dark," he murmured. "Jesus, ma'am. Will she die?"

It was no matter of dying, surely. Molly's case was, the midwife judged, more messy than desperate; the girl cried for a nurse if she suffered a hangnail, Hannah could witness, and besides, men always got liverish and histrionical at bornings.

But she let Jem stew for the good of his soul.

"Are you too weak a puppy to be any help," she said, "or must I send to the hayfield for my aunt?"

"Only tell me what is needed," he said soberly.

"Get some quilts from Mrs. Kemp, then. Clean ones. Lay a pallet on the floor there. Quick, now."

"But she'll die if we move her!"

Hannah turned on him. "Are you the father of this child, sir? Do you want it born alive?"

For a split second he paused, fists clenched. "I'll get the quilts, ma'am," he said, and was gone.

At all such times, Hannah was a calm, irresistible force and gave no order that did not further her purpose. While Jem was out of the way, she managed a cursory pelvic examination—a touching, the women called it.

The girl whimpered slightly and opened one baleful eye, but Hannah's hands were deft and skillful, and it took very little to discover the situation. The child would have to be breech born and it was laid slightly out of place, that was all, with one small foot clubbed back upon itself. No amount of straining was likely to shift it; the babe must be turned so that Molly could deliver it alive, and if it were done properly, gently, there would be no harm to the baby's soft bones.

Between them all, they moved Molly safely to the pallet, with even the protesting Mrs. Kemp giving a hand. "Should we not send for Dr. Clinch?" she kept saying. "Oh, do let me send for him!"

Clinch was the local barber-surgeon as well as the borough coroner, ill-trained and rum-besotted, too pompous to accept counsel and too thick-headed to profit by it. Since the night four years ago on which he had dismembered Charlotte Josselyn's child for want of the skill of turning it inside her—and taken a bash over the head with a basin from Hannah and another from her aunt—Samuel Clinch and Midwife Trevor had been less than the best of friends.

But she had no need to advise against sending for him this time. They had only just taken their places—Mercy and young Siwall kneeling to make a prop for the girl's limp body, Mrs. Kemp holding her hands, and Hannah squatting before the cocked, splayed-out legs—when the final spasm caught Molly Bacon. She was wide awake now, sounding far less ill than she looked.

"AAAAAaaaaaaooowwwwww!!! Aaaoow!!" she cried. "I shall die!"

"If you don't keep still, I shall drown you myself in a bucket!" Hannah snapped. "You've done this before, girl, don't thrash around like a codfish! Hold her legs open, Kemp, I said!"

When a child had to be turned, many midwives used a thin, cupped piece of whalebone, curved to the shape of the dilated womb and polished smooth. Hannah slipped it under the child's tiny buttocks and eased the bent leg straight.

"Now then, Mistress Molly Bacon, spinster," said Hannah formally. It was her legal duty in bastard births to ask the crucial question. "Who is the father of your child? Quick, now!"

"Damn and blast him, the rogue! He brought me a present of candied oranges at Michaelmas fair. 'Twas Jeremy Siwall. Aaaaaooooo—!" The yowl broke off as she caught sight of him. "Oh! God, Jem, are *you* there? Oh, Jem, I do love you sooooooooo."

"Will you swear it on him?" the midwife insisted.

"Yes. Oh, bugger! Aaaaaoooooowww! God! Oh!"

"Push, now!" Hannah grasped the child, her hands aligning it skillfully, easing the small body into a world that had no particular use for it. A son it was—a fine boy of perhaps six pounds, with a long, angular shape like his mother's, and Jemmy's mouse-brown hair.

"Do you accept the truth of it, Master Siwall?" Hannah asked him, as Mrs. Kemp and Mercy washed the blood and afterbirth from the baby. "Do you claim this child as your getting?"

For an instant, he hesitated. "I— Why, damme madam. I suppose I do!" he said, and his firstborn son took one look at him and began to screech.

It was a scene Hannah herself had not been forced to play when Jennet was born; Daniel had gone back to the War, and only Julia had been beside her. The crucial question had never been asked.

But something else, too, she had missed. She had listened in vain for the birth cry, and when her aunt laid the girl-child on her belly, Hannah was sure she had given birth to the dead. Even when her hands found the warm, slippery shape of a living baby there, it seemed to her an alien gift that had nothing to do with her own body nor with anyone else in the world—and was more precious, being only itself.

While the others fussed over Molly, Hannah went out to the well in the yard and washed, and when she returned to the kitchen for her things, she found young Siwall waiting.

"How much are you owed, Mrs. Trevor?" he said. He looked very pale, scoured clean—for the moment—of all his foppish mannerisms.

"I ask but six shillings, sir," she said. "It is my usual fee."

"But I can pay more." He smiled ruefully. "That's to say, Pa can."

Hannah considered a moment. The birth had settled her mind and focused her determination. "I want no more money," she said. "But if I might speak to you on a private matter—"

Young Siwall looked puzzled. "Sure you don't want Pa? He's in Boston, you know. General Court. Back tonight, I believe."

"Will you keep the child, Jem?" Hannah asked him suddenly. "Will you rear it?"

He considered. "Don't expect I'll be let, do you? Ma's bloody religious, if you take my meaning. Well, 'twouldn't do, black sheep son and so on, what? I'm no sort of use in the world. No money of my own, you know."

"But you have read the law."

"Oh, Pa made me, with old Napier, in the village. Nasty stuff, law. Bores the breeches off you. Napier's a sound old chap, though. Knows a good filly, too. Horse, that is. But do go on."

Hannah hesitated, uncertain. He seemed to take nothing seriously.

"I venture you're afraid, ma'am," Jem said at last, "that I ain't to be trusted. Oh, I do scheme and I do wriggle, and damme, I'm a devilish bad Christian. But why not have a go, what? Might surprise you after all, you know."

At this, she had to smile. "Very well, then. I wish to know something of the law where widows are concerned."

"As regards property?"

"As regards children. There is no property in the case."

"Ah. Nothing in trust? No present income?"

"Only occasional labor."

"Ah. Six shillings, what?"

"Can the law really take a child from its mother because she is poor?" Hannah began to pace. "Even though she asks no charity and works her own way in the world?"

"That's the devilish thing about law," he said. "Law can do whatever law wants, if it wants to. 'Specially with no property. What the world turns on, you know. Pence and shillings. Bricks and mortar. Pa makes a virtue of it. Grind, grind, grind."

"But it is absurd! My husband's property was taken from me by the Court, and now the Court will take my child because I have no property?"

Jeremy drummed his fingers on the table. "What you need is a guardian. Man to put up a hard-money bond. Trustee, you know. Have you no one? Your uncle or Mr. Lamb? Or Major Josselyn—"

"I am scarcely acquainted with Major Josselyn, sir."

"Ah. 'Course not. Forgot myself. Do beg pardon."

"And if there is no man?" she demanded. "And no property?"

"Then there's no justice," he replied softly. He paused a moment, then got up to stand beside her. "Or you might take another husband," he said, very quiet. "For, confound me—you're rather a dasher, you know."

Hannah turned on him, her eyes narrowed.

"Once upon a time, Mr. Siwall, I had a husband," she said, "and three fine children by him. Thanks to his tender providing, they died all in one summer's week. I will have no more of marriage, sir. I had rather be hanged."

❋ SIX ❋

MIDSUMMER FAIR

*T*here was a fortune-teller who wore a silk turban and a gold ring in his ear. There was a tiny little man who walked on stilts as high as a house front, and a dancing bear called Nicodemus and a Punch-and-Judy man and a singer of broadsides and a black man who swallowed fire and spat it out again like the mouth of Hell.

There were sailors and Indians and French trappers from Ft. Holland deep in the woods, come to sell their piles of mink and marten pelts. Black Caesar's wife, Tirzah, sold her willow baskets, and old Perkin, the button-maker, had hung up his strings of silver and shell and painted-clay buttons to glitter like raindrops in the sun.

In a makeshift sty of woven brush, Betty Garish kept watch on her father's black piglets; somebody else had brought guinea fowl and a dozen half-grown pullets, clucking and flapping. There were long trestles of ripe apricots and early plums and new potatoes. There was new-drawn honey and maple sugar loaves and cheeses and fresh eggs and beeswax candles and books from Boston, and blue-and-white Chinese cups to buy.

On the grass of the common they had whitewashed a finishing mark for the footraces, which were about to begin; at the opposite end, some woodsmen and one or two farmers and townsmen were shooting at targets for a prize of ten shillings hard coin.

"Meat pies! Fish pies! Buy my oyster puddings!"

"Oranges and lemons! Oranges and lemons! Seville oranges!"

"Great ale, small ale, elderflower wine!"

"Gingerbread! Raisins and ginger!"

And through it all, like a ship in a sea full of bright-colored flotsam, moved the ponderous black-lacquered sedan chair of Daniel Josselyn's great-aunt, Lady Sibylla.

Few people in Rufford had ever seen such an object as that chair, and indeed it was particularly grand—its doors painted with peacocks and Chinese pavilions in scarlet and jade green and gold, its bearing-poles polished mahogany with brasswork knobs, its windows hung with heavy crimson damask. Lady Sibylla called it Hobble, for without it she would have been forced to do so. Two aging footmen in red-and-gold-striped frock coats and powdered periwigs carried it—Jenks and Owen, who had borne their mistress from place to place longer than most carriage horses, and with greater devotion.

"Owen!" cried the old lady, and whacked at the roof of the chair with her stick. "Set Hobble down, sir! I seem to spy a business merits observation."

They were near the entrance to Lamb's Inn, just opposite the end of the common. Not far from the stocks and the rickety old pillory and the permanent specter of the gallows, a group of noisy, shouting farmers and workmen were gathered round a post driven deep in the ground. A dozen or more mongrel dogs snapped and growled, making feints at some animal attached to the post by a heavy chain.

"To him, Duchess!" cried the men, and, "Flash will have a piece of him next! A ninepence on old Flash!"

"Tyrrell, my dear fellow!" said Lady Sibylla, blinking owlishly in the bright July sun. She widened the crack in the red damask curtain and spoke to a plain middle-aged man in sober brown gabardine who had been walking quietly beside the chair, his hands locked behind his back as though they were shackled there. "What is it, pray?" she asked her secretary—for so he was, and had been for some three years. "I vow, sir," she exclaimed. "They are quite beside themselves!"

Andrew Tyrrell held a long-handled glass to one eye and peered through it. He had spent much of his life poring over badly printed books and now, at five-and-forty, he could not see more than a yard beyond his nose without a lens.

"What rural riot are these bumpkins about?" she demanded.

"Appears to be a baiting of some sort, ma'am." He lowered the eyeglass and shackled his hands behind him again.

"Baiting? But that is no bear, Tyrrell!"

"No, ma'am. Not a bear."

"And do not insult my reason by claiming it to be a bull!"

In truth, Lady Sibylla Josselyn's reason had never been subject to insult by any man. She was the only woman ever proposed for fellowship in the Royal Society, and though she had been, in the end, excluded, she was well known as a botanist of meticulous method and theoretical daring. She was nearly eighty now, a small, sturdy woman with a pile of snow-white hair laid in careful battalions of curls, amber bird's eyes with a hint of deep blue at their centers, and a nose that turned up at the end as though she were constantly sniffing the wind.

And so she was. Sibylla had known Boswell and given old Sam Johnson a piece of her mind. Alexander Pope had read her the opening of his *Essay on Man* no less than seventeen times before she would allow he had the meter right. She had named one of King George's fifteen children. ("Desist, sir!" she had told him. "You have now sufficient for a Christmas pantomime! Desist, before you are overwhelmed!") Handel had composed a cantata in her honor, and Romney had painted her portrait twice. She had fallen in love with her coachman at forty, and ten years later with a certain Benjamin Franklin, then resident in London. In her seventy-seventh year, Sibylla had read some poems by the fellow Burns and traveled postchaise to Scotland, with Hobble stowed carefully upon the roof, in order to meet the author and study his countenance. She had found his accent deplorable, and she could not understand three words of his together.

Besides, she was, she declared, too old to fall in love a third time. But there had been something in his eyes that made the trip worthwhile.

"Tyrrell!" she cried again.

"Ma'am?"

"The door, please, and your arm! I shall ascertain for myself what poor creature it is these boobies torment with such delight!"

The secretary bowed slightly and helped her out. Though she leaned heavily upon a glass-headed ebony stick, Sibylla's steps managed an odd sort of lightness, her robin's-egg taffeta gown rustling at every step and the ostrich plume on her striped turban headdress nodding. In the few years he had spent in her employ, Andrew Tyrrell had grown truly fond of the old woman. She could be difficult and imperious, but to her a man was as a plant was—beautiful or useful, a gift to the soul or a noxious weed to be rooted out of the world. All she demanded was truth to oneself.

Ah, thought Tyrrell, *that is a definition not so easily achieved*. If all his outworn and abandoned selves were laid end to end, they would reach from here to London and back again.

As the unlikely pair came nearer to the baiting, they could hear the low growling of the trapped creature and the high, excited yapping of the dogs. The circle of men had drawn closer now; their victim was almost broken.

Sibylla gasped in spite of herself when she caught sight of him, and her fingers tightened on Andrew Tyrrell's arm. She had never seen a wolf before, and this one was magnificent.

He was a big pale grey creature with a white muzzle;

they had chained him by his neck to the post and he was almost exhausted, his sides heaving. The mongrels had torn one ear to a ragged, bloody mess and ripped a great hole in his neck, trying to get at his throat beneath the leather collar that held the chain.

"Now, Sunshine!" cried a fellow in a leather jerkin.

"You! Bouncer, old boy! Ten pence on my Bouncer."

The dogs strained at their leashes, their masters scarcely able to hold them back. Suddenly the wolf dragged himself up, eyes wide and teeth bared, breathing heavily.

He lunged at the dogs and was stopped by the chain. Then he fell and lay still again, his chin on his forepaws, his teeth bared.

"He has a great heart, Tyrrell," said the old woman softly, and gripped her secretary's arm tighter.

"Jonathan Markham!" commanded a clear voice nearby. "Lend me your musket, Cousin!"

Sibylla looked up, startled. A woman in a plain brownish bodice and a cardinal-red skirt had spoken, a middle-aged woman with short brown wiry curls and spectacles and no decent cap on her head, nor a bonnet neither. She spoke to one of the target shooters, a dark-eyed young man who bore her some resemblance.

"I spy a wild orchid, Tyrrell," murmured Her Ladyship. "Do you note her? An orchid among these weeds."

Indeed he did note her. The secretary had not taken his eyes from Hannah for some moments. Sibylla smiled. So, then, a woman might still intrigue him. Tyrrell the rationalist was human after all.

And yet it was more than a mere admiration. His look singled her out most particularly.

"You know her, sir?" Sibylla asked him gently. "An old love, is she?" He had, now she thought of it, been eager to come on this journey.

"I have not the pleasure of the lady's acquaintance, ma'am," he said crisply, and turned his glance back to the wolf.

"On the count of ten, boys, have at him!" declared one of the baiters. "Five pence on Duchess's nose!"

"One!"

The dogs could scarcely be held now, and the men were drunk with their own power. Hannah recognized some of them—Phineas Rugg, the perpetual lounger, and stolid, hardworking George Anson, who did not seem to belong with the others at all. She caught sight of Ike Squeer and her eyes closed behind the shield of the spectacles, then opened again and looked away.

"Two!" cried the punter. "A count of two."

"If you please, Cousin," Hannah said urgently, taking Jonathan's arm. "Can you not put an end to it?"

Henry and Julia's youngest son frowned and glanced around him. Johnnie Markham was the town constable since winter, but he had never yet been tested by the need to interfere with his own pleasure or that of his friends.

"Now Hannah," he said under his breath, "for the love of God, let it be, can't you? There's no need to mix into it. It's only a bit of sport, that's all."

"Sport, do you call it?"

She seized the gun from him so fiercely that he dared not resist her. From the edge of the crowd, a man selling birch brooms watched them, his lips slightly parted as though it gave him trouble to breathe. He was tall and thickset, with a kerchief tied low over his forehead, and he had dark, greying hair that fell loose around his ears. Over the kerchief he wore a tricorne that might once have been an officer's; it had a military cockade of frayed scarlet ribbon and a narrow edge of gold lace braid around the brim. But it had not seen a hatter for years and the brim was unrolling, the fine felt matted and dull.

"Six!" shouted someone. "Seven! Eight!"

Musket in hand, Hannah moved quickly through the press of onlookers until she was no more than a foot from Sibylla and her secretary. The broomseller moved with her, skirting the crowd to keep her well in his view.

But Midwife Trevor did not notice him.

"Nine!" cried the punter, and a roar went up from the crowd.

"You, sir! Hold those dogs, there!" cried the old lady.

Before anyone could stop her, Hannah stepped into the center of the tightening circle of yelping beasts and walked toward the post where the wolf lay panting. His eyes opened and for one last time he dragged himself to his feet to face her.

A flicker of a second, only, she hesitated, the primed musket raised to her shoulder. Then she fired. The wolf fell dead on its chain.

The dogs barked wildly, and Isaiah Squeer and the others, robbed of their wagers, stood muttering angrily. Hannah lowered the gun and began to walk past them toward Jonathan.

What happened next came quickly, so sudden and from so many directions that she could not tell who began it.

"Death to all arse-licking Tories!" cried a man's deep voice.

"And shame upon whores!" a woman shrilled.

The first thing to strike Hannah was a half-rotten apricot; it caught her skirt and split open, the yellow pulp splattering her shoe. She stopped in her tracks, staring down at it.

"Enough!" ordered Jonathan.

A spoilt plum. A brace of rotten eggs. In her hair. Dripping down her forehead.

Andrew Tyrrell pushed through the crowd, took her hand and stood there beside her, feeling the charge of pride that came from her. A rotten egg struck his sleeve. Another fell short and cracked open in the grass.

Then it was finished, as suddenly as it began. Silence. Only the gabbling of the guinea fowl in their pen and the cries of gulls circling the wharf above the river. The clank of rigging on the ships at the dock. A sailor's accordion, playing "Lowlands."

Some of the onlookers moved away, their tails between

their legs. Phineas Rugg stood staring at a half-rotten potato still clutched in his hand, as if he had no notion how it had got there. George Anson's eyes met Hannah's and he drew the back of a sunburnt hand across them. Only Squeer stared boldly at her, sullen and unabashed.

Pelting, they called it. It had been a common amusement for idlers during the War, whenever Tory women did their marketing or ventured out alone to visit friends. But nobody seemed to be laughing now; they were surprised to find the old danger still there at their fingertips.

Jonathan disentangled himself from the crowd and came and took his musket back from Hannah, his eyes avoiding her.

"They'd rather hunt Tories than think about Debtors' Jail, and you're still Trevor's wife, is all. Better go up to our place now, and let my Sally make you decent."

He tried awkwardly to wipe her face with his own kerchief.

"I will be as I am!" she said, and pushed his hands away.

Tyrrell's blue eyes studied her like the page of a book as she turned and walked, clear-eyed and ramrod-straight, to where she had left her aunt's mare at the far end of the market stalls. The broomseller swept her a graceful bow as she passed, but she did not look aside at him.

"A great heart, Tyrrell," murmured Sibylla Josselyn.

"Hearts break, ma'am," replied Andrew Tyrrell softly, "and dogs eat them."

Already they had begun to butcher the wolf for his skin.

✕ SEVEN ✕

WHICH WAY THE WIND BLOWS, OR: WHAT THE COMMON-FOLK HEARD AT THE FAIR

*W*hy, Jamie Trevor were naught but a pimp, and he cheated me of ten pound at cards, once. Only I got it back, and I shall get more yet.

As for his woman, a Tory humped her and that makes her a whore. I seen a power of their women during the War, and they was all willing enough when it came to it.

I know what Mistress Trevor is, I do. Let her look to herself.

—Isaiah Squeer, Laborer

They be all coming home, you know. All them Tories that was drove out in the War. I don't know as I grudge them. But my Charlie can't come home, can he? They buried him somewhere in Virginia, I think, after Yorktown. Where be Virginia, sir, could you tell me? I'd be glad to know where he lies.

I have no house anymore, and no fireside. I wander and work, and winter with any who keeps me, as Lachlan McGregor does now. There was others before him, and he says they misused me sore. I was half mad then and I scarce remember. McGregor took me from them and steadied me, and he is kind and good.

I am with child now, and he would marry me, only I cannot. Oh, he may have the use of my body, for I scarcely live in it myself. But my heart wakes and watches and will not believe anymore in this world.

There be many like me, many dead women who walk about and breathe and work, and do not live. When we meet we know one another well enough.

—Mrs. Sarah Firth, Housekeeper
to Lachlan McGregor, Blacksmith

I threw no eggs nor pippins at her, mind. I would not stoop to such paltry doings. That she is a Tory is no matter, for Twig himself was a King's man when he lived. And of her winkings and grapplings and strokings, I say naught, neither, though I do know what I know.

But cropped hair and no kerchief and men's breeches in winter! I don't approve them. Twig, when he lived, would not have approved 'em. They are not to be borne in a Christian land!

—Mrs. Arabella Twig, Housekeeper,
Mapleton Grange

I say, take 'em all down, the rich buggers, for what we done to the Tories can be did again to them! We chopped open their doors with our axes and dragged out them and their women and stripped them, to show they was no different from us, see, for all their fancy clothes and their prating of honor. Some of the women we shagged and some we didn't. We drove them all naked into the river, afterward.

"Swim to London, Mistress, and warm a bed for the King."

Some died, I'm told, but that's scant matter. Caught the quinsy or such like, from the cold. Rich men and king-lovers and women is a measly, spindling, candy-arsed lot, on the whole.

—Jephthah Bacon, Groom, the Red Bush Inn and Ordinary, Father of Molly Bacon, Kitchen Maid

I was down the coast at Newington Fair a fortnight back, me and my poppets, and they'd caught a young Tory lad there, name of Will Giles. He got word in Canada that his old father was near his time, and he come back on the quiet to bid him farewell.

Well, they dragged him from the bedside and they hung him up by his hands from a ship's mast in the harbor. Give him the lash bitter hard, and not just on his back. His belly was red-raw, and his chest and his legs and his privates. He made not a sound, even young as he was, bless him. Never a sound.

And yet, you know, I heard him. My poppets, they heard him, and wept, though they are but wood.

They be damn fools for weeping, them poppets of mine.

—Francis Ledyard, Punch-and-Judy man

My brother went away up to New Brunswick in '79, him and his Jane and their little ones, but Canada's a hard land and Jed wasn't up to it. The young ones was near to starving, and his woman with child again.

Well, he killed them. Six children. His wife and the babe quick in her. Struck them down with a skinning knife while they slept, and then shot hisself with a pair of pistols, one in each ear. I blamed him at first, and did not understand him. But I think otherwise of it now.

Six winters ago, they come and put me in the Debtor's Jail at Salcombe. The cell where I slept held twenty-six men. We had no pallets, only straw to sleep in and straw to shit in and straw to clean ourselves with. My feet froze twice and I had gangrene. I've four toes on one foot, now, and but two on t'other, and it makes it pain to walk when the weather's ill.

And I thought as I lay in my piss in that straw, that if I had a knife and a gun and my woman and children by me that I love, then I should surely do the same as Jed, and put a clean end to us all. For I was no more use on the earth, and they at its mercy.

'Twas Daniel looked after my Susan and the girls and seen they had firewood and food. He wasn't so well off then, but he paid what he could of my tax and when I come out at last, he hired me steward. Siwall bought my own land for a third what it was worth, and since then he's sold it twice again.

It's that frights me, y'see. To be like my brother, and have no dirt under me that's mine. Land to put my blood in and feel my life fall down in the cold months and lie there sweet and secret as I shall lie in my good grave, and rise up in the spring. To lose hold of the earth and walk where there's no grass growing of my own planting—it's a killing thing to the heart.

—*John English, Steward, Mapleton Grange*

EIGHT

MIDSUMMER FIRES

*T*he day of the murders in the forest was Charlotte Josselyn's three-and-thirtieth birthday, and she spent it as she spent almost every other day of her life. She sat on the rose damask chaise longue in her bright, handsome bedchamber with a fine silk shawl over her lap, working an intricate pattern in crewel embroidery.

She made up the designs herself, and during the four years of declining health since the birth and death of her son, her combinations of twining leaves and fantastic fruits, animals and flowers had become more and more sinuous and difficult, as though she built of them a maze to disappear in.

When she married Daniel, he was an officer in Burgoyne's Horse, but more important, he was the third son of Lord Bensbridge, with six thousand a year, an Army commission, and a fine manor in Herefordshire. It was not a large fortune and he would never have a title, but it was comfortable and secure.

Of course, there were objections. He was eleven years Charlotte's elder; he was fonder of books than was fashionable, and his looks were not perfect. His nose had been broken in India and had thickened over the break, so that he had something of the peasant about his otherwise handsome face. And he never bothered to wear a wig, except with his regimentals.

Worst of all, he seemed to have little ambition and almost no taste for society. He preferred long, solitary rides to hunting or cards, and he was utterly hopeless at polite conversation across the dinner table. Still, he looked very dashing on horseback and he danced beautifully.

Charlotte was much spoken of as a beauty in those days—pale blond ringlets; blue eyes with long, dark lashes; a blush that rose to her cheeks at the slightest hint of excitement. She knew people of influence, and she might have guided Daniel's career to a general's command or even a life peerage, for society rather than service was the way such heights were scaled.

Only politics had been their undoing. Oh, men might call it justice or honor or conviction. But to her it was all politics, that wretched American war of his.

Daniel had written to her of his decision to leave Burgoyne and join the American side—a long, wrenching letter that took nearly two years to reach her. By then, however, the Army had already made her situation bitterly plain.

Charlotte had taken a house in London for the season and was dining alone when the footman came to fetch her.

"A Colonel Ashburton to see you, ma'am. Regarding Captain Josselyn."

She had thought, naturally enough, that Daniel had been killed; she went quickly into the drawing room and found the scarlet-faced colonel waiting for her, grim and furious.

He snapped to attention and bowed. "Sorry to distress you, madam, and so on," he said. "But it's my painful duty to inform you that your rascal of a husband has betrayed his King and his Country. If he returns to England, he'll be placed under military arrest."

They went through the house and took away all Daniel's letters, his medals, even the box of clothes she had been packing to send him. They emptied the bookshelves and shook out the books and slit most of the bindings, looking for evidence of treason. They confiscated his bank accounts, his shares, his house in Herefordshire, the grain in his barns and the old ewes in his meadows. Even Charlotte's carriage horses and her hunter, Halcyon, were seized and sold.

Daniel had invested her entire marriage settlement in trust under her own name, and it was enough for her to live on. Her parents begged her to divorce him, but Charlotte would not. How could she go home to them as if she had never been a married woman, and play whist in the evenings as she used to, and bear the condescending smiles of all her friends?

Daniel's British citizenship was revoked. He was dispossessed and disinherited. His father died soon after—of shame, it was whispered. Daniel's elder brother, Geoffrey, the new Lord Bensbridge, promised to shoot him on sight if he ever ventured to return. His mother mourned him and tried helplessly to forgive him, but only his grandfather, old Lord Robert, seemed to understand the turn of his mind.

"Have you read the letter, my dear?" the old man asked her as his sister, the formidable Lady Sibylla, settled a cushion at his back.

"I have, sir," Charlotte replied stiffly.

The old lady settled herself at the tea table and regarded the girl with a pair of hazel eyes as piercing as her brother's.

"Pray, what is your age, my dear?" she said.

"I am now six-and-twenty, madam."

"And when did you marry?"

"I was not yet nineteen."

Sibylla clucked her tongue. "Girls should not wed till at least five-and-twenty. It delays childbearing until the wits have settled and the blood has cooled. But, pray, do not have more than five. Be firm, and Daniel will defer to you. He is like my good brother, here, and knows when he is bested."

Lord Robert smiled. "My sister has an answer to every human dilemma, my dear Charlotte. But she is correct on one score, at least. My grandson has your happiness much at heart and must be deeply concerned for you now."

"I confess, sir," Charlotte said quietly, "I have not your confidence. His letter is all noble abstractions. I do not understand him, Lord Robert, and what I do not understand, I cannot forgive."

The old man nodded. It was as he had feared. The letter spoke vaguely of terrible things Daniel had seen, of horrors he scrupled to tell her or perhaps could not bring himself to remember and describe. He had written of them in tormented detail to his grandfather, and Sibylla, naturally, had read every word herself.

But Daniel could not tell Charlotte of the house he had stumbled across in a storm. He had found, in an upstairs chamber, the body of a pregnant Patriot woman of no more than twenty, stabbed a dozen times with bayonets. Tory raiders had cut the child from her body and hanged it from the curtain rod, and written with a burnt stick on the wall above her bed: *Thou shalt not give birth to rebels.*

He did not speak of the laughter by night of Burgoyne and his new mistress in a nearby tent, nor of the thirty carts of private luggage, nor the bottles of champagne and the French barber and the cut-glass decanters and the mahogany bedstead and the polished copper hip-bath.

And how could Daniel tell his wife or even his indulgent grandfather that when he slept and dreamed and saw himself among the causeless and disregarded dead of both sides—for soon after his change of uniforms, the opposing forces became indistinguishable to him—he would howl until the living men beside him shook him and battered him to make him stop?

Lord Robert had reached across for Charlotte's hand, then, and patted it and smiled. "A traitor, our Daniel. A husband who leaves you friendless and abandoned. Yet you scruple to divorce him. Now why is that, my dear?"

Charlotte's blue eyes opened wide and her slight body

drew in upon itself for shelter. "I do not believe he is a traitor!" she cried. "They say it is so, but it is all foolishness! Oh, sir! If he returns to England and offers to make some amends, then surely he might have his property back, and his commission restored him. Might he not?"

Daniel's anguished and idealistic decision seemed to her nothing but a willful indiscretion, like cheating unskillfully at cards and being caught in the act. Lord Robert glanced at his sister. Should the girl not be made to understand?

Sibylla gave him a slight shake of her head.

Let her dream and pout and embroider pincushions and pockets. Let her never know horror beyond a field mouse crushed under her carriage wheel. She would crumble like a teacake if she knew.

The hour was four o'clock, and as she did every afternoon, Mrs. Arabella Twig, the billowing housekeeper of Mapleton Grange, flapped into the bedroom with two glasses on a tray. One contained brandy, slightly warmed. In the other was a decoction of hops and burnet and Balm of Gilead—prepared by Midwife Trevor and discreetly delivered to the Grange by Susan, the hired girl from Two Mills.

Charlotte pushed away the medicine. "Give me the brandy, Twig," she commanded. "I will not take the other foul stuff tonight."

Tonight was her birthday, and she would have nothing near her that was part of her husband's lover.

"I vow, ma'am," clucked the housekeeper, setting down the tray on a cherrywood table with a piecrust edge, "I have never seen roses so fine as this year." She threw open the small window that overlooked the garden. "Do you catch the scent?"

Outside on the lawn, they were setting long tables for the haying supper and clearing the great threshing floor for the dancing to follow. Some of the traveling folk from the fair had come already—a gingerbread seller, the tumblers, the Punch-and-Judy man and the black man who ate fire. They had hung paper lanterns in the trees, the candles inside to be lighted at sundown, and there were torches planted all along the paths.

It was not true midsummer, for here in America they adjusted nature to suit themselves and Independence Day eclipsed all the rest. But the old ways still clung to them and though it was three weeks behindhand, they still must have their Midsummer Fair.

They had even built a great bonfire down on the riverbank. At home in England, in Herefordshire, there had always been midsummer fires on the hills, winking like beacons in the slow, greyish darkness. You could see them in the distance, hill after hill after hill, far away into Wales. It was an ancient thing, and sometimes they still drove cattle through the coals to scatter the light and bring good harvest.

As a girl, Charlotte had thought it a lovely custom. But the summer they wed, Daniel had taken her to see it close, walking arm in arm with her through the long, wet grass up to the brow of the hill they called Little Ben. To see the men and girls, bright-eyed and wild as they danced barefoot through the coals, the hands of each pair bound together with branches of blooming roses, white and red. The thorns bit into the flesh of their wrists and tore it, so that they kissed each other's blood away, laughing as they ran and scattering the embers in a shower of fire and ash.

Charlotte saw their eyes, reasonless and blind and a little mad with wanting. "What does it mean?" she whispered. "Do they not feel the fire?"

Daniel smiled and drew her against him. "Most of them are pledged and will wed before Lammas. It's an old superstition, to make the marriage fruitful."

They would spend this night in the open, making love wherever they fell down together—though he did not say so to Charlotte—and most of the girls would go to the altar already quick with child.

"It's horrible," she whispered. "Horrible."

"What is, dearest?"

She could not answer him. Daniel was not dressed like a soldier, nor even like a gentleman. His hair was loose to his shoulders and he wore no coat over his soft linen shirt. He was one of them, these shadowy people who moved laughing through the dark and were afraid of nothing, not even God's reproachful stare.

That was what frightened her. He carried the dark inside him and was alive to it everywhere, to the wordless, ancient, human root that lived in the dark earth and grew strong. And he knew, too, that it would shrivel and die in the narrow tunnel of bright light most people—including Charlotte—were terrified of leaving. He would pull her into the dark with him, and she would drown. Trembling, she turned her face away.

"Come, dance with me," he coaxed her gently. He picked up a fallen branch of red roses, twisted it into a coronet and set it upon her pale, soft hair.

Charlotte tore it away. "I cannot," she cried. "I cannot stay here. Take me back to the house."

"Am I such a terror to you, then?" he asked her, taking her by the shoulders and turning her in the thin dark to face him. "Why do I frighten you so?"

Charlotte did not reply, only pulled free and ran back to the house alone, a faint trickle of blood smearing her forehead where the thorns of the roses had pricked her.

Daniel came very late to their bedchamber, smelling heavily of whisky, and found her curled on the floor, her body wrapped in a heavy linen sheet. She felt him lift her up onto the bed and she thought he would come to her and make love to her and frighten her again.

And secretly, in spite of her fear, she wanted nothing so much as to love him, to forget herself and be free in her body like the daring, wild-eyed girls in the midsummer darkness, who walked through fire and were never burnt.

But Daniel did not disturb the armor cocoon of the sheet. He only stood for a while at the window, watching the last of the fires flicker on the hills and go out with the rising daylight. Then he went softly downstairs.

By the time Charlotte came down to breakfast, he had already left for his regiment. Relieved and happy, feeling a girl again, she went into the garden and cut a great basketful of roses and pulled off the petals to be dried for scenting the linens.

That, after all, was what roses were for.

"Close the window, Twig," she said peevishly, returning from her memories. "Roses have a heavy, mawkish odor. I wish my husband had not had them planted so near."

Mrs. Twig obeyed, but still she hovered. "I feel it my duty to tell you, ma'am," she said at last. "There's many as would shirk it, but I hope I may speak the truth, should it cost me my life!"

Charlotte frowned. These noble preambles of Mrs. Twig's invariably led to some fresh piece of gossip about Daniel and Hannah Trevor. "I do not wish to hear—" she began.

But Bella Twig could not contain herself. "They pelted her, ma'am," she said, licking her lips with the tip of a pink tongue. "That doxy Mrs. Trevor. With rotten fruit and eggs and I-know-not. At the fair this very afternoon." She pursed her lips and the mole on her cheekbone twitched with excitement. "Tory or not, she is a bold sinner, and what may be overlooked in the meek is not to be countenanced in the bold and forthright. They say that since the winter—" Twig paused.

Charlotte's eyes closed. "Very well. What do they say?"

"Why, ma'am, that she has hardly been out of your husband's company a single night these five months and is again with child!"

"Has Major Josselyn, then, a second self, so he may visit Mrs. Trevor and still sleep in his own bed and waken us all with his bad dreams?"

"No, ma'am, but . . ."

"Has Mrs. Trevor any sign about her of this child she is said to carry?"

"Such things may be concealed, ma'am! She is a clever minx!"

"Well, it may be," said Charlotte quietly, and did not argue further. Daniel often rode out alone in the darkness and was gone some hours. And Hannah Trevor was, as Twig said, clever. And strong, too. Strong as the girls who dared fire.

"And how did she bear it, this pelting?" asked her mistress quietly.

"Why, bold as bed-knobs, lady dear, as you'd expect." The housekeeper picked up the tray and began to sail toward the door with it.

"Twig!"

"My lady?"

"If Mrs. Trevor were less bold, I would not now be living." Charlotte smiled softly. "I beg you to remember that and hold your tongue a little. And Twig? Pick some of the roses from my garden and take them to Mrs. Trevor at once. I think they will suit her." Charlotte tilted her chin a quarter inch higher. "Take them yourself, if you please. But do not say they come from me."

✖ NINE ✖

THE SOLDIER AND THE
BROOMSELLER

"*O*h sir, I'm just bound on an errand and here comes a *creature* to the front door to speak to you! I bid him take himself off, but he would not, the impertinent rogue!"

Daniel looked up absently from the crate of books his great-aunt had brought him from London. "What is this, Mrs. Twig?"

The housekeeper sailed in at the library door, her kerchief flapping seductively and her formidable bosoms—the White Cliffs of Dover, the new boot boy called them—heaving so violently that little dust devils of lavender-scented cornflour rose from them. She bent over Daniel precariously and a veritable avalanche of chalk from the Cliffs descended on the red morocco cover of *Tristram Shandy*.

"I informed him as how you would not wish to be broke in on, sir, for I *know* how much solace your books bring you. Deprived as you are of the comforts of a brisk and healthy wife."

She twitched her cheek to give him an irresistible dose of her second-best feature, the small mole she called Nature's Embellishment, as a sound of footsteps was heard in the hall.

"There he is again, a-stamping about! He's a foul,

63

rough creature. I marked him a-selling of birch brooms at the fair.'' The housekeeper lowered her voice to a murmur. ''Shall I never get Harry Jax to fetch him a boot in the breeches, sir?''

Daniel stifled a sneeze and brushed the powder from his sleeve. ''I will see him. Show him in, Mrs. Twig, if you please.''

''No need to wax punctilious, my dear madam,'' said a man's voice. ''As you see, I am already in.''

The broomseller stepped into the room and took off his hat with a practiced bow. Daniel recognized the braiding and the cockade; but for the missing crest of three white feathers, the tricorne was that of an officer in the elite Prince of Wales's Own.

But the seller of birch brooms was no British officer, nor ever had been. He was grizzled, with long, lank hair hanging below the kerchief that covered his brow almost to the bridge of his nose, leaving his dark eyes to peer out from under a kind of escarpment of blue calico. The nose was thin and straight and perfect as Daniel's own was not, but the nostrils had been slit; usually it was the mark of a minor villain the law had caught up with somewhere.

Daniel ambled to the hearth and put his back against it, the fire irons comfortably within reach.

''Shall I not fetch Mr. English, sir?'' whispered Twig nervously. ''He is in the garden, I think, seeing to the supper tables. Oh, do let me call him, before I am off to Two Mills!''

Daniel turned on her. ''You go for the midwife? Is your mistress ill again? Why was I not informed?''

''Oh no, sir, only I was to fetch some flowers there, and—''

''Ah. I see,'' he said, relieved. The women at the Mills often bartered seeds and cuttings, and lavender for drying if the crop was good. ''You may go about your errand then.''

She sailed out with a frown and a sniff, and the

broomseller laughed. "Guards you like the dog Cerberus at the Gate of Hell, does that old lemon!"

A peddler educated in the classics? It had been meant to evoke a remark. Daniel did not oblige, but he studied the once-handsome face a bit nearer. "Have you a name, sir?" he said.

"Ah, I do beg your pardon. Major Josselyn, ain't it? Reuben Stark is my name." He peered at Daniel from under the fold of calico. "Familiar to you, eh?"

"No, sir, it is not. At one time, I knew several of the Prince's regiment. But no one named Stark. Perhaps it was after my time that you joined."

The man's shrouded countenance was impossible to read. He laughed softly. "You refer to my tricorne? Why, sir, I took this from a dead British officer at Ticonderoga. I had no hat. He had this one. By hap and by hazard we thrive, do we not?"

"We may," Daniel replied. "But the Prince of Wales's Own never fought at Ticonderoga. And nor, I think, did you." Daniel took a step in Stark's direction. "I am much engaged just now, Mr.—Stark, was it? State your business or else be gone."

The broomseller shrugged. "I'm in need of money, like most men."

Daniel relaxed, though the nerves along his backbone still jittered and jangled as they had before battles began.

"If by those words you imply a desire for work," he said tersely, "you must speak to my steward, Mr. English. When our first field of wheat is cut, in a fortnight perhaps, we'll need a good many men straight through threshing, and after that for the rye and the corn. But do you not move down the coast with the fair?"

"I travel where my profit is," he said. "But I have a woman, and she bides very near here."

He picked up one of the books from the floor and riffled through its pages, then looked up at Daniel, his dark eyes glazed like the blind.

"You say, Major, that you do not recall the name of

Stark. Is there any man hereabouts called Trevor whom you might know better? A man driven like the wind, and beaten and battered and cast away for the sake of a brave word in an ill season? A man of great promise and ill chances?"

Daniel's own eyes did not flicker. "We have in Rufford a midwife and nurse, a Mistress Trevor, but she is widowed. I never saw her husband. Otherwise, I know none of that name."

"Ah. The woman they pelted with rotten fruit today at the fair." The man's eyes narrowed and he took a step nearer. "They say she is a notorious slut and has borne a bastard to some great lordship hereabouts. Was it you?"

Josselyn's fingers closed around the fire poker. "Did she come to harm?"

"You are much exercised, Major. There is sweat on your lip and your jaw is hard-set. Now you want to taste vengeance, do you not? Are you quite ill of it? Shall I ring for Cerberus?"

The battle-nerves were growing more insistent. "What devil are you?" said Daniel. "What do you want of me?"

"Money, sir. Money. You have it. I need it. A man must provide."

Josselyn did not move, but his shoulders eased themselves a hair's breadth straighter, drawn up for inspection. "If you answer my question, I will give you a shilling. What harm came to Mrs. Trevor?"

"Oh, she is worth far more to you, is she not, than a single shilling? For ten, I will tell you and save you the ride across the river to see for yourself." The man smiled. "Besides, she is proud. She does not take kindly to pity. If she loves you, she does you an honor indeed. And we must all pay a high price for honor, must we not?"

Daniel strode to his desk by the window, unlocked a drawer, took the leather bag from which John English paid the day labor, and tossed Stark two ten-shilling pieces of silver.

The peddler bit each coin. "Twenty! And sterling, by

God," he said with a grin. "There's few men have such money nowadays, and fewer would spend it for love. I wish you joy of her." He paused. "And Mr. Squeer, I believe, has wished you the same."

Josselyn's eyes seemed to retreat a bit deeper into their sockets. "How do you know so much of Hannah Trevor? Damn you, who are you?"

To this Stark did not reply, only smiled and stared out the window a moment, toward the steep hill across the river, the path to Two Mills farm.

"Are you an alchemist, Major?" he said without looking at Daniel. "Can you turn shame into gold? It is a talent I might make excellent use of, if it were to be had." The broomseller put the two coins into his scrip. "I shall see you again, sir," he said. "You may count upon it."

"How is it with Mrs. Trevor?" Josselyn demanded. As always when he grew angry, his voice was very soft and level and his lips scarcely moved when he spoke.

"Why, 'twas only a bit of spoilt fruit on her shoulder, friend. She rode off home well enough."

Stark stepped past him and had reached the foot of the great staircase when Daniel's voice rang out into the hall after him, commanding and clear.

"What do you know of James Trevor, her husband? Where is he now?"

The other man turned. "Why, dead, sir," he said softly. "Dead as a rat."

When the strange fellow had gone, Daniel took from one of his desk drawers a small surveyor's lens cased in fine, tooled leather. Then he went straight to the stableyard and mounted the first horse he found not yet unsaddled. It was a sturdy little cob Andrew Tyrrell had hired from the stables at Lamb's Inn for his excursions after botanical samples for Lady Sibylla.

Daniel could not risk any more gossip by riding straight into Two Mills and paying Hannah a visit to satisfy his concern for her, and besides, Mrs. Twig had been bound there. But eight years' separation had taught him how to come as near as he might without being seen.

So he crossed the Manitac at the Grange Ford as always and rode along the South Bank almost to Gannett Cove, then turned the little horse sharply southwest, climbing a rocky path that wound in and out of wind-bent spruces and firs. It was steep going and hard for the pony to manage; the shoe was loose on its right forefoot and slipped dangerously on the outcroppings of granite and the loose surface shale.

At last they reached the level bluff above the village. Sixty years ago, during the French and Indian wars, the embattled settlers had built a rough lookout post of timber and stone here. It was no more than a tumble-down hut, now, overgrown with fireweed and bayberry and home to a family of ravens that gave the place its name—Rook's Nest. But you could still see anyone coming out of the woods from here, and any craft coming up or down the river. Best of all, you could see straight down into the yard of Two Mills Farm. Daniel took the lens from its case and put his eye to it.

There is silly old Twig, careening her way back down the steep hill with a cloth-covered basket on her arm—a new loaf or half a cheese for her trouble. Pleased with herself and purring, with some new tid-bit of gossip to spread.

Henry Markham, forking the last of the hay from an oxcart into the mow of his barn, mopping the sweat off his pate. Is there time for a pipe and a pint, and forty winks or so before we set off for the supper? He glances toward the house and sighs.

His wife is in the doorway, the Grand Duchess Julia, crackling-clean in her best sprigged gown and her finest lace cap and mitts. No, sir, we have not the time! No pipe for poor Henry. No pint to wash down the dust of the day.

Husband, it grows late, come and wash yourself! Where is your best stock-tie, my dear, and your buckled shoes for the dancing?

His feet drag the dust. She relents, her horse-face softens. Ah well, then, a few minutes more will not matter. Let me rub your poor neck where it aches.

On the washbench by the springhouse, with Arthur the one-eared tomcat beside her, Jennet, in her best dark indigo gown. *It makes the red hair darken to bronze and starts deep fires in the amber eyes. Jennet, my Jenny, my love.*

Her lap is full of roses, long canes thick with blossoms, crimson, white, damask-pink. *Only one place has such roses. So that was Twig's errand. But who has sent them?*

Charlotte. No one else.

Jenny weaves the roses into circlets, one larger, one smaller, one very small indeed. The middle-sized wreath she puts upon her own head, newly brushed and braided. The smallest she puts upon an indulgent Arthur. But enough is enough. He marches away, shaking his single good ear determinedly. *I am a cat, confound you, miss! I will not be a lapdog, not even for you!*

Many a crown has cost more trouble to get rid of; the wreath comes away from his thick orange fur and rolls under the oxcart. The nigh ox, old Redtop, puts his huge hoof down and makes mush of King Arthur's crown.

The third crown, the one of deep red roses that is made for a woman, what of that? Jennet takes it up and crosses the yard to the lavender bed, and tugs at the skirt of someone bent over a basin.

Hannah. Hannah, with an old brown skirt and only her shift for a bodice. She is washing her hair in a basin, water dripping down her face and neck as she looks up and smiles and sets Jenny's crown straighter. She bends over again and Bertha Pinch comes from the house with a bowl of warm water and pours it slowly, gently over the short, silver-brown curls, strokes them with her hand, strokes the bare, arched neck.

Accept this small comfort. This laying of hands. It is all I can give.

Jennet tugs at her mother, the crown of roses still in

*her hand. Take this. Mine. You are not hers, nor anyone's.
You are mine.*

*Hair still dripping, Hannah bends down and Jennet puts
the crown on her mother's curls. Susan and Parthenia and
Kitty pass by giggling, loading baskets of food into the
cart to add to the supper at the Grange.*

*Julia again. You are not dressed, Niece. Where is your new
kerchief, Hannah? Can you not wear a cap, at least tonight?*

*Hannah stands with the crown of roses on her head,
looking down at the beaten dirt of the farmyard, the water
still dripping into the dust from her curls.*

*How can I dance? They have put shame upon me like
a burden of stones, and no washing can help me. Take
back the stones.*

Daniel's hand let go of the reins and, eye still to the
lens, his fingertip traced in the hot late-afternoon air the
distant shape of Hannah's face. The slight lift of the cheekbones. The straight, dark, perfect brows. The hollows of
the eye sockets. The plain, thin nose that flared gently at
the nostrils. The bow-bend of the lips, always a bit parted.

*Hannah lifts her head, straightens her bent shoulders
to a soldier's stance. Then she takes Jennet by her two
hands and swings her, round and round in great wide
circles in the dust of the yard. Uncle Henry smiles and
Aunt Julia shakes her head and bites her lip. The oxen
stare. The hired girls giggle.*

*Jennet's eyes are wide with delight and Hannah is
laughing, laughing.*

*A straight back throws off a useless burden. I am what
I am, they may take me or leave me.*

And such as I am, I shall dance.

TEN

HOW THE DEAF CHILD
FELL AMONG THORNS

"*Speed* the Plow!'" cried Josh Lamb, and set bow to his fiddle strings. "One step forward, four in line!"

The dancers formed into long rows and bowed to one another, and the familiar measures began. The tune went back nearly two centuries, and everyone knew it and had danced to it, been born to it, would die with a whisper of it still in the bones.

Everyone, that is, except little Jennet Trevor. To her, music was a mysterious and amazing thing—not for its sound, since only a sort of buzzing penetrated to the silent precinct of her mind.

No, it was the effect on other people that astounded and delighted her. Big, solid Josh Lamb, the innkeeper, stood on a platform at one end of Daniel's threshing floor, tapping his great booted foot and sawing away at a strange piece of wood he had tucked under his chin, but there was no sawdust and the wood did not fall away into pieces. The drummer and the pennywhistle man were there as well, and towering Lachlan McGregor, the new blacksmith, who had a face like a statue and almost never smiled. But tonight his cheeks were puffed up like a pair of Yorkshire puddings and his eyes ran with delighted tears as he played upon a strange contraption of pipes and tubes and bellows. And he wore, of all things, a bright-colored skirt that was shorter than her own!

Fiddle. Bagpipe. Birthright. Ceremony. Dance.

Jennet knew none of these words, of course, nor even her own name—though Hannah had taught her to make the shapes of J and E with a pen, and she made a sort of fidgety effort at an N and a T as well. For the most part, though, she watched the distant, speaking world out of wide and stoical eyes and went her own way among grown-ups who spoke freely around her and did quite as they pleased, knowing she would bear no tales.

But when there was music, Jennet Trevor seemed to see it in the very air, and something that had slept in her since before she was born awoke and climbed the blank walls of her silence, demanding to be heard.

The little girl bounced up and down on Hannah's knee with excitement and clapped her hands, and her small mouth gaped open. Determined, she slid down and stood beside the chair, staring at the feet of the dancers; then she knelt down on the wooden threshing floor, her palms flat on the close-fitted timbers to feel how they shook with the rhythm of the thumping, bumping, joyous dance.

The lines squared and wheeled and squared again, then returned to the two long columns of men and girls with which they had begun. The couples began to weave in and out, crossing and prancing and taking hands and letting go again and changing partners, to return to their own lady or gentleman two or three places nearer the head of the line.

Henry and Julia danced, and so did their daughter Dolly Lamb, pink-cheeked and laughing, and Jonathan and his new wife, Sally, who flashed her black eyes and giggled at every man she took hands with. Mrs. Twig, beruffled and beribboned and simpering like sixty, had somehow entrapped Daniel. Sad-eyed Sarah Firth, who kept house for McGregor and his little boy, Robbie, and seemed to fear everyone, took hands at last with Abijah Teazle, the ancient sexton.

Mill hands and fishermen and men from the timber crews had come. Wives and daughters and widows and spinsters and wandering women who had no place at all. Even hunchbacked Bertha Pinch was there on the great torchlit threshing floor, dancing with old Enoch Luckett, who pranced and capered merrily—even though Uncle Henry's Sunday wig was perched atop Markham's own bald pate where it belonged, horsehair curls flapping to signal its owner's triumph.

As they had been at the haying, so they were now at the dance—no longer separate lives, but one thing. At other times they might sue one another and squabble and gossip and wrangle and dispute.

But the same grass would grow over them all in the end. And this was its festival.

To Jennet, it was a silent and magical pantomime. Little by little, her small feet began to move up and down, up and down, in a dance of her own. Faster she spun, wilder and wilder, mouth open wide, eyes rolling from dizziness.

People began to stare and mutter, and the Lambert twins were snickering and making monkey-faces. Hannah grabbed for the child with both hands, catching her around the waist to pull her back onto her lap.

But Jennet would not be hindered. She kicked and struggled and flailed, and a trickle of drool ran from the gaping mouth.

Daniel has given her silence, thought Hannah. *But this is my part of her. This terrible rage to be free.*

Indenture such a spirit, a thing as wild as the wolf in the common? Hannah's nerves convulsed at the thought of it and she bit her lip until it bled.

Josselyn had had no chance to speak to her since the Markhams' cart arrived. Catching sight of them now, he left Mrs. Twig and strode quickly toward where Hannah and the child were sitting. But before he could reach them, Andrew Tyrrell was suddenly there.

"If I may have this next dance, miss?" The secretary bowed very low before the little girl and offered her his hand. "I am sorely out of the habit, but I will make you the best foot I may."

Like a startled animal, Jennet stopped her struggling and Hannah pulled her close and kissed her eyes shut. It was always their signal. *Bedtime*, it meant. *Rest now, Flower. There have been games enough today.*

But the small body did not relax against her as usual, and Hannah could feel the pounding of her daughter's heart like a fist, slamming, slamming, slamming at the invisible door that locked her out of the world.

Again the silent mouth opened. Jennet's breath came hard and something like a sigh escaped her, a small explosion of air forced up through the straining throat.

But there was no sound. Nothing.

"She is simple, then?" asked Tyrrell gently.

"My daughter does not hear nor speak, sir." Hannah wiped the spittle from the child's chin and sat with her own eyes closed, arms locked around Jennet, body swaying softly to the ongoing rhythm of the dance. "Simple I would not call her."

Daniel stood watching them, pretending to talk to John English, as the first dance ended and Josh Lamb struck up "Haste to the Wedding." Dolly came back to her own chair nearby, winded and weary.

"Why, Hannah," cried her plump cousin. "I don't believe you've danced a step this night, my love, handsome as you look, too, with that crown of roses in your curls! You let me have Puss, now. She'll be no trouble, she's half-asleep already."

Indeed, the little girl seemed to have worn herself out. Tyrrell smiled shyly at Hannah. "In that case, ma'am," he said, "sleep has robbed me of my partner. May I beg the next with you instead?"

He was past his prime and had never been really handsome. But there was a winning simplicity about him in spite of his eyeglass and his careful speech, and Hannah felt herself drawn to him.

Tyrrell held out his hand and she hesitated a moment, then took it. Daniel closed his eyes and turned away.

Just then, Hannah caught sight of Preacher Gwynn; leaving his sister, he began to elbow his way through the crowd toward her. She suddenly wanted only to be out of the heat and the noise of clattering feet and the whining bagpipes and the flickering paper lanterns that seemed to violate the dark. Besides, one dose of pious lust was enough in a day.

"Pray, forgive me, sir," she said to Tyrrell abruptly, and let go of his hand. "I find I do not care for dancing after all."

Hannah moved away from him through the crowd at the punchbowl, and Andrew Tyrrell paused for a moment, uncertain and frowning as she disappeared into the dark beyond the torchlight. Then he turned sharply and went back to where his employer was sitting with Charlotte.

"I fear poor Tyrrell is something smitten, Lottie," said Lady Sibylla, laying out a pinch of snuff along her thumb. She gave two explosive sniffs and dusted her hand delicately with the feather fan. "Pray, who is she? The bold one I mean, with shorn hair and a gaze like a burning-glass." Sibylla peered at Charlotte and the blackbird's eyes sparkled in the torchlight. "She is tolerably hand-some—though she *is* as brown as an overbaked muffin!"

"Mrs. Trevor is a midwife and a nurse," said Charlotte blandly, "and travels in all weathers." She nibbled at a slice of fruitcake. "Her eyes bulge out too much, I think, for real beauty. And her mouth is over-wide."

Andrew Tyrrell was watching little Jennet, who had eluded Dolly and was now making her way purposefully through the crowd to where the fire eater was now turning cartwheels, his flaming rod clamped in his teeth. The broomseller, who had been taking coins for the tumblers, emptied his hat into a wooden box on the grass, then dodged out of sight behind the Punch-and-Judy stall.

" 'Harvest Home,' my dears!" cried Josh. "All address partners, if you please!"

They began another dance, formed in quadrille. The old lady drained a glass of wine and Tyrrell refilled it. But his bad eyesight made him spill more than half of it.

"I will just fetch a napkin, my lady," he murmured, and ducked into the dark.

"Besotted." Sybilla sighed. "I would not have thought it of Tyrrell. Still, they are a taking pair, that Trevor woman and her pretty child. The features put me in mind of someone, but I've taken too much Madeira to think who it is." Sybilla paused for another pinch of snuff and glanced at Charlotte sidewise. "Pray, which is the father, Lottie? One of these clodpoles?"

Charlotte pulled her Shetland shawl closer around her shoulders. "I think I should like to go back to the house," she said. "My head pains me. And the breeze has turned suddenly cool."

"Tyrrell!" cried Sybilla. "Ho, sir! Tyrrell! Now, damn the fellow. He has vanished like a ghost!"

Hannah, too, felt the wind change into the east and blow cool off the Newfoundland Banks. Lightning flickered low in the sky, some storm at sea that would bring little rain this far from the coast. A few drops tomorrow, perhaps, to make the women run for their washing spread out on the hedges. But nothing to signify. Nothing for the parched roots.

The new-mown field lay just over a small rise from the dancing, and the sweet smell of the hay had drawn her there. Though no torches flared here, the midsummer bonfire danced on the riverbank at the bottom of the hill, the field hands and their lasses laughing and singing around it, and the moon slipped in and out of thin clouds, making the summer darkness numinous and liquid, alive with movement just beyond the range of sight. An owl called from the small grove on the rise, and Hannah saw its shadow as it rose and soared, wings motionless, then swooped down on a field mouse or a rabbit with a hoarse, joyful cry.

She could still hear the fiddle music faintly, and she let it take her, let herself move to it as Jennet had done, turning in the darkness like the figure on top of the Dutch music box she had had as a girl. She wore her only good summer gown, a pale grey tucked linen much washed over the years, and cool. The skirt had been meant for old-fashioned pocket hoops, but Hannah never wore them; instead, the extra fabric hung in softly draped folds and as she spun it caught on the mown stubble, pulled free, then lifted slightly, as though the wind bore her up or the moon claimed her.

Suddenly she stopped. There was a sound of running feet and the shadow of a man appeared on the brow of the hill—a tallish shape, broad-shouldered but slender, and wearing no coat. She could see the full, white sleeves of his shirt and the uncertain shape of a hat of some sort.

"Daniel?" she said aloud, for he stood very still. "Is it you, my love?"

From the copse on the rise, she heard a horse nicker. The owl rose again, wings beating the dark, and soared again and struck. Distracted, Hannah glanced away, and when she looked back, the man's shadow had gone.

Perhaps it *had* been Daniel, and he had thought better of coming to find her. Perhaps he had changed since the winter, and regretted the unavoidable fact of her. Perhaps he believed Isaiah Squeer.

But no. Had he not sent her the armful of roses to make sure she would come?

And then, above the music, Hannah heard something crying. It was muffled and far-off and it sounded like someone being choked, strangled. There were no words, only the high, terrible cry torn from a tightened throat, pulled away like the branch of a tree in a storm that leaves jagged ends of living wood behind.

Again it came, and again, louder this time. It was shrill and wild, a terrified sound. *Jennet,* Hannah thought, and felt her chest grow tight and her breath labor. But that was not possible, for the child did not cry. Perhaps it was only some creature the owl had caught in his claws.

And then she realized that the fiddle and the pipes had stopped playing, and there was shouting in the distance.

Hannah got to her feet and started for the top of the field. When she reached it, she could see torches and lanterns moving in the garden beyond the threshing floor where they had not been before, and she heard Daniel's voice shouting, although she could not make out the words.

She ran lightly down the hill and into the yard, skirting the knots of buzzing neighbors, following the sound of the terrible cries. They were regular now, like sobbing, but there was an odd dry edge to them, a kind of monotone that did not rise or fall as voices are used to, but went on and on like her uncle's mill wheel when it turned.

The cries came from the rose garden, the arbor woven thick with thorny branches in full bloom. There were men's voices inside, and the hiss and sizzle of the pitch in their torches.

"Ah, Hannah-girl! Where the deuce did you get to?" Uncle Henry laid a hand on her arm.

"Who is crying?" she asked him.

"There's a man dead, my dear," he said. "Slit his own throat, poor devil." It was not the first suicide since the foreclosures began.

"Who is crying?" she demanded again. But she did not wait to be answered, only pushed between the murmuring men and went inside.

She saw Jonathan first, bending over the dead man. She recognized the broomseller's shabby cocked hat where it lay on the ground. But Hannah barely spared either of them a glance, for it was plain enough now where the strange cries had come from.

In a dim curve of the arbor, Jennet Trevor, wild-eyed and terrible, was giving her birth-cry nearly eight years too late.

"Nah, Jenny," said Daniel softly. "Shh, shh, Jenny, my Jenny. Shh."

Julia was there, trying to soothe the child, and Dolly and Josh and Mrs. Firth and Bertha Pinch, and the Punch-and-Judy man and some others crowded into the doorway, staring. But the little girl's screaming did not stop, could not. Daniel had her close in his arms, but she fought him, desperate and terrified, scratched his face until her kitten claws left a trail of blood along his cheek. She kicked at his chest till his ribs ached, and still he held her.

And still she screamed and screamed.

Jennet's hands were sticky with blood and her best indigo gown was smeared with it. There was blood in a pool on the grass-edged flagstones and blood on the white-washed lattice of the arbor and the crimson and white roses themselves seemed splashed with blood, grown out of soil that was blood and watered with a bloody rain. The scent of them was terrible, intense and dizzying.

"God Christ," said Jonathan. He got up suddenly from beside the broomseller's body and turned away.

But slender, soft-eyed Sarah Firth, standing a foot or two behind Lachlan McGregor and some of the other men, seemed unmoved by the blood.

"The child near went to sleep in Dolly's arms, ma'am," she told Hannah, "and we put her down on a quilt with Robbie and the littler ones. But she must have waked and gone to the Punch-and-Judy, and then stumbled into the arbor, here, and found—that."

A fresh bout of struggling had begun. Jennet sunk her teeth into Daniel's maimed hand and he cried out in spite of himself.

"Let me take her," Hannah told him. "Let her go."

He looked up at her. "Has she made sounds before? Any at all?"

"Never. Never."

It was all he could think of, beyond even the terrible dead body with its throat cut. *If she can cry, she can speak.*

"Let her go free," said Hannah.

Daniel nodded. He loosed his arms that had trapped her like iron, and Jennet lay still for a moment, surprised. Her mouth hung open and her eyes stared at Hannah as though they had never seen her before. But the terrible screaming stopped as suddenly as it had begun.

Hannah reached for her and Jennet's body found its favorite position, arms around her mother's neck and legs locked round her waist. She was big for it now, and nearly too heavy, but her mother lifted her with a soft grunt of strain and held her close. The child hid her face against Hannah's neck, and she could feel the spittle soaking her gown.

"Take her into the house, Mrs. Trevor, and bathe her face," said a soft voice from the end of the arbor. "Stay the night with her here. Twig will make a bed for you, and something warm to drink. If she sleeps, she may be calmed."

It was Charlotte. She leaned heavily on Tyrrell's arm, but she stood very straight and her blue eyes met Hannah's, unreadable and mild. Jennet's face was hidden in her mother's neck and she did not look at them.

"Some wine and water will settle her, perhaps," said Daniel's lady. "And you yourself should take something, some brandy or port. You are very pale."

"I thank you," Hannah replied. "But my aunt will take Jennet home. And I am well enough."

Charlotte nodded slightly, her eyes on her husband's face, and behind her Hannah could see the plumes on Lady Sibylla's headdress bobbing. Jenks and Owen waited while Andrew Tyrrell settled the two women in Hobble, and in a moment more they could be heard crossing the graveled path to the house.

Then Hannah's aunt and uncle were beside her, and Henry lifted Jennet into his arms and stroked her hair with his round, rough cheek. She lay quiet there, and made no more sounds.

"Let them send for Clinch, my girl, and come you away

home," said Julia in an undertone, avoiding the sight of the corpse. "I've heard how they served you at the fair. That's enough for one day. Let the men do whatever must be done here, just this once."

Hannah shook her head and the coronet of roses fell to the blood-stained floor.

"Nonsense, Aunt," she replied. "I am here, and someone must see to the dead."

Julia was bested, and could only shake her head and take her husband's arm and give way. When they had gone, Hannah turned to the others. "Does anyone know him? What is his name?"

"Reuben Stark," Daniel told her. In front of the others, he could say little more. "He came today asking for work. He said he had a woman hereabouts, though he didn't say where."

"I know myself where they live. I have tended his family," said Hannah. "His wife must be told, and his children comforted. I'll go with you, Jonathan, she knows me. Though I never met—"

Her voice strangled, for she had looked down at the dead man's face and saw him clearly in the light of a lantern they had set by his head. His cocked hat lay on the bloodstained flagstones beside him, next to it the razor with which his throat had been slit. The blue calico kerchief had slipped away from his forehead, and his greying, dark brown hair had fallen aside.

Hannah felt her body shudder at the sight of him and cave in upon itself.

None of the others would have known him. He had been handsome and vain of himself when they saw him last, and worn a fine powdered wig in company and a diamond pin in his tie.

But God had scourged him bitterly since then.

He had run away hoping for safety, but somewhere they had caught him, in some pisswater village or some back alley in Boston or Philadelphia where he tried to disappear. "Damn the Tories!" they cried as they stripped him and beat him and dragged him through the streets on a rope. Laid the whip on him, perhaps, or rode him on their shoulders, a sharp rail jammed between his legs until he bled from the groin and his sex hung wooden and dead.

They had cut off his ears and left great gaping holes there, like caverns. Clipping, they called it, and made jokes about how the fashion would catch on and King George himself would demand to be clipped. Sometimes they stopped with the earlobes or cut small notches, only. But with him, they had done their job well, and his nose, too, had been slit like a convict's. The scar on his forehead was long-healed, now, but still a dark crimson, and the shape of the brand they had put on him was plain enough to read.

TORY, it said. It had once been a name he boasted of foolishly, drinking the health of the king.

Only his brows were still the same. They had greyed and were not so dark as before, but the left still grew straight and perfect, while midway through the right there was a broken space, a scar where the hairs would not grow. It split the right eyebrow into two clean halves, like the skip of a badly dipped pen that draws a line and falters.

It was by that broken line she knew him, for she had given him the scar herself.

Hannah heard a voice, then, that was surely not Jennet's and did not seem to be her own. It made a low sound, as though her lost girlhood were mourning him, and her heart's blood and the years she had wasted in hate. She felt some human shape move close and stand beside her, felt an arm steady her. She did not know if it was Daniel or Jonathan or Mrs. Firth who held her, or her mother who was nearly twenty years dead or her father who had died when she was ten.

All Hannah Trevor knew was that the dead are never dead and they do not let go of the living.

"What is it, my heart?" said Daniel's soft voice, so near it seemed to come from deep in her bones.

"My husband," she whispered. "It is James, who was dead."

ELEVEN

Piecing the Evidence: In the Matter of James Trevor

Item the First: Notice of Eviction

Upon Ten Acres Farmland and Forest, with a Cabin and Stable, One-Half Mile West from the Falls on Blackthorne Creek, Marked Section Twelve, Lot Seventeen. Hamilton Siwall, Esquire, owner, having these Four Months failed to collect Payment of Rents amounting to Four Pound, does demand that the Tenant, one Reuben Stark, shall vacate the Property forthwith, and that his Goods be distrained and sold toward the Rents outstanding.

—Served by Jonathan Markham, Constable
This Ninth Day of July, 1786

The foregoing was found folded in the dead man's scrip, with twenty shillings in silver and half a veal pie, the missing part but lately eaten. Upon the reverse, in a man's schooled hand, the following:

If I have done great wrong, so it has been done me by many. I am undone, and the Devil take my soul.

Item the Second

Cocked Hat: Prince of Wales's Own Regiment, 1781, Welch Fusiliers Being A Round Black Cap with Tricorne Brim, having Gold Lace to its Binding, the Cockade Scarlet

Item the Third

Razor: The Blade of Sheffield steel, set with a Carved Bone Handle. Along the Blade Engraved, the surname TREVORE, and the Mark of a Pine Tree, Being the Hallmark of Mr. Merridew of Jermyn Street, London, Barber, Made by Him, 1733.

Item the Fourth

A Woman's Mourning Kerchief, White Lawn, worked in Black Silk upon the Verge, the Threads counted in Crosses and Plain bars, with the motto:

> *Hannah Trevor James Trevor*
> *In Love We Wed, To Love Forever*

❊ TWELVE ❊

PIECING THE EVIDENCE:
What a Fellow He Was

Letter of Mr. James Trevor, Esquire,
to his Wife, Hannah Trevor
At Rufford, Maine, County of Sussex
Written from Salem, Massachusetts,
the Tenth Day of October, 1780

My Sweet Wife, etc., etc.

Having been hounded forth from my own bed to great peril here abroad, I at last reached the safety of my friend Mr. Baggett in Boston. There I stayed some months, making my way as I could, till my funds were exhausted.

Thinking to restore my finances by the sale of my furniture left behind in the house on Batchelder Street, I went there secretly by night to write a catalog of my goods. I found them in possession of a rough fellow who said my house was now his, and drove me with pistols from the door. I know you will appreciate, my Own, the desperate state of my feelings, to see in the hands of a ruffian that particular chamber in which are contained such tender memories of my delight in your arms.

Provided with letters of introduction from Mr. Baggett to a loyal subject of His Majesty King George in the town of Salisbury, near Salem. I passed some months there in quiet, acting as clerk to this gentleman. I had for a time a small house and cherished some hope of sending for you, so that we might celebrate that tender, that delightful restoration of conjugal relations to which I shall always aspire.

But alas, it was not to be. I am at present in Salem, and so desperate is the temper of the rabble hereabouts that I must again take flight. I shall go to London, where I have many friends already gone and I may make my way by my wits. A substantial sum will be needed, my Own, to outfit me for this arduous journey and provide me with a good horse and with proper apparel upon my arrival, which will set me in a way to prosper among the best classes there.

Sell at once my two carriage horses, Castor and Pollux, and my chaise. In so small a place as Rufford, you have no need of a carriage, and they should bring a good sum. Sell also the pearl ear-drops I bestowed at our marriage, and send me the money straightaway to: Baggett and Sons, Esquire, Agents and Commissioners, 33 Fountain Lane, Salem.

It is a husband's duty to remind his wife that his honor is couched in her obedience, and though I be gone, I have yet the right to command loyalty and faithfulness of my beloved wife, as she may rely upon that of

Her fond Husband,
James Ramsay Trevor

Post Scriptum: If the sale of the ear-drops and the greys do not bring two hundred pound, sell up the household goods and dispatch me the money. You may stay, I trust, with your aunt and take service with her, or learn some useful trade to provide for your wants, and what you earn in addition may be sent me to whatever lodging I may find, once I am settled in London, so that I may restore you to my bosom the sooner.

Do all as I tell you. Act quickly. I would be gone.

N.B. The preceding is the only letter received by Hannah Trevor from her husband after his flight from Rufford. When asked why she had preserved it, she replied that if and when she were ever again free to marry, she would use it as a caution against the folly of trusting any man at his word.

Mrs. Trevor adds that the pearl ear-drops were her mother's and were not a gift of James Trevor, though they were sold at auction with his goods. The matched greys, Castor and Pollux, and the chaise, are now in the possession of Hamilton Siwall. Baggett and Sons is well known for its dealings in smuggled rum, tobacco, contraband British goods, slaves and indentured servants.

✖ THIRTEEN ✖

JAMES

*I*t might almost have been suicide.

He lay on his back with his eyes closed, the mourning kerchief clutched in his left hand, the open razor near his right on the flagstone floor. One arm was thrown upward as though he were reaching for something, and the other was laid out primly at his side.

They *might* have fallen so after he had slit his own throat, in the long warm moment of dying when the mind has gone but life has not and memory has not left the muscles and the bones. In that moment, the body has a kind of will of its own; Hannah had seen it often, the hands of dying old women knitting away with invisible needles, men raising invisible pipes to their mouths and puffing as though a last whiff of tobacco might save them from the wrath of God.

James Trevor *might* have laid himself down so to die. His legs were straight, the heels of his worn old riding boots close together. The boots were long and cuffed at the top and reached above his knees, and when Hannah knelt down and put her fingertips to them, they were damp almost as high as the cuff. A few strands of mown hay had stuck in the arch where the sole and boot heel met. Surely he had paced along the riverbank and then through the newly cut meadow—not more than an hour ago, or the boots would have dried in this heat.

Had he gone to meet someone there? Or had he seen her alone in the hayfield? Had he paused on the brow of the hill and thought to speak to her?

Hannah bent low over him for a moment and seemed to be listening, waiting for something to come to her that he might have said. Was it repentance? Some useless desire for a belated amends? A confirmation of her own bad memories?

And how, how, how *dare* he have cheated her so long even of his own honest death?

She looked up at Daniel and at her young cousin Jonathan, the constable. Many of the rest had gone, though a good number still lingered outside, talking in low tones of suicide.

"I cannot credit it," she said quietly. "It is no self-murder. He was always afraid of knives."

James Trevor was a few years younger than Daniel, forty or thereabouts. He wore no coat, only a long leather jerkin over his grey homespun shirt and rusty black knee breeches. The scrip at his waist was the kind both armies had issued to hold musket balls and provisions, but he had no weapon of any kind except the razor that had slit his throat.

Mr. English had set more of his guards, now, at the two ends of the rose arbor to keep out the curious, and Jonathan had sent for the coroner, Dr. Clinch. The flaring torches had been quenched and several lanterns of pierced tin now gave a steady light in the narrow confines of the place. The young constable's lean, dark-stubbled jaw was set with determination; he must be nobody's cousin now, and nobody's friend—especially Hannah's. It frightened him, this loneness, and he turned grim and fierce. He picked up the black-bordered kerchief and frowned at the sight of her name embroidered there.

"What do you say to this, madam?" he said, and handed it to her.

Hannah stared at it dully. "Why, nothing."

"Nothing? Are you blind? Your name's on it, and his."

"Yes," she said vaguely. "Mrs. Pitt worked it for me, after I had the letter in February saying he was dead. I meant to make a new border but—"

"To hell with embroidery! How did it come here?"

She turned and looked away from it. "I cannot say. I had laid it away in the chest in my room." Her voice drifted. "I'm sure I had. I'm sure I had."

"Did you lock it? It's your custom to lock it, I know."

As a boy, he had once put a bull snake in among Hannah's linens for a joke and got a whipping for his pains. Ever since, the chest was kept locked.

"Did he not meet with you here? He was about the fair all day, and here at the dancing. Surely you knew him, just as you know him now."

"I believed my husband dead, and how should I look to meet him around every corner?" she said. "I saw and did not see. With that hat on his head, I had no thought he was James. He was a hat, that's all. A bunch of brooms."

"Hannah. Listen to me. If you dropped the kerchief here, you must tell me. Before Clinch comes. Before Sheriff Tapp. Once they are here, I can do nothing for you."

Suddenly she seemed to remember where she was, and who. She flared up and turned on him.

"I know what you are thinking! But if I murdered James, why leave a kerchief behind with my name upon it to accuse me?"

"*Did* you lock the linen chest?" the constable repeated.

Her focus slipped away again and her voice grew soft and dull. "I—I do many things in a day. Perhaps I neglected the lock. Perhaps I dropped the kerchief on the stair and someone picked it up."

"Who was in the house today, aside from the family and the hired girls? Had you any visitor?" Daniel asked her. "Anyone you do not know well?"

"Only Preacher Gwynn. But surely—"

"Was he at any time alone in the place? Did you go into the yard and leave him in the kitchen?"

"I went to the stillroom for a glass of buttermilk to

give him. But it was not enough time to go looking for
kerchiefs, or anything else. And why would he wish to
lay guilt upon me, when he meant to—''

She broke off, but Jonathan would not have it.

''What? Meant to what?''

Hannah glanced at Daniel. ''When he meant to marry
me,'' she said.

''You? Wed Preacher Gwynn?'' Jonathan was
dumbfounded.

Daniel said nothing, only walked a few paces, turned
and came back again.

''Mrs. Trevor is quite right,'' he said at last, his voice
cool and formal. ''Mr. Gwynn would have no way of
knowing she even possessed such a kerchief, nor where it
might be kept.''

The constable's dark eyes were frightened. ''If it
weren't for that damned kerchief, Trevor—or Stark or
whatever you may call him—would be just another broken
man that took his own life. As it is, with you saying he
would not have used a blade . . .''

''There is more,'' she said, ''and you may as well hear
it. The throat was cut in a single smooth stroke. But when
a man sets about to cut himself, he most naturally fears
it. He makes one or two small cuts, getting used to the
pain, before the final deed.'' She rolled back the long linen
sleeves of her gown and held out her wrists to her cousin.
''See there,'' she said.

On the insides of both wrists, beginning at the base of
her thumbs, there were two narrow, snaking scars. At the
thumb end of the scar on her left hand, where she had
begun, there were three smaller scars like healed gouges.

''I was afraid, in the moment of doing,'' she said softly.
''I bungled it. The knife was dull.''

Jonathan could only stare at her, and Hannah stood with
the scarred wrists dangling limply at her sides. There was
more, but she could not give it.

She sank down on one of the benches, her hands in her
lap, gripping each other hard, and Daniel came and rolled

down her sleeves one after the other and buttoned the tucked cuffs carefully over the scars. He had seen them before, like lines on the map of her body, and deluded himself that they came from some mishap, some tangle with brambles or broken glass.

But in the winter past, she had told him. How James had abandoned her in Boston at the outbreak of War, a Tory's wife to whom merchants would sell no food. How she had shut herself up in the dark house because if candles burned they would see her and remember she was alive and come for her. How she had blamed herself for the deaths of her three children and cut her long hair and slashed her wrists.

Much of her pain she had given him to help her carry.

But not all. Never all. There would always be some part of Hannah that belonged to no one but herself. It was what had turned Trevor against her, that she would not be owned. She would keep one last sliver of truth to herself, the worst and the sharpest, able to sever all bonds.

Forgetting the dead man at his feet and the young constable beside him, Daniel kissed her hands one at a time, sheltered them in his own for a moment, then laid them gently in her lap and stepped away.

"Why would James come back here, where I am?" she whispered. "Surely not out of love?"

Daniel sat down by her side, not touching her. "He did very ill by you. Perhaps he felt it, after all. The note makes it seem so, does it not?"

If I have done great wrong, so it has been done me.

But the crucial word was *if.*

"It is most surely in his own hand," she went on. "Yet I cannot believe he would take his own life. It is wrong. All wrong."

Johnnie bent over the ruined body. "I served the eviction upon him three days ago and I didn't even know him. He's been here among us for months!"

"You were only a boy of eight or nine when he left," said Daniel. "And he could easily avoid those with fresher memories if he kept to the woods and sent his woman to do the errands. Or traded at Fort Holland with the Dutchman. Even if he risked coming himself to the village—by night, in the smoke of Edes's tavern or among the crowd at the fair—that outlandish costume would take the eye and lead it straight away from his countenance, as Hannah says. He looked like a traveling cutpurse, and not many would linger in his company.''

Jonathan frowned. ''But if Hannah knows him dead, how is it she did not know him living? At the fair, or here at the dancing?''

''He was much changed,'' she told him. ''I would scarcely know him even now but for the scar on his brow.''

She did not tell them how James had meant to come to her bed a week after the deaths of her children.

I require no more than your duty, madam, he said. *We may have another child by the spring.*

She had found the fire shovel, then, and struck him full in the face with it. Nose broken, blood streaming, he had lunged at her, toppled her with a fist to her belly. Hannah did not cry out, made no sound when she lay at last on the floor with his furious sex crashing into her again and again until her body was a silent wound in the earth.

No, it was James who was sobbing, tears streaming from his eyes.

I forgive you, he had whispered when at last he finished, stroking her forehead and kissing her gently on the lips. *I love you, my dearest. Why do you make me hurt you so?*

''Will you hold the lantern closer?'' she said at last, tearing herself from her memories. ''I must look at the damage more carefully before Clinch comes, if we're to find out how he died.''

''The devil with it! He slit his throat with that razor, he must have done!'' cried Jonathan. ''It makes no matter how the kerchief came here! I'll burn it and be damned to it! I served him with Siwall's eviction, and he fell into a madness.''

"I tell you James would never kill himself with a blade," she insisted. "He would have feared it too much."

"After what had been done to him?" said Daniel. "You cannot know his mind."

"Can I not?" She almost spat the words at him, suddenly furious. "This is his razor. Oh, I know it, it was his father's, brought from London. But if scraped chins had not been the fashion, no blade would ever have come near James. You may take my word, for I shaved him myself with it often enough."

She seized the lantern and held it close to the gaping wound that ran across the dead man's neck from one to the other of the naked, cavernous ears. "Look there," she said. "That is where the blade drove into him, that cut like a bird's wing. It began at the right, not the left. Don't you see? My husband was right-handed, sir, as I am! Could he cut his own throat backwards?"

Hannah stood up from the body and walked a few steps where the lantern light could not find her. Daniel could hear her breathing, short and sharp and painful. But she made no move towards him, held out no hand.

She is gone, he thought.

Gone.

Hate him though she might, James Trevor dead had done what James Trevor living would have had no hope of. He had taken back his wife again.

The arbor was built like a long, narrow hallway of blossoms with arched doorways at either end. Overhead, the rose canes grew in and out of whitewashed wooden lattice to make a roof of flowers, and the side walls—also lattice—were the same. They had pruned the canes to keep them from overwhelming the four wooden benches that faced each other on both long sides, but the luxuriant growth of the plants would not be entirely contained and they grew out around the benches, forming small, curved bays.

Too many people had been in and out that night to gain

much of the truth from the flagstones. The grass that grew between them was trampled, of course, and pitch had dripped down from the torches. The canes had been scorched badly in places and shriveled rose petals lay thick underfoot, the heavy scent of the flowers mixed with the bitterness of ash.

In the far corner, the gardeners had carelessly left behind a hoe and a basket half-full of weeds.

There were no signs of violent struggle, no breaks in the lattice where someone had fallen against it, no overturned benches. But blood stained one bench and the lattice behind it, and spattered some of the canes of white Versailles roses that curved onto the path. One or two were broken and smashed, as though his body had fallen on them.

Painstakingly, Hannah began to reconstruct, to build the pattern of James Trevor's death.

An hour ago, no more, he left the dancing. They were still at supper then, at several long tables surrounded by torchlight. No one need see him slip away into the dark.

Meet me at the river's edge, someone had told him. Or had he himself appointed the meeting? *I must see you. I can stay hidden no longer in the cabin. Eviction, I need money. A lot of money, and soon.*

It had been his way, she had heard him speak so a thousand times, dreaming of the wealth he would have, the investments he would make in Barbados sugar, tobacco, rum—even in the slave trade. There was always some grand scheme afoot, and he did not scruple over principle. His grandiose dreams swept it easily away.

He would buy a Virginia plantation and live like a lord. He would take her to England, buy a partnership in some thriving legal practice, run for Parliament.

Not for James Trevor the slow labor of earning. *Now. I must have it now.*

He had used up the comfortable dowry Hannah had brought him in less than a year after their marriage. *Speculate to accumulate. No, no, the velvet coat with the double*

cuff, tailor. It cuts a much finer figure, I'm sure you agree.
One sound roll of the dice, a good hand of whist, and I
shall be able to buy those Spanish leather boots, my love.

As for the note on the back of the eviction paper, that,
too, was like him. She had found many such stuffed in
his waistcoat pockets, scribbled on the backs of winemer-
chants' bills, notes-of-hand for his gambling debts, once
even a challenge to fight a duel with the husband of one
of his flirtations.

"If I have compromised your honor, 'twas only because
I overlooked its existence, being too small, on the whole,
to be seen. To the Devil with you, and as to that old ewe,
your lady, she smells of civet abed and has a nature like
piss-warm tea. Any money or gifts she gave me, I have
more than earned."

This Hannah had found crumpled up beneath her husband's pillow when he returned from one of his months-
long absences. "Business" often called him away to Philadelphia or New York at the height of the season of races
and balls. At first he wrote her fond letters, but after a
time they grew less frequent, more terse, more arrogant—
though always bedecked with fine phrases of courtship.

He did not fight the duel. It was not a matter of coward-
ice but of relative value. What woman, after all, could
have been worth the risk to him? Surely not his wife.

That was the James she remembered. A talent for flat-
tery, seduction, even blackmail. An endless craving for
buying, selling, buying again. An endless ability to use
and discard other lives.

What torture it must have been to him to have nothing,
far worse than the slitting or the branding. *If a man has*
nothing, he is nothing, he had used to say.

So. Money. Clothes. A good horse.

She had heard a horse in the wood next to the hayfield.

It was the first flicker of rational pattern. A neat triangle—garden, river, arbor. He had met someone at the river,
made his demand for money, clothes, a horse. *Bring me*

*the horse to the woods and tether it. Then come with the
rest to the arbor. I will wait for you there.*

But who? And what could James have offered in return?
Silence? A promise to disappear and never return? Some
telltale letter, some proof that would ruin the killer?

"He must have known the one who killed him, or been
expecting him," she said. "Else why did he not cry out?"

"Above them pipes of McGregor's, who'd have heard
him?"

"But you all heard Jennet." She began to walk back
and forth, her skirt catching on the rose canes.

Josselyn stared down at James Trevor's dead body, trying to imagine that face before the damage was done it.
Below the ruin, it was handsome—high-boned and arrogant and hard, with heavy dark brows and ruddy cheeks.
And yet for all that, there was a distance about it, something unformed and indistinct, like a painting washed over
with turpentine so that only a ghost of a picture remains.
Daniel had noticed it that afternoon in the library—the
face of an unfinished man, eternally innocent, eternally
selfish. A boy-man who could do great harm and leave
chaos and ruin behind him, and yet swear the blame was
none of his own.

"You left the dancing, Hannah," persisted Jonathan,
"just before he died."

His voice was distant and formal and not at all like the
boy she had carved pumpkins for at All Hallows and
chased through the woods at sugaring time.

"Dada went to look for you," he went on, "but you
weren't to be found. You must tell me now where you
were when James died."

She stared at him. "Oh, Johnnie. You cannot truly think
I have done this."

"If you killed him, I will trust he deserved it and call
him a suicide, and there's an end. I will say nothing to
Tapp when he comes in the morning! Daniel will say
nothing. We will burn the kerchief and bury it. Only you
must tell us the truth of it now, so we may help you."

Hannah spun round to face Daniel. "And you, sir? Do *you* believe this?"

He would have spoken to reassure her, but she gave him no time.

"Well, then. I have my answer," she said, and clasped her hands tighter together.

"Where did you go when you left the dancing? Was anyone with you, my dear?" Daniel spoke gently, careful to keep his voice level.

"I went to the hayfield," Hannah replied. "Alone, but for a mousing owl." She looked up at her lover. "But did *you* not come after me, sir, to the meadow? Watch me from the hilltop? Had you no horse tethered near there?"

Daniel shook his head, puzzled. "If some man watched you," he told her, "it was not I."

"Make way! Make way, there!" bellowed a voice from outside.

It was that paragon of Science, Samuel Clinch, coroner of Sussex County, randy and rum-breathed at sixty-odd. He lurched to a halt, listed dangerously sideways and was caught by his black servant, Caesar.

"You, madam?" roared Clinch, spying Hannah. "Take yourself off, you are no use here!"

But Hannah did not step aside. "You know well enough, sir, that tomorrow I must witness the dissection of this man's body. It is the law."

Because male doctors had been known to drink and swear at autopsies, and to make wagers on the internal condition of the dead, the law required a midwife to be present as a civilizing influence.

"What's the use of it?" he grunted. "See that brand there? See those ears? Tory scoundrel, ma'am! Coming back in their hordes now, damn 'em. Boston papers full of it. Good riddance, I say, and be done!"

"You intend no dissection?" said Daniel.

"He don't deserve it, sir. Bloody waste of time."

"What are you paid by the county to perform an autopsy?"

"You are an impertinent puppy, sir!" blustered the old rumpot. "A presumptuous hound!"

Caesar, who had been standing silent in the shadows, stepped close to his master, murmured a word or two, then retreated into the half-dark.

"Hmmph! Well, then!" Clinch scuffed his boot on the flagstones. "My customary charge is, er, thirty shillings. One pound ten. Modest, I think? Equable? But the county's at present embarrassed, sir. Taxes, you know. People won't pay 'em. County won't pay me. Living or dead, I don't cut till I'm paid."

"And the dead may go unjustified and murderers go free?" said Hannah.

"You are insubordinate, madam! Magistrate Siwall has returned this night and make no mistake, you shall be summonsed!"

"Ah, but surely, Mr. Clinch," she said, stepping very close to him so none of the others could hear, "surely you have seen to *one* summons already. Have you not?"

All the afternoon, Hannah's mind had been sorting her friends from her enemies like the colored pieces of one of her quilts, for she was certain the Orphans' Court would not have bothered with her even now but for the interference of some meddling busybody.

But Clinch did not seem to understand her. "You are barking mad, ma'am," he said. "Clear away! Clear away!"

"Constable Markham," Daniel began formally. "I hold you to witness that I offer Mr. Clinch three pounds to perform a dissection on this man in the usual manner." He turned to Clinch. "Is that sum sufficient, sir, or must I double it again?"

"Oh, plague it!" said Clinch, with a snort. "We'll cut him up tomorrow noon, confound him." He paused for a pinch of snuff. "What was the beggar called when he breathed?"

Hannah glanced briefly at Daniel. "He is James Trevor," she said, "who was once my husband."

Clinch's eyes bulged and his face grew as purple as beet-root. "Then, pray, Madam Midwife," he said, "how is it that you and your paramour are not yet in shackles and under arrest?"

�֎ FOURTEEN �֎

GRACE AND HER CHILDREN

*A*s they had mown and as they had danced, so they went together to tell the news to Trevor's other woman, the lady who called herself Mrs. Stark.

It was too dark for horses in the woods, and they traveled on foot in a straggling column, with Daniel and Hannah and Jonathan walking ahead of the rest.

Then Josh Lamb, the innkeeper, close behind, a brother to them all.

Sarah Firth and hunchbacked Bertha Pinch. McGregor, huge in the flickering light of the torches they carried, his fingers scarcely felt where they lay on Sarah's arm.

Gwynn, the minister, and his sister Merriam, fierce-eyed and silent and pale.

Hosea Sly, the ferryman, awkward and ill-at-ease on dry land.

Even Mrs. Twig was there, picking her way in the dark and gripping for dear life the sturdy arm of old Enoch Luckett.

And quietly, with no torch and no lantern to guide him, Andrew Tyrrell walked with them, head down, hands locked tight behind his back like a man on the hangman's cart.

They crossed the river on the great rafts of lashed logs that floated at the mill dock, the women kilting their skirts up around their waists, the men squelching in sodden boots. Past the turning mill they went, where the night sawyer still minded the great groaning blades. Then past the flax field, pale silver in the darkness, all its morning blossoms spent. Across the sheep meadow and on, into the woods beyond the little falls on Blackthorne Creek.

A long crooked column of small lights in the darkness they made, no steadier than the heat lightning that still flickered in the eastern sky above the sea.

There was a narrow footpath to the cabin, just visible among the trees and the high ferns and the thickets of wild raspberry and mountain holly and bush cranberry. The branches of cedar and spruce and white pine grew together over their heads, hanging so low that the torches had to be doused to keep from setting the trees afire.

So the light they made grew more feeble, and the huge dark gnawed at them, and they danced now upon the jagged edge of the secret world whose questions are huge and without answers.

God had put out the stars like blind men's eyes. Even the lightning no longer reached them. There were only the bobbing lanterns, fisherman's buoys in the sea of dark.

"We must go back!" wailed Arabella Twig, who had stumbled and fallen into a nest of brambles. "I am not a woman to shirk my Christian duty. Major Josselyn knows it. T-Twig, when he lived, often said so. But ch-ch-ch-charity obeys the l-limits of reason! And it is sooo veeeery daaark!"

"Now, now, me old darlin'," said Enoch Luckett, and heaved her up for the third time, an arm around her ample waist. "Don't be 'feard."

"Why, bother you, Twig, you silly old pumpkin!" cried the voice of Bertha Pinch out of the dark. "Can you not see it's broad daylight here in the grave? No one be lost here. No one falls but he be lifted. No one breaks but he heals as good as new. And better. Better. For you grow straight in the grave, you know. They do not build coffins crooked, with great silly humps upon 'em for the likes of me. They build 'em straight and true and sweet."

Mistress Pinch's legs were short and her back was bent and the one shoulder sank down under the weight of her hunch and the other rose up as though it would lift her feet from the ground. She was stunted and thick, like a tree that has girdled itself at its roots and grows by fits and starts, one limb full-leafed and perfect and the next one crooked and bare. She could not keep up the pace and walked now beside Tyrrell, a few yards behind all the rest where the light was dimmest.

But her eyes gleamed bright in the darkness and her hair was long and fair as a girl's and flowed out from under her lace cap to overwhelm her shoulders and fall halfway to the ground down her back. There was nothing she could not do with a needle, and she was famous for her lace-knotting and her fine quilting stitches, which she made at random without patterns or lines, forming perfect circles and coronets and wreaths of feathers from the strange geometry of her uncrippled mind. The gowns she made for the women needed no patterns to cut by, and were as fine as any from Philadelphia or London.

It was the third summer she had spent with them in Rufford, working a few months for one family, then a few more for another, taking orders for her sewing and stitching far into the night when the households slept. No one seemed to know her age nor where she went in the winters nor where she had come from so suddenly. Since the War they were not questions you asked of lone women, if you were kind.

"They who be trodden upon in the darkness, Pumpkin-dear," she told Twig, "shall be raised up furious in fire and light." She cocked her head, studying Tyrrell's silent form as they moved through the dark. "Have you a name, sir?" she asked him. "Are you furious?"

"My name is Tyrrell," he said.

"If your mother told you so, my pretty gentleman, she deceived you. I know your name. It is Riddle, for you are a question without an answer. Give me your arm, now, Riddle. Walk with me kindly and keep me upright. For I tilt sorely sideways, and one day I shall slip straight under the ground if I don't watch out.''

He linked his arm through hers and she leaned on it heavily. "That's a good Riddle," she murmured. "A kind Riddle in small things. But what of the great things? *Are* you furious? Shall you rise up in fire?"

"Ah," said the secretary softly, "if I am a riddle, then you must find me out."

So they trudged on.

A small field had been marked out to one side of the path and the trees felled, the stumps still standing waist-high. Hannah knew the place and she walked ahead, with Jonathan on one side of her and Daniel on the other, holding a lantern high to find the path. She spoke to no one, took no one's arm; she was thinking what she must say to the woman who had taken the place she herself had prayed to be freed from—the empty half of Jamie Trevor's bed.

Behind them, a woman's voice began to sing a psalm, and another took it up, and then Lachlan McGregor's deep bass and Josh Lamb's tenor.

> *Our God, our help in ages past,*
> *Our hope for years to come,*
> *Our shelter from the stormy blast,*
> *And our eternal home.*

As they passed a thicket of scrub birch, Jonathan stopped. He bent to pick up some object that had caught his eye as the lantern light struck it—a gold piece. "Spanish?" he said, peering at it. "Or king's sovereign?"

Most of the gold coin in circulation came from the Indies, through the rum trade, and was Spanish in origin. But except for rampant smuggling, that trade had been at a standstill during the War, and the Treaty of Paris had done nothing to restore it. Gold coins were rare birds indeed these days.

"It's strange in such a place, surely," Daniel replied.

"And gold suits very ill with foreclosure. This is a hard, bare corner."

He had brought no weapon, for since the War he avoided anything you might chance to do harm with. Unless he went hunting or had the militia company to train, his musket and sidearms were kept locked in a box in the stables at the Grange, along with his swords.

But something in this place made him wish he had brought them, all of them, and more.

There is an energy the dead transmit to the living, to men who have seen much of dying and have killed in their turn, and to women like Hannah who have watched many souls out of the world. Not ghosts, for Daniel did not believe in them, except in the hearts of the living. Not even the cold hand of God, for having made the world, He had surely set it adrift.

So Daniel had no name for what he felt. But in a place where someone has lain dead, even weeks or months before and is long gone and buried, it still remains in the air—this fragment of displaced life that refuses to surrender and harbors itself like a seed in the heart of the world, waiting and warm. It was what Hannah had felt as she sat listening beside James's body.

And it was here in this clearing, Daniel knew it. Before his feet stumbled over the heavy ax. Before he glimpsed the quilts spread upon the dead bodies. He felt the muscles clutch tight across his chest and his senses grow keener— the darkness smashing down upon him, the lantern light blinding, the scent of the pines unbearably sharp. Suddenly he grasped at Hannah's arm and pulled her hard against him, not for her sake but for his own.

> *A thousand ages in Thy sight*
> *Are like an evening gone,*
> *Short as the watch that ends the night*
> *Before the rising sun.*

"What is it?" Hannah said. "Daniel, let me go."

He could not keep her, then. She pulled away from him and walked a few paces ahead. But at the edge of the clearing, she stopped. Behind her the others ended their singing, the only sound a low, fruitless rumble of thunder from somewhere beyond the woods.

Daniel held the lantern higher, and Hannah saw what it was that had made her stop. A wolf sat on his haunches in the middle of the yard, motionless, staring straight into the dark as though he had been waiting for her. He was old and grizzled, with a brownish muzzle, and he stood perfectly still there, watching soberly over the dead.

They could smell the corpses plainly now, for the day had been hot. A heavy, sweetish smell, it was, like roots left too long in a cellar, but with a sour edge that cut into the nose and the throat and made the eyes water and weep. By the lantern light they could see the dried blood that had soaked the faded quilts, and the shapes of the human things that lay underneath them. But nothing had pulled away the coverings, neither raven nor fox nor bear nor opossum in search of easy food.

Nothing smells death more keenly than a wolf, and nothing knows better that life feeds upon its own ruin, that the dead must be used and not wasted. Still the big animal had not torn at them, had not even nosed away the quilts. He was their guard, and he made no move to leave them now.

"Fire will drive him away," said Josh Lamb. "Fetch a pine bough and we'll set it burning!"

Hannah took another step and the wolf bared his teeth and growled. He made a feint towards her, but she stood her ground, with only a few feet between them.

"They who be trodden in darkness," said the sweet, high, fearless voice of Bertha Pinch, "shall be raised up in fire and light. Ain't that so, my fine Towser? Come, dog-dear. Come away, now."

Still arm-in-arm with Andrew Tyrrell, she stumped forward through them all. When they reached Daniel's side, she slipped free of her guardian and went to where Hannah stood alone in the dark, a small hand upon the midwife's arm.

"Nothing falls in the grave, my dear," she said, "but what is lifted. Nothing is lone, but it has much company there. Towser knows, don't you, my darling? Towser has his corner, and must keep it safe till we come."

The wolf stared at her for a moment. Then he turned and trotted away into the trees and was gone.

For a moment it seemed that he guarded them still. No one moved.

" 'The s-souls of the righteous are in the hand of God,' " said the unsteady voice of Reverend Gwynn, " 'and no torment will ever touch them.' "

"Amen," said Josh Lamb.

The rest was done in silence, as it was owed to them.

Daniel went from one of the covered dead to the other and lifted the quilts away; it was not easy, for the blood had stuck them down when it dried. But he took pains not to worry the bodies, to leave them what peace he could. The small lanterns made circles of light that seemed to float through the darkness in no living hand, and what soft sounds they made as they hunched over the hacked bodies were not weeping nor praying nor mourning as the dead are easily mourned. They were the sounds of breath that has no right to come freely, of hands reaching out to grip the air because there is nothing else left in the world.

Sarah Firth knelt beside the two small ones and took the dead baby up in her arms and held it against her breast, and McGregor bent low over the little girl, his face hidden in her blood-soaked hair.

Tyrrell sat with his back against the cabin wall, holding Grace's dead hand in his own, lips moving silently. Preacher Gwynn stood benumbed in the center of the clearing, unable to remember any more prayers. A few yards away, in the shadow of the corn patch, his sister

Merriam sat blank-eyed and isolate, keening softly, and Bertha Pinch rocked an invisible child in her empty arms.

Daniel had found the ax and picked it up gingerly. It was a felling ax with a long helve, the head heavy and brutal. The weight of it alone would have smashed those delicate skulls. Their killer had only to raise it above them and let it fall without aim or decision. Perhaps without will, thought Daniel. They had been there, that was all, in the path of death like a church in the path of cannon fire.

Josh and McGregor had lit the torches again to make a better light, and Daniel could see fresh hoof marks in the hard-beaten dirt before the door. A horse had been there, from the depth of the hoofprint a nice sturdy little cob, strongly made and stocky. A driving horse, most likely, for carts and carriages, but used as a mount when need be. A hire-horse from one of the inns.

His breath caught, and he bent to look closer. It favored the right forefoot slightly, for the print of the shoe was jagged and missing one of its nails. It was the same horse Daniel had borrowed to ride up to Rook's Nest that afternoon. Andrew Tyrrell had been here, there was not the slightest doubt.

Still, Josselyn *did* doubt that his aunt's secretary had done the murders. The woman had had no time to run inside and bar the door against their killer, had not even left off her work when he struck. And on a horse, through such dense woods, you could take nobody by surprise.

He looked around for Tyrrell and saw him enter the cabin alone, a lantern held high. Daniel followed, hoping to ask about the hoofprints he had found, but Jonathan, too, was inside. He held his tongue and waited, hoping Tyrrell would speak of his own accord.

"Look here, sir," said the secretary, and held up his lantern to better illumine a spot on the dirt floor. It was pounded hard as stone and carefully swept with the birch broom that stood in the corner. There were several others stacked together nearby; it was evidently a small family business.

James Trevor, solicitor-at-law. James Trevor, peddler of brooms.

It was not an uncommon declension for a Loyalist. Half of England's great houses had Harvard-educated servants since the diaspora after the War. Poets, philosophers, statesmen—they had all fled or been expelled and impoverished. The king had promised them pensions to reward them for their loyalty to the crown, but the Royal Commission in charge could not help everyone. The strong survived, and some flourished. But many exiles had ended, Daniel's letters told him, in Bedlam, as mad as wild birds. Or had gone—as James had—to the Canadian wilderness and, near to starving, killed their helpless families and then themselves.

Surely, surely James Trevor had done the same in this place. Daniel ached for an answer that would sweep Hannah clean of it and leave her some peace.

But the hope of a simple solution faded quickly as Jonathan stared down at the beaten earth where Tyrrell shone his lantern. The partial shape of a woman's bare right foot was twice stamped there, just inside the door. It grew fainter with the second step, like a signature too much blotted and half worn away. The ball of the foot was clear enough, narrow and slender, and the outer edge long. The shape of the heel was barely there, not borne down upon. There was a third print as they followed her, a small, shapeless blot in the dust.

It led to a rough-hewn table against the far wall. A leather razor strop hung from a nail and a cheap, smoky shaving mirror leaned against the wall. On the table was a set of good brushes, tortoise-backed and inlaid with silver, though their bristles were almost worn away. Beside them stood a shallow wooden dish of soft homemade soap, the sort poor men used for their shaving.

But there was no razor to be found.

The three men looked at one another.

"Only a wet foot could leave prints on this pounded earth," said Tyrrell quietly. His eyes were huge and his

hands shook; he locked them again behind his back.
"There has been no rain and scarcely any dew this morning. She must have stepped barefoot in the blood before
it was dried and brought it in with her unknowing." His
eyes met Daniel's. "When she came inside for the razor.
And the quilts."

"Jesus. A woman, then," murmured Johnnie Markham.

"Oh, yes," said Tyrrell. "It would take a woman, you
know. To think of the quilts."

Hannah had scarcely spoken since the wolf left them.
She moved from one of the shattered bodies to the other,
touching each in their turn. The others watched her and
one or two put out a hand to her. But at last she stood
alone in the middle of the clearing, turning round and
round in the dim light, confused.

"Who is it?" she said aloud. "Who is hurt? Jennet?
Jenny!"

She was spinning, then, bumping the sharp edge of the
darkness like a moth against fire and falling into the
light again.

"I have lost her! Where is she? JEEEENNNNNYY-
YYY!" she screamed.

Hearing her, Daniel forgot the secretary and the footprints in the dust and came out of the cabin, half-blind in
the dark, the flickering lantern behind him.

Twig bustled over to Hannah. "No, no, ma'am," she
said. "It's not your little one, she's safe at home, she—"

"Get away!" Hannah flew at her. "You don't know!
Let me go to her! Let go!"

Suddenly she turned like the wolf and ran headlong into
the darkness.

"She is possessed!" wailed Twig.

"Let her be, Pumpkin," said Bertha Pinch gently. "The
dark will bring her back again sooner than we."

But Daniel snatched the lantern from Tyrrell's hand and
was gone.

*　　*　　*

He found her on the bank of Blackthorne Creek, hunched and silent. She did not cry, and whatever wild fear had come over her had ebbed quickly away.

"I don't want you," she said. "I don't want anybody."

"You've seen too much this night."

"No. I can look at anything."

"Oh, I know your 'anythings.' Come, let me hold you."

"I don't want you! I don't want holding!"

"Christ, Hannah," he whispered. "I do."

He stood apart from her, his shoulders bent and his knees giving way, the earth not enough to sustain him. He slumped down with his face in the grass, weeping as men weep, and some few women. Like a bone through the heart.

In a minute he felt her hands stroke his back and her head lean against him. It was nothing to do with any love of him, he knew that at once. It was how she touched the dead when she washed them and laid them out for burying, to smooth the pain and the fear of passage from their limbs, and the last of the life-fever.

As she had touched him on their first night together at the Forge, with the distance of the grave between them no matter what their bodies did.

She took both his hands in her own.

"And do you think I killed *these,* too, then?" she said.

"No. Christ. No."

"And James?"

"On my soul. No."

"Because you don't want to think your mistress could kill?"

His voice came, very low and soft. "You are no mistress. You are my home."

He looked up at Hannah and his eyes were translucent in the darkness, washing her like cool water.

"Others will say I am guilty," she said. "And you with me, do not doubt it. You heard Clinch. You heard Johnnie. My own Johnnie."

"I know, my love," he said. "I know."

And so they sat side by side on the bank of the small stream that ran mourning beside them, hands clasped and bodies parted by the grass. Insects moved in the dark, and away in the woods a nighthawk swooped and dived, and the claws of an opossum scuttled up a tree trunk and then were silent.

Josh Lamb grew afraid for them and left the dead to find them, and the young constable with him. Mrs. Twig puffed and jostled along with them, subdued and afraid. And Bertha Pinch, too, like a pale, crooked shadow in the lantern light.

"There!" said Joshua, catching sight of the two. "Dan's found her. I'll leave one of these lanterns with them."

"Let them be, man," said Jonathan gruffly. He himself would have given much for a hand to hold, and he would not break in upon them now.

"They'll find their way as they came," he said, and stalked back to the cabin.

For a moment longer, Mrs. Twig stood watching. "They touch sweetly," she whispered to Bertha Pinch. "Why, I had never thought—"

But when she looked round, the little seamstress had gone.

Daniel and Hannah did not notice the lantern light nor hear the voices of their friends. For a long while, they did not speak. Then she turned to him at last.

"Help me," she said, very softly. "Or else I shall drown."

"I am here," he murmured.

They stood up and began to walk toward the clearing again, where the others were carrying the bodies into the cabin. It would be no use sending for Clinch; the manner of their deaths and the heat of the day had put them far past the reach of dissection. The most they could do was what the wolf had done—watch over the dead until their coffins could be made.

"Someone must stay with them," said Jonathan.

"It is my duty. I shall watch and pray," replied Reverend Gwynn. "If only some of you will see to my sister?"

"Never you mind, friends," old Luckett said, a big hand on the minister's shoulder. "Go you all home and rest if you can, and pray by your own firesides. I've buried seven babes and a wife, and three grown sons. I sat up with they, and I shall sit peaceful enough with these."

They lighted a betty-lamp that hung by the cabin hearth and set stumps of candles by the dead. Daniel and Hannah, returning, saw the lights flare and steady.

And then, clear and high, they heard from somewhere in the near distance a woman's voice, singing.

> *The cuckoo loves the summer,*
> *The wild goose loves the fall,*
> *The lady loves the blood red rose*
> *That climbs upon the wall.*

FIFTEEN

SWEET HERBS AND LILIES

*A*ll the doors of Henry Markham's house were open to the cool night air when Hannah came in, and candles still burned in the workroom and kitchen and in the bed-chamber upstairs where Jennet lay. It was bright and safe and welcome in the old farmhouse, but after the dead and the darkness even this stronghold seemed fragile, able to be overcome at a breath by whatever monster was abroad.

Uncle Henry was dozing on the great high-backed settle beside the hearth, his stockinged legs stretched out before him and his long-stemmed clay pipe still tucked in the corner of his mouth. Hannah did not wake him, for it would have meant more talk, more protestations and sup-posings. Tomorrow, when Sheriff Tapp arrived, there would be questions enough.

What she needed was to suspend all conscious thought and let the mad pieces sort themselves by shapes and col-ors so that some fabric of sense could be made of them. She longed for time alone with her quilt, where she might at last see a pattern come clear in her mind.

But even more, she longed for Jennet. Hannah did not tarry to snatch up a candle to light her way, but charged straight up the stairs to her bedchamber, where Aunt Julia, barefoot and in her ruffled tent of a nightdress, still watched over the little girl.

"The poor dove's been quiet," she told Hannah. "I

can't say she sleeps. You know her, she cannot be read plain and she does as she pleases—like another I might name.''

The old woman sat in the rocking chair, the only thing Hannah had salvaged from the seizure of James's possessions. A single candle burned on the table, the post Reverend Gwynn had brought that morning lying within the circle of unsteady light. The second letter was still sealed, but the other—the summons from the Orphanmasters' Court—was in Julia's hand.

''Oh, yes, I have read it.''

The older woman's eyes followed Hannah as she stripped off the soiled grey gown and bent to get clean working clothes from her chest. It was not locked. She had forgotten to lock it when she took out her best gown for the dancing.

Dear God, how many other times had she forgot?

''You meant to keep this to yourself, did you?'' Julia demanded, tapping the summons on the tabletop. ''And what did you think to have done? Dare the Court to take her from you, because Mistress Hannah Trevor is not like other women and will not be ruled? Or have you been less of a stiff-necked fool than I think you? Have you gone to Dan Josselyn and asked him to take her as his ward? He would do so in an instant, and surely he has paid for the right.''

Hannah said nothing, only finished her dressing and broke the seal of the unopened letter. Then, absently, she laid it down again.

''You must bend in small things, Hannah,'' said Julia softly. ''Or be broken in great ones. I know, it's his wife that worries you. But if you won't let Daniel take the child, then go to Siwall. He has a softer eye for you since the death of his brother, and he has great influence with the equity courts.''

Hannah smiled, in spite of her weariness. ''Shall I go to him stripped and willing, then? Or may a dollop of fainting and fluttering serve to excite his soft eye?''

"Joke if you will. But I'm an old trout and I've swum about a little. A poor woman has few weapons but her body and little power but what use she may make of it. Ask Sarah Firth! Housekeeper, indeed! Have you not seen she's with child by McGregor?" Julia sighed and shook her head. "Your uncle and I are too old to be Jennet's guardians, and I fear the Court would not have us even without our debts. Josh and Dolly have not the money to spare. No, my dear. You yourself are your only weapon. Do not scruple to use it. The protection of a man of influence is what you need, and if it may not be Daniel, then it must be another. Matters will be even worse for you now, what with this business of ax murders and throat slittings."

If most gossip in Rufford proceeded from Bella Twig and her circle of cronies, then all honest news seemed to come to Julia Markham's door to be judged and balanced.

"Bertha came back from the woods wild-eyed, poor thing," she went on. "She told us what's been found there. And about James. Sweet God, I'd never have known him. And that hat, a jade's trick of his, that was! Well, he was ever a practiced deceiver. I pity the poor lass he betrayed."

The old lady finished braiding her hair and pushed a few stray locks back from her forehead, wiping her eyes surreptitiously.

"Did he never come to you, my love?" she asked gently. "Did he never tell you he was hereabouts?"

"If he had, I'd have been gone the next day. No, he dodged me and laughed at me behind my back, no doubt, when he succeeded. But I never knew he was here, or even alive in the world. And—I did not kill him, Aunt. Do you not believe me?"

"Why, what a question!" Julia got up from the rocker and put her arms around Hannah, heat or no heat, and kissed her. "You are my sister's child and as good as my own, and I know nobody kinder. Except Husband, and he cannot help himself, for I haggle him into it!"

She let Hannah go and stood by the window to catch the faint breath of wind from the east. The hope of rain had all but gone, now, though there was still low thunder from far away at sea.

"You have been more at peace these last months," said Julia, "and I thought you had partly forgave James. But why did he come back here, do you think?"

"I don't know, dear Aunt. I don't know anything. I'm a great sinner, and the sky has fallen on my head this night. I'm too tired to think."

Hannah climbed the bed ladder to sit beside Jennet. The one-eared ginger tomcat they called Arthur had found his usual spot beside the child, but another human in the bed was one too many and he jumped down with a thump and went to sprawl before the window, where there was a hint of breeze.

Feeling him gone, Jenny opened her eyes and saw Hannah kneeling next to her in the wide featherbed. The little girl's mouth gaped and she sat up, suddenly afraid again, her arms held out for rescue.

"Anh," said Jennet Trevor. "Anh."

It was raw and painful, but it was not a scream made in fear, and though Hannah had no idea what it meant, she knew well enough what it was.

It was a word, the first Jenny had ever spoken.

"Annnhhh," said Hannah softly, learning the sound herself. "Annnnnhhhhh."

She put Jennet's fingertips to her throat and made the sound again, so the little girl could feel the thrill of the vocal cords deep in the sheath of nerves and muscles along the neck and breast. The child put both hands upon her own throat, then, eyes very wide.

"Annhh," she said. A half-smile came to her face. "Annhh . . ."

But then Jennet's fingers began to move. Delicately, slowly, they drew themselves across her own throat from right to left. Her lower jaw dropped and her eyes rolled and her mouth gaped open. Her legs began to kick and thrash, and Hannah pulled her close and rocked her back and forth.

"What is it?" said Julia. "An apoplexy?"

"No! I don't know! She's gone wild again."

The old woman bustled into the hall. "Husband!" she cried. "You're needed! At once!"

In a minute Henry's stockinged feet came thudding up the steps. Other feet could be heard coming down the stairs from the attic where the hired girls had their beds, and in a moment more, Kitty, Susan and Parthenia put their heads in at the door and Bertha Pinch stumped unevenly up the back stair. Still Jennet thrashed and flailed and battered her small fists against Hannah.

"It's how she was in the arbor," said Henry, trying to get a grip on her. "But I vow it's worse this time. What brought it back again? She was sleeping peaceful, Mother said."

"She woke and saw me put my hand to my throat," Hannah told him. "And then she seemed to remember something. Oh, Uncle. I think— I think she has seen James's throat cut."

"Annnnhhhh!"

"No, Flower! Shhhh!"

Jennet's thrashing grew suddenly worse. Her lips were a strange blue-purple and the vein at her temple stood out under the delicate skin, the blood slamming angrily against the fragile wall that contained it. If she were not calmed soon, there might be convulsions. Brain fever. Damage to the heart.

"Never mind the dead!" cried Julia. "Hannah, you cannot hold the child. We must tie her arms to the bed!"

"No! Go down to the stillroom. On the second shelf, near the back!"

"Sweet woodruff, of course!" Julia cried. "I'd forgotten! A strong tea and some honey to make her drink it down!"

"And some of the lemon balm and primrose flower, too. And bring me the valerian, I want too little of it to explain the dose. If we use too much, she will never wake.''

"I'll go!'' said Kitty.

"I'll boil the water!'' said Parthenia.

"I'll fetch the honey crock!'' said Susan, and the three of them flew anxiously away to the kitchen stairs.

Mrs. Pinch and Julia sat on either side of the bed, trying to calm the child, and Henry Markham laid a hand on his niece's shoulder. Between them there were few deceptions, whatever face they might put upon things in public.

"Shall I not fetch Daniel, child?'' he said, very soft.

For a fraction of a second, Hannah hesitated. "No, Uncle,'' she replied at last. "Don't send to him. He knows how it is, he will come if he can.''

"But you will not ask it of him?''

"That I will not,'' she replied, and bent again over the floundering child.

In order to keep it as best they could for the dissection, Clinch's servant and some of the women had laid out the body of James Trevor in the small icehouse at Mapleton Grange, with a watch at the door and a torch burning outside. But the great house itself was dark and silent by the time Daniel made his way upstairs at last.

He went straight to his wife's bedroom and felt his way in the dark to her bed. He often came in as she slept and looked at her, or stood in the door and listened for the safe sound of her breathing. It was more than the dangerous bleeding that came if she moved about too much; since the brutal siege of labor, her heart was damaged, the beat too fast and not regular. He feared the effect of the night's disruptions upon her.

But Charlotte was sleeping quietly, her fair hair loose and spread across the pillow like spiderwebs, so soft it was. He thought of the dead woman at the cabin, how she had lain so, perhaps, her loose hair swirled on James Trevor's chest.

Daniel had seen many women die in the War, and chil-

dren too. One small girl of four or five he had kept alive
for nearly a week, separated from his company and wandering with her in the woods. Picking berries and mashing
them for her to eat. Snaring rabbits and squirrels. Sleeping
with her thin, frightened body held close against him, his
cloak wrapped round them both. Murmuring old stories to
divert her, singing children's songs—"The Happy
Farmer" or "Banbury Cross." Rocking her for hours, till
his arms ached with the weight of her and she lay fast
asleep on his breast.

Then, at the end, his horse dead under him, Daniel had
run with her in his arms, skirting the British patrols and
the villages where you never knew what side it was safe
to be on. He had heard a cow lowing from a farmhouse
one early, wet morning, and gone to steal some milk for
the little girl, leaving her wrapped in his heavy wool cloak.

Lily, he had called her. *Lily-flower.*

When he got back to where he had left his child—for
so he thought of her—carrying the stolen milk gingerly in
a small leather cup, Daniel Josselyn had found his Lily
lying uncovered in the rain, a single bullet in the middle
of her forehead.

Someone had killed her for the cloak.

Human creatures could kill for anything, and so it was
not the deaths of the woman and children they had found
in the woods that surprised him. It was how gently they
had lain, and how long. Covered with weighted-down
quilts, as though their killer cherished them.

But a man who loved them would have struck them
down in their sleep, surely, or at least carried them inside
the cabin after, and not been satisfied with quilts in the
open. And there were the footprints. Whether she killed
them or not, there was some woman at the heart of this
business, and it was not Hannah.

And where had the woman and children come from that
Trevor lived with as his own, calling himself Reuben
Stark? Had he found them as Daniel had found Lily? And

who was this Stark, if there really was one? Where was he now?

What of the gold sovereign—for so it had proved? An old coin, it carried the head of the second George, not the third, the reigning king. What need had a man with gold of selling brooms at a fair?

And what of the wolf that had guarded the dead? Some of the others had taken it for a portent, but Daniel did not believe in visions. Many of the trappers and woodsmen kept tame wolf pups and made dogs of them. Surely, he thought, he had seen the animal somewhere before, he was sure of it.

And the kerchief. The damned black-edged kerchief.

In love we wed, to love forever.

Needing to feel himself closer to Two Mills, Daniel left Charlotte sleeping peacefully and went down to his library. Twig had drawn the curtains across the long window that faced the river and the mill, but he opened them again. A candle was burning in the upstairs window of the Markhams' farmhouse, where he knew that Hannah and his daughter lay.

"You are still waking, Nephew?" said a voice behind him, and Daniel spun round as though a sword had pricked his spine.

But it was only Sibylla. In the shadowy hall beyond them, he could see the outline of Hobble just out of earshot and the figures of Jenks and Owen, who had borne her down the stairs.

"I have spoken to Tyrrell," she said. "A wretched business, these deaths. He is badly shaken, good man."

The old lady took a step and stumbled in the dark room, and Daniel reached out a hand to her—his sound one. But she would not take it.

"No, sir, let me have the other," she said. "Without that everlasting glove of yours! I am not Charlotte. Come, now."

Daniel took off his glove and offered her his hand. The

ring finger and the middle finger had been hacked off just below the knuckle. "Many have suffered far worse," he said. "I grow quite used to it now."

"Who did it? Some savage?"

"A woman. A child, almost."

"And what had *you* done to *her?*"

"Nothing. What I was or had done did not matter. What I seemed—that was enough."

Sibylla let her own soft, dry fingers travel over the ruins. "Does it pain you?"

"Sometimes. In dirty weather." He took his hand away again and slipped on the glove. "But it's nothing to fret over now, my dear. I'll walk back upstairs with your chair and see you safe to your bed."

"First we shall talk a while."

Daniel smiled in the darkness in spite of himself. When Aunt Sibylla's voice had that peculiar tone in it, nobody argued. His grandfather had used to compare it to the sound of a pickax breaking rocks.

"You must know," she said, "that I did not sail all the way from London to watch Charlotte work pincushions."

"I thought you were bent on a visit to Philadelphia. Your old beau, Mr. Franklin."

"That is as may be." She walked a few paces, then stopped again. "In the main, I am here because my poor brother Robert, your grandsire, gave me upon his deathbed a most solemn commission to you. I had no one to carry it out in my stead."

"Not even Mr. Tyrrell? You seem to place great faith in him."

"Tyrrell is paid to do as I bid him. He keeps my notes and gathers plants for my botanical studies. He has a good eye and a knowledge of science. He is my legs and arms, as he was tonight. But he is not my mind, nor my memory. Nor my affections. So I am come myself."

"Where is your secretary now, Aunt?"

"Why, abed, sir. Have you need of him?"

Daniel considered telling her about the telltale hoof-prints, but he did not wish to alarm the old lady.

"It will keep till daylight," he said. "But what is the commission from my grandfather, if I may ask?"

"You may not. Not tonight." She took her nephew's arm. "You are spent, and I need more time to sort things through and tell the weeds from the simples. But it does me good to see you, Daniel. Though you *are* a selfish scapegrace, and snatched up all dear Robert's brains and left none for your brothers, the oaf and the milksop." Sibylla reached up and let her hand travel lightly across his features. "Oh, you are very like my brother. I miss him sorely."

"He was my friend," he said softly. "Best friend."

Without intending it, he glanced across the river to the house on the opposite bank, where the candle still flickered in his daughter's window.

"And there?" said the old woman, pointing her walking stick toward the small light at Two Mills. "There is another friend, even a better one. Bold Midwife Trevor, who has borne you a daughter. Has she not?"

Daniel's temper flared. "And this you were told by your pair of extra ears, Mr. Tyrrell? He has been listening too well to Mrs. Twig!"

"You offer no excuse for this miserable liaison?"

"I love her dearly. For that I owe you no apologies."

"Confound you, sir, I speak of coupling, not of loving!"

"You speak of what you know nothing about!"

"Nothing? Pah! Did you think you invented it?" Sibylla laughed. "You may bank your fires, sir. I did not like to believe you a mere trifler, and I am glad to find you are none." She paused, then began again, more imperious than ever. "But you raised your voice to me just now, Nephew. Do not do so again. I wish only to do you good. Remember that."

"Forgive me," he said, and gave her a stiff little bow.

"Well. We shall see if I do."

He turned to go, but she stopped him with her stick.

"You must know Charlotte will not live much longer," she said. "I've seen many like her, and I know. Six months, perhaps eight. A year, if she's not excited."

Daniel felt panic and guilt wash over him. "Is there nothing I can do? Some medical man, someone you know of in London?"

"Some plants choke on their own roots and strangle themselves of the effort of growing. If it had not been travail that ruined her, Charlotte would have found some other way. There is no medicine for it. Let her be, and comfort her as you can."

Sibylla gave Daniel's arm a fond pat, then started toward the hall where Hobble awaited her. But partway there, she paused. "You believe there is more to these killings you have found tonight than meets the eye, I think."

"Indeed, many things do not ring sound."

"And there is some danger to you?"

"Sheriff Tapp arrives tomorrow, and he is a hard man of few scruples. Mrs. Trevor is already suspected, and perhaps I may be myself."

"Ask Tyrrell's help, then. I called for him before the child cried out, but he was gone like a will-o'-the-wisp. It was not above a quarter-hour until he was beside me again, but much may be seen and done in a quarter-hour."

"And throats may be slit?"

"Oh, I do not suspect him. But though he has been near three years in my house, I know no more of him than I do of the king of Ethiopia. He sees more than he says, and he may know something that will aid you. He seemed—oddly excited tonight, at the dancing."

"He has hired a horse for his use, Aunt. Was it for your purposes, or for his own?"

"I believe they often coincide. I took him on because he wished to return to America."

"Mr. Tyrrell is American?"

"His speech scarce betrays it, I know, but that is true

of many of your new countrymen. I took great care in planning my little expedition. I cast about for a guide familiar with the native ways and plants, and schooled enough to keep my notebooks and attend to my correspondence. Tyrrell presented himself at my door, and I hired him on the spot. As to the horse, I told him he might surely ride upon some animal of yours, but he would have none of it. He is independent, and brooks no charity. And he seemed to know who Mrs. Trevor was without the telling."

Again Sibylla pointed to the window of Two Mills.

"A light is still burning in that chamber there. Is that why you are not in your bed? Does she wait for you?"

"The lady does not keep lights in the night unless someone is unwell."

"And you fear for the small one? My great-great niece." The old lady smiled in the darkness.

"Jennet was badly shaken. I had thought they might send for me to come, but—"

Sibylla's white head shook with irritation and she lifted her stick and brought it down with a whack on his shoulder. "Why will men always sit about like slugs on a garden wall, waiting an invitation?" she cried. "*Go there,* sir, and be a proper father to your child!"

✖ SIXTEEN ✖

SHADOWS

*D*aniel raced up the steep hill to the Markhams' farm-house as though it were afire, only to stop short at the open back door. This was Hannah's place and she had not sent for him; he paused on the sill, uncertain.

"If he should do her harm," said a soft voice from inside, "I shall take off his head with a sickle and rake him up for hay! If he grinds her down to shame, I shall issue forth thunderbolts wholesale. Oh, how shall I not, for such as him?"

Bertha Pinch seemed to have no companion in the work-room but herself. She was in her nightdress, which was long and loose and made for a woman twice as tall. It lay along the floor at her feet like a coronation train or a christening gown; there was a capelet of fine snowy lace over the shoulders, and lace hung like icicles from the sleeves and the hem, and lace stood up like sharp slivers of ice round the neck. On her long, fair hair she wore a cap of lace, too, and in the pale yellow light of the single candle that flickered on the bench at her elbow, she herself might have been made of frost or of snow, or of strange white flowers that bloomed only by night.

"I shall smite sore if he fails her," she said. "Oh, you know I shall cudgel and thrash."

She sat by the cold hearth stitching, a length of rose-colored wool cloth draped over the settle by her side and a half-dozen pins tucked neatly in the corner of her mouth. On a wooden trencher on the table, a picking of purplish-red, overripe raspberries had been laid out painstakingly to dry. Someone had begun to string them on a linen thread in the fashion of a necklace, but the end of the thread hung down from the table, the needle swinging faintly in the draft. A rush-seated chair had been drawn up opposite Bertha's place at the settle, and on it lay a woman's plain grey shawl, neatly woven but unlike any he had seen the Markham women wear. No one else was in sight; perhaps it was Bertha's own.

Still, lest he intrude on some women's confiding, Daniel knocked on the door frame before he stepped inside. But Bertha Pinch's eyes did not leave her sewing.

"You see I sat up for you, Shadow," she said, taking the pins from her mouth. "You are dreadful late, and if time were convenient, I should be sharp with you. Sharp as coffin nails."

"To whom did you speak, ma'am?" he asked her. "Before I came in, you had some other here, did you not?"

"I? Why, I do not speak. I am silent, like poor little Childie. Oh, but sometimes my straight self speaks loud, though, and threatens dreadful and stamps her foot and shouts down the wicked to hell."

"And which are the wicked, my dear?"

"Never make me your dear!" she snapped. "I am too crooked to be dear but for pity, and pity *she* will not have! *She* shall rise up and nip you if you call me dear anymore." Bertha smiled up at him then. "You may be *my* dear, Shadow. Only I may not be yours. I wasn't brought up to it, you know. I don't expect it. I am used to the other. I like it better by now."

"What? Other?"

"Why, scoffings. Fleerings and hootings. Stones bouncing off my old hump like hailstones. Rotten eggs and apples from behind hedges in broad daylight. I am used to such. But *she* never was, and I fear for her."

Daniel laid a hand on her cheek and she bent her head

against it. Something glinted on her lace cap in the candle-light, and he could see now that all the fine lace was stuck at random with pins and needles, some large, some small, some bent and some perfect.

"Do you mean Mrs. Trevor?" he said. "But who shall fail her? Not I?"

"There, it's made your eyes grow great and round, because you doubt yourself! Well now. If I must choose between a riddle and a shadow to lean on, I shall have the shadow every time. For a shadow cleaves to its honor, which is to be where it need be. But a riddle, now! Why, a riddle is a dodgy thing. 'Tis near as bad as a sermon."

She took his arm and held it hard.

"Promise me not to put faith in them!" she whispered. "Promise, for your life and for hers!"

Her breath came shallow and she clung tight to him. Whatever her strange talk meant, her fear was real enough.

"I'm thick-headed," Daniel told her. "You must speak plain and make me understand you. What man do you fear so?"

She did not answer for a moment. "I gabble as it takes me," she said at last. "Perhaps it is nothing. Perhaps I am daft as barn owls."

Where her hand held his arm, he felt cold. He laid his other hand, the damaged one, upon her. "It was you who sang in the woods last night, was it not?" he asked her. "At the last, when we were bound for home? You have a sweet voice for a song."

Bertha laughed again. "Do I look like a nightingale?"

Daniel smiled. "Like a changeling, I think. But had you been there before, to the cabin? Did you know Mrs. Stark and her children? Her man—did you not know him? Did you know he was Mrs. Trevor's James?"

"I know everyone a little and myself least. God, I do not know at all. But He made the acquaintance of my mother briefly, and left her this gift to place upon my back. Is it not graceful? Do you not think me a beauty?"

He watched her turn in the candlelight, and although

her poor body was crooked and stubby, her face was finely modeled and handsome and her hands were long-fingered, delicate. As she turned, they seemed to float free of her and ride of themselves upon the air, edged with the snowy lace she had made and jeweled with the pins and needles that flashed and caught the light and loosed it free again. There was a tender grace about her as she danced with her own shadow in the flickering light.

"Where do you come from?" Daniel said. "Where is your home, where you winter? And your husband, where is he?" She was *Mrs.* Pinch, or so the other women sometimes called her.

"You are a dreadful, pesky shadow this night," she replied, suddenly sharp. "And I have enough of your questions. Off with your great clumping boots, now. You must walk soft here."

While Daniel did as she ordered, the little bent woman fetched a candle from the box on the wall and lighted it from the stub of the one that still burned on the table. Then she led the way up the narrow back stair to a door of pine planks with a sound iron latch.

"Don't tarry too long," said Mrs. Pinch, handing him the candle and opening the door without a sound. "For we must all be somebody else in the daylight, you know, and the sun will be up before long."

Daniel stood outside the door until he heard her uneven footsteps die away down the stairs again, and then the soft murmur of her voice as she took up her work. He went into Hannah's room and closed the door and looked around him.

The window was wide open to the night, where bats squeaked and circled, diving close to the eaves and away again, drawn by the small light. The candle on the table was almost guttered and a cloud of tiny midges flew around the flame, some left struggling in the soft tallow that had dripped onto the saucer below.

He snuffed it and set the one Bertha Pinch had given him in its place.

There were some letters on the table, but he did not read them nor even glance at the handwriting. They were a landmark of the room, that was all, like the midges and the candle and the two or three pictures on the wall draped with cheesecloth and the bright-colored quilt draped over the rocking chair.

The bed was high and old, with a frame of rails above it that held curtains for warmth in the winter. The hangings had been removed for the summer and the bare scoured rails laid narrow bars of shadow across the bed below where Hannah and her daughter were sleeping.

The little girl lay on her back in the middle of the rumpled featherbed, the woman on her side with her arms clasped round the child and her face against the fine reddish hair. Jennet slept, but now and then her feet still thrashed about as though she were running and her small hands opened and closed into fists.

Daniel stood for a long time watching the two, then sat down in the rocking chair. The old cat who slept by the window woke and came to sniff him over, then curled itself against his feet. The night was very still, without even a breath of breeze; his clothes felt heavy upon his limbs, as though they might smother him.

In the east the lightning could still be seen far, far out at sea. Even the Night Watch had made its last round, and the watchman's lantern was a tiny speck of light in the distance as he rode back toward the jail along the village high road. The last shift at the mill was long over and the great wheel silent; there was no light but the dull pewter gleam of the Manitac and the brighter polish of the mill pond at the top of the sluice.

Then something moved at the edge of the pond. At first Daniel thought it might be some animal come out of the woods to drink—a venturesome buck or a moose, perhaps. But it was human, a tall, slender shape, a woman or a boy. It eased into the still water with scarcely a sound and for a long time it stayed down and did not break the surface.

At last the long slim body came up from the pond and stood on the far bank, outlined against the pale sheet of lightning in the western sky. It was a woman; Daniel could see the soft droop of her breasts as she turned and lifted her arms up, outstretched to the sky.

There was another shape on the bank beside her, a twisted, crouching shape, thick where it should have been thin and thin where it should have been supple and curving. It wore a long gown of white that glittered by the blue flare of the lightning—the pins and needles that adorned the crooked shape of Bertha Pinch.

My straight self, she had said, and he had thought it a fancy. But surely this was the woman who had dropped her grey shawl when she heard him and fled.

Then both women were gone into the darkness, as suddenly as a pair of revenants. It put Daniel in mind of the old stories of silkies, seal-women who came to land and mated with men, and then slipped away again and their human children with them, to find comfort among their sisters in the sea. And yet there were stories, too, of how they came back to their true husbands, found them drowning in storms and lent their life-warmth, and buoyed them up again to living.

Daniel got up from the chair and went to the bed and lay down opposite Hannah, the child between them.

Help me, else I shall drown.

"I am here," he said very softly, and took hold of her hand.

Daniel did not remember sleeping, but he was not sure how long he had lain there when he felt Hannah's fingers touch his face. He let his own fingertips tangle in her short, dark curls and lie there for a moment. He felt deeply at peace now, with Jennet's body curled close against him, as though he had lived here always with them and his other life were a dream.

Life. Marriage. Husband. Peace.

This was what the words meant, this room and this bed. The law would scoff at it. The church would condemn it. Hannah had wanted no more marriages, no more yokes upon her she could not remove. And he himself, if he had been free to do so, would have been reluctant to risk marriage again.

Now here it was, grown like a tree from a wind-planted seed. This quiet, small place. In this bed, they were as truly married as if they had knelt in a church.

And yet, the ancient words mattered. *Thereunto I plight thee my troth.* The ceremony of honor pledged. He was still too much an Englishman to shrug it off.

"How is our girl?" he asked quietly, and kissed his daughter's forehead in the flickering, liquid dark.

"I've given her medicines," Hannah said. "But she was wild, Daniel. Worse than before. I think— I think she *saw* James killed."

"And saw who killed him?"

"And *was* seen, I fear. Jenny is known to have no words, so the killer would have thought it safe enough to leave her, perhaps. Until she made sounds. But now—"

If she can scream, she can speak. If she can speak, she must die.

Daniel's arm closed tighter around the child. "Christ," he said.

Hannah eased herself out of the bed and stood up. He lay still, watching her, feeling the sense of connection drain away from him. Awake she seemed smaller, more self-contained than elsewhere, all her careful defenses in place again. She sat down in the rocker and took the old cat on her lap, her hands stroking him from nose to tail and nose to tail again.

"Daniel?" she said quietly. "What would become of you if you never saw us again?"

He came away from the bed and crouched beside her chair. "We'll find out the truth of this business in a day or two, my heart. Don't fret so. I'll send a man to watch over Jennet, shall I?''

Hannah shook her head. ''Even if there were no James and no Mrs. Stark. I think I must not stay here longer.''

''Have you grown ashamed of me?''

''God forbid.'' She kept her face turned away from him. ''But I took too much upon myself.''

Once James was gone, Hannah had wanted a child of her own, one that had nothing to do with any husband. She had taken careful stock of the men in Rufford and chosen the strange, damaged Englishman who worked at Quaid's Forge. She had never intended to commit the folly of loving Daniel Josselyn, and when she realized she had done so in spite of herself—that all her ironclad rational plans and deductions were founded on the quicksand of passion—she had sent him harshly away. For eight years, until the winter just past, the delusion that she needed no one and nothing had grown up like a safe wall between them. That wall, too, had been her doing, not his. Her pride. Her fear of weakness. Her refuge against memory.

In the winter it had all come tumbling down, and now she ached for the old wall to lean on.

''If I do not leave here, I shall marry Matthew Gwynn,'' she said.

Daniel's eyes closed. ''If that is what you choose, I have no right to hinder you.''

She handed him the summons from the Orphanmasters' Court that had lain all along upon the table. He read it, silent, squinting into the candlelight. Then he laid it aside.

''Gwynn is cold and smug and I don't like him,'' she said, ''but I see no way else, unless Jenny and I leave here and go where I am not known. Even if I were not half-suspected of these deaths, I could not find enough money to satisfy this Orphanmasters' Court—''

''Is that all? Christ God, I'll give you a thousand pounds tomorrow, as soon as I can write a draft on my bank in Boston! What use is money to me without you and Jennet?''

"Hush, sir," she said, and laid her hand on his face. "They'll hear you. My aunt and uncle sleep beyond that wall."

She folded the summons again. The unopened letter lay just beyond the candlelight; she took it up now and began to unfold it.

"There's that timber land I've put aside," Daniel told her. "I shall only have to post a bond with that and the court will accept me as Jennet's trustee. She will stay with you just as always and nothing more said of it."

"But legally, she will be under your control. And Charlotte's."

"Ah. So that's it."

"I don't mean that Charlotte would harm her, but—"

"But you don't trust me not to raise her as Charlotte's daughter instead of your own."

"I do trust you! That's not fair! Only—"

"Shhh. Shhh."

"But to risk losing her now, just now, when James is found dead upon your doorstep with a trifle of mine in his hand! So many dead," she whispered. "I cannot grasp it. What kind of creature could kill as those in the woods were killed?"

Daniel frowned. "I have been thinking. The kerchief, the quilts—they are a woman's thought and a woman's deed. And we found the print of a woman's foot in the cabin. But *could* you handle such a great ax? Are you strong enough? Is any woman?"

"An iron stewpot full of hot soup weighs forty pound, my love. A boilerful of wet wash fifty or more. I have felled trees in my time. So have most women who live in rough country and are not born to a houseful of servants."

"Well, if it was a woman, then other women know her." He was thinking of Bertha Pinch and her friend. "There is a kind of sisterhood among you, of stitchers and quilters and weavers and hired women and wives."

Hannah's fingers traced the stitches of the light summer quilt on the rocker where she sat. It was not a pieced pattern of squares and triangles, like the one of Red Roses in her frame downstairs. This was another sort, made of irregular scrap pieces laid down on a muslin backing and fitted together as best they might be, the jagged edges trimmed or turned under and embellished with bits of lace or ribbon or embroidery to disguise the joins and keep them from raveling.

Maid of Bedlam, they called it, or sometimes simply *Crazy Quilt.*

Broad end to narrow. A woman with a short, thin foot. A lone woman, expected by no one, missed by no one if she does not arrive on time. And yet, perhaps, welcomed because she is kind.

Narrow to broad. A woman who works hard for her keep and is stronger than she looks. She knows the woods, wanders in them. She has no fear of anything or anyone but of those who have power, because she is poor and alone.

Hollow to heart. She goes barefoot in summer, for she has but one pair of shoes and must save them against the cold months. Many things she does because she must, no matter what they cost her in pride or discomfort or disgust or guilt. A poor woman. A weary woman, worn thin as a wire. A woman with only her body to buy her survival, who uses it as best she may.

Heart to hollow. A woman well enough known to raise no suspicion if she enters this house—or any house—and is seen. Known and unknown, seen and disregarded. All women are nobody. Poor women are nothing at all.

If she kills, she is a woman ground down to nothing, who carries a banked coal of rage deep and low, as I do, like a child in the belly, and gives birth to it suddenly, without warning. A woman mad in her birth-pangs.

It is someone I know, and more like me than different. A tiny fleck, only, to set us apart. Something pushed down and down till it smothered and died there, and made a grave of the heart.

"Would James have covered their bodies himself if he

killed them?'' Daniel asked her. "Had he such tenderness in him?''

Hannah stared at her lap. "When my children died,'' she said, "he would not come to their bedsides for fear of the fever. He left me alone with them, in their chamber. It was summer, as now, and I had had the sitting room sheeted and the floorcloth taken up. James sat there, waiting for the fever cart to come for them and haul their bodies away. One by one, they were all taken. After the last, I came out of the chamber and down the stairs. I heard the men's feet clumping on the floorboards. I heard the door close behind them. They were carrying Benjamin. My strong little hobbyhorse. My little boy. I stood there, listening to the wheels of the cart in the street as they drove away. And there was—a sound then. I have heard something like it from you in your sleep. A great howl that made the candle-glasses rattle. No words. No prayer— he was not a man for praying. Only a howl, like the end of the world.''

"So. He loved them after all.''

Hannah looked up at him. "He dragged them back to Boston to die of fever when I would have brought them here to Maine and kept them living. Love them? He hated God, that is all, for proving me right. He howled out his hate, and in a week he was ready to get me with child again. It was his best means of punishment. But even that I refused him. I went to an old black woman, a runaway slave who knew many remedies. She gave me some oil from the root of a certain plant. It made me very ill. When it was over, the child was no longer in me. This I did twice. I have told you before, I would not bear him another child if I died for it.''

Daniel wanted to touch her, but dared not. "Could he have murdered them so? With an ax?''

"How can I say? Only he wanted my death as much as he could ever want anyone's, of that I am sure,'' she said. "And yet he struck me but twice, in anger. He was not brave enough. And besides—''

She broke off and sat silent. There was something, still, more bitter than she could bear to speak of. But he did not press her to tell him.

He put his two hands on her shoulders. "We'll have the truth of it," he said. "That I swear."

"I care only for Jennet." Hannah sighed. "We need time, but there is less than a month till I must face the Court, and if there is a charge of murder upon me they will take her, money or not. And tomorrow comes the sheriff's questioning. He will set Johnnie aside and carry all before him, of that I am sure."

Daniel let his hand stroke her cheek. "I heard of the pelting. That lout Squeer taunted me at the mowing." He paused, wondering how far to press her. "Do you know the man, my love?"

She glanced at him. "Has he said so?"

"He has an idle tongue. I faced him down and his friends took you to task for it at the fair. They are torn by their debts and their fears, and all the old anger is rising again."

Hannah stared down at her hands in her lap.

"Will there be another war?" she asked him. "I have heard my uncle talk of it, and Josh. The militia is raised already in Massachusetts, they say."

Daniel shrugged. "Men know when they have been sold and betrayed. They will bear it so long, and no longer."

The sky was growing pale and a soft ground fog lay on the mill pond and the river beyond it. In another quarter-hour the sun would be full up and the heat would come back again.

"I must go," Daniel said. "But— Hannah?"

"Sir?"

She kept always this small refuge from him, as most women did from their men, this tiny edge of formality that could shut you out in the blink of an eye. *Husband,* they said. *Sir. Keep your distance. I can do quite well without you if I choose.*

"If you must leave here, send me some word. I won't

come after you, I promise. But I beg to know if— If I am to be alone.''

He stepped to her and kissed her lightly on the forehead, paused for a moment beside Jennet's bed, and then was gone, soft-footed down the stair.

And then, by the first pale light of that storm-breeding July day, Hannah opened the letter that had lain in her room since the previous morning. If she had read it sooner, she might have left Rufford before the sun was high in the sky on the day of the haying, and never seen Daniel again.

SEVENTEEN

Piecing the Evidence:

Letter of Mrs. Grace Stark, Dated 5 June, 1786

To the Midwife Hannah Trevor at Rufford, Province of Maine

I trembled to call upon you in sickness, for though he speaks very ill of you, that you have killed his three children in Boston, he says you are his true wife and I sinfully take up your place in his bed. But now I have seen you in my sickness, and know you, how you are kind, I can leave you no longer in the bonds of untruth.

James Trevor, your husband, is yet living and names himself Reuben Stark.

He did wed me two year since in Canada and got there a child upon me, and he told me but lately he had a wife in this same place yet living. And he took my dead husband's name upon him to be safe when he came here, for there was no treason ever cried upon my Reuben.

And so it is as though my own dear husband did never walk upon the earth, and he is utterly gone down unto the dark.

But I think Mr. Trevor will leave me and have you back again for all that, for my little money is used up. And though he may name you a whore and beat you when he drinks and rages, yet he is sorry after, and gentle enough when he is sad. And you must pity him then in spite of all, and do what you may to pleasure him.

I have writ to my own husband's brother, but if he should fail us and the winter come upon us here, and Mr. Trevor leave us for you or some other, my babes and I are lost. For we are now very poor.

He meets wild men in the woods and I fear them, for they care not what they do.

> Grace Stark, Unwedded Wife to James Trevor

Think of me as a sister, for whom you must pray.

✖ EIGHTEEN ✖

PIECING THE EVIDENCE:
On the Nature of Disregard

The woman who had killed Grace Stark and her children in the early morning remembered nothing of it after she left the woods to go to the haying. Where she had first heard the old love song that battered over and over again at her mind, she did not recall. She knew nothing, either, of the chamois-skin pouch with the gold piece in it, nor the black-edged mourning kerchief she had brought from her grave in the woods, nor the razor she had stolen. They lay wrapped in her shawl, in the draw-chest where she kept what little was her own, and when—that heavy, hot afternoon before the haying supper—the man found them among her things, she could not say how she had come by them.

"Why did you steal this?" he shouted, shaking out the pouch onto the table and laying the kerchief smooth. "I'll have no thief in my house!"

He had come home dejected and angry and shrunken, and his sorry eyes looked out upon a desert life that stretched blankly away before him with only death for a landmark. She saw it and knew that despair had made him dangerous; he had never so much as shouted at her before.

"How did you come by a gold sovereign?" he cried. "Where have you been?"

The woman said nothing, only stepped near to him and stroked his face and his chest. Gently she undid the flap of his breeches and slipped her two hands inside them, where his sex had already grown hard from his rage.

"Whore! What man have you been with? This razor is his." He squinted at the name engraved on the blade, but his eyes were bad and he could not make it out. "And how did you come by this kerchief?" he shouted as her slim hands explored him. "It is Hannah Trevor's!"

"She gave it me," the woman told him.

She slid down onto her knees between his long legs, slowly, slowly parting them, turning him to her and rousing him, humming softly as she worked, as though she were carding or spinning or plucking a goose.

"There is no other man," she said when she had finished. "Only you. I love you. You will not send me away now. I will do whatever pleases you. Only I will never marry you, that I have sworn."

"Oh, my dear," he whispered, his hands stroking her hair. For he did love her. "What have you done?"

In his voice there was pride and a kind of worship, and she knew that he would do anything to keep her, now, and would always be hers no matter who else he took to his bed.

"I am," she said. "I love you. I am."

And she pulled his face down to her and kissed him tenderly, and was at peace.

But peace was her enemy. Whenever she drifted upon it like the shore of an island, she lashed and flailed until her moorings broke again and the huge, faceless sea of her rage set her free.

In the peaceful kitchen garden of her father's house, near the lilac hedge, there had grown a strange, squat plant with broad hairy leaves. Horses trod on it and men drove oxcarts across it and children ran over it. Still it thrived and was mown off and thrived again, ugly and useless.

One day, an old woman of the neighborhood came asking to pick up the wool their sheep left on the briars and hedgerows, and she saw the plant and clapped her hands together.

"Give me but a root of that comfrey," she said, "and I will work for you two months and ask nothing more for my pay."

"Why? How is that?" said the girl.

For she, too, had sprung up in the place in spite of disregard, and though she was poorly made and unhandsome and her brothers railed at her because they could not marry her to rich, self-important men who wanted only pretty wives, she was strong in herself, and secret and true.

But no one would have paid two months labor to have *her*.

"Such an ugly, scant thing precious?" she said, amazed. "It has not even any flowers."

"If you have an ache that will not comfort," said the woman, "or a sore that bleeds and will not heal, comfrey will cure it. For it has God's grace within it, so it does."

The girl was surprised, for she had thought the grace of God an invention of preachers, to keep people happy and themselves sleek and fat.

"Or if you have a bone of you broken," the woman went on, "and a battered place that will not be tamed, then lay a leaf or two of this upon you, and it will make you whole."

So that night the girl took a leaf of the plant and laid it on her breast while she slept, where her own heart should have been, and where her soul should have had its hiding place.

But she woke as empty as ever, and believed the plant had failed her, and God had failed her. For she did not know that the soul is an empty cup that must be filled with grief to be seen, and God is the broken shards of grief that fill it. She believed that He, too, disregarded her and drove over her with the huge wheel of His indifference.

She poured tallow on the comfrey plant and brought

fire from the kitchen hearth and burnt it like a living torch, leaf to stem and stem to root and deep below the root, into the empty cup of the grieving earth.

Then she said the word to herself.

Nothing. I am nothing human. I am a weed to be torn from the world.

Her father had died a month before she was born, and her mother was a thick, simpering woman who spent all her attention upon her five handsome sons. She flirted with them as though they were her suitors and pampered them even more than she did her lap dog, Fudge.

One by one they all sickened and died of her smothering, and only the girl was left.

She was sixteen when her last brother died, killed in a duel over a married woman he had chosen because he knew she would drive him to death. They brought him home to his mother's fine parlor and put a coffin on the backs of four harp-backed mahogany chairs and laid him inside it with his pale hands folded on his breast where the wound had been bleeding. There was a triumph written on his face, because he had set himself free at last.

When the girl came into the parlor to see him, her mother was bent beside the coffin, a piece of linen edged with black needlework held to her eyes. She had no love for the boy; love was beyond her. But he had let her possess him and rule him, and she did not possess the girl, who was distant and calm and had known he would die as the others did, because he could not escape by any other means.

"What do *you* want here, you horrid girl?" shouted the mother. "You are no good to me! Go fetch me a cushion for my back and then walk to the village and bring back the post."

It was more than six miles, and she had made one trip already that day.

"I will take the ponycart," said the girl.

"Ponycart? You? What are you, that I should indulge

you with ponycarts and carriages? You are not made for a lady. You shall walk, as the other servants do.''

''Then if I am a servant, I will not go unless you pay me.''

''Not? Will not?'' The old woman's face grew red and she tore the black-edged piece of linen in half. ''No, you will not! You are no use to anyone, not even in small things. Ill-made and stupid as you are, I cannot wed you to a decent fellow who will look after my property. If anyone marries you now, it will be some wastrel who takes you for the money that should have been your brothers'! Who would have a thing such as you in his bed for any other cause?'' Her eyes narrowed and grew sharp as the lash of a whip. ''Go to my chamber and fetch me another mourning kerchief. You have made me ruin this.''

''I will not,'' said the girl, and did not move. ''My brothers did not fetch for you, nor walk to the village for you, nor brook your disparagements. I suppose I am as good as they.''

''You!'' cried her mother, her hand upon the dead boy's coffin. ''You are to blame for this! My life began to die on the day I conceived you! My poor husband could not live in the same world with you! My sons are all murdered and gone!''

''You killed them,'' said the girl. ''The weight of you upon their hearts! I have no heart. I will live.''

''Murderess!'' shrieked the mother. ''My sons are all murdered and gone!''

The housekeeper and the parson came in and tried to silence the old woman, but she continued to scream. ''Murderess! Cold-hearted brute!''

The girl stood silent in the middle of the room. It was raining outside the windows, a cold November rain that slanted down onto the pond at the edge of the brown lawn and the dark pines beyond it, with white crooked fingers of paper birch at their edge.

''Bitch!'' screamed her mother. ''God sees you! Every breath you draw on the earth is an abomination! If any man takes you, may God look down and curse your womb and make your husband deceive you and your children all breech and miscarry and die!"

The old woman sank onto the floor in a stupor and did not seem to breathe.

"Is she dead?" asked the housekeeper.

"I fear so," said the parson.

"We must pray for the grace of God upon her soul," said the housekeeper.

They bent their heads over the mother, but the girl stood still, looking down at them from a great distance. She began to laugh at the thought of the grace of God, and her laughter was high and sweet and beautiful because she had never laughed before in the world. Still laughing, she went to the fireplace and took up a heavy poker and raised it above the parson and the lap dog and the housekeeper and the body of her dead mother.

"Get out!" she said aloud. "Get out of my house! It is my house now. I will use it as I choose!"

She struck hard with the poker and split the top of a walnut table. She struck again and broke open the cushions on her mother's French brocade lolling chair. Again and again she brought down the poker on the things that had been her mother's and none of her own.

"She is mad!" cried the housekeeper.

"Possessed!" whispered the parson. "Driven wild by her grief!"

When they had run away, terrified and wailing, the girl went upstairs and took the fire ax from the hallway and went into her mother's chamber and chopped open the three feather ticks that lay on the bed where she and her dead brothers had been conceived. She chopped up the drop-front desk and the crewelwork chaise and the japanned blanket chest at the end of the bed, and the lap dog, Fudge, who had run there to hide.

Finally she chopped out the window glass and the rain came in and found her face and washed her clean. She stood a long time at the window, watching the grey sky clench itself against her like the brow of God.

Then she went down the stairs and into the kitchen. All the servants had run away, frightened, and only the dead were left in the house. She took tallow from the barrel and melted it over the fire and poured it in a narrow trail from kitchen to workroom and workroom to parlor and parlor to library and library to music room. Then she took fire and set it alight and went out of the front door into the garden, where the rain was still falling.

The pond was clear as fine pewter and she walked to it calmly, as the fire ate room after room of the great house her father had built for his strong, handsome sons.

But she hardly looked at the fire. The girl unlaced her bodice and took it off and folded it carefully, and laid it on the dead grass, and took off her stays and her skirt and petticoat and her stockings, and folded them, too, and made a pile of them with the other. At last she took off her shift and was naked in the rain, her small breasts with their rose-colored nipples grown hard and pink in the cold.

" 'Breech and miscarry and die,' " she said softly to the rain, and laid her hands on her belly and stroked it and knew her mother's curse would come true.

A thin coating of ice had formed on the surface of the water, but she slipped into it like a seal that loves the cold and dived deep, deep, straight to the bottom, looking for her new self and her soul that was gone.

It was there, and she saw it. A homely plant with charred leaves that grew stubbornly upward. A battered cup overflowing with tears.

"I am," she said. "I am."

NINETEEN

THE GOOD GRAIN AND THE CHAFF, OR THE MAGISTRATE'S RETURN

" '*F*or shame, Mr. Punch! You should regard me as good as yourself!'

'Regard you? I shall beat you and break your pate and beat you, beat you, beat you, you dreadful Judy, you! I shall cudgel you sore!'

'Ow, ow, ow, ooooooowwwwwwwww, Mr. Punch! You have killed me with your cudgel! Your spiteful old cudgel has broke my poor head!' "

A small crowd had gathered outside Lamb's Inn to hear the puppet-master, but almost nobody was laughing. Even the faces of the children were blank and frightened, as though Punch had struck them with his club. Inside the inn parlor, the mothers, too, looked big-eyed and fearful, and they glanced at the men with furtive, suspicious eyes. But the fear was not only of axes and knives.

It was ten o'clock and still too early in the day for drinking, but Lamb's was as much a public gathering place as a tavern and hostelry. In the corner near the big walnut case clock, a dozen grim-faced farmers and townsmen sat on benches, waiting to take their turns at the table where Gabriel Bent presided with his tax book and his money box. He was a pale, thin fellow in his forties, with a lame right arm from the War.

George Anson, who had a small, rocky farmstead near Maid's Hill on the South Bank, was at the taxing-table now. He was a tall man and heavyset, with a long, lugubrious countenance and grey eyes set deep in his skull, like musket balls in a bore. He emptied a heap of crumpled paper bills onto the table.

"There, now," he said. "There's near a thousand in Continentals. Army pay, and I was long enough getting it. But take them and be damned to you."

Gabriel Bent's dark eyes were dead and black as two lumps of charcoal in his pale face. "You know I can't, George. Continentals and scrip is no good here. I must have a hundred and ten pound hard coin."

"Wait a bit, Gabe," said Ralph Bunce, always moderate. "Siwall's come back in the night, so I hear. P'rhaps they'll be issuing new bills that's sound, now the General Court's heard our petition, and all will be square again."

"And pigs got wings and fish got fingernails." This came from Freddy O'Neal. "Even if they issue new money, they'll not trade us even up, man, you know that. It'll be ten new bills for a hundred of ours that we bled for."

"Could you not take a signed note-of-promise, Bent?" asked one of the moderates, Nathan Berge. "Half in this room'll be in Debtor's Jail before Michaelmas else."

But a tax gatherer agreed to collect a fixed sum for each township according to its rates, and if he failed to arrive at the Excise Office with the proper amount, he had to pay what was lacking out of his own purse. Gabriel Bent had signed for more than four thousand pounds. If he gave way, he would end up in jail himself.

He shook his head. "I must have hard money for taxes. And I must have it now. 'Tis the law, and none of my doing. A hundred pound, George. I shall knock back the ten, but that's as much as I can manage. I'm that sorry, but there it is."

"Oh, aye? And shall I piss hard money? Or pick it off the trees?"

Anson glanced across the room at his wife. They had eight children, the eldest not fifteen and a girl. The wheat was not yet cut and the corn barely tasseling. Without him, how would they bring it in? Or cut firewood for the winter? Or butcher the black pig and salt it down?

He stared at the table before him, his big hands turning and turning, as though he might wring hard money out of his pores.

Rufus Penny picked up a Boston newspaper from the bench beside him. "You need wait for no help from the Court, friends! They scorn laboring men as much as ever the king of England did."

He began to read, in a loud, barking tenor that cut through the tobacco smoke like acid.

" 'These countrified plough-plodders who whine over the payment of a fair tax in recompense for our glorious freedom must learn to live by their means. What need has Madam Plodder of a pearl necklace and a taffeta gown? Let her learn her station in life and forswear vanity for her country's good and her husband's self-respect!' "

"Polly, girl!" cried Anson, and his wife, who sat sewing with some of the others, looked up, shamefaced and afraid. "Show the tax gatherer your pearl necklace, my darling! Why, it shines out grand when she's digging potatoes! Show him your taffeta gown, now, and your velvet slippers and your diamond buckles and combs that I gave all my self-respect for!"

Polly Anson's skirt was washed thin and her boots were her husband's old ones, cut off at the tops and run-over at the heels, and the nearest thing she wore to a jewel was a raveling bit of pinkish ribbon folded and stitched into a sort of cockade to cover a nursing stain on the breast of her gown. She looked down at herself, laid her sewing on the settle beside her, and put both hands to her cheeks. The men stared at her and a few laughed and murmured.

Then Dolly Lamb came to stand by her, and Freddy O'Neal's Annie and Mrs. Firth. Even Squeer's slattern wife, Nell, came across to them, and Ruth Dowell, and some of the women from the fair. Under the eyes of the men they drew close together, as though their bodies were one body and their bones one bone.

For who knew but themselves that they walked nearly twenty miles in a good day's spinning at the great wool wheel? Or that flax hetcheling left their hands raw and split and bleeding, or that long after their babies were weaned, they kept their breast milk flowing by putting puppies or young lambs to their nipples in secret and nursing them? So long as her milk was good, a woman was less likely to find herself with child again, and most had borne five or six, many ten or twelve or fifteen.

One after another, more and more women joined the group around Polly Anson. Scarcely seen by the others came Merriam Gwynn, the minister's sister, her pale, squarish, scoured-out face circled by dirt-blond hair plaited and pinned in a nimbus, like a tall, gaunt, absent-eyed madonna.

"There's sixpence, Gabe," said George Anson angrily, and threw a coin onto the floor at the taxman's feet. "It's all the hard money I've got. Take that, or take paper."

"Or take a coat of tar and feathers for the sake of Liberty!" cried someone at the back.

"Up the Regulators!" cried another.

It was Ike Squeer, his voice like turned vinegar. He moved to the middle of the inn parlor and some of the other men followed him, dogs to a bait.

Just then Jonathan Markham stepped in from the porch. He looked nervous and spent, and carried a musket at rest across his arm. With the other, he ushered Hannah Trevor in at the door. She did not move to join the women, but stood by herself near the cold hearth in the side parlor.

"Another mention of Regulators," the constable said, "and you'll all spend the rest of the fair in my jail, playing checkers with mad Dickie Bunch! They dragged two of the sheriff's men from their bed at the Cat and Drum in Wybrow last night and beat them senseless, and they burnt Toby Dunn's barn and all his animals besides."

Dunn was magistrate in the nearby village of Snaresbrook, on Mount Sable, one of several islands near Gull's Hook where the Manitac began to widen toward the sea and the larger port town of Wybrow.

"Aye, to the devil with him, and all magistrates like him!" shouted somebody. "We're dirt to them, and we may go beg for a living! They're worse Tories than the Tories ever was!"

"If Tapp's deputy dies, as he's likely to," said Jonathan, "there's them in this room may have to answer for it."

"And who shall answer for *that,* then?"

Through the open door, a heavily laden oxcart could be seen making its laborious way along the near side of the common. In the cart lay four coffins. The weather was too hot to keep the bodies of Grace and her children any longer, and they were to be buried early that afternoon in the little walled graveyard between Preacher Gwynn's house and the church.

On the largest of the four coffins the felling ax lay like a crucifix, a bundle of fireweed and Queen Anne's lace wilting in the sun beside it.

Squeer scowled and his eyes grew slitted and piggish as he pointed a bony finger at Hannah. "There stands the slut that did for Trevor! Aye, and that poor woman and her young ones, too!"

Hannah turned to confront him, feet braced, eyes wide and unblinking; her breath was quick and her head trembled slightly.

"Why do you hate me so, and abuse my good name?" she said. In spite of her unsteadiness, her voice was very clear. "All here know I am not what you call me."

A murmur. A few nods. Sarah Firth smiled and came to Hannah's side. Even some of Squeer's friends looked shamefaced.

"To some men, all of my sex are but wantons," she went on. "If that is how you regard us, sir, then we may all be pelted and called sluts."

Squeer snorted. "Regard you? I don't trouble myself to think much of women at all."

Hannah smiled and bit her tongue, and her fists clenched tighter. "Perhaps you find it overtaxing to your brain, sir. But I know my sums, if you do not. And I pay my debts prompt."

Her hand came suddenly out of her pocket and connected hard with Ike Squeer's face in a resounding slap, and then another, and yet another, like three musket shots in the quiet room.

He swayed a bit, then righted himself. Hannah stood her ground and he grabbed her and pulled her hard against him, his voice a low rasp in her ear.

"How if I tell your fine lordship what I know of you, eh? Do you think he'd be so tender of you and your brat if he knew?"

The organ-grinder was playing outside, his parrot chattering and fidgeting. Nobody spoke.

"I— I—beg your— Pardon. Sir," Hannah said aloud.

Ike Squeer let her go. Her eyes were blank and unfocused, and she fumbled rather than walked past them all, until she reached the door to Dolly's stifling kitchen. She opened it, went inside, and closed it soundlessly behind her.

Alone in the kitchen, she took a dipper from the pail of water and poured it into a basin and washed her face where Squeer's breath had touched her, and took off her bodice whose sleeves he had soiled with his hands and put it onto the cooking fire and watched it catch light.

"Ah, Jesus," she said, and sank down on her knees.

And then Hannah Trevor, whose weeping no one but Daniel Josselyn had ever heard before, began to sob, great smothering sobs so loud you could hear them everywhere in Lamb's Inn.

Out in the kitchen garden, Delia the hired girl heard her and looked up from emptying the potato peels and grew afraid.

Up in the sleeping rooms, Captain Christian Fairway of

the brig *Intrepid* heard her in his sleep and clutched his pillow against his face and murmured, "Now, now, my love. Now, now."

Down in the cellars, the mice heard her and thought it was the spiders mourning the short lives of their delicate webs.

And out in the inn parlor, the men and their wives and the children and Mr. Punch himself heard her and fell silent and stared at the floor. Squeer subsided into a corner with a tankard of Josh's beer, smirking and hard-eyed.

Sarah Firth pulled her shawl close around her as though she were cold, and Dolly got up to go to her cousin. But her husband put up a big palm to prevent her.

"Let her be, pet," said Josh gently. "Give her a moment in peace."

But if Merriam Gwynn heard him, she paid him no heed. She moved very softly, and Hannah did not know she was in the room until she felt something brush her shoulder.

"How is the pretty child?" said the minister's sister in her odd, sweet voice.

"Still sleeping, I hope," Hannah told her. She could not yet stop the tears, but she swiped at them, determined. "She was badly frightened at what she saw."

Mistress Gwynn took her two hands and put them suddenly to Hannah's face and stroked the wet cheeks with her fingers. Then she put her fingertips to her own mouth absently, tasting the tears. "And you? How are you?"

"I am—" Hannah would have said "well enough," as she usually did. But the wide blue eyes would not let her. "Badly frightened, too," she said.

In a split-second she was in the other woman's arms, smashed tight against her. Merriam's long, slim body was taut and hard, every nerve and muscle concentrated. She laid her face against Hannah's bare neck in the same way Jennet had, and Hannah felt the soft brush of the woman's lips against her skin and the thin hands stroking her, travel-

ing gently along her back and shoulders under the thin
shift she wore.

Hannah disentangled herself from the strange embrace.
Suddenly shy, she took one of Dolly's shortgowns from
the basket of clean laundry beside the ironing-table, put it
on and buttoned it. It was some sizes too large in the bust
and her ludicrous appearance seemed to break the spell
between them.

"Merriam? Ah, there you are."

Without bothering to knock, Matthew Gwynn strode
into the kitchen and took his sister's arm. There was a
burst of shouting from the inn parlor, and the crash of
crockery onto the wood floor.

"They are beside themselves," he told Hannah. "Mr.
Siwall and the sheriff have just arrived."

Hannah sat down heavily on Dolly's cushioned settle,
her hands gripping the edge of the seat. Sheriff Tapp had
sent Johnnie to bring her for questioning, and now he was
here at the most inopportune moment. She looked about
for some water to bathe her eyes, so he might not perceive
she had been crying and use it against her.

She had been a fool to indulge in it. Weeping was
always a mistake.

"I must attempt to calm them, but . . ." Gwynn paused,
his eyes searching her face. "You look very ill. I think
you have not slept."

Hannah did not reply.

"In regard to what we spoke of—" he said.

But she did not let him finish.

"Truly, I cannot wed you, sir," she told him.

"Not that. It was— I was foolish. But there is something I must tell you. I— I will speak to you again," he
said, and hurried out to the parlor, Merriam's thin arm
through his own.

Hannah collected herself and went to join the others;
their attention was all upon Hamilton Siwall now. But
Josh Lamb came quietly beside her and drew her back to

rest against his arm. From the other side she felt Dolly's hand grip her own and hold it hard.

Siwall was a stocky man in his early fifties, red-faced and excitable and unskilled at disguising his loyalties. He was not cut from the cloth that made successful politicians, but he had a taste for power—perhaps, thought Hannah, more taste than talent.

But today she barely noticed him, for with him was Marcus Tapp, Sheriff of Sussex County. She had seen him often enough when she was called to give testimony at inquests and hearings, but until today she had had no need to take his measure carefully.

He was younger than she had realized, no more than forty-five, with curling chestnut-brown hair worn long and tied back at his nape. A broad face, high-boned and somewhat too flushed across the cheeks, as Siwall's was. Brows growing grey and throwing his face slightly off-balance, its whole focus on the startlingly pale blue eyes, almost like the painted china eyes of blind men.

But Marc Tapp was anything but blind. He glanced in her direction, bowed slightly, and gave her a quick, sharp little nod.

He had the brutal, ascetic manners of a lifelong mercenary; he had fought for the Spanish in Portugal, the Swedes in Denmark, and the Russians wherever they ravaged. During the War in America, Tapp had indulged himself and fought for the sake of principle—though which one, it was never quite clear. Nobody was certain of his private beliefs nor where Siwall had met him, but they knew well enough why he stayed.

Hamilton Siwall spent money to make money, and once he had made it—however he made it—he called it God-given and used it to make more; Marcus Tapp was what it had bought him.

"Read the document again, Constable," he ordered.

"What need have we to hear it?" cried Anson. "We shall pay and they shall play, and that's the way the world wags!"

"Friends! Friends!" cried Reverend Gwynn. "Let the man speak, for your own sakes! 'Render unto Caesar the things that are Caesar's.' "

The crowd was very angry, and Jonathan looked pale and young and frightened, his hands gripping his musket hard.

"Read, damn your eyes!" roared the sheriff. The men fell silent.

" 'It— It is the judgment of the General Court of the State of Massachusetts and its Upper Province of Maine,' " began Jonathan, " 'that taxes cannot be lowered if the state and the province are to meet their obligations to the Confederation. There are great war debts owed to the French for military pensions—' "

"To the *French?* I lost a leg at Saratoga, and devil a pension *I've* seen!" cried Harry Finsley, who farmed a patch near Gull's Hook.

"Nevertheless," Siwall replied calmly. "There can be no amnesty on debts. Such a measure is certain to damage trade even further—"

"And take money out of *your* pocket, you mean!"

The magistrate raised his voice a bit more. "A new issue of currency is useless without the hard silver to stand behind it. Silver we cannot have without trade, nor gold neither, gentlemen. Surely you must see that. And if we are to have sound trade, debts and taxes must be paid and paid promptly."

"So you say. Only I can't pay if I'm locked up in Debtor's Jail, can I?" said Anson. "And them that owes me is locked up, too?"

"Aye, the Regulators have the right of it! An end to this begging! What we need, we must take!"

"We struck once at tyrants in high office, and we shall strike again!"

"Calm yourselves, friends! That is treason!" cried Gwynn, and tried to climb onto a chair to be better heard. Somebody yanked it aside and he sprawled onto the floor;

for a moment it seemed the crowd would fall upon him and batter him.

"Enough!" shouted Tapp, and he aimed his musket at Rufe Penny's chest. The preacher scrambled to his feet.

"Out, you rounders!" roared Joshua Lamb, wielding the trusty belaying-pin he kept for subduing rowdies. "If it's brawling you want, do it outside my doors! And you, Mr. Tapp, may lower that weapon! Sheriff or no, this is my house and my wife's, and my guests will have no guns aimed at them for the sake of a rash word."

Marcus Tapp's pale eyes barely flickered. He turned the gun away from Penny and for a split-second it was aimed straight at Josh. The big innkeeper did not blink. Tapp cradled the gun at his elbow and gave another short, businesslike bow.

"I cry a town meeting, friends!" shouted sensible Ralph Bunce. "Let us do as we did when the British trampled us! By process of law!"

"Siwall's law!" cried Rufe Penny. "Tapp's law! Not mine nor yours!"

"I second the cry," said Josh. "If the General Court will not hear us, then the Congress must be petitioned!"

"Josh is right!" cried another. "I'm no barn-burner, and my tar mends my roof and my goosefeathers goes in my old woman's mattress! Town meeting it shall be!"

"Meeting!" echoed the others. "Meeting and vote!"

Tapp lowered his musket, his cold eyes without expression. The Penny brothers and Freddy O'Neal looked at each other, uncertain. Squeer gave a nod and they marched sullenly out, trailed by a half dozen more.

"Let us have a psalm, brothers," said Reverend Gwynn. "And a blessing on all just endeavors."

The men rose—even Gabriel Bent at his table full of tax notices.

" 'Blessed is the man who walketh not in the counsel of the wicked, nor standeth in the way of sinners,' " Gwynn began, " 'nor sitteth in the seat of the scornful.' "

His quiet voice trembled with concentration, his eyes

closed and his pale face flushed. He had the disciple's passion, and there was great beauty in his speaking of the ancient verse.

" 'And he shall be like a tree planted by the rivers of water, that bringeth forth his fruit in his season; his leaf also shall not wither; and whatsoever he doeth shall prosper.' "

Here he paused. There was silence in the room. Across the bowed heads, Tapp's eyes met Hannah's again.

" 'The— The ungodly—' "

Gwynn faltered. Merriam stood beside him, her eyes half-closed and her cheeks flushed a deep rose against the close-fitting white lace of her cap.

" 'The ungodly are not so; but are . . . are like the chaff that the wind driveth away.' "

Again he broke off, looking at the faces around him.

"Right you are, sir! Amen!" said Josh Lamb at last, with the hint of a twinkle in his eye. If the fellow had stuck to "The Lord is my Shepherd," he'd not have gone wrong in his lines.

The minister and his sister went out and Sheriff Tapp set off with Siwall, bound for the jail to begin his inquiries. In another minute Johnnie would come to escort Hannah there.

"What will you do now?" whispered a soft voice at Hannah's elbow, and a hand slipped round her waist. It was Sarah Firth. "If they come for you, where will you go?"

"I don't know. Boston, perhaps. I have very little money. I must work."

"There is a house on Gull's Isle, down the river a way, near the Hook," said Sarah. She was plain and slender, but under her gown her breasts were already swelling softly in readiness for the child she carried. "Spruce Cottage, it's called, an old house that hangs over the inlet with its back to a church, and an old woman keeps it. Mrs. Annable is her name. If you must go, go there. She helps many and she will help you."

Jonathan had been speaking to the tax collector, but now he came across the room and took Hannah's arm.

"Tapp's waiting, madam," he said formally, and she could feel the slight pressure of his hand. Power, it meant. And fear, lest she drag him down with her.

For a moment Midwife Trevor's much-vaunted boldness failed her. She must stay at a distance from all of them, now, lest she ruin everyone she cared for. She must give them all up, and be alone.

But not Jennet. Not my Flower. Not till they tear you away.

✖ TWENTY ✖

PIECING THE EVIDENCE:

Enquiry into the Guilt of Mrs. Lucy Hannah Trevor, Wife of James Ramsey Trevor, Deceased Made by Sheriff Marcus Tapp, Recorded by Peter Fellingham, Clerk 13 July, 1786

*S*HERIFF TAPP: You identify the body of the man known as Reuben Stark to be your husband, James Trevor?

HANNAH TREVOR: I do.

T: You say you have believed him dead since February. In what year did he part from you, and why?

HT: Early in 1778. There was a warrant for his arrest.

T: He worked for the king, did he not?

HT: My husband worked for only three things that I know of. Money, position, and pleasure.

T: You have no great respect for him.

HT: I have never known death convey sainthood. Nor does it alter my memory, nor addle my wits.

T: He was wearing the cockade of the Prince of Wales's Own. Do you think he had enlisted in the king's army?

HT: I do not. He feared blades of every sort, and most other weapons.

T: Would you subscribe him a coward?

HT: Such words have a meaning only to men's vanity, Mr. Tapp. James never considered consequences, if that is what you imply. He was often rash and took desperate chances with his own life and with others. Usually for money. Often for pride. He was—romantic. He drew a grand character of himself and lived in it and when others did not see him as he saw himself, he raged and many paid the price of it. His fancies made him a most attractive and poetical suitor. Mr. Trevor could be most charming, most gentle. His manners were excellent, when it served his idea of himself.

T: Did you not perceive this flaw before you wed him?

HT: I was barely eighteen and I saw him only four times before my marriage, never other than in company. It is, as you may know, the manner in which courtships are often conducted in the city. I had a respectable dowry from my father's will, though he was only an apothecary, and my mother was altogether dazzled by Mr. Trevor. He was a lawyer. He had many influential friends among the British in Boston, or so he said. I saw little enough of them once we were wed, and I cared nothing for politics and causes. But my dear mother distrusted nobody, and all her friends considered him a fine catch. They persuaded her. I would they had wed him themselves.

T: You say he was not without virtues. But it was not a kindly marriage, I think?

HT: I said nothing of virtues, only manners. He fancied himself undervalued in general and much put-upon by me. I am plain spoken. It is not a good quality, they tell me, in a wife. No. It was not kindly.

T: Did he strike you?

HT: Once. Twice.

T: Did you complain of it? What did you do?

HT: I struck him back, sir.

T: Did he use other women?

HT: Use?

T: Whores? Streetwalkers? Tavern girls?

HT: At times.

T: How many times?

HT: I did not keep a tally, nor go with him and peep through their windows. I do not see—

T: He beat you and betrayed your bed. Men have been murdered for less.

HT: Oh come, sir. Betrayed my bed? After the first year he might have coupled with apes and parrots, so he had left me alone.

T: And did he? Leave you alone?

HT: I bore him three children, Mr. Tapp. Judge for yourself.

T: So. You were wed to a man you despised, whose attentions were unwelcome but constant. And yet I think you are not a woman to deny the delights of the flesh. You are, if I may observe, handsome.

HT: You may observe as you wish. I would prefer that your hand were farther from my lap.

T: Clerk! Strike that reply from the record! Hem. Now, then. Did you not take a lover, madam? Did you not revenge yourself for your unhappiness?

HT: The question is impertinent.

T: Did you not hold Trevor guilty of the deaths of your three children?

HT: God may judge. There was fever in Boston. He forbade me to bring them here to stay with Aunt Markham, where it was safe. He sent constables to bring us back, because I had disobeyed him for their safety's sake. Within a fortnight, they were dead.

T: And so you harbored this grudge against him.

HT: Grudge, sir? On the Sunday I had three healthy children. By the Friday they all lay dead. I could not save them. I could not even see them buried, I— The fever dead were carted away and burned in a pit. They took my children and hauled them away like the carcasses of cattle, they— Grudge?

T: Clerk! Get some brandy from the inn!

HT: Forgive me. Please get on. I want nothing.

T: Very well. Did he write to you from Canada?

HT: No, sir. From Salem. He had gone to friends there.

T: In what year did he write to you? How often?

HT: In 1780. He wrote once only. Asking for money to leave the country and go to London.

T: Did you send it?

HT: I had nothing to send. They seized everything.

T: They?

HT: The Rufford Committee of Public Safety. My husband's great friend Mr. Siwall sat at the head of it, after he returned from Saratoga.

T: Ah. But surely they left you your dower, right? The third of Trevor's goods?

HT: Like yourself, sir, they were adept at turning words to their own purposes. They said I was no wife, for Tories kept no laws and could have no legal wives. Tory whores, that's what they call us even now. Oh, but I was wife enough for them to claim his debts of me. I am working to pay them yet.

T: Had you known of Trevor's return before tonight? Received any message that he was yet living? Any recent letter?

HT: None.

T: He made no approach to you? Did he not wish to know who fathered the babe you bore in his absence?

HT: James Trevor was her father! I was with child when he left me!

T: It's said in the town that Major Josselyn is the girl's father, and not Trevor at all.

HT: It is said the moon is cheese, sir, and pigs talk French on the eve of Christmas. I do not credit it, myself.

T: But how if Trevor believed the idle gossip he heard at the fair and came to look for your lover? Demanded money, perhaps. Major Josselyn is rich. He admits Trevor paid him a visit in the afternoon.

HT: Question him, then. I know nothing of it.

T: Believe me, I shall. Mrs. Trevor, I put it to you plainly.

When you thought your despised husband dead, you were glad to be rid of him. But he showed himself alive and made demands on you. Wished to return to your bed. Claimed his right as your husband. Intended to avenge himself on Josselyn. So you arranged to meet him in that arbor, and you cut his throat. Perhaps with help, or perhaps alone. And there you dropped in your frenzy this kerchief, worked with your name and his own! Do you deny it?

HT: I do not deny it is mine. I deny that I dropped it. Have you a pocket Testament about you? I will swear.

T: You deny that you knew he now called himself Reuben Stark and had another woman and brats by her, and was living in the woods not three miles from your uncle's house?

HT: I do deny. I knew nothing of it.

T: But you were called to nurse this woman, Mrs. Stark, in the spring. Surely you did see her husband then?

HT: I saw no sign of him. She said he was in the woods, retrieving some furs he had cached in the winter, that he often went off for many weeks at a time and stopped at Fort Holland, with the Dutchman, in order to trade for supplies. He disliked coming into the town, she said. I had no notion it was to avoid meeting me.

T: How long did you tarry with her?

HT: A day and a night.

T: Long enough to find the razor you remembered as his father's and to realize who Reuben Stark really was. Long enough to know that your husband had taken another woman and kept her and her children, while you must keep yourself and pay the price of his treason! I say you thought on it these many weeks, till you'd maddened yourself with it. Then yesterday morning, you went to the cabin and picked up the ax from the woodpile and killed Grace Stark and all her children.

HT: You cannot have it both directions, sir. Did I kill James because I did not want him back, or did I kill his woman and babes because I could not bear to let her have him?

T: You did not know what you did, or why! But when they lay dead and broken, you came to yourself and went and got quilts and covered them. There is a woman's footprint in the cabin.

HT: Match my foot to it. I am not afraid. My feet are wide, and I bear down heavy on my heels, and my second toe on the right foot was broke when I dropped a flatiron on it, and it knit crooked. It would leave a strange impression indeed. Shall I take off my boots and stockings now, so you may see?

T: Minx! You killed them! Her three children for your own three that died!

HT: No, sir. Calm yourself. Mr. Clerk, perhaps that brandy now?

T: I will not have this, madam! You found his razor in the house and took it with you, and when you met him at the fair you engaged to come to him at night in the arbor. And there you came softly and slit his throat where he sat on the bench, waiting for you. You have been weeping not long since, Mrs. Trevor. I can see you are swollen-eyed. Were they not tears of guilt?

HT: I have denied and denied, but you do not hear me. Will you hear facts, now, or am I to be hanged without a hearing?

T: What facts? I have presented you with all the facts.

HT: You offer wild inventions, but they will not do. I have sat corpse-watch with many dead, sir, they are old friends to me. As for Mrs. Stark, she had been past this life many hours when we found her and her children, at something after midnight. Their limbs were entirely stiff, but the small muscles—the eyelids and the cheeks and jaw—had begun to resolve themselves and grow slack again. They died, I should say, sometime before the mid-morning. Fifteen, perhaps sixteen hours would be needed for such a condition to be achieved. A little less, as it was such a warm day. Eight or nine in the morning, perhaps?

т: Well? I am told you didn't go to the haying this morning.

нт: I stayed behind to do woman's work, and woman's work is my defense. I rose at four with the rest and we stoned cherries for preserves and cordial. It was but newly in the kettle when the others left for the meadow at six with the oxcart. I stayed behind, meaning to go later on foot, once my preserving was done. Cordial must be simmered slowly, a good four hours on a low fire, to reduce the juice and give good flavor. A low fire dies easily if it is not attended; you must feed the wood slowly and swing the pot aside from the new flame to keep it from scorching, and rake out the spent coals a few at a time to keep a distance from the pot. The bottles were only just filled and cooling on my aunt's table when Mr. Gwynn arrived at our door at near ten. Now, sir, tell me. If I had been striking people down with axes in the forest in the meantime, then how did the cherries stone themselves and the cordial bottle itself up? You may ask my aunt's hired girls if there was any part burnt in the kettle when it was washed. Did the fire keep itself stoked? And I turned the cheeses, too, you may ask my aunt and the girls how they lay. While the cherries cooked, I dressed a fine big turtle and baked it for our gift to the haying supper. It was there in the oven when they returned. Oh, and I did the churning, as well. There is some buttermilk less in the crock, for I gave some to my caller, but there was none at all when they left to make the hay. Pray, ask my aunt. Or Parthenia, or Mrs. Pinch.

т: Preacher Gwynn was there with you, you say?

нт: And not a half hour after he left me, Mercy Lewis came to fetch me to Burnt Hill to a delivery. Molly Bacon's child, a boy, by Jem Siwall.

т: And they will all swear this? The preacher and all?

нт: How could they not? But only I have no proof where I was tonight when my husband was killed, sir. The dissection is to be performed at noon, and it may tell us more of him than I know myself after eight years' absence.

T: You left the dancing at the precise hour of his death. Why?

HT: I saw Mr. Gwynn coming to speak to me. There was— a particular matter upon which he desired a reply, and I was not yet prepared to answer him.

T: What matter?

HT: It is of no concern to you.

T: So long as you are suspect, madam, all that concerns you concerns me. I am the law.

HT: No, sir. You are the sheriff. But I will tell you. Mr. Gwynn has asked me to be his wife.

T: Hah! You! The wife of Siwall's tame preacher?

HT: I am glad it provides you amusement. But as to the kerchief, our door is never locked and many might have slipped in and taken it. What reason would I have had to carry it with me to the haying supper?

T: To front Trevor. Taunt him with its loving inscription. If you were maddened and out of your wits—

HT: Oh, indeed. If I was maddened and out of my wits, you may invent any wild tale and paint me with it and be credited! But I am not mad, for I still know the difference between a clean gown and a bloody one. My own last night was of a pale color. Ask Constable Markham if he saw any blood on it when I came into the arbor from the field. Ask any who was there. Mrs. Firth. Mr. McGregor. Lady Josselyn saw me plainly, surely you may trust her word.

T: You might have covered yourself! An apron or a smock, or some such gear. Hidden it away, meaning to go back and burn it or bury it. We will find it out.

HT: And what of my shoes? There was much blood on the flagstones. My shoes are dancing slippers, sir, with linen tops. Examine them yourself, if you wish, I will bring them you. They are near ruined by that walk through the fern and bramble last night to Mrs. Stark's house. But you will find precious little blood on them. I picked my

way round it as best I could, but how should I have
been so careful if I was slitting throats and dragging
corpses about?

T: You could've taken off your shoes! Your gown, too,
for the matter of that.

HT: Would you like to examine my shift, then? Or do you
suppose I killed him barefoot and bare-breasted, in the
midst of a company?

T: A tantalizing prospect, madam. But not impossible.

HT: Sheriff Tapp, I have listened to enough of your inventions. I have a dissection to witness at noon, and my
daughter is ill and in need of me. Either lock me away
at once, or let me go home.

T: You will keep within the bounds of Rufford township.
I ask no bond of you as yet, only parole. Your word,
that is.

HT: I know the meaning of the term. I give my word freely.

T: Sign the Bounds-Book and be gone, then. Are you able
to write your name?

HT: Indeed, sir. And though I am no man, I know a fox
that is hunting chickens by daylight. You are fiddling,
Mr. Tapp, and you know I have done nothing. Why not
admit it and help me to look for the truth?

T: You are bold and clever, madam. I admire you. But I
wonder if you are wise.

✖ TWENTY-ONE ✖

Piecing the Evidence:

Testimony of Major Daniel Josselyn, Esquire
Mapleton Grange, Rufford,
13 July, 1786
Marcus Tapp, Sheriff

TAPP: Did you know James Trevor before he left Rufford, sir?

JOSSELYN: No. I had been in the town but a short while before the warrant was issued for him. He did not visit the Forge, where I worked at that time. He was a solicitor, I believe, by profession, and kept his horses elsewhere.

T: But you already knew his wife?

J: She was a friend of Mrs. Hetty Quaid, the smith's wife. I saw her when she called.

T: That is not the question you were asked, Major. I will advise you when you may improvise upon the theme. Did you know James Trevor's wife before he left Rufford? Did you have converse with her?

J: I believe she came once for a pot-hook to be bent for her aunt's hearth. It was necessary that I speak to her then.

T: You have an excellent memory, sir. A pot-hook, after

eight years' lapsing? Did you debauch her immediately, or did you wait until Trevor had gone?

J: You lay very plain snares, sir. But I am no rabbit. I have nothing to do with the lady, nor have ever had. I never saw her husband until yesterday afternoon, when he called upon me under the name of Stark.

T: Very well, let us go down that alley instead. When James Trevor called upon you yesterday, did he say nothing that led you to suspect who he was?

J: He did not.

T: Nothing of his wife, Hannah Trevor?

J: No.

T: Why, then, did you cry out after him, 'Where is James Trevor?' Do not trouble to deny it. You were overheard by your servant, sir. A Mrs. Twig. Had you not then perceived that Reuben Stark was James Trevor?

J: He— It was my understanding that Stark traveled widely. I thought he might have had some knowledge of the gentleman.

T: It has been thought since the winter that Trevor was more than a year dead, in Canada. What made you suppose he was not?

J: It was only— Mrs. Trevor's uncle, Mr. Markham, the miller and sawyer, is now a partner in my business. He informed me that she had received several previous reports of her husband's death which proved unfounded. Such doubts can be most tormenting. Some substantiation might, I assumed, be welcome. That is all.

T: But scarcely enough. What did he reply?

J: That he understood Trevor was dead, as we all did.

T: And what else?

J: He asked for work and said he had a woman nearby to support. A wife, I assumed.

T: Did he say nothing of his real wife, Mrs. Hannah Trevor?

J: I have told you. Nothing at all was spoken of her.

T: Did he not accuse you of making her your mistress? Of fathering her child, Jennet?

J: If he had made such accusations, Mr. Tapp, he would have undergone my challenge. If you were not protected by your office, you would undergo it now.

T: Come, Major. This is not London or Paris. We are yet a rough country, and I daresay a man may grease the thighs of a country slut and button his breeches upon his own honor after. Trevor had himself taken other women. I doubt he set much more value on one of the creatures than another. But you do. If he threatened to expose her to a worse calumny than a pelting, you would think it your duty to protect her, would you not? You are rich and you could afford to pay for his silence, pay him to disappear again and go on playing dead. Did he not attempt to extort money from you?

J: I have said. He asked for work. I referred him to John English, my bailiff. I believe he did not pursue the matter with John.

T: Why work, if you would bribe him? The servants say that the money-pouch was open on your desk when Trevor left you. There were twenty shillings in silver found upon his person. A gold piece in his yard.

J: There was also half a veal pie in his scrip. I do not sell pies. I did not give him gold.

T: No harsh words passed between you? Nothing of personal significance or of interest to the Court?

J: I was much occupied, and I spared him little time. I took him for a vagabond.

T: I put it to you that you knew who he was and informed your lover, Mrs. Hannah Trevor, who had already—perhaps unknown to you, I will grant you that much—savagely murdered the woman Grace Stark and her children in a fit of madness! I submit to you that you and your mistress conspired together and took James Trevor's life for the sake of your own reputations and the continuance of your adulterous pleasure!

J: And I submit to *you,* Sheriff Tapp, that the people hereabouts are incensed and most of their anger has your friend, Mr. Siwall, as its target. And you with him. He has pushed them and squeezed them, sir, and you have been the rod he has beaten them with. I caught him trying to steal from me and deceive me and I broke with him in the winter. They all know of it. He represents them because only rich men with great lands may sit in the General Court. But they trust him no more than I do myself. They know he went to Boston on his own errand and none of theirs, and now they despair. They may care little for Trevor, but they need to see some scrap of justice for Mrs. Stark and her children, who were as helpless as they are. They want someone punished, and you and Mr. Siwall would prefer it not to be yourselves.

So you rush justice and think to hand them Mrs. Trevor or myself. It would please Mr. Siwall to take some revenge on me. He has lost rich timbering contracts and trapping rights on several thousand acres of upland property, thanks to his falling-out with me.

And you must please Mr. Siwall, must you not, sir? If you are to keep your sheriff's seal for another quarter?

T: Mr. Clerk! Strike that response! Enough, Major. You will observe the township bounds and supply a bond of five hundred pounds to the constable's clerk.

J: You have not sufficient evidence to demand either bond or parole, sir. People hereabouts already think you a villain. Can you afford to make yourself look a fool to them, as well?

T: Hmmm. Where were you at the hour of Trevor's death, then? Be precise, and take care!

J: On the threshing floor, sir. Precisely. Dancing with old Mrs. Markham, and seen by thirty or forty guests and my own family.

T: Well, then. That is nothing, wherever you were! You have servants will do your bidding for enough silver, even to slitting a man's throat.

J: Produce them. Name them.

T: I shall do my utmost, sir. You may depend upon that.

TWENTY-TWO

MY LADY'S CHAMBER

*I*t was past eleven that morning when Hannah's interview with the sheriff was over. She had hoped to ride home again and spend an hour with Jennet before going to the dissection of her husband's body, which was to be performed at Clinch's surgery on the North Bank at noon. If the child's drugged sleep had dulled the terrible edge of her memory by now, she might perhaps lead them to some clearer understanding of what she had seen in the arbor.

But there was no time to go home, no time to be with her daughter yet.

It was a motive that had run through Hannah's existence for two days now, and she knew she must soon come crashing against the hard stone fact of it. At the back of her mind, it had been there since winter and, indeed, long before that—since James's desertion, since Daniel.

No more time. No time.

Instead, she only stopped at Lamb's Inn and let Dolly pin the borrowed bodice tighter. Then she mounted Flash—astride, as usual, with her skirt hiked up and her white stockings shockingly exposed above her boots—and set off, deep in thought, for the South Bank ferry dock.

Like most ferries, Hosea Sly's craft was only a railed wooden barge attached by leather loops to a rope stretched across the Manitac and manipulated by means of a pulley and pole, the rope reeled in whenever a ship demanded passage upriver or down. One day, the townspeople had always promised themselves, they would build a proper bridge, when there was time and money to spare for public works. But for now, the rickety old contrivance carried passengers easily enough, or a chaise and horses or even a heavy sledge full of wood, if need be.

The merchant docks were nearby, and along them stood a number of poky, cramped, unhealthy dwellings to let, where the sailors' and longshoremen's families lived. In one of these latter, James had left Hannah to the mercy of the Tory witch hunts and the reprisals that followed them. They had never been as vicious in Rufford as in Boston; a few were tarred and feathered, one or two families stripped and beaten and dunked or driven to the coast and abandoned.

But in secret, over their quilting or spinning, the women still whispered of impoverished wives sold or kidnapped or forced by their debts into indenture, or into the beds of British officers or the brothels of Philadelphia or Boston. Some—men, women, children—had been dragged off to the Outward and hanged, it was murmured, their bodies cast into chasms or bogs. Tales of haunted ruins like those at Rook's Nest became commonplace as the outcasts took shelter where they could; when they had none, they ran wild. There were some even now in the deep woods, it was said, who did not know the War was over—and would not have believed it, were they told.

Thanks to the respect in which the Markhams were held, Mrs. Trevor had escaped such trials, but rocks had come crashing through her windows one night soon after James had gone. Next morning, Uncle Henry had fetched her to live at Two Mills.

Ever since she had read Grace Stark's letter, a question had been gnawing at Hannah's mind, and the sight of the dockside house where she had endured more than a year with James Trevor after their flight from Boston made it too plain in her mind to ignore. If he had really come for her and claimed her back again—as Grace had believed he intended—what would Midwife Trevor have done?

Live with him? Cook for him? Sleep with him? Bring Jennet to live as his baggage? Or had he perhaps changed, and grown kind?

From all she had seen and heard, all she remembered, Hannah was sure he had not.

James Trevor had been horribly marked and disfigured, yet he had charmed Grace Stark into a bigamous marriage. He had struck her, lied to her, manipulated her, got a bastard upon her by deceit, and then proposed to leave her bed and return to a wife who could not bear the sight of him.

Yet Grace had pitied James and felt tenderly toward him.

And he, no doubt, had believed he loved her, and half a dozen other women he had stumbled upon in his wanderings. It was the imposture he lived by—a man of feeling, a charming gentleman whose conquests were tender and generous gifts. If boundless damage was the fruit of them, it was surely no fault of his own.

I forgive you. I love you. Why do you always make me hurt you so?

Where had he been these eight years? Where was the damage done *him,* and by whom? And how many had he ruined in his turn?

Two women in Rufford she knew of—herself and Grace Stark. Might there not be a third? Mrs. Siwall, perhaps? He had, she knew, gone to card parties at Burnt Hill, scraping acquaintance with quality. But Honoria Siwall made a positive fetish of propriety; surely the very idea was snatching at straws.

Still, the jagged shapes that melded themselves into the quilt called *Maid of Bedlam* must somehow contain the more rational squares and triangles and circles of sensible piecework, that frail stitched-up illusion that covered the truth.

Some mortal quilt, surely, like the one of *Red Roses,* the flower of love and the color of blood.

Three women flattered, used, abandoned. Grace Stark, Hannah Trevor. And one more. One more.

Hollow to heart and heart to hollow. Narrow to wide and wide again.

Three roses on a lattice. Each rose of three petals. Each petal a triangle stitched to the next.

And the fickle stem of them all was James.

On the North Bank, Sly's ferry bumped the dock at the foot of Burnt Hill Lane and Hannah nudged Flash gingerly ashore again, picking her way between heaps of fish heads and guts, black with flies and pawed over by nine or a dozen half-wild cats. It was here that the drying racks were set up for the summer's catch of cod.

There were lobster aplenty, of course, but most had no liking for them; they were the food of the poorest classes, and when the servants' gorges began to rise at the sight of them, they were fed to the dogs or the flesh used for bait.

But cod, now. Why, cod was the king of the sea. When the boats came in, the housewives scurried to get the pick of the haul, then gutted their purchases on the spot, salted them, and laid them out on the communal racks in the baking sun. At least three or four barrels of salt cod were required to see a middle-sized family through the winter, and it took a large part of spring and summer to accomplish the job. Small boys were hired to shoo the raucous mobs of wheeling gulls away from the drying fish, and hired girls or the housewives themselves came every day or two to turn them and collect the well-cured fish in baskets and take them home to store.

Samuel Clinch's house and surgery lay perhaps a half-mile up a narrow lane from the drying yard, and Hannah held her breath against the heavy smell of salt and dead fish as she passed.

"Hallo! Mrs. Trevor!" cried a voice. "Will you wait, ma'am? Please!"

Mercy Lewis, Madam Siwall's serving maid, threaded her way between the racks and ran to where Hannah had pulled up her mare.

"Oh, ma'am," she said, breathless and frowning, clutching her basket of fish to keep it from spilling. "Here is such a to-do at the Hill!"

Mercy's cap had slipped off and her neatly-braided brown hair was damp with sweat. She glanced round at the other women, then lowered her voice almost to a whisper. "Pray, will you come to my mistress? She says I am to watch for you and bring you, and no one must see you, especially Master, and I must tell nobody, not even old Biddy Kemp!"

The uppity Madam Siwall wishing to see her? Portents and wonders, indeed! But Hannah did not remark, only helped the girl up behind her, then nudged Flash's warm, round sides again and turned into Burnt Hill Lane.

"Is your lady ill?" she asked the girl. "I have not my medicines with me, nor much time to spare."

"Oh no, ma'am," Mercy told her. "Mrs. Pinch is with her, pinning and stitching upon her new gown for the party. Master is come home last night, a-lashing of his tail and storming, and he says young master must be married by Michaelmas, and there will be a great ball for the bridal."

"Married to whom, Mercy?" Hannah could not resist a little teasing. "Ah, well. To Molly Bacon, I expect."

Mercy blushed crimson. "Oh, no ma'am! He will wed a grand young lady from Boston. Miss Harriet Smith, her name is, a niece of Mrs. John Adams, I think. Or Mr. Samuel Adams. Or some such a great one. I know not which from which." She paused for breath and her small hands gripped Hannah's waist a little harder. "Only I think it is bitter hard on poor Moll, for she's to be turned out, and her pa won't have her back, the old stoat!"

"Indeed, Mercy, that is hard. And what does Jemmy say to it?"

"He sits in the best parlor with the curtains drawn, and

calls now and then for a bottle of spirits. Poor gentleman, I don't think he cares a pin for this Miss Smith. They did argue all night something dreadful, and came almost to blows. But there's no gainsaying Master when his mind is set on a thing.''

Especially, thought Hannah, when the thing has a good dowry attached to it. A niece—even a niece by marriage—of John Adams, who was now ambassador to the Court of St. James? Why, upon such powerful coattails, Siwall could ride straight into a seat in the Congress or an ambassadorship of his own—if the Regulators did not ride him first upon a rail.

For as they arrived in the yard, Hannah saw that a group of sullen, muttering men had gathered outside the back door of Burnt Hill Manor, and there were most certainly Regulators amongst them.

"What is it, Mercy? What's happening?"

"Master has common court this morning," said the girl in a whisper. "And there's four men up before him for debt, that could not pay their tax. This way, ma'am. Hurry, if you please.''

They did not go through into Margery Kemp's overheated kitchen; instead, they turned into a narrow, breathless passage. A bell rang upstairs, then another. Two big footmen pushed past the women and up a steep flight of unvarnished steps.

As they brushed by her, Hannah felt the cold, hard pressure of a pistol upon her arm: Siwall's footmen went armed against his neighbors. The magistrate was in fear of his life, and well he might be.

At the top of the steps was a heavy oaken door; Mercy Lewis could scarcely push it open, but once she did, Hannah heard men's angry voices and the scuffling of feet. Something crashed to the floor and broke, the sound of crockery and metal. Another footman rushed past them, a musket cradled in his arm.

Hannah knew the hallway. It was handsomely designed, a kind of long gallery with archways that led the eye toward each room in its turn. The library was second on the left, a high-ceilinged chamber of considerable size, paneled in dark, carved wood and hung with rich mallard-blue draperies. It was not remarkable for the number of its books, but it was far too well known for other reasons. It was the seat of the Magistrate's Court, where she had often been a witness.

"Friends, I beseech you, let us pray!" cried the muffled voice of Reverend Gwynn from inside the room.

"Piss on your prayers! And a pox on you!" shouted Rufus Penny.

"The courts are all knaves! Our sweat has bought this house for you ten times over, Siwall, and what have we to show?"

"There is one more stair, ma'am," murmured the frightened little servant. "Quickly, please!"

Uneasily, Hannah followed Mercy up another steep flight at the end of the corridor and out into another handsomely appointed hall. The ceilings were high and finely plastered, and the walls wainscotted with oak planking painted a gleaming white. Above this, a silvery-green silken fabric covered the upper walls, and many pictures, portraits, and framed mirrors lent elegance—though little warmth.

Madam Siwall's boudoir was quite another matter, and Hannah took stock of it with some amusement as Mercy trotted silently away to the safety of Mrs. Kemp's kitchen.

Honoria Siwall had started life as a draper's daughter in Derbyshire, and her notions of beauty seemed directly derived from a talent for cramming as much merchandise as possible into a shop window. There were folding Chinese screens and small tables with silver bowls of dried lavender, and silk fans and damask draperies and hangings, and clocks and ewers and empty birdcages and china shepherdesses and stenciled firescreens. A pair of awkwardly carved rose-damask lolling chairs took up the middle of the room, with one or two upholstered joint stools, a tangle of embroidery frames, and a chaise longue like a Roman senator's couch.

Beyond this muddle of worldly goods, the great tester bed—its hangings still in place in the middle of summer—stood squashed into a far corner, as though the lady hoped that her husband, navigating the place in the dark, might abandon the pursuit of her company and lie down to sleep where he fell.

Near the door, a sleepy black boy of six or seven stood waving a huge palmetto fan up and down, up and down, though there was no window open and the air was dank and suffocating as a shroud.

"Mrs. Trevor!" said a loud, deep female voice from somewhere in the surreal hodgepodge of the room. "Judah? Is that Mrs. Trevor's step I hear?"

"Yes, ma'am!"

"Go and fan in the great hall, then."

"Nobody in that hall, ma'am!"

"Do I require to be controverted with? I shall fetch you a box on the ears!"

Without another sound, the boy ran off with his fan flapping behind him.

A silence ensued, during which Hannah heard the distinctive sibilance of someone pissing into a chamber pot. Crockery clattered. The wooden door of a commode stand clapped shut.

"Now, then!" said the booming voice at last. It issued from behind a cubicle of dressing screens at the far end of the room. "You, Mrs. Trevor! Come here at once!"

Two eyes of an indeterminate shade of puce peered over the edge of the screen. Suddenly they opened very wide.

"Blast you, Pinch!" cried Honoria Siwall, and her heap of powdered curls shook with outrage. "Do I stand here like Lot's wife half the morning that you may stick pins in my nipple?"

"Hold still, then, you old muffin, or I'll stick you in t'other one!" replied Bertha's undaunted voice from somewhere lower down. "A tough, overbaked muffin, at that," she mumbled. "*I* wouldn't have such a nasty muffin for a gift."

"I have a dissection to attend at noon, Madam Siwall," Hannah said coolly. "What is your business with me?"

"Come here, I say! I am not accustomed to being ignored nor debated!"

Hannah stood her ground. "And I am not your servant, madam, to be ordered about!"

There was a moment of silence. "*If* you will oblige me, Mrs. Trevor," said the deep voice, only slightly humbled. "Come where I may see your face."

Hannah sighed. "Oh, very well."

She stepped behind the screen and was treated to the spectacle of Lot's wife standing on a low footstool in her shift and petticoat and stays. There were at least a dozen oddly-shaped pieces of unbleached linen pinned here and there about her bony person, while Mrs. Pinch fitted and snipped and basted and pinned again, until at last something like the bodice of a stylishly low-cut gown began to emerge. With this linen pattern, the expensive lemon-colored Mantua silk that lay spread upon a nearby table would at last be cut and stitched by hand, nine yards or more for a single gown.

Fifteen shillings the yard, by Hannah's calculations. With careful economy, Grace Stark or Polly Anson might have fed her children upon the price of one yard for the better part of a year.

From the floor below, the men's angry voices rose and fell and rose again, each time louder, each time less hearkened to.

"Justice!" shouted one of them.

"I shall not have a lace stomacher," said Madam Siwall. "My daughter writes me from New York that they are sadly out of fashion. Now it is all wide sashes and triple-draped sleeves in the French manner. You shall make me a triple-draped sleeve, Pinch. See to it. With velvet ribbons. And the Antwerp lace for a cap. Or perhaps

I shall fancy a wide bonnet with egret feathers. Caps are very countrified, indeed. I do detest a cap.''

Honoria Siwall eyed Hannah down a nose so long and thin it might have served a heron for a beak.

"Madam," she said, "I am told Preacher Gwynn has foolishly asked you to wed him. It was most ill-advised. You will not, of course, think of accepting him."

"Whether I do or do not, it is no concern of yours."

"Such a union cannot be allowed to take place. Your reputation is entirely unsuitable for a clergyman's wife. You will refuse him at once. Well?"

Hannah drew a breath and held it. "Your presumption, Mrs. Siwall, is quite beyond my power to believe. I bid you good day."

In a swirl of skirts that toppled a pair of china shepherdesses on a side table and sent the pieces flying, she turned to go.

"Wait!"

The word was an entreaty, not a command, and suddenly the deep voice was a ragged shriek. Hannah paused where she stood.

"I will listen," she said. "Be quick."

The voice of Lot's wife sank to all but a whisper. "You— You are accused of your husband's murder, are you not?"

Hannah spoke calmly. "There is nothing but flimsy circumstance against me. No charge has been brought."

"Ah, but Tapp is clever! He will tangle you if he can! My husband desires it, because he fears you. And what he wishes, Tapp will contrive!"

The long, angular body seemed to drift in midair. Then it lurched dangerously.

"Here now! Muffin!" cried Mrs. Pinch. "Come down a bit! Come down!"

Pins and pattern and all, Honoria Siwall stepped down from her pillar and crumpled onto the ugly chaise longue.

"What has Mr. Siwall to fear from me?" Hannah asked her. She found some smelling salts on the dressing table and held it under the woman's nose. "I have no power over him, surely."

"He thinks you know something to damage him." Mrs. Siwall's eyes closed. "His ambitions in politics—" There was a long moment of silence. "I knew your James," she said quietly. "I—was much taken with him for a time."

Hannah bit her lip and kept silent. Was this the third woman after all? The puritanical lady who—so the servants joked—sang a hymn under her breath while her husband did his clockwork office between her sheets?

"Ah," said Bertha Pinch, with a sharp snip of her scissors, shaping the air. "He capered his way onto your pillow?"

"Not that!" Honoria Siwall sat up straighter. "I did not want that, I—" She glanced at Hannah and broke off, knowing she was not believed. "My husband is a good provider to me; but Siwall is not a man to make a companion of his wife."

"Nor was James," said Hannah tartly. "How did you first make his acquaintance?"

"He called to see Mr. Siwall on some business. My husband was from home and I received James myself. After that— I gave him no cause, but Siwall came to . . . to suspect me. I believe he signed the warrant for Mr. Trevor in order to rid me of temptation."

More likely to rid himself of the taint of a Tory acquaintance, thought Hannah. But she let Honoria Siwall go on.

"Two days ago, on the day before the fair began, Reuben Stark came to call upon me. As soon as he spoke my name, I knew him. He was so spoilt from what he had been. So horribly ruined. I pitied him greatly."

"And he asked you for money," said Hannah. "Did he not?"

Mrs. Siwall looked up at her. "I offered it freely, such as I could manage. He was still the same, you see. Sweet-natured. Gentle. Charming. His troubles had not soured him, and my heart could do no less for him."

"And besides," grumbled Bertha, "you had to be rid

of Master Charming, for if that red-wattled turkey cock your husband got wind of him, he'd put you both on a cake of ice and float you away!"

"How was it arranged?" Hannah persisted.

"He meant to take ship at the Head for London. I gave James fifty guineas and one of my husband's horses. In the saddle sack, I provided an old suit of Jeremy's, some good linen. A more suitable hat."

"Then and there? Or did he come back to collect the things?"

"My husband was expected at any time." Honoria Siwall put her fingertips to her temples as though her head might explode. "James said he would go to Major Josselyn's haying supper, that he would slip away and wait by the Grange ford for my messenger, who would leave the horse tethered in the copse above the meadow."

It explained James's damp boots and the hay stuck to them, and the horse Hannah had heard. But why had he not taken the horse and the money and ridden away? Why had he returned to the arbor to wait for his killer?

"This messenger, who was he?" she said. "Your steward? Or one of your footmen?"

"Oh, no. They are all my husband's men, they would have told him the moment he returned." Honoria twisted her petticoat in her hands. "I prevailed upon Mr. Gwynn. But he returned me the horse and the money. He said James had never appeared."

Hannah frowned. James Trevor not turn up, with money and new clothes and a good horse in the offing? And what of the wet boots and the straw? The pieces did not match.

"When the servants returned, my maid told me. The arbor. Horrible."

Mrs. Siwall began to weep softly, a lace-edged handkerchief held gracefully to her nose. For all these years since James's leaving, she had fancied herself the heroine of a great romance like the one Matthew Gwynn had tried to play with Hannah; it had filled the empty spaces of her life as the Chinese screens and the brass bowls filled her boudoir, and James's death was the last act of it. She might as well have been the china shepherdess, lying in pieces on the floor.

"You say your husband fears me and wishes to silence me. What does he think I may say?"

"Why, this that I have told you. How I loved your husband and he would have left you for me and taken me away with him to France, to a house he would take in Paris!"

"James promised you that?"

"He— He intended it. I am sure of it. He spoke often of it."

Hannah passed a hand over her eyes. "He had no money, Mrs. Siwall. He gambled. James Trevor could not have bought a ticket on the Salcombe coach, let alone passage to France."

"That is not true! He had expectations of two hundred pounds and more. Much more! He was a clever man, and capable! No one knew his true value!"

A door slammed downstairs. In the yard, the sound of horses' hooves on the cobbles.

"Did James tell you how he came by his scars?" Hannah persisted.

"A Whig mob outside Salem, he said, on the coast." The woman was silent for a long while. "He could scarcely tell me. It was a great pity to see him so comfortless. If he did wrong, he was driven to it."

"And did Mrs. Stark drive him to entrap her into bigamy?"

"*You* were never a wife to him!" cried Madam Siwall. "You have not a spark of womanly tenderness in you! He often spoke of your lack of a proper regard!"

Hannah said nothing.

"But still, you did not kill them, I think," Honoria Siwall went on, her voice very soft. "And James was too gentle-hearted to take his own life or anyone else's. There was not such selfishness in him, I know."

Again Hannah said nothing. What shall we live upon,

if even our delusions are stolen from us, that we breathe like the air of our souls?

But it was too much for the little hunchbacked seamstress. She got up from the floor and stamped her small foot.

"Is not a man a dark, secret thing with a heart like a riddle? You cannot answer for any man, you great silly biscuit, you maple-sugar candy, you Shrove pancake, you! He will break and run and leave you to whippings and kickings and peltings and marchings! He will preach you a noble tale by night on your pillow and leave you cold as the devil's eye in the dawn!"

She stumped furiously out of the room and down the stair. From the library, the two women could still hear the angry voices of the men downstairs.

"You're a walking dead man!" somebody cried. "We'll have no more of your governance!" Hannah knew the voice. It was Anson.

"Sedition, sir! Take him, Constable!" shouted Marcus Tapp's deep voice. "Chain him, the traitor!"

"Chain him yourself, you weasels!" cried another voice, younger and clearer. She knew it, too, quite as well as her own: Jonathan. "I'll have no more of you, law or no law!"

Then the voices rose all together and joined into a great wave, and there were no more words, only the wave of rage that climbed and climbed and broke at last. Hannah heard feet running down the hall, and a musket fired. A door kicked in. A shattering of window glass.

A footman looked in at the chamber door, his red-ribboned peruke badly askew and a cocked pistol in his hand. He bowed deferentially and closed the door again.

"They will kill Husband, surely," whispered Honoria Siwall. "He says it is economy, and it will do good to the country, and I do not know what other fine words. But he has made them hate him so."

She sat foolish and forlorn, the muslin pieces of Bertha's pattern pinned absurdly here and there.

"And do you love him?" Hannah asked her softly. "Will you weep for him as you have done for James?"

The red-rimmed eyes stared blankly at her for a moment more, and then the heavy lids lowered again and flickered shut.

For a long time they stayed so, but at last they opened and stared at Hannah as though no word of James Trevor had ever been spoken, and no war was brewing in the library down the narrow stair.

"Where is Mrs. Pinch gone now?" said the lady of Burnt Hill Manor in the same cold, harsh voice as before. "Come here, Pinch! Do you think I mean to be kept waiting by a beggarly seamstress? Here, in my own house?"

❈ TWENTY-THREE ❈

PIECING THE EVIDENCE:
What the Neighbors Said of Master Charming

QUESTION: Did you know James Trevor before he left Rufford?

ANSWER: In here most every night, wasn't he? Fancied quince flip, I remember. Milk punch. Lily-arsed kind of drinks for a man. But once he was half-seas-over, 'twas Scotch whisky and rum, and the devil take it.

Q: Was he known to gamble?

A: Not here, Master Sheriff! There's a law against gambling in taverns, ain't there?

Q: Mmmm. But there is a room at the back of your bar-parlor, and many men make straight for it when they come into the Red Bush. Did Trevor not make his way there now and then?

A: Aye, well. Let me put it like this, Mr. Tapp. If Jamie Trevor spied two ants crossing a road and a horse pissing in the middle of it, he'd have wagered on which ant was like to get drownded first. And he'd've lost, by God!

—*William Edes, Innkeeper, the Red Bush Tavern*

A nice, polite, Christian gentleman, he was, and I don't care if he was a Tory or not, for he always brought me a sweetmeat or a posy or a ribbon when I pleasured him! It's a pity to think of him, lying in his grave with his ears cut off and God knows what else. I hope they hang that wife of his, so I do, for she never was kind to him, and he said for two pins he would sell her on the block! So there!

—*Bella McKee, Barmaid, the Red Bush*

Now, now, Mr. Tapp. Likely she was thinking of Phinny Rugg or some other, and not Trevor at all. Bella's a kind-hearted lass, but she's been on her back with so many, she gets them muddled up a bit. Ask her the cracks in the ceiling of Bill Edes's back bedroom by candlelight, now, and you may trust her wits better!

Trevor? I never knew him in them days, when he was grand. Stark, now. He was a rogue and a bounder, always cooking up some stew with that blackguard, Ike Squeer. Come to think, *he* come back here about the same time as Stark turned up. Four months ago, maybe five.

Tumble Ike Squeer? I, sir? Why, I'd as soon lie down to a bull in season! Though Stark, now—he had a gentleman's manners for all his ill looks.

What's that? Oh no, sir, I don't sleep upstairs. It's the small room aside of the scullery. Down the three small steps and turn left.

Oh, tush, you are a tease, Master Sheriff.

Knock twice and ask if the moon's up, so I know it be you.

—*Patsy Innes, Barmaid, the Red Bush*

Q: Did you know James Trevor, Mr. Sly?
A: Crossed on my ferry like everybody else, didn't he? Pay me a farthing, I'd pole the Devil t'other bank over.

Q: Had he any friends hereabouts that you know of? Particular friends?

A: Didn't give a rat's fart, did I? Don't give one for you, neither.

Q: Answer the question, you old rogue, or I'll have your barge pole up your backside! Did Trevor cross often with anyone? Was he known to meet anyone here, on one dock or other?

A: Oh, aye. He used to come down to meet the blockade runners when they come upriver by nights. Fast cutters brought in British goods to Wybrow Head, and sent it upriver by longboat. Smuggling, see. Not much he wasn't up to, him and that rum article, Squeer. Prophet, he called him. Isaiah the Prophet.

—Hosea Sly, Ferryman, Lamb's Inn Dock

Man was a trickster, what I knowed of him at the fair. Every trick got two things to it. Thing you see. Thing you think you see. I open my mouth, I lift up the firestick. Nitre flames up. I bend back my head, look like I be swallowing that fire. Air eats the nitre, fire dies.

A trick gives a man power, makes him more than he is. Do my trick, I feel like I never got to die. Just go on and on. Burn up the old man. Build me up new again in the dark, the long sleep.

Hard thing is, sometime you forget the trick is there. You believe in that power, like you can do anything. Do any kind of harm and walk home free.

That's when it burns you. That's when the trick takes you down.

—Brutus Daylight, Fire-eater, Midsummer Fair

Q: What was the charge against James Trevor when he was warranted by the Committee of Public Safety?

A: Treason, sir, as with all recalcitrant king-lovers. He had on many occasions drunk the health of King George III in public places. He had many known acquaintances among the British officials in Boston. He perjured himself in signing the Oath of Loyalty and persisted in the purchase and consumption of tea and Scotch whisky. He was heard to say that General Washington was not fit to empty Burgoyne's chamber pot.

Q: Heavy offenses indeed.

A: There is worse, Mister Tapp. He was accused of selling contraband English goods.

Q: Which goods? Where sold?

A: Tea. Barbados sugar. Rum. Bound servants. Men and women, children. From England, Jamaica, and some indigents picked up along our own coast.

Q: Tory prisoners?

A: Prisoners were not sold, sir. They were treated in the manner befitting traitors, and taken to centers of incarceration established for their detention. None were mistreated.

Q: Tory women, then? Families displaced by the seizures?

A: I have no specific information, sir. Some may have been. We were at war, and we had not the leisure to be nice. If such women were taken into service, they did so of their own will, as a means of survival.

Q: But traffic in such was illegal, was it not, once the War was declared?

A: That is a point of law, sir. The importation of servants from England, like other salable British goods, was illegal. The king was emptying his prisons upon our shores, as you know! Sending out the refuse of the old world to pick our pockets and infect our young men with pox and the clap!

Q: Indeed, Mister Siwall. So I have heard. But since my own father was kidnapped by black marketeers in the streets of London and taken by force to Virginia as a lad of nine years, you will grant me a grain of good salt to take with that story. But what of the sale of American-born servants?

194   MARGARET LAWRENCE

A: That was, and is, a perfectly respectable trade, provided papers can be offered to ensure the free consent of the object.

Q: Object, Mister Siwall?

A: The thing sold, sir. Man. Woman. Child. It must sign or make its mark that it be not enforced to the bond. Any may sell his labor as he chooses, by wage, by contract, or by indentured bond.

Q: How did Trevor dispose of these—objects?

A: They were taken by cart through the woods, we believed, and from there to the post road, and Boston, where they were sold through a certain firm of importers. Baggett and Sons, was the name. It was a difficult maneuver, but brilliant. No one expected them to move such goods overland. Most clever sleight-of-hand. And very lucrative. Great shortage of decent servants just then, what with the War. Still is.

Q: A pity, sir, that your own great Christian probity forbid you a part of those profits. Or did it?

A: Remember your place, Mister Tapp, and how you came by it!

Q: I am obliged for the reminder, Mister Siwall.

—*Hamilton Siwall, Solicitor and Magistrate,
Burnt Hill Manor*

❈ TWENTY-FOUR ❈

GRIND, GRIND, GRIND

*T*rue to her promise of secrecy, Hannah went quietly down the narrow back stair again and, snatching up a spare maid's cap from a row of hooks in the entry, pulled the ruffled disguise down over her unruly curls. She made for her pony and was about to mount when she caught sight of her uncle and Jonathan standing a little apart from the others.

But they were far too busy arguing to notice her; the old man's round cheeks were flushed and his hands were balled into fists, and Johnnie's black eyes were as hollow as caverns. He turned away from his father, and Hannah saw Uncle Henry clutch at him as she had done at Jennet when the little girl was half-wild at the dancing.

But Jonathan shook off his father's broad hand and, with a single dagger-glance of the black eyes, he turned and walked away to where the Penny brothers and some of the other Regulators stood, near the entrance.

"Pa's been a-grinding again, ma'am," said Jem Siwall's lazy, drawling voice beside her.

"What has happened in the court?"

Hannah turned to look at the boy. In spite of his bemused manner, he was very pale; it had been two days, she knew, since he slept.

"George Anson is sentenced to prison," he said. "Your cousin would not put the irons on him when Tapp ordered it, and Pa took his constable's office away." He grinned in spite of his weariness. "He made a devilish bad constable anyway, what? Never a grinder, was Johnnie."

"Make way!" cried a man's voice from the doorway.

The two armed footmen came out of the house and took up positions on either side of the path, livery gleaming in the sun-baked yard, muskets shouldered, eyes wide and frightened.

Behind them walked George Anson. His hands were shackled in front of him; around his ankle was another iron attached to a long chain wrapped round the arm of Sheriff Marcus Tapp.

Such durance was unheard of with debtors. Felons were chained even in their cells, but debtors were treated mildly until they reached the overcrowded, fever-haunted jail up in Salcombe. Tapp was making an example of George Anson for the benefit of any Regulators in the crowd—or for some private reason of Siwall's.

Across the yard, an oxcart waited. The three other prisoners were already in the back of the cart, heads bent, eyes averted.

On the other side of the path stood Polly Anson, George's wife, with a small boy clinging to her skirt and a child of perhaps eighteen months in her arms.

"There, Poll," said Anson softly as he passed her. "Take care to mend the chimneypiece before autumn. You may do it yourself, if you get good stones and—"

"God!" she cried. A high, sharp cry that cracked the blue glass of the sky and brought it raining down in broken shards upon them. "God!"

"Ah, my poor love," said the big, stolid man, and took a few steps toward her. "My heart."

Marcus Tapp's pale eyes snapped shut, then open again, and he jerked hard on the chain attached to Anson's right leg. The big man toppled, but he gave Tapp no time to come down upon him. In an instant, George Anson scrambled to his feet and charged at the sheriff's legs.

They fell together, the chains rattling, the two furious

bodies rolling in the dust. Siwall came out of the house door with Reverend Gwynn beside him.

"You, there! Stop them!" he ordered the armed men by the path. There was fear in his voice, and shock. Whatever he had thought to begin, it had gone far beyond him. Now he could only shelter in his arrogance.

The footmen stared. They were, after all, only hired servants, not soldiers. What had they against George Anson? Siwall did not pay them for shooting their neighbors. The big fellow on the left side of the walk yanked off his powdered peruke, threw down his musket and ran pell-mell from the yard. The other let fall his weapon and stood like a statue, pretending to be invisible.

Some of the others ran to part the battlers, but suddenly Tapp was down and Anson's hands were at his throat. One by one, he threw them all off him, and still the big hands bore down. Tapp's face was grey-blue, and his chest made a rattling sound.

Hamilton Siwall stamped down the path and picked up the footman's abandoned musket. "Traitor!" he cried.

For a split-second George Anson did not realize the word was meant for him. Had he not fought against Burgoyne at Saratoga and weathered the winter with General Washington at Valley Forge?

Traitor? Where is a traitor?

He seemed to realize the truth of it then, that he had gone past stopping. George Anson looked round at his wife, his hands still choking the life from Marcus Tapp.

But in the great scheme of his own private struggle with the sleek and the strong, she no longer existed. Whatever he did, he must do alone.

"Christ forgive me," he said, and went back to his work. Siwall raised the musket and fired.

The shot struck Anson in the temple, just in front of his ear. For a moment his already-dead body hovered there, curved backwards from the blow of the musket ball, his hands still locked tight around the sheriff's throat and his eyes open wide. Tapp lay quiet, his mouth hanging open, half-dead himself, but still watching the face of the dead man who held him.

At last the hands let go. The body toppled and lay still.

Polly Anson did not scream nor run sobbing to throw herself upon her husband's corpse. For a long, breathless moment nobody in the yard made a sound. There was only the clucking of hens in the garden, and the drift of hot breeze through the box-hedge, smelling of Mrs. Kemp's venison stew.

"Come, Neddie," said Polly Anson at last, and took her little boy's hand. "We must go home and make Dada his supper. I think we shall have roasting ears, if the 'coons have not stole them all from the husks."

For a moment more she stared blank-eyed at George's dead body, as though it were a rock or a tree stump in her path. Then she hiked the baby up onto her shoulder and walked straight past her husband and out of the yard.

The men stared. Hamilton Siwall let the musket slip from his fingers and crash to the ground; his florid face was white as paper and nearly as brittle, able to be crumpled by a fingertip.

"Murderer!" cried somebody. "George was shackled and chained! You need not have killed him!"

"Aye! 'Twas plain murder!"

They would have closed on Ham Siwall then and there, Hannah was sure of it, and beaten him to death. Beside her, everywhere around her, she could feel the suffocating heat of the men's anger, as though they were all shut together in a box and must break out of it or die.

But in a single smooth motion, Marcus Tapp was back on his feet, sword in one hand and pistol in the other.

"Take up your dead and get out!" he commanded.

He spoke quietly, well aware that even the slightest hint of his usual impudence would push them past stopping.

"War!" shouted somebody. "Where's Josselyn? Let him call up the militia and help us!"

"Come, lads," said Uncle Henry. "One dead is enough now! Let's have no talk of wars!"

Jonathan was kneeling beside Anson's body, but at the sound of his father's voice he looked up.

"Will you not go home with me, my son?" said Henry softly.

The young man got up and stood for a moment, wiping the blood and the dust from his hands.

"Up the Regulators!" he roared. "God burn all tyrants in hell!" Then he leaped onto his horse and spurred it and rode at a breakneck gallop from the yard.

"God damn the magistrates! We shall govern ourselves, as we was promised! We shall have no more judges and sheriffs to ruin us!" shouted the others.

"Justice for the poor! Justice for Anson and Stark!"

Ah, thought Hannah, they had forgotten he had ever been James Trevor. Trevor was a Tory and there was no pity for Tories, but Reuben Stark was a poor farmer, a hacker of tree stumps, a scrimp-and-saver with a dirt floor and a weary wife and three hungry children. Whatever James Trevor had been, Reuben Stark was one of *them*, as George Anson had been.

Still crying justice for all the dead, the Penny brothers charged away out of the yard, and most of the others with them, even a few of the moderates. Henry Markham, his shoulders hunched and his blue eyes brimming, mounted his own horse and rode straight past his niece without seeing her at all.

The forgotten prisoners in the back of the oxcart stared at the body of George Anson where it lay, with somebody's leather jerkin laid over it for decency. Tapp's deputy, a scrawny little fellow with a cast in his eye, arched the goad over the back of the nigh ox and the cart lumbered out of the yard in the direction of the Salcombe road.

Shaken as he was, Siwall did not give ground and go back into the house for safety. He and Tapp, with Gwynn hovering beside them, stood by the well-sweep, heads high, until the others had ridden out.

Then Jemmy Siwall turned back to Hannah.

"Take your daughter and go, Mrs. Trevor," he said in

an urgent whisper. "Pa will grind me and he will grind Moll, and he will grind you, too! And that one will help him."

Hannah looked at the face of Matthew Gwynn where he stood with the forces of law and justice beside him. It was pale and set, the fair skin pulled tight across the high forehead, and this time he made no effort to pray over the dead. He looked up and must have caught a glimpse of her, for he looked quickly down at his hands, ashamed and silent.

"He will betray you," Jem said softly. "He is weak, like myself, and we wet-legs know one another."

Every nerve in Hannah's body told her to ride home, snatch up Jennet, and run. But it must not be done so wildly and openly, or they would only find where she had gone and drag her back.

"What will you do, ma'am?" Jem asked her, helping her up onto Flash's back.

"Just now I am waited for at the dissection of my husband's body," she said. "It may tell me something to help me." She paused. "What will you do, you and Molly?"

He looked up at her. "I suppose I might dash off and wed her. Take her off to some patch of rocks and tree stumps in the woods. But Molly likes company and a bit of fun, you know, and she'd be miserable. Inside a month, she'd run off to warm some lumberjack's bed and leave me cold. Unless I starved the pair of us first, for I'm a lazy fellow, damn my eyes." He looked up at Hannah. "So I shall wed the snow-white maiden from Boston, I expect. The dowry I get with her will buy Moll a snug little cottage, and she may set up for herself, and I may see her whenever I like. Better that way, what? Happier on all sides."

"Grind, grind, grind," said Hannah, and urged Flash to a trot.

✖ TWENTY-FIVE ✖

PIECING THE EVIDENCE:

Results of the Dissection Performed Upon The Body of James Ramsay Trevor 13 July, 1786 Rufford Township, Maine, Upper Massachusetts

*T*he man's body bore many old scars, chiefly upon the face and head, of clipping, branding, slitting, et cetera. The occipital bone of the skull had been but shortly before the hour of death further degraded by a strong blow from some heavy rounded implement, which struck by measure four inches above the base of the neck, at the most weakened part of the skull. It is to be assumed that this blow was sustained by the body just before death, as much blood was found in the hair and upon the back of the neck so far down as the scapula and the collarbone.

Upon the back and buttocks were seen the healed scars of at least two receipts of the lash. One layer lay close upon another, so that the number of strokes was not possible to determine, but the latest perhaps twenty or thirty, as of a moderate punishment for theft or fornication, and all suffered some five or seven years since.

The third and fourth ribs upon the right side were cracked, and the fifth rib broken. When the cavity of the chest was cut open, this rib was found protruding through the right lobe of the lights, or lungs. As there was no bleeding found within the lung nor around it in the cave of the chest, it is probable that the rib was broken by some insult to the body after its decease, as by a fall or a blow of a nature similar to that sustained by the occiput just before death.

The inner organs appeared in good health, except the liver and kidneys, which gave great evidence of the ill effect of strong drink taken for some years to excess.

Death resulted immediately from a single cut made clean across the throat with great and sudden force, severing the large vein and laying open the windpipe, which caused suffocation and further great loss of blood. The cut gave evidence of an angle of ninety degrees or thereabouts, and began at the man's left side, as by a right-handed person bending over him.

When the brain was removed from the skull, there was a quantity of blood found within the brain-pan, as from a great hemorrhage suffered because of the blow to his head at or before the moment of death from the knife. The deceased, it is believed by all the undersigned, could by no means have survived such a damage, whether his throat had been cut or not, so that the murderer's blade did, in effect, kill one already dead.

To this we do give and subscribe as true.

Samuel Clinch, Coroner and Physician
Hannah Trevor, Witness
Julia Markham, Witness

✖ TWENTY-SIX ✖

THE JOURNAL OF HANNAH TREVOR

13 July, the Year 1786

Since my last writing, I am determined to leave this place forever, and my daughter with me. Where I shall go I know not, for the only place sure is the grave and there I have no mind to travel yet awhile.

I have seen my husband's body this day, how he was set upon and made naught of, as though he was no human thing. And yet he left upon my own heart scars invisible, deep as his own and full as bitter, and upon Grace Stark, too, and upon one other yet adrift in the mists of this world, as I believe.

For no matter what others have done to him, I will not have James Trevor innocent by virtue of his dying.

God may forgive him for the sake of his sufferings.

God was never his chattel nor his wife.

My Aunt came most kindly to be at my side through the dissecting of the corpse, and her strong heart was my comfort and stay. Where now shall I turn for good counsel when I have gone from Two Mills?

What is found by Clinch's knife is the pitch of my danger. They will say I came to James in the arbor and struck him down from behind with some bludgeon so I need fear no struggle, and then cut his throat with his own razor that I took from Mrs. Stark's house in the morning, once she was dead. And Preacher Gwynn will say he was not with me and never offered me marriage, and Squeer will perhaps bear some other false witness against me.

I have not long to remain here, and some other must find out the truth. Only before I go I must run and see Mrs. Hinkley, whose breast is abscessed, and change the bandages on Abiah Foster's arms where she burned herself singeing her hens, and attend Mrs. Thatcher if I can, for she is very near her time. And I am promised to attend Mrs. Hewins and three or four others next month, and how shall they be safe delivered, with Aunt fretted past endurance for Johnnie, and Clinch snatching and stamping about as he please?

Shall leave for Mrs. Foster some comfrey root and colts-foot, which are sovereign for burns.

My cousin Dolly Lamb and some other of the women will watch this night with Mrs. Anson, lest she do herself some ill.

I fear also for Daniel, that he may be drawn into this new war they will make, the poor against the rich. For how should I breathe if he were no more sweet and whole and living in the world?

I am very ill with the headache. When I shall write again upon these poor pages, I know not.

Though I may not stay to finish the work upon it, I record here the pattern of my quilt of Red Roses, for my Daughter's sake, when she be grown. And wherever I may go, if it be not to some prison, I shall make up my pattern again.

God smash apart the fist of power that beats upon the poor.

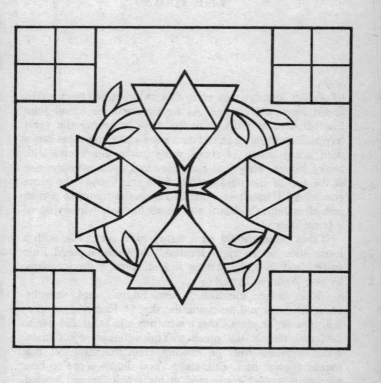

✖ TWENTY-SEVEN ✖

THE EXILE

*D*aniel Josselyn rose early that morning and paid a visit to his steward's cottage. As he expected, he found John English hard at work with his crew, covering the great haystacks with huge tarred canvasses and tying them down with a crosshatch of ropes weighted at either end with heavy stones. They had built the stacks just over the rise at the top of the field not far from the house—the same rise where Hannah said she had seen the figure of a man just after James's death, and heard the soft whinnying of a horse nearby.

If that horse should be a sturdy little cob, now, with a loose shoe on its right forefoot? A mild-tempered little mare hired from the stables at Josh Lamb's inn, perhaps, by one Andrew Tyrrell?

"Rain before nightfall," John English said, straightening his back and assessing the sky. " 'Red sun at morning, thunder at night,' that's what my old Dada did use to say, and there's not much a Yorkshireman don't know about weather. Ants be making great mounds, too, that means a great rain. But, there. You didn't come to hear me prophesy." He squinted at his employer and smiled, briefly. "What's wanted, sir?"

"I'll be heading upriver at midday, John," Daniel told him.

"Thought you might." English pulled a stem of hay

from the stack and began to chew on it thoughtfully. "That old heathen up at the Fort will know if there be anything stirring in them woods that ought not."

When anything untoward happened in Rufford that could not be otherwise explained, there were two directions from which the damage might have come. One was downriver—the sea, and the ships that came up the Manitac once the ice had gone out of it, and the sailors and passengers they brought with them. The other, upriver to the north and west, was the giant shadow of the Outward, the great primordial forest.

A narrow logging road ran through it parallel to the river, and a few settlers' tracks branched away from the main trail—the Trace, as it was called. But beyond that, the forest was unmapped and unknown, keeping its own secrets, swallowing many who ventured into it unprovided.

The old Dutchman Piet Soutendieck, manager of Daniel's cutting crews, lived with his Indian wives and a gaggle of half-breed children at a trading post called Fort Holland deep in the woods, where he ruled like an absolute monarch over trappers and logging crews.

The Regulators were said to meet somewhere in the Outward, riding or rowing downriver by night to strike at their enemies, and gangs of robbers prowled through the dense bracken and fern.

All in all, it was not a place to venture alone. John English looked at his master's determined countenance and frowned.

"Bad time to go, sir," he said, with a glance toward Two Mills.

It was to the steward's own cottage rather than the Grange that Parthenia or Kitty had brought Jennet nearly every day this spring and summer, where Daniel could see her and learn to know her, and teach her what he could without causing more talk than necessary. John had grown fond of the child; when she was late turning up, he fussed and fidgeted like a grandfather.

"I would not leave them now, John, if there were any

other way about it,'' Daniel told him. "But Trevor hid in those woods, and those he brought back with him died there. Some part of the truth lies there still, and the sooner we find it, the sooner we'll be clear of it. If I take one of the canoes, I should be home by dark.''

The steward nodded. "I hear Siwall's back. The news from Boston's sorry, and that'll give them other meat to chew on for a bit.'' John English bent his shaggy head and rubbed the sleeve of his blue-checked homespun shirt across his forehead. "But one more thing you best know, sir, before you go. Ned Hatch was in that arbor yesterday, pruning and weeding and what not, and he tells me he left his tools standing about—well, you know old Ned. No better hand with a garden, but a memory like madam's old stewpot, all full of holes.''

Daniel smiled. "I saw them, a hoe and a weeding basket. Tell Ned not to concern himself. It's no matter.''

John frowned. " 'Fraid it does matter. Maul's gone missing, you see. Ned bethought him where it must be and went to look in the arbor. Found it gone.''

When the old gardener had to pound down a stake for a plant or mend a fence post, he preferred that ancient implement, the maul—the heavy bole of an oak tree, stripped of bark, sun-bleached and hard as iron. It would fell a man in a minute—especially a sitting man with his back to the entrance. After that, kneel over him, take the razor and slit his throat.

Daniel frowned. "Look for it, John. If it's anywhere about, we must put our hands on it.''

Tapp would be quick to accuse him of concealing it otherwise.

But English shook his grey head. "First thing I'd do, sir, is sink it. That river's held more than one bludgeon in its time.''

"Still, we must look.'' Daniel glanced at the sun, which was now high in the sky. "And I must be gone.''

"Been some while since I was up to Fort Holland,''

said John. "And that canoe'd pull a sight sweeter with two men at the oars. Let me go with you, sir."

His master smiled. "I need a safe hand here, my friend," he said. "You'd best keep the guards on the house and the barns. And—keep an eye on *them*, John. Stand between them and harm."

He clasped the older man's shoulder in farewell, but John English did not let him go yet. "Take weapons, Daniel," he said. "I've a bad feeling in my belly about all this."

Josselyn could not remember when the steward had last called him by his Christian name, and he felt again the prickling of battle-nerves rising along his spine. "I'll take a musket and a sidearm," he said with a smile. "Who knows but I may have a chance of some hunting while I'm there?"

"Take a sword," English commanded. "Most men can handle powder and shot. You're at home with a short sword, you was trained to it, and that's your advantage. Not just something fancy, mind. Take a strong blade. One that will cut deep, and kill."

The steward said no more, only walked away toward the stables, and Daniel was free to make his way to the copse at the upper edge of the field—the same copse where he had seen Bertha Pinch chopping kindling for the cooking fires.

Somehow the business was all bound up in the ways of women, in their loves and hates and their comings and goings, and in the men they trusted or despised.

Sarah. Bertha. Dolly. Merriam. Julia. Grace.

In Daniel's mind, their names formed a litany that sang its way into his footsteps as he walked through the mown stubble to the copse.

Grace. Merriam. Sarah. Bertha. Charlotte. Jennet. Hannah. Hannah. Hannah.

*   *   *

The grove of maples and beech trees was thick with flies feasting on the remains of yesterday's meal. The cold ashes of two or three cooking fires lay at the edge of the trampled grass, and some child's forgotten cup-and-ball had been laid with care upon a fallen log, in case he should come back to claim it.

Daniel got down on his knees and crawled the few yards at the edge of the field. Animal tracks—squirrel, mostly. One or two deer. A family of raccoons. The neat little leaps of a weasel. Field mice, mad and scurrying.

Ah, there they were! Hoofprints, indeed! And the heavy droppings of a horse that must have been left here some time. But the prints gave no sign of a loose shoe, and they were deeper and broader than those of the little hired cob Andrew Tyrrell rode.

"The horse was not mine, sir," said a deep voice.

Daniel got up from his knees to face his Aunt Sibylla's secretary.

"You have seen the prints of my mare at Mrs. Stark's cabin and recognized them, have you not?" said Tyrrell. "I surmised from your manner last night. Your scrutiny strips a man's bones, Major."

Daniel smiled faintly. "I saw the print of a small horse with a loose shoe in the dooryard," he said. "But there is more than one such in the world."

"I *was* there, very early in the morning," Tyrrell told him. "But when I left her, Grace and her young ones were yet living. And so far as I know, James Trevor also. That I swear upon my soul."

Daniel wanted to believe him. Andrew Tyrrell's sober face was composed enough now, but there was a puffiness around his eyes that made it plain he had not slept. He had pondered all night upon his duty, and now he had come to perform it.

Or had he been racked with guilt?

"I did not think it wise to speak to you last night, in front of so many," said the secretary. His shoulders hunched slightly, a scholar's stoop, and his hands were clasped, as always, behind his back. "Besides, Lady Sibylla was already upset by the course of events. She is not so strong in body as her temper leads one to believe, and I— I am fond of her. So I determined to approach you privately today, and to take whatever course you advise where the law is concerned."

Daniel nodded. "You went to the woods collecting plant samples for my aunt's notebooks?"

"Only in part. I had a more urgent affair of my own at the house of Mrs. Stark. She—she was my brother's wife."

Andrew Tyrrell sat down heavily on the fallen tree where the cup-and-ball lay, his body bent almost double, his hands bracing themselves on the rough bark at either side of him, the eyeglass on its ribbon dangling from his collar almost to the ground.

"I had never seen Grace," he went on, "until yesterday. My name is not Tyrrell—or was not until I went into exile at the end of the War. I . . . had lost myself, I— Ah, how could you know what it is to feel the world shatter to pieces around you? To be suddenly poor and friendless in a strange country, and called traitor to everything you have loved and spent your life upon?"

Daniel's brandy-colored eyes collected the sunlight and flamed up for a moment. "Many these days know what exile is, Mr. Tyrrell," he said in his quiet, steady voice. "And so do I."

Tyrrell glanced at him, bowed slightly, and continued.

"I was loyal to His Majesty. I believed we could cleanse the bond which the greed of a few powerful men had fouled, that we need not discard our great heritage. Edmund Burke believed so. Many spoke for us in Parliament, your own grandsire among them."

It had been almost Lord Robert's last public duty before his retirement to his country seat. He had sent a secretary's copy of the speech to Daniel, who was then with General Gage's staff in Boston.

"Besides," Tyrrell continued, "it was in the nature of

my profession to preserve the tie with Britain. I was a vicar, sir. A small Anglican living in Cambridge, near Boston. I had established a school. It was very dear to me, my work with the children.''

He stood up and began to pace through the long grass of the grove.

''My dilemma was a harsh one. I had many friends who wished me to join the American cause, but the Church of England is, of course, established and protected by the Crown. I could not retain my profession and sign the Oath of Loyalty demanded by the new Patriot government. I refused to swear. My friends in the district protected me for a time, but in the end, I fled. I was arrested. Carted through the town with a sign around my neck and tried— or so they called it. I was four years a prisoner in the Simsbury mines. You have heard of the place?''

Daniel nodded. It was a copper mine used as a prison for Tories, a terrible watery catacomb. William Franklin, bastard son of the great Benjamin and Tory governor of New Jersey, had spent five years there. Only a handful had ever escaped it, and many had died.

''Upon my release,'' Tyrrell continued, ''I was shipped off to England, which I had never set eyes upon—I was born in Boston and educated at Harvard College. I hoped to continue in my profession, but I soon learned the English church had no livings kept vacant for outcast Americans, no matter how loyal they were. I drove a freighter's wagon for a time, but other men, local men, had no work themselves and resented the upstart. I was beaten. Robbed of what wage I had earned. I tried next to go into service as an underfootman, but by then my appearance was that of a ruffian. The poor, you know, are seldom dirty by choice. The price of a cake of soap was beyond me, and clean linen . . . I used to dream of it as a child dreams of sweetmeats. For a time I worked as a bootblack, and then as a stableman. But again I was driven out by hungry men stronger than I. Until I happened upon the good will of your aunt in London, I was in a fair way to starve to death." He stared at the hard, dry ground. "My church, my friends write me, is now a tavern, and the school a livery. What has become of the children I taught there, I do not know."

For a long moment, neither man spoke.

"So, then. You are Andrew Stark?" said Daniel at last.

Tyrrell nodded. "I had word of my poor brother's death two years ago from Upper Canada, a sad letter from his widow, Grace. I sent her what small aid I could muster. She was rawly left, I knew. But seven months ago another letter came, and it was then that I determined to risk returning to America."

The flies buzzed thick around them, gobbling up a crust of bread and butter someone had tossed away. Tyrrell kicked it aside, then began to pace again, back and forth on the trampled grass.

"My brother was many years older than I, and also loyal to the Crown, but he took a different course. He enlisted in the British army in the hope that his wife would be safe behind the lines. They had married in the Carolinas. Reuben had a small tobacco plantation there."

"He enlisted in the Prince's Own?" asked Daniel.

"Ah. You have seen the tricorne Trevor wore?" said the secretary eagerly. "It was my brother's. Reuben was invalided out of the regiment early in the War, and Grace took her children—there were five at the time, but three died of fever upon the journey—and went to join him. After several false starts, they settled in Upper Canada, to the north and west of Quebec. Two years ago, Reuben also died of a putrid fever. It was then that James Trevor took my brother's name."

"And buried Reuben Stark in his own, as James Trevor," said Daniel. "To free himself of the warrant upon him."

"It is an isolated country, and nobody knew them. Trevor had been with my brother's family for some little time," said Tyrrell, "as a hired man. He was an educated fellow, well spoken, and my brother grew fond of his society. They drank together every night, mourning their losses.'' He glanced down at Josselyn. "As I observe, Trevor's were great indeed. I have met his lady."

"He could blame that particular loss on no one but himself," said Daniel in a cool voice.

"James persuaded my sister-in-law to wed him soon after Reuben's death. She knew nothing of the imposture he had managed with the burial. Trevor was kind enough, known to her, and he offered her protection if she would return with him to Maine. She thought it prudent to accept."

"But he did not tell her he had a wife yet living here."

"Not until a few months since. Then the whole of it came out."

Andrew Tyrrell paused in his pacing, and again he was silent for a long space. The air was hot and very heavy in the little copse, the leaves above them scarcely stirring.

"Once they arrived here in Rufford, he could no longer hide Hannah Trevor's existence. He spoke very ill of his wife, but Grace was much troubled by her sin, and afraid. He spoke wildly of reclaiming his wife, or extorting money from her uncle or from yourself. He drank more and more. He meddled in smuggling, the selling of stolen goods, contraband. His confederates were rough men, and they treated Grace with disrespect."

"And so she wrote to you in England, begging assistance. And you gave it. The gold piece at the cabin?"

"There were nine more, sir, of your aunt's generosity. Ten sovereigns in all, in a fine chamois pouch with a silk lining. I told Lady Sibylla I had a longstanding debt to clear before I left America, and she most kindly obliged me with a loan. How could I refuse Grace? I have no other family living." Tyrrell stared ahead of him. "*Had* no other family. Sweet Christ. When I saw them last night—"

"Did you speak to Trevor when you went to see Grace? Quarrel with him?"

"He was about to leave for the fair. He said they would not stay much longer here, that he would soon have enough money to quit the place. I assumed the source was his smuggling.''

"Did he say anything then of Mrs. Trevor?''

"I told him he must go to her and confess himself living. Encourage her to divorce him if she could. Then, I said, he must offer Grace honorable marriage.'' He sat down again on the log and studied Josselyn's face. "She loved him, you see. In spite of all.''

"And what did he say to that?''

Tyrrell wiped his face with a handkerchief. It was utterly breathless, and a bank of heavy clouds was building thunderheads.

"He laughed, and went on chopping stumps out of the field.''

Daniel's eyes did not focus, except upon the building thunderheads. "What did you say when he laughed?''

"I said I would go myself to Mrs. Trevor. Mrs. Twig pointed her out on the day we arrived, and I would have spoken to her at the fair, but—''

"But the pelting prevented you.''

"Yes. Even so, I felt I had to act quickly. Grace could not have borne her shame much longer, and I knew it. I told Trevor that if he did nothing to right matters, I would take Grace and her children away to London. Dear God, if only I'd taken them with me that morning.''

"Did you speak to Trevor again at the dancing?''

"I left Lady Sibylla for a few moments to look for him, but he had gone. He must have been already in the arbor.'' Tyrrell shuddered. "I did not go inside it myself.''

"And you saw no one else?''

"Mr. Ledyard, the puppet-master. Mrs. Pinch. Mrs. Firth. Several of the women and children. The fire-eater was there, I believe.''

"And at the cabin, once Trevor had left you? You saw no one else about? No woman?''

"You are thinking of the footprint. No, I saw no other woman than Grace,'' Tyrrell told him. "But I did hear a woman's voice, singing. Above me, very strange and sweet, like a choir in its loft.'' The secretary turned to look at Daniel. ''An old song, it was, I'm sure you know it. From the dance we did as children—they call it 'Blood Red Roses,' do they not?''

TWENTY-EIGHT

PIECING THE EVIDENCE:
The Litany of Lost Women

Sarah Jane Firth

*W*idow, Age 33. Occupation: Itinerant weaver. Presently common-law wife of Lachlan McGregor. Born Sarah Jane Tompkins, Stratford, Connecticut, 1753. Illiterate. Signs by means of a mark of parallel lines with a cross through them. Married Charles Firth, farmer, August 18, 1773. One child, Betsey. Husband served in Connecticut militia, killed by a bayonet thrust, Yorktown, 1781. Farm foreclosed and sold for debt, 1782. Daughter, Betsey Firth, age seven, indentured by Orphans' Court to Geoffrey Merker of Bell's Forge, New York, March, 1782, until her majority. Sarah Firth is blind in her left eye from a blow.

Found her wandering, I did, down near Wybrow Head. Beaten and half-mad, turned out by some bastard, once he'd had his pleasure of her for a few days and knocked her about to prove himself a mighty fellow. When I made to help her up, she stuck a knife in me, poor lass. But I've blood to spare, for all that. The McGregors be outcast from Scotland since Rob Roy, and I've been myself a wanderer and borne a false name for-why my own was outlawed and might not be spoken in all Scotland on pain of prison. I felt for Sarah. I'm big and ugly, indeed, but I'm

217

not past feeling. I could see how fine she was, under her fear. How gentle-fine her heart.

So I took her up and carried her to old Lady Annable, at Gull's Isle. It's a place nothing touches, and I've took other women there, for they'll turn none from the gate. I've seen as many as eight or nine at a time there, pulling flax in that wee patch of a field. Spinning. Weaving, like Sarah. Biding their time and licking their wounds.

I left Sarah there a month to harbor and get back her quiet, and then I came to seek for her. I did not knock at the door, mind, nor speak to her at all. Only sat there on the cart like a great scruffy lump of ill-leaven, without the heart in me to lay claim to her or even ask her own will. After a time, Sarah come walking out to me and climbed up beside me, and my lad Robbie to the other side of me. And so we came away here, to the Forge, to start up new together, and no more word said of the past.

Where was my Sarah in the morning, when the poor lass and her childer were hacked down in the woods? Why, she was late a-bed yestermorning. She was greenish, and I bid her never trouble with Robbie and me, and she didn't rise till near ten, for I heard her upon the stairs.

Ah, the Devil, man, I may as well tell you! She's fresh with child, is my Sarah. She's my true wife by common law and good Scots custom and whether she'll wed me before some lag-tailed parson or no, it makes little odds to me, for I'll have none other till I die.

To say true, I'm that glad of the bairnie. It warms me to think of it, lying soft in her body. Lone things must shelter each other. Or what else is there on the earth?

—Lachlan McGregor, Blacksmith and Ferrier

Merriam Susanna Gwynn

Spinster, Age 31. Gentlewoman. Presently housekeeper for the Reverend Matthew Ezekial Gwynn, her brother. Born Winslip, Massachusetts, 1755. Illiterate. Signs with the mark of a cross and star. She is an excellent housekeeper, but she suffers violent headaches during her monthly courses, which are very irregular and painful. She has a faulty memory at all times, and has been known to mistake her own name and that of her brother, and to wander abroad. No more is known of Merriam Gwynn.

She's a flighty one, and no mistake. Sets out walking west in the early morning and sometimes near to twilight, too, like she was bound for China and meant to make the waters part for her and the trees bow down and curtsy! And Black Caesar's Tirzah, that works for Mrs. Pratt, says she caught her one day in the spare bedchamber, just lying there on the bed with her eyes shut, and little Martha held close and scared half out of her wits! And my own Dolly come in our back parlor one evening, and there sits Miss Merriam, a-spinning on the wheel and singing soft to herself, that old song of London Bridges. And when Dolly speaks her name, Miss Merriam turns about with the thread in her hand and, 'What do you make here, mistress?' says she to Dolly. 'I will have no beggarwomen in my house!'

Well, I ask you now. No, sir. No thin, pale, nerve-soured spinsters for me, by Harry! Give me a round, warm lass like my dear Dolly—eh, my pet?

And yet—

And yet I do pity the heart of Miss Merriam Gwynn, for it shines out through her eyes at odd moments, cool and tender. I have seen others like her, in war and out of it. Women who labor away their lives and pay a high asking for such scraps as God throws them. When they die, they do not leave the earth, for it has taken them captive. They are the ghosts of us all.

—*Josh Lamb, Innkeeper, Deacon of Rufford Congregation*

Bertha Pinch

Married woman, Age 38. Occupation: Itinerant seamstress and lacemaker. Born Bertha Jouet, Pawhasset, New Jersey,

1748. Able to read but not write nor cipher, and signs her
name plain in a good square hand. Apprenticed to Mrs.
Farnham of New York, lady's dressmaker, until the age
of fifteen. Employed by that lady a further twelve years,
till the outbreak of war. Returned to Pawhasset to work
as hire-seamstress and lacemaker. Father's house raided,
looted and burned by men calling themselves Patriots, October, 1777. Father died of stroke, December, 1777, leaving no property and great indebtedness. Bertha Jouet
married Nathan Pinch, a blind itinerant musician and sing-
ing-school master, 1782. No children. Abandoned by Nathan Pinch, November, 1782, outside Battleborough,
Maine. Bertha Pinch is a hunchback and has one arm
shorter than the other, and halts sorely when she walks.

*Well, he's stone blind, is old Nathan Pinch. I'm a singer
myself, and I knew him. He come here to Rufford one
winter and gave sing-school at the Meeting House evenings, and we had some fine songs indeed. He was a man
of past forty and he hadn't had a woman since he were
a lad, I'd wager. Not many wants to lumber themselves
with a blind man. And she's a sweet voice, has little Bertha. He took to her kindly, and she to him.*

*Only he couldn't see her, you know, and she never let
him lay hands on her till they was wed, except upon her
face. Well, now. It was the shape of her broke him. When
he come to her abed to do his office that first night, and
touched her and felt the hump on her, Nathan Pinch begun
to shout aloud and tear at his blind eyes and weep, and
cast blame upon her and upon the God who made her.*

*For he saw plain enough the ache of her that made her
voice so sweet. Saw what made her hide and tease and
talk riddles and grow wild in the night.*

*But in one thing he was blinder than stone, for he saw
no sweet woman there to want and be wanted. Confound
him for a fool!*

*In the War, raiders burnt her pa's house, and they
stripped her and beat her and made sport of her body,*

under the eyes of her old father and all. Well, it was the way of it them times, and women paid a high price though they carried no muskets and swords. They used her, I reckon, though she could not bring herself to say so. Most women don't, and it seldom gets spoke of nor wrote down proper.

Well, she never told Pinch of it, but she told me, for we are the best of friends. After he left her, she was the first winter a-wandering the river down by Gull's Isle, but I have sheltered her every winter since, though I keep it my secret, for my wife is gone under the ground and my house echoes with no other voice in it but mine now my children are grown, and them gossips in town would make much of it if they knew. But my sight's not so good as it once was, and if I but squint a bit, I can scarce notice Bertha's shape. And I need not lay hands on her, neither, unless it's to dance a bit with the poor bird, for, bless you, I'm long beyond wiving and bedding!

Though I think if I was not, a bit of a hunch and a hobble would bother me little enough!

'Tis a great thing to be said for old age, you know. You may let people be as they are, and not scorn them nor judge them. You may let lust wash away from you, and greed and pride, and think only of kindness. Ha, ha! When you're my age, nothing human is fearsome, and there's no crooked monsters to shout "boo" in the dark.

—Enoch Luckett, Farmer

❈ TWENTY-NINE ❈

UPRIVER

The canoe was birchbark—Indian-made, light and well balanced—and Daniel was at home with the oars. After his own interview with Sheriff Tapp, he lingered only long enough—keeping his usual distance—to watch Hannah cross safe on Sly's ferry on her way to the dissection. But it was already past noon when he at last set out, the air heavy with storm.

Where the river narrowed, it was overhung with boughs and the tall ferns and scraggly wild plums and elderflower bushes grew almost into the main channel in some spots. The source of Blackthorne Creek was one such, and there he passed through a fierce cloud of stinging, biting mosquitoes that got into his eyes and ears and mouth and down the neck of his shirt.

There was but one quick way to get the stinging pests off. Resenting the waste of precious time, he pulled the canoe onto the creek bank, his weapons still inside it, and dived into the water breeches and all, to emerge dripping and shivering—for even in hot weather, the uncleared woods were cool and the water downright cold.

He shook himself dry enough for the heat to finish the job, and was about to launch the canoe again and set off, when he smelled the sweetish fragrance of tobacco smoke. Before he could move, a heavy hand descended on his shoulder and another grabbed his wet shirt. Daniel snatched up his sword and spun round, still dripping, to confront the barrel of a long hunting rifle in the short, stubby hands of old Piet Soutendieck.

Oncle Pierre, he was called, or Uncle Piet, or half a dozen other names, some not so pleasant. He was barrel-shaped and fiftyish, with corn-colored hair in a shoulder-length fringe round his bald spot. As usual, he was smoking a long-stemmed clay pipe, and a tame grey squirrel sat bright-eyed and nattering on his shoulder. Piet was never without some wild creature about him, but he did not wax sentimental about them. If game was scarce, his Indian wives served them up in a stew.

"So, Dah-niel my friend," said the Dutchman with a grim cackle. "You want to chop me to pieces like that brood at Stark's cabin?"

Daniel picked up his sword, but he did not put it back into the canoe with his musket and pistol. "How do you know about Stark? And what brings you so far downstream from your lair, old man?"

"Come with me once, and I show you. You can leave your chopper here. Little Jean will watch it."

He nodded toward a slender young man who had appeared from among the trees. He was no taller than five feet three or four, brown-skinned and black-eyed, with heavy dark hair knotted at the nape of his neck and tied with a red kerchief and one or two owl feathers, and a gold ring through the lobe of his ear. Daniel knew him, of course. He was Jean le Petit, the half-breed runner who traveled back and forth from Piet's stronghold to the town with messages when the lumber crews were cutting. He spoke a garbled French and knew the Indian sign language, but for the most part he ranged the woods alone, watching, spying out profit for the Dutchman—and no doubt for himself when he could manage it.

By his side was a big grey wolf with a brown muzzle, the same that had sat in the clearing and guarded the bodies of Grace and her children.

"*Eh, bien, Jean! Il est à vous, le grand chien-loup?*"
Daniel asked him.

Is the great wolf-dog yours?

The half-breed glanced at it. They were uneasy allies;
fondness had nothing to do with either of them. The wolf
studied Daniel for a moment, then sat down on the
bankside and laid his nose on his paws, snapping now and
then at a marauding insect.

"*Un loup est seulement de soi-même,*" said Little Jean.

A wolf belongs to no one but himself.

"But he obeys you," Daniel said with his hands. "You
set him to guard the dead. Was it you, then, who killed
them?"

Little Jean laughed, a soft sound like wind in bare
branches. "*Je ne tuer pas des femmes,*" he said. "*Les
enlever dans les bois. Les coucher bien. Les vendre vite en
Canada, si ne sont pas belles. Les bambins aussi-même.*"

*I don't kill women. I take them away into the woods. I
fuck them good. If they're not pretty enough to keep, I sell
them off quick in Canada. The brats, too.*

The Dutchman chuckled. "My Jean is no fool, Dah-
niel. Them British and French pays good money for bound
women up north, good as Boston did before the War. Ten
pound sterling for a homely one, and not young. Twenty,
thirty for a young one, if she's good looking maybe. I'd
sell them one of my wives; that Louisa, she's got a temper
worse than my Dutch wife back in Amsterdam!"

"There was gold at Stark's place, Uncle. Somebody
took it. Was it you?"

Piet's blue eyes narrowed and became all but invisible
in the weathered mask of his face. "How much?"

"Nine sovereigns." Daniel glanced at the runner. "The
gold was gone from Stark's house. But Little Jean's wolf
was still there."

Soutendieck's face turned a shade pinker, and he tossed
the squirrel from his arm. There were only two rules in
Soutendieck's kingdom: never disobey Oncle Pierre's orders, and never steal unless you give him his share.

"What has my Little Jean got in his pretty scrip, now?" said Piet, and with a single swift movement he grabbed the half-breed around the knees and toppled him, a huge heavy foot on his ribcage. Taking the hunting knife from his scabbard, he cut the leather thong that slung a handsome beaded-leather pouch across Jean le Petit's heaving chest.

Leaving his big moccasined foot where it was, the Dutchman seized the pouch and turned it upside down onto the creek bank, no more than a foot from the dozing wolf. It merely looked up and flicked its ears in boredom.

The contents of Jean's scrip was an odd assortment. Three painted deer's joints for the game of toss-bones the Indians and trappers played for whisky. Some jerked venison. Two or three corncakes, moldy but nourishing. A pouch of tobacco and a short-stemmed clay pipe. Flint and steel in a small firebox. A dozen musket balls.

A fragment of beavertail, for virility. A bear's tooth, for courage. A bit of stag's hoof, for swiftness. A scrap of gilt-and-silver snakeskin, for shrewdness.

And eight gold sovereigns, for the dangerous pleasure of getting one up on Oncle Piet.

"Goddamn it, Jean," said the big Dutchman. He swooped down again and the tip of his blade was at the half-breed's Adam's apple.

"Put the knife away," said Daniel in his quiet voice. His own sword's point was inside Soutendieck's ear.

For a split second, he thought he would have to drive it home. There was no sound but the rushing water of creek and river and the buzzing of the insects around their heads. Then, at last, Piet lifted the knife and relaxed his foot on Little Jean's breast.

Daniel drew a deep breath, but he did not return his sword to its scabbard. "Once I have what I came for," he said, "you may stretch him, skin him, boil him, and serve him for stew for all I care. But not yet."

"And what the devil you want, then? To save your woman from a rope? Georges Dumaines was in town drinking last night when they come back from that cabin.'' Piet laughed softly. ''I never seen no woman hang. That would be something to see, all right. Maybe I don't sell that bitch wife of mine. Maybe I stretch her instead, yah?''

Daniel pushed the point of the blade another fraction of an inch into the Dutchman's ear, letting him feel it. ''What do you know about Reuben Stark?''

It was dangerous to bring such a fellow meekly to heel, especially in front of one of his men. But he had brought no money with him for bribes. A flicker of indecision shadowed Daniel Josselyn's broad face, and his eyes glazed and grew blank. Then he slipped off the gold wedding band from his right hand and gave it to Piet.

The ring that had been Charlotte's wedding gift to him, Daniel had lost when the fingers were taken from his left hand. When she came to Rufford to join him, her first act had been to send to Boston for another ring, absurdly engraved with the outcast's family crest and motto:

Beyond Life, Honor.

''Will that suit you as payment?'' he said, lowering his sword from Piet's ear. ''It's worth a hundred sovereigns, at least.''

The Dutchman studied the ring, bit it, shined it on his breeches. Honor was a different commodity in the woods. Satisfied that he suffered no loss of it in the exchange, Piet nodded sharply and slipped the ring into his own scrip. Jean le Petit scrambled to his feet.

''Where is the bag you stole with them, Jean?'' Daniel demanded, his fingers forming the words. ''*Un petit sac?*''

''*Sac?*'' said the half-breed. ''*Sac, non. Dispersées sur la terre.*''

There was no bag. I found them scattered on the ground.

''Come now,'' said the Dutchman. ''Let me show you what else Little Jean found. We talk on the way.''

The Stark cabin was a little more than an hour's walk behind them and to the south, down Blackthorne Creek in the direction of the town.

But they did not follow the usual trails. Piet had chosen a roundabout route that led them to a spot almost within view of the place, but just above it. They clambered over outcroppings of granite and shale, hacking their way through clumps of fireweed clouded with yellow and blue and black butterflies, and disrupting the dinner of a pair of black bear cubs suckling their sow.

At last, climbing a jutting bluff thickly grown with cinnamon fern and buckthorn, they reached a small natural meadow above and behind the Stark cabin, ringed with raspberry bushes that thrived in the sunny open space. The country was high and heavily wooded, but here and there the great glaciers had gouged and smashed away the ancient Precambrian rock and weighed down the earth to the level of the underground streambeds, forming unexpected bogs and marshes on what was otherwise high ground. Waterfowl nested in them, bayberry and blueberry bushes nearly covered them, and water grasses made them look on the surface like perfectly solid meadowland.

Only the smell betrayed it—heavy and voluptuous, rich and rotting and biting the back of the throat. The air the dead must breathe in their graves. Daniel knew of the place; they called it Triler's Bog.

In spite of his girth and his rocking waddle, the old Dutchman was deft and graceful as he picked his way round the edge of the marsh to solid ground. A big maple grew quite alone at one end of the small meadow, and it was there that Piet halted. He said nothing, only pointed down into the long grasses where the trunk spread out its great roots like twisted claws.

"A grave?" said Josselyn.

It was long and narrow, but too shallow for a decent burial place. Too shallow for anything he knew of—a man-trap, a cache for furs. Even as a child's hiding place, it was insufficient.

Piet bent down and lifted away the branches that covered it. At one end, wrapped in a fold of oilskin, was a sort of packet. The Dutchman lifted it out and laid it on the grass to unfold it.

Daniel stared down at the collection of objects, as ill-assorted as those in Jean's medicine sack, but perhaps of as much significance to whomever had hidden them here. And to Dan Josselyn, too, they had a meaning—a heavy one, at that.

A wooden bird with its wings painted crimson and blue.

It was Jennet's; he had made it for her himself and let her splash it with bright paint as she chose. When you pulled it at the end of a string, its wings fluttered on tiny wires.

A book.

The well-thumbed copy of Shakespeare's *Sonnets* he had sent to Hannah after the winter. Still inside was a slim piece of foolscap, meant for a bookmarker, on which he had written *Knowledge is Freedom*, in his careful spikey hand.

A blue-and-white china cup.

Dolly Lamb served her special friends tea in such cups at Lamb's Inn; they were not common, but there were also a few in Julia Markham's kitchen at the Mills.

A bit of lace with the bobbins still hanging from it.

Mrs. Pinch's lace, it must be. But it was a child's cap, of a size to fit Jennet.

A carved rosewood locket on a black velvet ribbon.

Inside the frame was a miniature painted on ivory. It was a portrait of a young girl with brownish curling hair, an overwide mouth and large brown eyes.

He recognized it, in spite of the clumsy strokes of the itinerant painter who must have made it. It was Hannah, as a young girl.

They were the bits and pieces of her life and of Jennet's, and only another woman could have taken them. The same woman, surely, who had left her bare footprints in Grace Stark's cabin. The woman who had taken Hannah's mourning kerchief as she had taken these other things—

building a life from the disregarded scraps she stole, harboring it here for her comfort.

A child's toy for innocence. An ancient book for wisdom. A cup to hold sorrow. A lace web for beauty. A locket to close up the picture of the past.

"Jean found the trash. Nothing to steal, so he left it. He was going to that fair of yours to sell his furs, and he passed this way about noon, him and the wolf."

"And it scented the dead and led him to them. Down there." Daniel nodded downhill toward Grace Stark's cabin. "Was it Jean who covered their bodies, then?"

"Nah. Dead is dead to him. Only the wolf wouldn't come with him, call it or curse it. They take crazy notions sometime."

Daniel slipped Hannah's locket and his daughter's toy into the scrip that hung from his belt. Then he folded the other things up again in their oilskin and knelt down beside the shallow, gravelike cache. It had been carefully lined with grasses and fresh boughs, the cuts not yet entirely healed over. The sides sloped inward and were not cut off as a spade or a shovel might dig them. They appeared to have been clawed out; there were tunnel-like tracks where spread fingers had worked at the earth when it was still damp enough to dig, before the present drought set in. Aside from a useless shower or two, it had not rained in nearly six weeks.

She has lived all this time through a window, thought Daniel, *as I have. Through a secret lens, to be part of their lives. To become Hannah, perhaps even to love her. To have Jennet for her own child.*

But in time, a window is a prison. You must smash it to pieces or die.

And so she had begun to do.

On the morning of Grace Stark's death, something had happened to change the madness that took only laces and books and lockets and toys to another sort. Cool. Strong. Pitiless.

Something red caught his eye in the bottom of the

clawed-out grave, and for a split-second his own mind
betrayed him.

Sweet Christ. It is Hannah, he thought, and his lungs
ached as though they might collapse inside the cell of his
ribs. *She has caught her red skirt on the branch and left
a scrap of it behind.*

But when he reached among the pine boughs that lined
the grave, his hand did not find homespun. He felt something soft and wet, and closed his fingers gingerly upon
it. When he opened them again, he found a soft, pulpy,
half-spoilt mess upon his palm, and a little juice oozing
through his fingers. He smelled it, then tasted it.

Raspberries. She had picked raspberries and put a handful here with the other things to keep them, like a careful
housewife putting up preserves for the winter.

But it meant nothing, surely. It was the season for fruit,
and many women came out gathering in the woods. Why,
even Bertha Pinch had been stringing a child's necklace
of leftover raspberries last night at Two Mills, when—

Daniel stood up from the grave, the handful of fruit
dripping musty juice like blood onto his white shirt.

Some woman had been there with Bertha. She had
dropped her shawl when she ran from him, and left a
half-strung necklace of wild raspberries, the needle still
dangling. She had gone out to the pond and dived down
and Mrs. Pinch had gone after her.

*A wooden bird. A lace cap to fit Jennet. A child's neck-
lace of dried raspberries. There are no raspberry bushes
at Two Mills. No raspberries.*

*Jennet was safe because she could not speak. Could not
say, I am not your own child. I will not have you for my
mother instead of Hannah.*

"Jenny!" he cried aloud, and the overhanging trees sent
it back to them.

The Dutchman stared.

"I— I must go back at once!" Daniel told him. "At
once!"

Already the sun was lowering. It was well past midafternoon, and would be twilight before he got back to the Grange. It would be quicker to leave the canoe and go on foot.

Piet read his mind. "There's a path, my friend," he said. "It will save you more time than the river."

It led almost straight down, at first, through rocks and dense trees and ferns. Then halfway down it branched, taking a more gradual course into thinning woods that must at length come out somewhere near Henry Markham's sheep meadow. The other branch led straight to Grace Stark's dooryard and the scrubby patch of kitchen garden that bounded it.

Sarah. Charlotte. Bertha. Hannah. Merriam. Jennet. Grace.

"Send Jean down to the Grange with my canoe and my weapons," Daniel said, gripping the Dutchman's arm. "You said you knew something of Stark. What was it? Quickly."

Piet shrugged. "Only that there's more trade in these woods than furs and tree trunks, and Stark had a finger in it—or wanted one. Him and the Prophet. That bastard Squeer."

"You think Squeer might have killed them?"

The Dutchman shook his head. "Stark maybe, but he'd do it here in the woods, not in your fine garden. Sink him in one of these bogs. The woman and her brats—them he'd sell." He considered a moment, studying Daniel's face. "You and Siwall, you still got a fight between you?"

"If he makes one."

There were heavy clouds in the northeast, now, and the sun had gone. It would grow dark early, but in another good hour's brisk march Daniel could be with them, with Hannah and Jennet, and see them safe. He turned to go.

But Piet Soutendieck stopped him. Reaching into his scrip, he rummaged a moment and came up with Daniel's wedding ring on the end of his thick, calloused finger.

"It don't fit me, English," he said with a grin. "My

fingers are fat. Besides, I don't want no more wives. Five is plenty.''

The number went up, Daniel had noticed, with every winter that passed. Uncle Piet handed back the ring and laughed his great laugh.

"*Beyond death, honor*? Piss! If you save her white neck, you bring your second woman and live free in my woods. I give you a nice warm bed, you can let them fight their new war by themselves.''

Daniel's eyes narrowed. "Surely there won't be another war. Will there?''

"If you chop a tree and stand under it in a northeast gale, will it fall on you?'' Piet clapped a hand on the younger man's shoulder. "You stay inside, my friend. Fuck your woman. Keep out from under trees. And this I tell you for nothing. That Prophet, Ike Squeer? He might wear the pine in his hatband and ride with the Regulators when it suits him. But he's Tapp's spy. And Siwall's.''

❊ THIRTY ❊

HOW THE DEAF CHILD
HID FROM THE MORNING

*J*ennet Trevor did not wake from her drugged sleep till near six that evening, but in the clock of her bones it was morning still.

The light was very bright through the north-facing window, but the sun did not slant in from the east as it should have. It came from low in the west, crooked and crippled by building clouds and tangled in the branches of the old ash in the kitchenyard. This sudden departure from the usual frame of the world made the child feel alien and afraid.

Even when the eardrum is pierced and the inner ear totally useless—which Jennet's was not—there remains a tympanum of the mind, some frail membrane of sensation and intellect that no anatomist could possibly discover. Reason would scoff at it, Science deny its existence. But for a creature robbed of sound, this invisible tissue of selfhood records the impressions of all the other senses—a slant of sunlight, the bright red color of a woman's cloak, the softness of cat's fur, a taste of sour pickles or sweet maple sugar, the parabola of wheeling gulls—and makes them echo in the mind like sound.

Something beautiful, fearful, delightful, terrible, comforting. Something urgent as a warning shout, that demands response.

The brightness is in the wrong place, thought Jennet even before her eyelids fluttered entirely open. *They have made the world go wrong.*

She sat up in her bed and looked around. Arthur's sleeping-basket by the window was empty; a cat likes to be out early on his morning prowl, after all, and then nestle somewhere in the shade for an afternoon's quiet philosophizing. But Jennet had lost time, and the comfort of habit. She did not know it was no longer morning, nor even afternoon.

The soft one is not here. He has gone early to the sheep meadow, looking for mice and moles.

There was no word in her mind for *cat.* Daniel had taught her to wiggle her fingers, and she knew to what persons or objects or animals the motions referred. But words, implications, relationships—of those she had no notion. She saw little use to the sign language, but Daniel was her friend and it pleased him. He would pick her up and carry her, swing her about and laugh. She could feel his laughter when she laid her face against his chest— much as she heard Arthur's purring, with her delicate muscles and nerves—and her secret mind heard it and remembered it. She was safe and glad and strong in his arms.

We are two, she thought, and hugged her own arms around her as though they were Daniel's. It was the shape that meant *love.*

Alone in the big featherbed, Jennet opened her mouth wide in a silent laugh and jerked the muscles of her chest in and out as Daniel did. Then, as she had done in the arbor, she forced sound from her belly and throat and up through the mask of her face. She could not hear the strange gulping laugh she produced, but there was a funny buzzing that vibrated against her palate and the root of her tongue, and made her small chest rise and fall.

She sat up and looked around, surprised at herself.

I am new, like the sunlight from the wrong direction. I am more than I thought.

Her mother had been there while she slept; the inkstand

and quill were still on the table, but the raggedy old sewn-together journal was gone. On the empty pillow next to Jennet, Hannah had laid a handkerchief lady, a tiny doll with a knot for a head and a scrap of lace for a bonnet, and a blue hair ribbon tied round her waist.

The child took up the limp little doll and rocked it, nursing it against her chest. Then suddenly she pushed it away.

Ignoring the bed ladder, she kicked her feet once or twice for the feel of the air moving fast and cool across her bare legs, like water in the mill pond. Then she spread her arms like a bird's wings and jumped down to the scoured plank floor. They had scrubbed it with sand to make it white, and her bare feet landed with a gritty bounce.

Susan and Kitty, the hired girls, who were down in the kitchen taking their cornbread from the iron spider on the hearth, heard a thump overhead.

Kitty frowned. "She's awake at last. Oh, if she do start that wailing again, I don't know what I shall do!"

"Go and see to her, love. I can manage," said Susan.

But Kitty—round as a dumpling and covered from top to toe with cornmeal and flour and freckles—was already halfway up the stair.

Once on the floor, Jennet got down onto hands and knees to check under the high bed for the errant cat.

Not there. Wrong.

She scowled and thunderclouds gathered on her brow. Arthur was always there in the morning, waiting to lean against her bare legs and slide himself down to her foot. But today he had left her, like all the others. Even Hannah was gone.

Jennet's mouth formed the two equal shapes of the word. *Han. Nah.*

"Annnhhh, ahhhhh," said her new voice. It made a tight, scraping feeling in the back of her throat, but she pushed the word out again, harder, straining to hear what she said. "Annnnnhhhh, ahhhhhhh."

It was just then, the front half of her still under the bed and the back half aimed at the open window, that Jennet saw the door swing open. A brown homespun skirt swished in, meaning business.

The little girl scuttled under the bed, her eyes wide with mischief. If it had been Hannah who entered, Jennet would have darted out, grabbed for the familiar pair of scuffed boots, and latched on like a sand crab to be pried away and tickled until she surrendered.

But the boots were not Hannah's, nor Aunt Julia's. Jennet knew them.

Silly-boots, that was her name for Kitty. She was younger than Parthenia—who was soon to be married and leave them—and not so clever as Susan. When you played hide-and-seek with *them,* they would find you in no time and set you to polishing pewter or sorting out the stabbed potatoes from the whole ones.

Silly-boots was more fun to tease, for she forgot the good hiding places as soon as she learned them, and then she stamped her feet and made her mouth go little and tight, like sour gooseberry juice.

"Jenny?"

The word cut through the blanket of silence and found Jennet somehow, as her own name always did. Perhaps by sound, for she sometimes heard faintly, much as a man with profoundly bad eyesight can discern the dim glow of a candle when the room is dark enough. She knew, for instance, that lightning was followed by a low, dull rumbling sound, like the cat's purring or the laugh in Daniel's chest. Thunder. She would wait for it, braced against Hannah's arm, and when she heard it she would run to the window and put her face against the glass to feel the pane tremble slightly.

So it was with her name. When Hannah spoke it, the child would turn and gaze at her.

What is wanted? What have I done?

"Oh God, she's gone!" cried Kitty. Silly-boots was always quick to panic, that was what made it such fun to tease her. The worn boots turned nervous circles in the middle of the bedchamber floor, the brown linen skirt tangling and twisting. "Jennet! Child!"

Jennet pressed herself back under the bed as far as she could go, into the shadowy corner nearest the wall. Sillyboots would look under the bed first, then go out into the hall and open the big cupboard—Jennet hadn't hidden *there* since she was four!—and then go galloping down the stairs to look in the workroom under the big loom.

"Susan! Susan! The child's gone!" screamed Kitty, now nearly beside herself. She yanked the sheet back from the bed and looked behind the big draw-chest in the corner and turned the rocking-chair upside down. Then at last she remembered to look under the bed.

Nothing but dust-mice, and not many of them.

Susan found her friend on her hands and knees, tears rolling down her face. "Oh, what shall we do?" wailed Kitty. "Whatever will Mistress say when she comes back and finds I've lost Jenny?"

The dissection completed, Hannah and her aunt had come home to Two Mills weary and grim-faced, but neither had stayed long. Julia had gone to the burial service for Grace Stark and her children, and then to sit with Mrs. Anson. As for Hannah, the two girls at their work in the kitchen had heard her moving restlessly about overhead, in the room where the child still lay sleeping. She had taken a quilt-covered parcel with her when she left an hour later, and said only that she was off on some errands and would return before dark.

"If only her ma was here," moaned little Kitty. "She'd never have strayed, if Hannah was by!"

Susan peered under the bed herself, just in case. But neither girl noticed a pair of wide eyes the color of fine dark ale peep in at them through the hinge-crack of the door, then disappear. She had invented this game, and she changed the rules faster than anyone else could learn them.

"Oh, what shall we do if we don't find her? Wild as she was in the night, she may drown herself in the mill pond or fly off the top of the barn! Or run away into the Outward and be eat by a bear!''

Kitty collapsed in another fit of hysterical wailing, but Susan was not so easy to fool.

''Why look there, you poor goose!'' she said. ''Here are her petticoat and skirt, still, and her everyday bodice. And her stockings and boots, where her ma laid them out for her. She's not let to run barefoot, you know, like a beggar child! Do you think she'd get far without boots? Stop your caterwauling and search the other rooms upstairs. I'll go down.''

''She loves to hide in the parlor behind the firescreen,'' said Kitty, somewhat comforted. ''Or perhaps in the cellar! 'Tis cool in there on such a hot day as this.''

When the two girls had gone huffing away, the child emerged from beneath the lowest shelf of Julia's punchwork airing cupboard under the attic stair; she went determinedly back into the bedchamber and dressed herself. Then she sat down on the linen chest to pull on her long white stockings and her low-heeled calf-skin boots, whose laces she never quite properly tied.

But what of the loose ends of her memories? Jenny had not forgotten what she had seen in the arbor the night before. The drugged drink and the heavy sleep had closed like a comforting door upon her vivid senses, but the colors were all there—red, white, brown, blue, black. The sticky feel of the blood. The faces. The shapes. The light and dark.

Slowly it came back to her, and the light brought it. The punched-tin lantern someone had set in the door of the arbor.

She had found the puppet show tiresome, and the tumblers' tricks were no better than any child could do in his sleep. But she had seen the dancing lantern-light fall through the lattice; it made magical patterns on the darkness, and the sweet, dazzling scent of the flowers drew her. Eluding the grown-ups as usual, she went softly into the arbor and hid herself behind the heavy branches, where the lantern light did not reach.

The man in the tricorne was there, sitting hunched on the seat between the swooping, twining canes of white roses. White flowers, and the liquid dance of the lantern light, and the white oval face of the man that seemed to float in the dark. His white teeth when he laughed.

He was talking to someone behind him, a woman. A white cap and kerchief. White hands that seemed to move of themselves.

And then the darkness began to move, too, and to thrash, and it crashed down on the back of the hunched man's skull as though the roses battered him. Something tore at the flowers, and Jennet felt the lattice shake.

He lay dazed and bleeding, tangled in blood and blossoms, slumped against the bench. The gaudy tricorne hat fell to the floor and lay there upside down, like the open palm of a beggar's hand.

But there was somebody else. A white shirt front. The long blade that shone in a white hand. The quick, hard pull of the razor. The rush of the blood, not red but black in the dim light.

Something heavy smashed down on the fallen man's chest and his body jumped, jerked, lay still.

A skirt swooshed past Jennet in the dark and disappeared outside.

White hands took the body and dragged it, laid it flat on the floor, with the hat and the shining blade beside it.

A pair of man's boots stopped at the doorway to put out the light and his eyes saw her crouching there, her mouth wide open with fear when the lantern light fell on them both.

A moment he paused. *She has seen. Must I kill her?*

No, no. Why bother? She is mute. She can do me no harm.

But she had seen the face looking down at her. A dead face, oddly peaceful and kind.

*   *   *

Jennet glanced out the window. There were men in the yard, riding up from the mill on great horses. Men she did not know, strange men with blank faces and eyes that stared. John English was there, worried and stolid, and the crooked woman, too, away by the mill pond, watching.

And someone else, there in the yard. A shape that opened the terrible door which the night's rest had closed. A face she knew and did not know.

Jennet's small mouth sagged open and her breath came fast. But this time she did not howl.

I will hide and not come out. I will go where the soft one goes, where it is dark, and I will wait there till the morning comes back as it ought to. I will go where my woman-friend is.

It was how she thought of Daniel and Hannah. Not father, not mother, but friend.

"Annnnnhhhhh. Ahhhhhh," she said to herself. "Anh-Ah."

She went to the door and looked out, but there was no sign of Kitty or Susan. Stuffing the handkerchief doll inside the laces of her bodice, Jennet crept down the back stairs, but although she had not eaten since the haying supper and was hungry as only a child can be, she did not go into the kitchen for a piece of the fragrant, warm cornbread.

She slipped instead into the stillroom, where her mother's herbs hung in great bunches from the ceiling and many pots and baskets and leather bottles stood on the shelves and hung from nails on the walls.

I will have to put the soft one in something, she thought. *I will not go without him. Where I go, he must go, too.*

She dragged a joint-stool over to the spot, climbed up, and lifted a large basket down from its nail. It had a hinged lid she could close to keep Arthur safe. Clambering down, she emptied out the bunches of dried pennyroyal onto the floor, hooked the basket over her arm as she had seen her mother do, and went through the small, low-cut door that connected the stillroom with the springroom beyond, and the dairy.

The stone-walled springroom was built into the hillside itself, and from the clean granite of the fourth wall a small trickle of ice-cold water bubbled out and fell down into a narrow channel that carried it away in a paved trough under the wall, to end at last in the millrace outside. If you wanted to keep food cold, you set the crock into the stream, where the running water kept it fresh and sweet.

In one such crock, Jenny found some of the leftover baked turtle, in another some soft farmer's cheese, nicely-peppered and flavored with cumin. She stuffed the food into her mouth with her fingers until she was satisfied. A bit of the baked turtle she put carefully into the basket; it would help her persuade Arthur to come.

Besides, he was fond of turtle, and she was fond of spoiling him.

She found the old cat in the dairy, engaged in licking the last of the morning's cream from one of the milking pails before he went out to make the rounds of his kingdom. Scooping him up, Jennet held him to her face for a moment, stroking his back and ears until she could feel the deep rumble of his purring. It calmed her to feel it, and made her less afraid.

"Chuuurrr, chhhuuuurrr," she said, making the rumbling sound with the back of her tongue. It felt rough and strong. *We are two.*

Arthur squirmed, and she put him into the basket with the morsel of turtle meat; while he was busy sniffing it over, she closed the lid on him and fastened it down.

Out in the yard, more men had gathered. Kitty and Susan were talking to a big man she did not know, a dark man with eyes that had no color in them. She did not know Marcus Tapp, the sheriff, but by instinct Jennet feared him.

And then she saw the other one again. The face behind the closed door of her mind, the one she had seen in the arbor.

Her mouth opened wide and she clutched Arthur's basket hard against her.

Run, now. Go quick. Hide in the secret place. This morning is wrong and they have broken it. They have taken away the good light.

Tongue between her teeth, panting softly, Jennet slipped out into the heavy, stifling air of the now-crowded farmyard, the basket of cat on her arm. The woodpile was no more than a few yards away, and once she reached it, she could keep to its shadow and make her way behind the barn, between the ripening wheat field and the orchard, and onto the high road. When her mother returned from wherever she had gone to, she would almost surely come that way; Jennet often met her in the small grove of red spruce beside the path that led to Rook's Nest, where Arthur liked to hunt field mice and ground squirrels.

The cat in his basket was clawing at the withes now, but Jennet ignored him, running, dodging into shadow, crouching low, then running again.

"Jennet!" cried Kitty, catching sight of her.

The little girl stopped in her tracks and looked round. The muffled shape of the sound was right, but the edge of it was wrong. It made her nerves jump when she heard it, like the slap of Hannah's open hand when she was spanked.

She ducked away into the orchard and was gone.

When the dissection was finished, Hannah Trevor had ridden home to see if Jennet would be well enough to travel by nightfall. Finding the child still asleep, she took the time to pack some few clothes and her journal in a small parcel wrapped in the Maid of Bedlam coverlet; then she knotted the twelve shillings that constituted her life's savings into the hem of her gown and rode off to Mrs. Hinkley's house to lance the stubborn abscess on her breast, and then to Abiah Foster's, to change the dressings on her burns.

When she left the Fosters', Hannah turned Flash's nose south, to the small unconsecrated potter's field just beyond the militia arsenal, where the oxcart had taken James Trevor's dissected remains—still coffinless, wrapped in a fold of worn canvas—to be buried where suicides and felons lay unforgiven.

But Tory or not, bigamist or not, villain or scoundrel or rogue, Uncle Henry Markham could not let any man be cast into the earth unprovided; he had worked all the morning, sawing and hammering clean pine boards into a plain coffin, and it lay waiting beside the grave as Hannah slid down from the pony's back.

Most of the village had turned out to weep for Grace Stark and her children, and it would be much the same for George Anson when he was buried next day.

But only a few stood by Trevor's grave that sultry late afternoon—Uncle Henry; Josh Lamb and his warm-hearted Dolly, who could never leave anyone to mourn or to be mourned alone; and Sarah Firth with McGregor's lad, Robbie, beside her.

Hannah stood a little apart from the others, hands at her sides, eyes fixed straight ahead of her.

They laid James into the coffin and Josh nailed it down. Then they eased it onto the ropes slung across the open grave and lowered it, with a fine rain of dry earth as it went down.

A little wind had begun to blow from the northeast where the thunderheads were rising, and it tossed her short curls about and caught at her skirts like the dry, spiky grass underfoot.

Hannah passed a hand across her eyes and walked away.

But there was one more thing she must do before she left Rufford. She had written a note of farewell to Daniel on a page torn from her journal, and leaving her uncle and Joshua to cover the grave, she set off to deliver it when she heard shouting behind her, and the sound of a horse's hooves moving fast along the hard, dry high road.

Jem Siwall pulled his grey gelding up so short beside her that the bit drove into the animal's mouth and blood mixed with the foam of its spittle.

"Don't go home!" the boy cried. He was almost as wild-eyed as the horse that strained and panted under him. "Tapp and his fellows have gone to Two Mills to search your belongings for proofs of your guilt!"

Hannah smiled. "I wish them success. They will find none."

"Did I not say that the law may do what it wishes? He's taken the proof with him! I heard them in Pa's library. I listen at keyholes, you know, for they never tell me anything otherwise."

"What proof?"

"A gold piece, a sovereign like the one found at Stark's cabin. He'll lay it among your things and say you had hidden it there. They'll put you to trial on the strength of it, ma'am, and hang you inside a week!"

Hannah gripped the reins tighter. "Where did this gold piece come from? How did Tapp come by it? What—"

"There's no time for whys and hows and wherefores! They are grinding already. You must go!"

The clock that had been ticking so urgently at the back of Hannah's mind for the past two days had struck at last, and broken its spring. The painstaking labor of quilting and piecing and stitching up the truth was torn suddenly from her hands.

"My daughter!" she cried. "I will not go without her!"

"I'll tell Josselyn. He'll see to her."

"No!"

"If your neck is not stretched, you may come back for her once you are cleared of all blame, or he will bring her to you!" He looked up at her, boyish. "Please, ma'am. Pa's blind and bamboozled, and I'm a damned rogue. But we ain't bloody. Tapp is, though, and he's calling the dance now. I beg you to go."

Hannah's body straightened itself in the saddle. "Very well," she said, and reaching into her basket, she handed him the carefully sealed note. "Give this to Major Josselyn, sir, if you please."

She turned Flash's nose toward the ferry, but again he stopped her. "Wait! Let me give you some money! Six shillings don't go far, what?" He smiled. "I stole it from Pa's dragon-horde. Come, now, be sensible. You'll take it, will you not?"

Hannah looked down at what lay in his hand. It was ten pounds in good sterling, more than she earned in a year. But it was stolen, and if she were caught with it, the gift might prove a millstone indeed.

"I thank you, Master Siwall," she said, with a hand on his arm. "But give it to Molly, to christen her son."

Naturally Hannah had no serious intention of going a mile out of Rufford unless Jennet was with her. Besides, it would be folly to ride out in broad daylight on a horse well-known to be her aunt's and with Tapp's men no doubt watching the roads. She must find Jenny, see her safe until after nightfall, and then seek out some better means of transport. They would go downriver to the Head, buy passage to Boston on the next coastal packet, and then be gone.

The old watchhouse at Rook's Nest was tumbledown and vermin-ridden, but no one would think to look for her there. It would do until dark; then she might slip back to the Mills and get Jennet, once Tapp and his fellows had gone.

But when Hannah reached the crossroads and the grove of red spruce near Cove Creek Bridge, she heard something that made her tug on the reins and turn Flash in among the trees. It was a scratching sound, and with it came a frantic and familiar yowling.

A lidded basket stood upon the thick carpet of needles under the trees. It rocked back and forth wildly, and a strong smell of furious tomcat came from it, as well as the yowls and the scratchings.

Next to the basket was one of Jennet's calf-skin boots,

and a torn bit of white stocking. There was a stain on it, but though it was small, Hannah did not need her spectacles to see it.

It was almost the color of the ribbons Matthew Gwynn had brought her as a courting present. The color of the pieced roses made from Aunt Julia's discarded bed curtains and stretched on the quilting frame at the Mills. The color of Charlotte Josselyn's sweet-smelling blossoms, white and damask and red.

It was the clear, undried crimson of fresh blood.

"Jennet!" she cried out, forgetting her own danger. "Jennnnnnyyy!"

And suddenly a small, sturdy body—with one shoe fallen off and a torn, dirty stocking that had trodden upon a rock—came hurtling out of the undergrowth and fastened itself around Hannah's waist like a sand crab, and would not let go for its life.

"Oh, Jenny," whispered Midwife Trevor, and laughed with relief. "My wild heart. My silly love."

"Annnnhhhhhh. Ahhhhhhh," said the deaf child.

The world is right again. We are two.

THIRTY-ONE

Flight

Dark fell early, slipping unnoticed behind the great woods to the west.

Hannah and Jennet stayed hidden within the crumbling walls of Rook's Nest until almost the same hour that Daniel Josselyn returned from his trip to the Outward, but they caught no glimpse of him. The clouds were now very heavy and lightning streaked sidewise through them from time to time, but there was no rain yet. The air was dense and very hot, and the small wind had been smothered.

Below them, the farmhouse at Two Mills was brightly lighted and Tapp's horse was still in the yard. Hannah could see the faint glow of his men's pipes in the darkness as they paced and smoked, and she knew she must not risk returning to borrow her uncle's skiff for the journey as she had planned.

There were other lights, too. Torches and lanterns moving along the North Bank and the lamps of carriages and carts crossing by the ferry, making their way along the high road. Hand in hand, she and Jennet skirted the road and made a zigzag path through fields and back gardens, but when they at last reached the village, Hannah saw that the meeting house, too, was brightly lighted, its door open wide and a ragged stream of farmers and sober-faced townsmen entering by twos and threes and talking in low murmurs. Her uncle and Josh were not among them, but she saw Mr. Bunce and Enoch Luckett and a number of others she knew. The moderates were having their town meeting sooner than promised, it seemed; Ham Siwall's chaise was stopped at the door.

On the common, the last stragglers of the fair were making ready to leave, and she spied Mr. Ledyard, the old Punch-and-Judy man, putting his puppet stage into a bright-colored caravan, a lean, spavined horse already hitched to it and grazing wearily, in no hurry to depart.

Head down, Hannah scurried with Jennet across the open space of grass to where the old man was packing Mister Punch and Mistress Judy and the Constable and the Butcher into a basket-trunk.

"If you please, Master Ledyard," she said. "Where are you bound next?"

The puppet-master looked up. "Why, to Bridgewater Fair, mistress. Downriver a bit, and round the Hook, and cross the Narrows Ferry, and there I shall be, safe and dry! 'Tis a fine fair, is Bridgewater. My poppets be fond of it, and so am I."

"Would you carry two passengers?" Hannah made an effort to smile. "I can pay, sir. Will a shilling for both be enough?"

Just then Arthur the cat, who had surrendered to the inevitable and fallen asleep, awoke with a loud burst of feline profanity and a renewal of clawing at the badly-splintered basket withes. Mr. Ledyard smiled and bent down to peer over his spectacles at Jennet.

"And who have you in there, my little lady? A lion? A tiger? A leopard, by chance?"

"My daughter does not speak, sir," Hannah told him.

"Not speak!" he cried, and slapped his thigh with delight. "Why, by Jove, then I *shall* take you along, ma'am, with all my heart! And she shall be company for Brutus. Brute! Brutus! Where be you, man? Come out now, confound you, for I have found you an equal!" He leaned close to Hannah. "Brute don't speak much neither, for the fire have so parched up his throat that sometimes the words, you know, comes out burnt to a cinder! But he talks to them he trusts, and we travel together and are company for each other by the way. Come now, Brutus! Don't shilly-shally! Be bold, man! Be bold.''

A door opened at the back of the caravan, and the face of the huge black man who ate fire peered out. He was dressed all in red like his fires, and he wore a small gold ring through one ear and a large one through the other, and carried a birch wand, peeled and polished until it shone like ivory. Brutus's white teeth smiled brightly, but his great, mournful eyes studied Hannah's face suspiciously.

A runaway slave, she thought, *from somewhere to the south.*

"How do you do, sir?" she said, and stepped to the doorway to offer him a hand. "I saw you perform at the fair, and again at the haying supper. You have a great mystery, indeed. But my child and I will not pry it from you. We seek our freedom in some less fiery path."

Brutus smiled, leaped down from the wagon, turned a cartwheel or two, and then, leaning his head back, he opened his mouth wide. Fire blazed up at the end of the birch wand and he gobbled it down and laughed.

Two horsemen rode up to the open door of the meeting house and dismounted. One of them, Hannah recognized as Sheriff Marcus Tapp. She stepped into the shadow of the caravan, pulling Jennet with her.

The black man broke off in the midst of a somersault and swung a bedazzled Jennet up into the wagon, then disappeared inside it himself.

"Come, ma'am," said the puppet-master softly. "I think we must go. We've stayed too long as it is, but Brutus has folk hereabouts."

Hannah had noticed a marked resemblance. "He is the brother of Caesar, is he not? Mr. Clinch's servant?"

"Aye, ma'am. And you—" His eyes narrowed in a frown. "You are the Tory woman, eh? Mrs. Trevor, the murdered man's wife?"

"I've done no crime, Mr. Ledyard."

The old fellow nodded. "We traveling folk have had scrapes enough to misbelieve guilt when it's smacked down on any Christian too sudden and too tight. Keep your shillings, my dear. You may come with us freely."

And so they left the town, the old horse plodding with maddening slowness along the South Bank road.

In the first hour, they saw men riding like shadows on the opposite bank. A cart passed them, breakneck, and nearly forced them from the road. There were two men inside, their faces smeared with red, white and blue warpaint, and they had tied feathers in their long, unfastened hair.

"What's afoot?" Ledyard called to them.

"Liberty!" cried one man. "We're burning the stacks! Our sweat will fatten no rich man's carriage horses this winter!"

"Make way, there!" cried the other. "We have Freedom's work to do!"

In the second hour, the wind came up, tossing the trees that hung over the path. Below the steep road, the river roiled and churned, and a boat crossing it with four men inside ran aground on a fallen spruce near the bank.

Ledyard stopped and he and Brutus pulled the men from the water, breathless and sodden, but scant of their thanks. They had sprigs of long-needled pine in their hatbands—the badge of the Regulators. Peering out from the back of the caravan, Hannah recognized Rufus Penny's squat shape and balding pate among them, and the lank, sullen figure of Isaiah Squeer.

And there was another, too—Jonathan, her cousin, with a sprig of pine in his hat like the rest. Not constable now, but rabble-rouser. After this night, she feared, outlaw as well, till they were all caught and thrown into prison.

"Will you take some rum, friends, to warm you?" offered the old puppet-master.

"We've no time to waste," said Rufe Penny. "We'll be warm soon enough!"

"There's a boat at Redferns'!" cried Squeer. "Let us take that, and cross down by the cove!" And they ran off at a lope, scarcely able to keep upright for the wind.

For, oh, it was a hot wind, and a sour wind. Before the second hour was out, Hannah could see fires blazing up on both banks—the new-made haystacks burning. The wind fed them and the wind ate up the sweet hay, and the wind blew blazing faggots onto the roofs of the houses and set some of them aflame by accident. They heard shouting, and the screaming of horses and women, and the wind carried the screams on its back.

Hannah thought of her uncle's stack that stood near the barn, and of Daniel. She could almost see the shape of him there, straining and struggling, battling the wind and the fire. But quiet in himself. Braced for burning.

Though I have gone, she thought, *I am not gone. Some part of me I have left behind and I will never get it back again.*

Without him, I shall bleed at the roots.

In the third hour, they passed through a village. It was too small to have any name. There was a great tree and they saw by the flicker of lightning the shape of a man hanging there. They had stripped him naked and painted him with pine tar and covered him with goosefeathers, and though he hung by his hands, there was a noose round his neck, too, so that if he should get his hands free somehow and try to move, the noose would strangle him. He swung in the wind and when they passed under him, they could hear his low moaning, as if the tree had a wound in its heart.

Ledyard pulled up the wagon and Brutus leaped out, but suddenly a musket ball screamed past his head and plowed a thin furrow of blood along his temple.

"Your life if you free him!" cried a voice from the cottage beyond.

"What's he done?" shouted Ledyard above the wind.

"Broken many. Killed some. Starved others."

Hannah looked up at the face of the hanged man; it was Gabriel Bent, the tax-gatherer. His eyelids flickered open and he stared into the storm.

Hannah climbed out, the wind whipping at her skirts. There was a woodpile nearby, and an ax beside it; she could cut both the ropes with a single stroke and set him free.

"No, mistress!" roared Ledyard, and Brutus pulled her out of the way of another musket ball just in time. It lodged itself in the helve of the ax and split it neatly in half.

"You think I won't kill a woman? Begone about your business and don't meddle with men's rightful work!" cried the voice from the cottage. "Next shot won't miss."

The wagon pulled away again, into the storm.

At last the rain came down upon them, falling in dense sheets like pitted glass. What was left of the burning haystacks hissed and smouldered, but they could scarcely see it; the river was only a roaring beside them and the pathway a rope on which they danced. When they crossed Whitebird Creek at its mouth, it was full to its banks, and the lightning and thunder were one now, very near on either hand. Jennet, huddled against Hannah in the back of the wagon, buried her face in her mother's skirts and clung tight.

One bolt tore the darkness above the Manitac and left it hanging like crooked scraps of burnt paper, to clatter down to the water below. The wind blew down a big maple behind them and another shaft of lightning struck not ten yards from the caravan.

It was too much for the old horse. He reared in the shafts, screaming, eyes wild and a thick cream of foam dripping from his mouth.

"Down, Soldier!" cried the old puppet-master. "Do you know me? Down, sir!"

But Soldier knew only the lightning that shook the

ground and the rain that made his hooves slip in the mud and blinded him, and the wind that blew his straggling mane in his eyes. He reared again, then bolted away down the road.

At a mad pace, the caravan swayed wildly from side to side and was whipped with sodden, low-hanging branches. Bracing herself against the floor of the wagon, Hannah grabbed for Jennet, who had been thrown flat against the opposite bulkhead; the cat in his basket was wailing his death-song and rolling from side to side. They were almost at Jedd's Cove, less than five miles from the Hook, and the road cut sharply inland toward the village of Oxford.

Just as they reached the turn, a bolt of lightning slashed into the flax field to the right of them. The wagon tilted horribly sidewise and Hannah could hear the old horse, Soldier, screaming, screaming in the wind.

"Jump, ma'am!" cried Ledyard. "He'll turn us over! Jump!"

With Jennet clinging to her skirts, Hannah felt her way to the back of the caravan and tried to throw open the door, but the wind was too strong. It blew the door shut in an instant, and one instant was all that was left them.

The horse screamed again. The wagon leaned crazily, then shot forward. There was a crack like a gunshot as the off wheel broke. Hannah dragged Jennet as best she could to the upward side of the wagon, where the worst of the wreck would not fall on them, and held hard to a fragile beam that supported the roof.

"We are finished!" cried Ledyard.

Daniel, Hannah thought, *I am dying.*

There was no time to think of God.

The fall was slow as her memories of childbirth, or so Hannah recalled it afterwards. A fraction of an inch at a time, with Jennet's small fingers clawing into her, trying almost to climb back inside her body and be born again.

And then the end of the world. The cracking of the

boards in the roof and walls, and the terrible crash against the hard ground that blotted out everything.

A great death-scream from the horse as he fell.

Then silence. The wind blowing the rain against the splintered wood. Something touched Hannah's face, stroked her closed eyes.

A voice spoke, and she thought God had become the rain and passed judgment upon her.

"Where do you live now, pretty mistress?" it whispered. "Oh, you shall sleep cold in Dog's Alley tonight, where the poor maids go to mourn."

And, then, in the flicker of a second before her body claimed her and blotted out her mind, Hannah Trevor heard another voice, another kind of word.

Annnnhhhh! Ahhhhhh!" it cried against the wind. "Annnnhhh! Ahhhh!"

But Hannah could not reply.

If Ledyard had not clung to his driver's seat to urge the terrified horse a few yards more round the turn, they would have gone down into the swollen river and almost certainly drowned. Instead, Hannah woke to find herself lying in the midst of a field of growing flax plants; had they been dry and ripe for pulling, it would have been as bad as landing on a bed of sharpened sticks set upright in the ground. But green, soft, still blossoming, the bushy clumps made a springy cushion that had kept her alive.

It was still dark, but the rain had nearly stopped and the lightning was growing distant, traveling upstream now toward the forest.

Hannah tried to move and found she could not. Part of the caravan roof lay across her chest and legs. When she moved, a hot pain shot through her right forearm; a nail had left a deep gouge, and there was blood in her mouth and half-clotted blood from another cut on her forehead.

She used her left arm to lift away the wreckage, and found she could stand. "Jennet!" she cried. "Jenny! Where are you, Jenny?"

But no small, warm body came hurtling out of the darkness to find her this time.

Hannah turned in a desperate circle. "Jennet!" she cried again, and fell.

Crawling, then. "Jennet! Jenny!" But there was no reply.

Something stirred among the ruins of the caravan and in another moment Brutus fought his way free of the splintered chaos of boards and household goods and puppets and costumes. In his arms, he had Hannah's quilt-covered bundle and Arthur the cat, who was digging his claws ruthlessly into the big fellow's chest.

"Girl gone, lady," said Brutus. The crash, it seemed, had loosened his tongue and the rain put out all his fires. "Be nowhere under there."

"And Mr. Ledyard?"

"Dead. Neck broke, like the horse."

He began to slosh through the deep mud between the rows of flax plants; Hannah tried to follow, but her legs would not hold her. She struggled up again, fell again, and was raised by a strong black arm.

"No sign of her," he said. Brutus's voice was very low and soft. "I take you far as that village yonder. Be an inn there. In the morning, they find her."

"She's not dead!" cried Hannah. "She was there with me, after the wagon fell! I won't have her be dead!"

His long black fingers stroked the pale fur of the cat. He unloosed Arthur's claws from his chest and handed Jennet's pet over to Hannah. "She'll want him, when you get her back."

He went to the ruined caravan, poked about for a moment, then disappeared. In a moment he was back with one of Mr. Punch's costumes, dripping with cool water from the river.

Gingerly, at arm's length, Brutus tipped back Hannah's head and inspected the cut, which was still bleeding slightly. He washed her face with the cool, wet rag, then laid it against the gouge on her arm.

The clouds showed a crack of clear sky, now, and a sliver of moon with a star in its arms. Brutus bowed very low in the darkness, his gold earrings glistening.

"Pray God for you, my lady. And for the girl."

"Stay! She hides when she's frightened, that's all! When she could not rouse me, she thought she must hide!"

Hannah said nothing of what Jennet had found in the arbor. But Brutus had been there, with Ledyard and the other folk from the fair.

"She got voice," he said. "Just like I do. I heard her when Stark died. Heard again when the wheel break. She make herself known. If she can." The black man hesitated. "Stark be rightly *your* man, eh?"

Her back straightened a bit and she pushed away a stray curl from her face. "By law, he was my husband," she said, her eyes fixed steadily on him. "That same law that made you a slave. If you know something that may free me of the taint of these deaths, you must tell me. I have some few shillings, but I will not offer to bribe you. I think you are a better kind of man."

His face was impassive. "I seen Stark there, seen him go in that arbor. That the word? Arbor? Where the sweet flowers be?"

"Arbor, yes."

"I could see but the farther end of it, away from the people. For a bit I was busy helping old man with his puppet-box. Then I see the woman. I knowed her before, see, and I can't afford to forget what I know. I kept out of her sight best I could."

"What woman? What is her name?"

"Name mean nothing. Call her Mary Ann when I knowed her. Don't know what she be called now."

"Did she go into the arbor?"

"That I did not see. She was watching the children. She was ever a gentle creature. I seen her, and I knowed her plain. Mary Ann, that was bound servant in Boston. I stop there awhile. Met the old man there, him and his puppets. Never seen her again till last night."

"She was a bound servant? What does she look like?"

"White woman. White skin."

"What color is her hair?"

"Wears a cap, most times. Hair's not so dark as yours, now."

"Fair, then? Blond hair?"

Bertha Pinch had pale cornsilk hair. Sarah Firth's was middling light brown, but it might be called fair by a man so dark as Brutus. Who else? Zilpah Cummins was black-haired, but was there not a new servant in Mrs. Twig's kitchen, called Thankful or Needful or—

Hannah's head ached fiercely, and she felt dizzy and sick. What did it matter who Twig's servant woman was or what she looked like? There was nothing to connect her to the deaths. It was another straw in the wind and she had grasped at it, but she was too weary to keep hold. "Please," she said quietly. "Help me to look for my daughter. Stay with me a bit."

Brutus looked away from her and shook his head.

"No, mistress. Sheriffs be out after last night, looking to take somebody."

"Why do you run? There are no slaves in Maine. Your brother is no slave."

He shrugged and his white teeth flashed a sour smile. "Serve a fool for a shilling, I don't call that free. Man, woman. Black, white. You got no hard money these times, you somebody's slave. Don't need to write it down to make it so. Ask them ones with the evergreen stuck in their hatbands. They tell you true." He let the back of his hand brush across her cheek. "You see they bury the old man with his puppets, my lady. He'd like that."

"God speed you," she whispered. In a blink he was gone.

Alone in the fading darkness, Hannah sat down on the muddy ground, tearless and silent, to wait for the light to come back.

If only I had left her with Daniel. But not I. I must risk her, I must have her on my terms, if she die for it. I must be I, and give not a morsel away.

She wished for him, then, for his stillness to clean the wild fear from her and his heart that could track down the truth of her own.

But since the first year of her marriage, nearly twenty years now, Hannah Trevor had feared love more than she needed it, and called the fear precious freedom. Now she ached to be able to give it away.

God protect you. I am gone, she had written on the note she sent Daniel. She had given him too little light to find her by, surely.

"Jennet!" she cried, and the word closed in about her like fog and overwhelmed her in the prison of herself.

I am. I am. I am. I am.

THIRTY-TWO

PIECING THE EVIDENCE: On the Nature of Prisoners

They marched us seventy miles or more, across country. Eighteen of us, our hands shackled and the shackles roped together. The end of the rope was tied to a horse, so that if the first man fell and was dragged, we all fell. Were all dragged.

When we reached Simsbury, they undid my shackles and dragged me into a hovel built over a narrow shaft cut straight down into the earth. I could see nothing but darkness. They put my arms into a harness attached to a windlass and shoved me through the hole. The Mouth of Hell, they called it. I could hear the tackle grating, grinding and grinding. My own body was no longer part of me. My legs flapped like a puppet's. I could not stop retching and my own vomit covered me. I could smell the stink of shit and I knew it was mine, but I had no sense of my body's releasing it.

My brain had severed all connection with me. The words of every prayer, every psalm I had ever known—gone. Out of the depths have I cried unto thee. By the waters of Babylon, there we sat down and wept. All gone. I had no knowledge, no memory, no profession, no pride and no shame. No faith and no lack of faith. I had ceased to exist. God had ceased to exist. There was only the shaft.

It was solid rock, very narrow and deep, forty feet or more. Water trickled down it constantly. Traces of copper still gleamed from the cuttings, like eyes in the breathless, wet dark.

At forty feet, the windlass stopped. A guard unhooked the harness and took off my shackles so I might move. Off the small landing were shelves cut into the rock face, and he marched me down them, shelf by shelf, another thirty or forty feet into the earth. I could hardly stand up, but if I had not marched, I would have fallen off into the bottomless hole.

At forty-five feet, we came to the prisoners. Many prisoners, reputable men. The mayor of New York was there. Mr. Franklin, the governor of New Jersey. Physicians, lawyers. Clergymen like myself. Sea captains. Farmers. Merchants. We lived on a platform, with a few boards above us to keep off the foul water that dropped from the copper seams. Charcoal fires for heat and to sweeten the air.

They had bored a small hole in the rock many yards above us, to let the smoke out and give us some air. From one spot on the platform, we could see this hole clearly. A pinprick of light, but to us, it was the world.

We took turns at it. Some prayed to it. Some called out the names of their wives and children. Some cursed. Some made love to each other for comfort. Some sang old songs or spoke verse they recalled.

Some battered others to rob them of their turns. That is the nature of prisons.

When the last of us is dead, they will seal up the Mouth of Hell and plant rosebushes there and when someone speaks of Simsbury to write down its history, they will tell you it did not exist, that it was some mad tale put about by the Tories to gain themselves pity.

I was there four years. Some part of me is there even now, waiting my turn to look up at the hole. We survive, and we do not survive.

I am prisoner still.

—Andrew Tyrrell, brother of Reuben Stark

I was born in Rufford, where my father was master shipwright, and there is my heart's home. In my seventeenth year I did wed Mister Kendall, for my father commanded it, and he was rich and had great properties. And for my father's sake he was kind to me at the first, though he would no more allow me to read books nor to write many letters as my father had encouraged me, for he said learning in a woman was not a respectable thing and he would not countenance a lettered wife. And he took also my mare, Star, from me, that my father had given me, and sold her, and said I would make a display of myself if I ride her abroad.

Before Husband wed me, he had lain many years with his housekeeper, and had got her three bastard sons. And he would not turn her out when I came to him, nor cease to use her abed and fondle her before my face and take her in his lap by the fire, saying it was none of my affair. But when he came to bed me, he said I showed him too little of willingness and did not tender him as she did. And she scorned my governance in the house and made great mock of me when we two were alone. And when my father came out for the King's side and was fled away to London, Husband did lock me in a cold chamber for some days together, and after he did beat me two days of seven with a birch, for he said he must drive out the Tory from my blood, and so he advertised me in the papers as a recalcitrant wife and bid others shun me.

Which I knew was to keep himself from taint with the Committee and keep safe his property.

For to him I was nothing, and had not a heart nor a brain. Yet he could not stop my thinking, and my hate for him grew, and I do not repent though I am damned.

I was wed to him twelve years and I bore him four children. I am now nine-and-twenty. In the War, there came to our house a young Patriot soldier, John Ensley, sore wounded, and I nursed him and loved him, and I did lie with him and fall pregnant by him, and Husband said he would accuse me a whore and have Mr. Ensley whipped, and so I struck Husband down with the ax that lay by in the woodyard, and pushed him into the well, and the housekeeper, too.

This I do not deny, nor ask any pardon. Only I plead for the child, that I may live in this durance till it be born.

The appointed physician, Dr. Samuel Clinch, affirmed to the court of Sussex County that Mrs. Kendall was not with child, and could not therefore "plead her belly." Judge Horatio Evander denied her plea for a stay of execution, and she was hanged at the public gibbet upon Salcombe Common on the tenth day of July, 1785. Dissection performed after the body was taken down revealed that her womb contained at the time of her death a fetus, male, near five months grown.

—*Petition of Bathsheba Whitbread Kendall, Salcombe, Province of Maine, for Stay of Execution for the Cruel Murder of Her Husband, Thomas Kendall, Merchant, June 1785.*

Mr. Ashley Farragut of Boston will pay a reward of two pound for the return of his female servant, Mary Ann, bought for seven years from the dock at Salem, 1779. Able-bodied and hearty, a good spinster and puts her hand to most work with a little correction. Exceptionally tall, about five feet ten inches in height, though slender. Unhandsome, of a pale complexion and fair-haired, of little schooling, about thirty years of age. She has been but twice whipped for disobedience and lying, and of this bears some marks. At the time of her departure from her master's care she was with child, and a further seven years is owed upon her bond for the child not supplied, or twice the value of her service-bond.

It is believed she has gone to seek for her lover, of whom she speaks much. Mary Ann Stokely has a fine singing voice for the entertainment of any master, and may teach singing to children. She was believed to have taken away with her at the time of her flight one Euphemia Lester, aged five years, child of Mr. Robert Lester of Portsmouth, who was later found and returned.

If any shelter Mary Ann Stokely, he shall pay the twelve years yet wanting upon her bond and the defaulted child's not born, and shall answer the charge of theft against her master.

—*Advertisement for the Return of Mary Ann Stokely, Runaway Servant, 1782.*

✖ THIRTY-THREE ✖

THE BURNING OF THE GRASS

*H*is sword slapping at his side in the wide braided leather swordbelt that crossed his chest, Daniel set himself a steady, Indianlike lope and cleared the last of the woods just as the sun went down, then broke into a run across the Sheep Meadow, to arrive weary and sweat-soaked at Two Mills.

There were two strange men in the yard. They had bayonets fixed to the ends of their muskets and they were tossing something back and forth between them and laughing, one man spearing it and tossing it up, the other running to spike it as it fell.

As he came nearer, Daniel could just make out the object they tossed. It was Henry Markham's Sunday-best wig, in which he had meant to be buried.

"What are you doing here?" Daniel said. "Who are you?"

They laughed. "Evening Your Lordship," sneered the smaller man, a weasel called Ketchell.

"If you've come for a hump and a cuddle, you're too late," said the other, called Tully. He was gap-toothed, with a greasy mane of dirty-blond hair and a belly that hung over his breeches. He tossed the wig in the air again and let it land with a plop in a fresh pat of horse-droppings.

The scrawny fellow speared it with his bayonet and held

it toward Daniel, oozing muck. "Look there, sir! 'Tis your sweet-smelling mistress!"

"Mrs. Trevor, ma'am," said the weasel, and made a bow to the shit-smeared wig. "Why, I thought you was run away!"

Daniel's big right hand sprang forward and Tully staggered, then toppled, landing with a squelch and a plop in the worst of the horse dung. Blood streamed from his nose and mouth. Ketchell shook off the wig from the point of his bayonet and circled. "Duncan!" he cried into the darkness. "To him, boy!"

Before Daniel's sword could clear the scabbard, the third man struck him from behind, a hard blow on the side of the neck that put him on his face in the dust. He took a kick in the ribs and another in the temple. He grabbed for Ketchell's boot, caught it, felt the man stagger.

In another minute two bayonets were poised at either side of his neck.

"Your sweet bird has flown, Major. But we will net her in a day or two. And then we shall have some sport."

Sheriff Tapp strode out of the workroom door and gathered the reins of his big black, tethered at the mounting block near the well. Daniel could not move; he lay on his belly in the dirt, the bayonets pricking him, but his eyes never left Marcus Tapp. Every wasted movement, every lapse of judgment, every chance relaxation, he recorded.

"If she's gone," he said, thick-tongued and tasting blood in his mouth, "why do you linger here?"

In their shallow sockets, Tapp's pale eyes were flat as window panes. "I was waiting, sir. For you." He smiled. "I suppose you know I could put you in irons. You've just attacked the sworn representatives of the law, after all. Are they not noble fellows?"

The bayonets were still pricking Daniel's neck.

"But I don't want you caged yet. You will lead us to your hag." He clapped his hands sharply. "Let him up, you ill-sorted dogs!"

Daniel got to his feet and looked round him, eyes still

blurred from the blow and ribcage aching. "Where is Mrs. Trevor's child? Where are the miller and his wife?"

"Here, sir!" cried Hannah's uncle from the doorway. "He has searched my house without a warrant or a by-your-leave!" Henry Markham's clear voice shook as he marched angrily out into the dooryard, a heavy ash-plant staff in his hand. "He's insulted my womenfolk!" the old man said, and raised his stick to strike at the air.

"Go in, old man, and be quiet," Tapp told him.

"That I will not! You have spilled out my barrels of meal and salt cod and broke open my casks in the cellar! You have ruined our winter's stores, and where shall I go for redress, sir?" The old fellow turned to Daniel. "Why, this bold-faced knave, he has torn open the ticks of my niece's very bed!"

"And found there the proof we sought." Tapp smiled.

"What proof?" said Daniel. The bayonets were still at his back.

The sheriff slipped his hand inside his jerkin and produced a small chamois-skin pouch lined with fine green silk. Inside was the only sovereign yet unaccounted-for of the ten Aunt Sibylla had lent Mr. Tyrrell. One they had found at the cabin. Eight Jean le Petit had stolen.

Here was the tenth. Daniel fought for his breath in the stifling near-dark.

"A gold piece coined the same year as that found at Stark's cabin." Marcus Tapp nudged his horse a few steps closer so that he forced Daniel to look up at him. "Your murdering love had sewn it into her featherbed, Major Josselyn. Where you, yourself, no doubt have nestled snug a night or two." He leaned down from the horse. "Tell me, is she yielding? Or does she make you labor for it? I rather fancy an unwilling woman. A sweet pudding needs a touch of bite."

Daniel lunged at him, and at his back he heard the muskets cocked.

"You, sir! Master Sheriff!" came a shrill hoot from the doorway.

Julia Markham had her husband's own ancient musket to hand, soundly braced on her shoulder and primed. Her back straight as a ramrod, she stepped into the dooryard.

"I have had enough of your sneers and traducings! You've done what you came for. Get you gone!"

"My men will remain, old woman. The lady may come back here for refuge and if she does, we shall have her."

Suddenly Tapp dug his heels into the horse's sides and the animal shot forward, straight at Julia. Daniel dived to pull her out of the way, and Henry would have taken his ash-plant to the sheriff if she had not restrained him.

Marcus Tapp reined in his mount and turned to Daniel. He bowed mockingly and smiled. "We shall no doubt meet again, Major. On the day I take Mrs. Trevor."

In spite of the muskets aimed at him, Daniel's deep-set eyes blazed in the gathering darkness and his voice was even and calm.

"You'd best bring a sharp weapon that day, sir," he told Tapp. "And cleverer dogs than these."

Julia's well-kept workroom was a shambles. Tables and chairs were overturned, crocks of cherry preserve smashed and cordial bottles spilled out on the floor. They had taken their bayonets to Hannah's handsome new quilt in its working frame; it hung in great strips of pieced red and green and gold and white, the wool batt dangling like spilt guts from between the layers of fabric.

Henry fussed over Julia and Julia fussed over Henry; Kitty sat sobbing in a corner, with Susan bending over her.

"Come now, love," said the older girl. "It's never so bad."

But the sobs only came harder, broken and comfortless.

Daniel hunched down on his heels beside them. "Have they done her harm?"

Susan looked up at him, furious. "That randy little weasel had one hand in her bodice and the other up her skirts, and if I hadn't near bit off his ear, he'd have done what he planned on!"

"He's still there! He's out there!" Kitty sobbed.

She was very young, not yet sixteen. By night, she still lay, no doubt, in her clean sheets dreaming of boys near as innocent as she. Likely no man had ever yet laid a loving hand on her. And now she would take even the gentlest touch for the gropings and pawings of lust.

Was this what Charlotte had seen in *him* on their wedding night? Daniel wondered.

What secrets lay in the delicate bones of women. What fierce pride kept them silent. What rage.

"I h-hate him," said the girl, and looked up at him. "I hate men! I shall never marry, never!"

Daniel put out a hand to touch her and she drew back. "No," he said. "No. Hold still now, Kitty. Please. Please. They are *not* men, my dear."

She hung back, braced against the chimney corner, her eyes staring. He brushed his fingertips across her brow, touching her lightly, no more than the draft that came in through the wide-open door. He pushed back the damp hair from her forehead and let his palm lie soft against her cheek.

"Oh, sir," she said, and threw her arms round his neck, sobbing. Beside them the other girl, Susan, drew close and put her own arms around her friend, so that they made a shelter, the three of them, two roses and a lattice, like Hannah's ruined quilt.

Across the kitchen, the old couple sat in one another's arms; outside Tapp's men were laughing in the dark. Daniel stood up and walked out again into the yard.

"You, Ketchell!" he roared. "You're handy enough with young girls and old women, and striking men down from behind!"

He was no farmer now, but the soldier who had fought on as many killing fields as Marcus Tapp. And though the Dutchman far away at his own hearth might almost have heard his shouting, Daniel was as still in himself as when he whispered to Hannah in the dark.

"Show yourselves, or I will rake for you!"

One by one they appeared, their pipes glowing in the dark. Lightning cut jagged lines across the low clouds and disappeared behind the forest. Daniel drew his sword from the scabbard and held it straight out, aimed at the three distant shadows of the men. It moved slowly from one to the other, then back again. The lightning shone off the blade, sparking fire. His voice was calm and clear, cold as the sword's edge.

"Touch any in that house again," Josselyn said, "do any more damage here, make sport of any, put any at risk—as God's my judge, I'll find you and feed the fish with your guts. I don't boast, I'm not known for it. What I promise, I will do."

No one answered. At the far end of the yard, the three red coals that were the men's lighted pipes retreated slowly, hidden in shadow once more.

Daniel turned to go inside again and found Julia waiting. He took her hand for a moment, then let it go. "Where is Jennet?"

"Gone. Bertha Pinch saw her run off through the orchard when Tapp's men came. And the cat is gone, that the child dotes on."

"And Mrs. Trevor?" He still kept the deferential distance between them.

"She is belied!" Julia said. "But you know that. She took some clothing and that journal she keeps. I pray the child made her way to her, but where they have gone, I know no more than you."

"I've done her great harm," he said, and his eyes looked aside from her.

Julia laid a hand on his battered face. "Has she bound your honor to do nothing and let her go off alone?"

"Aye. That she has."

Her eyes narrowed. "And will you go after her in spite of it?"

"Can you not see, ma'am?" he said. "I am already gone."

*   *   *

Daniel hurried away down the hill path, crossed the river on the rafted logs and made for his own house; there were many things to attend to before he left, for he had not the slightest idea whether he would ever return.

As he rounded into the stableyard, he heard a shout go up in the distance. Two of his field hands ran past and he snatched at the sleeve of the second.

"Fire, sir!" cried the man, barely aware whom he spoke to. "They've set light to the stacks!"

It began with a crackling and then, almost in an instant, the fire gave a great roar as the draft caught it and the whole of the largest stack was ablaze. Across the river, Daniel could see men moving, dark shapes on horseback. But he had no time to waste watching them; he ran for the house, boots pounding the gravel path, and before he could reach the side door the new haystack at Two Mills was blazing, too. Downriver, they had set three others alight on the South Bank, and on the North he could see flames coming from Siwall's great barn.

The landing horn at Lamb's Inn, which served for a fire warning, was blowing wildly now that the wind had come up. Men streamed out of the meetinghouse, running for home to protect what they could. The church bell began to ring.

The fires were a signal, surely, like the tea they had dumped into Boston harbor thirteen years ago. After them would come the grand rhetoric, the fine words.

Resist! We will not be the slaves of the proud. Liberty or die!

And soon the old question would come again.

Which side, which side? Whose be you? Friend or enemy? Whig or Tory? Which side are you on?

But this time there was no king to blame it on and use as a rallying cry. No king's men and patriots, no noble causes. This time, it was rich against poor. Taker against taken.

Still wearing his hunting sword, Daniel raced into the house and up the stairs to Charlotte's room. He found

Sibylla with her, and when the old lady caught sight of him she dropped her hand of whist and stood up, gripping her stick like a weapon.

"How now, sir?" she said, her eyes as bright, almost, as the burning haystacks. "Armed and wild-eyed? What's afoot?"

He was winded, his hair stuck to his forehead with sweat, his chin stubbled with the long day's growth of reddish beard. There was blood on his face from the beating and whenever he drew a breath he felt a sharp stab of pain from the kick in his ribs they had dealt him.

But he forced himself to regain his control. For Charlotte's sake, he dare not be too rash or abrupt, lest her strained heart could not endure it.

"Forgive me," he said. "But the new hay has caught alight, and until my men can extinguish it, I fear you must allow me to take you downstairs, into the back parlor."

When he had seen them safely installed there with Dragon Twig to guard them and Tyrrell to carry Charlotte to safety if need be, Daniel tore out again into the yard.

The storm was drawing closer, but there was no rain yet to help put the fire out. Men, women, stablehands, bootboys, kitchen maids—they had formed up a bucket brigade in a long snaking line from the well in the stableyard to the hopelessly blazing haystacks, and were handing the water along the line in every container they could find. Leather pails, tin kettles, stewpots—everything that would serve to carry a drop in to put out the flames.

A second line was passing more buckets to the house, and two men on the roof drenched the wooden shingles with it, stamping on the wisps of burning hay as they fell. Daniel cursed himself that he had not sent to Philadelphia for slates instead, and ran down the yard to the heart of the fires.

"No good, sir!" shouted John English. "We've lost the great stack already, and the two smaller ones are near gone, too. We're three hands short, I sent them out to

look for you when— Daniel, the sheriff's been at Two
Mills—''

"I've just been there. I know.''

"Soak them old rick-covers and bring 'em up here!''
shouted English to a passing hand. "Not at the well, you
fool! Take them down to the river! Run! We might save
this stack yet!''

Some of the trees in the grove had caught, now, like
the spread fingers of burning hands held up to the sky,
and the stubble in the meadow had burnt halfway down
to the riverside. Daniel slapped at a bit of burning straw
that had landed on his sleeve and set it smouldering.

The wind was high and the lightning was very near.
Horses screamed, men shouted, and everywhere was the
sound of the fire itself, roaring, snapping, searing the mind
till it lay dry and wasted in its hollow of skull.

The hay they had cut together the day before and cele-
brated at the dancing lay charred and wasted. The bond
that had joined them was burnt away—or so it seemed for
a moment.

"Look there!'' cried somebody. "God save us, the
mill's a-light!''

The last of the stacks had burned down now, and the
fiery shower of straw ended almost as soon as the sodden
canvases were spread on the last stack to catch. No more
of the trees in the copse had caught.

"I think we've had the worst now, sir,'' said English.
"By your leave, I'll take some men and—''

"By all means, John! Go and help Henry! I'll come
directly, once I've seen to my wife.''

The steward struck off across the meadow and most of
the other men with him. Others were arriving in haywains
and oxcarts from nearby farms; if the mill burned, no corn
or wheat would be ground for the winter's provisions, no
logs would be cut and sold, no profit would be made from
the summer's labor, and taxes would be even harder to
pay. War or no war, they could not do without a mill.

Daniel had just set off for the house to tell the women

their own danger was past and to take Charlotte back upstairs, when a cart came rattling at a wild gallop into the yard. In the back of it, her bed gown flapping and her hair streaming on the wind, sat Madam Honoria Siwall, the driver her black-sheep son, Jem.

He jumped down and ran to meet Daniel. "They've burst down our doors, sir," he said, "and tried to take Pa from his chaise as he crossed on the ferry! Regulators! God knows I think they meant to hang him for the death of George Anson in our very yard, but Tapp got wind of it somehow and was waiting for them. He's taken two of them, one of the Penny brothers and some other."

Squeer's work, thought Daniel. Had Uncle Piet not said he was Siwall's spy, and Tapp's? Ride with the Regulators and name them to Tapp, and line his pocket with Siwall's good silver all the while. But what part had Trevor had in it? Squeer was his confederate, his drinking crony, his friend.

"Is your father badly hurt?" he asked Jem. "And where is Tapp?"

"Gone after the rest of them. He says they've a hiding place near the Hook nobody knew of."

Daniel's mind was racing. He was almost certain Hannah would not have risked taking Jennet into the Outward. She would stick to the roads, or take a wherry downriver to the coast once she had cleared the clutter of islands and villages that crowded around Gull's Hook.

But in this mad riot, caught between Tapp and the Regulators—what chance had a woman and child?

And somewhere was the lone woman who had gathered the bits of their lives to her own, whom they might trust and let near them for comfort, not knowing she might any moment strike them down.

"I must go back and help Pa with the fires," said young Siwall. "The barn's lost and the east wing of the house is still afire. *He* would not ask you, but— Will you shelter my mother here, Major? Those fellows— They pulled her out to the yard and tore the clothes from her back till they had her near stripped. As though she was a—was a—''

"Tory woman?" said Daniel quietly. "Or only a poor man's wife?"

The young man shuddered. For a moment he stood silent. If his father had grabbed up the property of the strugglers and grown fat upon it, Jeremy Siwall had gamed with it, drunk it away, seduced any number of maids with the presents it bought them.

"I'm an ass, sir," he whispered. "You don't like me, and you've good reason. But there's something I must tell you. About Trevor. Stark, that is. I knew him no other way."

"Say it quickly. There's no time."

"A month ago, just after Pa left for Boston, Stark was in Edes's one night, very late. We'd been dicing—that room at the back, you know, where the law can wink a bit. Stark lost to me that night. Heavy, sir. I knew he couldn't pay. Didn't really expect it. I said he might wait to cover his losses till we played next, but he'd have none of it. He called for paper and ink and wrote me out a note, Major. Surety, he called it."

"He had money? Property somewhere?"

"No, sir," said Jem, very quietly. "He offered to give me his wife."

Daniel scarcely breathed. "Grace Stark?"

"Yes. He said nothing of Mrs. Trevor. I did not know his real identity until—"

"You say, 'give.' Did he mean merely—"

"Not just a tumble, no sir. He meant sell. In exchange for his losses." Jem hung his head. "I have taken some thoughtless pleasure in women. But most were as thoughtless as I. Even Moll, though she's warm and fond . . . But damn me, Major Josselyn. Men have not sold their wives openly in this country these fifty years."

"Not openly." Daniel's mind ticked like a clock.

I don't kill women, Jean le Petit had said. *If they're not pretty enough to keep, I sell them off quick in Canada. The brats, too.*

Ten pounds for a homely one, Piet had told him. *Twenty, thirty for a young one, if she's good-looking. I'd sell them one of my wives.*

"Stark laughed about it. Perhaps it was only the rum toddy, but— He hinted," said young Siwall, "that he'd done it before. Surely he could not have meant—"

Hannah. Hannah. What else have you hidden away?

"Go help your mother down from the wagon, Jem," said Josselyn, "and take her up to the house. She is welcome to stay." He grasped young Siwall's arm. "Listen to me, boy. Don't try to stand off these Regulators. If they come again, send to Mr. English for help and tell him I've offered it."

"Will you not stay? You're a soldier. I'm no use with a gun or a sword."

Daniel shook his head. "I captain the militia, Jem. If I act against these men as a soldier, then we're at war."

Which side? Which side are you on? To say the truth, Daniel could not yet be sure.

Jem bowed stiffly and drew out Hannah's note from inside his shirt. He ran off to see to his mother, and Josselyn broke open the seal at the torn edge of the soft, cheap paper. By the light of the smouldering fires, he could just read Hannah's spidery writing.

God protect you. I am gone.

It began to rain in earnest, now, great heavy sheets of rain slanting from the northeast. The lightning came down like a jagged sword plunged into the river. Sheltering the precious note to keep it dry, Daniel hunched down by the side of the cut field—beaten and drenched, staring at the ruined haystacks, their embers steaming in the downpour—and gave himself up to the rain.

"She is gone with the puppet-master in his caravan, Shadow," said the voice of Bertha Pinch almost in his ear; he put up his arm to shield her from the beating rain.

"But you must go quick, now. For there is one that will snatch and snatch and snatch her away!"

"Speak plain, God damn you!" he cried, and took her by her crooked shoulders. "Who did you let up to Hannah's chamber to take away her things? What are you? Whose crimes do you hide?"

"Ah, how should I say, for good men look to me like devils, and sinners like creatures that God has forgot and forsook! Oh, you may shake me till you shake loose my bones from my body. But it will do you no good. He wronged her and used her and he is dead and well served. She must go free now. She will do no more harm."

"You cannot know that! Whoever she may be, she is mad!"

"Oh, ho, and are you not mad yourself? Your eyes are wild and your hands grip like iron and if you had a club to bash in my head, you would not stint! Look! Let my eyes be your mirror! In a minute you will do murder on me."

Daniel closed his eyes against her and stood still, the rain washing over him. Bertha Pinch was weeping now.

"What is she to you?" he asked her more gently. "Cousin? Sister? Lover? What is her name?"

"She gave me comfort when I had none!" cried the little seamstress. "I would not have had her go with him, not for the world, for I do not trust such jigmakers! I would he were dead and in hell!"

He held her close against him, rocking her slightly, side to side.

"Will you not tell me where she's bound? If I promise I will do her only good, and see her to safety? If I swear so upon my honor?"

"Have I not honor the same as you? Has *she* none? No, sir, I have spoke too much already. You may pull out your sword and spit me upon it like a rabbit, but I shall tell you not one word more!"

✖ THIRTY-FOUR ✖

STICKS AND STONES

"Tut, ma'am, such a night we have had!" said Mrs. Twig as Lady Sibylla was carried back up the stairs to her room. "I shall fetch you some hot milk and a bowl of gruel to give you strength till the morning! For a body of your age, such a night may be your undoing unless we take care!"

This discourse was accompanied by a frenzy of flappings and twitchings and a thundercloud of chalk from the Cliffs as Hobble reached the landing at the head of the great stair.

"Owen! Jenks!" shrilled the old lady. "Set down here, my boys, and then be off to your beds. I shall need you no more tonight. Unless," she muttered under her breath, "it be to pour a bowl of gruel on the head of a dunce."

Andrew Tyrrell returned from carrying Charlotte to her own room.

"The rain has quenched all but the worst of the fires, ma'am," he said. "The mill, I believe, will be saved, though a pile of the sawn boards is gone."

"And my nephew? Is he burnt to a crackling?"

"Why, 'tis sure Major Josselyn has gone by now!" cried Twig. "Have you not heard that Hannah Trevor is fled, and her bastard with her? I cannot think but the major will go after her and fetch back the child to raise it, for though it be dumb, 'tis a sweet child, and if the mother

277

be a wanton and a Tory and a murderess, still it is no blame upon the child.''

"Will you hush, you great booby?" hissed Sibylla under her breath. "Stand a foot from your mistress's door, and prattle so!"

"I beg your pardon, my lady," said Twig. "I speak but from duty. Twig, when he lived, desired plain-speaking above all things. But in truth, I do not think so ill of Mrs. Trevor as I did. Indeed, I wish I had not been so hasty as to—"

Sibylla's sharp nose lifted. "As to what? Have you been meddling?"

Twig's lips pursed and her eyes brimmed with tears. "I believed it my duty! For the sake of the poor child—"

"What have you done, you fool?"

The housekeeper sniffed. "Why, only write to my friend Mrs. Whinnet, whose husband is Clerk of the Orphanmasters' Court, that there was a case hereabouts might bear looking into! There is no harm in my writing a word to a friend, ma'am, I hope?"

The old woman raised her stick and her eyes blazed. "Wretch! This is what your prating and gossiping comes to! If I were mistress of this house, you should not sleep another night in it!"

Twig stifled a sob and flounced away down the hall to the chamber in which Madam Siwall had been installed, no doubt to lay the groundwork for a new position, just in case. Sibylla lowered her stick and leaned on it heavily.

"Shall I seek for your nephew, madam?" Tyrrell asked her.

"No, my friend. Be away to your bed now, you are far spent."

Indeed, he did look ill, worse and worse these past two days. He seemed to have taken all this business very much to heart. She dismissed him with a nod and the secretary went off to his own small chamber at the opposite end of the hall. In another moment, Sibylla saw the light of his candle appear, almost die, then grow steady and bright.

He would read till near morning; it was Tyrrell's way—
as it would have been Daniel's, had he the leisure for it.

The old woman sighed. It seemed nobody was likely to
sleep much this night. The door to Charlotte's room stood
open, and the little maid, Abby, had lighted enough candles inside to make it welcome and bright even though it
was now past midnight.

Charlotte sat at her dressing table while Abby unfastened the elaborate arrangement of curls and tiny braids to
let the fair hair fall loose around the narrow white shoulders. The pale blue silk gown had been unlaced and removed, but the maid had had no time as yet to fetch the
cream-colored dressing gown of fine lawn that lay folded
at the end of the bed.

Sibylla stood for a moment in the doorway, her small,
bright eyes absorbing the sight as she might have looked
at plants in a border. It was the same way Hannah regis-
tered the patterns and colors and shapes of her quilts—
blocks of color set together and the neutral ground they
played upon, broke apart, then drew back together to make
a pattern in itself.

The light blue of the discarded silk gown. The cream
of the bedgown. The faint pink of Charlotte's stay-cover
and petticoat and shift. The white of her skin and the pale
gold of her hair.

Illusion. An unreal image of womanhood imposed by
custom, fashion, convenience. Why, even poor Twig indulged in it, this froth of perpetual virginity thrown like
an insufficient veil over the hard fact of the used and aging
flesh and the ever-narrowing mind. A long, lonely dream
of innocence, it was, that pale figure that sat so demure
at the dressing table.

Beyond her, the darker shades of the crewelwork were
everywhere in the room—deep rose, crimson, willow, soft
blue, burnt gold, topaz, bronze, spruce green. Sibylla had
always scorned women who spent much time on embroidery; in her girlhood, they had tried to force it upon her as

a more respectable pursuit than observing the reproductive habits of tulips visited by energetic bumblebees.

But these embroideries of Charlotte's were more than a sedative. In the flickering candlelight, the birds and animals and fantastic tendrils seemed almost to live and move. Daniel's wife was a puzzle, indeed—a tame kitten that sat trembling with fear at her kind master's window, and dreamed of running wild in the woods.

"I will do that, if you please," said Sibylla.

She stumped into the room, took Charlotte's hairbrush from Abby, and resumed the rhythmic strokes, scarcely missing a beat. A hundred before sleep, another hundred upon waking, that was the rule. But illness had made the locks brittle. They broke and came out in the brush after even a dozen strokes.

The little maid dropped a discreet curtsy and scuttled out, closing the door behind her. The rain had turned to a mist that whispered softly against the window panes. The porcelain clock on the mantel ticked solemnly. Down in the yard, a hound bayed and another answered him.

"Lottie, my dear?"

"Yes, Aunt?"

"What are you now to my nephew? Wife? Companion? Friend?"

Charlotte turned to look at Sibylla, her blue eyes pale grey in the candlelight. "Why surely, madam, I have earned the right to be called his wife."

"That depends. Do you love him?"

"He— He is very dear to me."

"I had a spaniel was dear to me, and a finch in a cage."

"You mistake my words on purpose! I love him, of course."

"To be loved 'of course' is no better than kennels and cages. But let us say that you do. How much of him do you love? For which of his parts?"

"Why, for his excellent mind. His brave spirit. His good heart."

"You say nothing of his man's body."

"You are unkind, madam. You must be aware that for the last four years I have been unable to pay him a wife's duty."

"Oh, do not ruffle yourself like a grouse, my dear, and grow missish. I do not mean merely that somewhat grotesque appendage referred to as his manhood. No. I mean that frail shell we all live in. All flesh may be as grass, but you cannot have Daniel a pleasant, reliable wraith with no case to hold him, like a genie in a silver jug. Had you chosen more carefully, you know, you might have done. Some men you may love quite well enough on principle, as you would approve a fine sermon, and let the rest go. You may bestride the bodies of others and care not a pippin for their souls—it is all they deserve of you, and more. But Daniel is all of a piece. Mind, heart, spirit, scars, sins, dreams, terrors—oh, I know he can be bitter hard at times. Who cannot, who has had to take men's lives in an instant or lose his own? So, my dear, you may love some things and wink at the others and be his good friend, surely. But bedding or not, you will never be his wife if you take him less than whole. Violence and all, and make it as much your own as his."

"And must I make Mrs. Trevor my own as well?" Charlotte sat studying her own face in her mirror. "Don't pretend you do not know of her. Twig will surely have seen to it by now."

"Twig! What has she *not* seen to?" muttered Sibylla under her breath. "You must comprehend the part of him that loves Mrs. Trevor," she said aloud. "That is father to her child."

"I cannot approve his adultery! Why should I?"

"To comprehend is not to approve. It is to accept and to forgive. Tell me, have you ever asked to look at his wounded hand and know how he came by it?"

"I—cannot."

"No. You cannot. I have watched you. You would keep him by you for comfort and he would stay for kindness, for loyalty—for the parts of him you would deign to approve of and open your eyes to. But in time, you will tear him in two.''

Charlotte turned away from her mirror and faced the old lady. ''I am not the only one who tears at him. Go and say as much to Mrs. Trevor!''

''She is gone. Run away.''

''Because she knows he will follow her!'' Charlotte grasped the edge of the dressing table, her knuckles sharp and white. ''She misleads him and lures him, and yet you make *me* to blame! Besides, how do you dare speak to me of the duties of marriage, you who will die a maid at eighty-odd?''

''Though I was never a wife, I am no maid, I assure you. At forty-two,'' said Sibylla, ''I bore a child. To my coachman, Frederick Watt. I had delayed the claims of passion too long, thinking I would be safe from its dangers at such a ripe age. I was afraid of it, you see. Of childbirth. But I conceived, absurdly enough, very quickly. A girl-child, born dead.''

The younger woman sat silent for some moments. On the tables and the mantelpiece the candles dripped wax into their saucers and wisps of burnt tow flew up from their wicks like black birds.

''Did you love him?'' asked Charlotte at last. ''This fellow, the coachman? Mr. Watt?''

''Oh, too much for reason. It was no sensible dalliance, to be disposed of with a shrug and a few coins. But not enough for equal passion. I was no match for him, in that. Only I could not send him away. I was still afraid, you see.''

''You? Never!''

''Of dying alone?'' said Sibylla. ''How should I not be? Nothing lives that does not fear that. I was better matched, of course, with Mr. Franklin. I wanted a child by *him*, but I was past conceiving then.''

''What became of Frederick Watt?'' Charlotte asked her.

''He began to drink and to frequent the card-tables. He

fell into debt and demanded large sums of me. For a time, I paid his debts. He had a wife, a decent woman. Stronger than I was. She forgave him everything. She might have kept him whole, but I ruined him. He drifted away somewhere. Escaped us both.''

"It is the way of people when they are smothered," whispered Charlotte Josselyn. "They go looking for free air to breathe.''

When he left Bertha Pinch, Daniel took time only to go to his own chamber, change his drenched clothes for a dry shirt and breeches and a sound oilskin greatcoat, and write a careful list of instructions for John English. Tyrrell's room was dark and quiet and Charlotte's candles were snuffed for the night, though he could still hear Twig's heavy footsteps as she ministered to Madam Siwall.

When he had finished the note to his steward, Daniel folded it and wrote another—briefer, but far more difficult.

My dear Lottie. I must leave you, but I beg you to believe you have not been abandoned. Mrs. Trevor and the child are at great risk, and I must do what I may for them. You have a generous mind and a kind heart, and I hope for your forgiveness, though I do not deserve it. If I do not return, write to my lawyer, Mr. Hedrick, in Boston. You are well provided for there. I leave you in the kind care of my aunt and Mr. Tyrrell, whom I think you may trust. Your husband, D.

"Will you come back, my dear?" said Charlotte's voice behind him. "Or not?"

Somehow, God knew how, she had made her own way along the hall from her room to his and stood gripping the cut-glass doorknob for support. Her face was very pale, except for two sharp blots of scarlet on her cheeks. Where her nightdress fell open at her throat he could see the great vein throb under the thin, fair skin.

"If you find Mrs. Trevor and the child, will you not take them and go away? I know you have been thinking upon it these months past," she said. "Oh, I have not come to dig my claws into you. I am not angry. Between us, we break you in pieces. Your aunt has made me see that, I think. And yet— You are dear to me. I cannot help but ask what you will do.''

''My aunt should not have spoken so.''

''She was quite right. I have been long enough in a dream.''

She seemed to reel and almost fall, and he took a step toward her.

''No! No more of your pity!'' she cried. ''I am quite poisoned with it, and so are you! I need—''

''Charlotte, for the love of God—''

She sank to her knees, sliding slowly, helplessly, along the heavy oak door. Daniel swooped down and picked her up and laid her gently on his own bed. He could not remember that she had ever lain there before, even when the house was first built and she was not yet ill. Whenever he spent a night with her, it had been in her own room, with her own things around her, as though he had invaded a country to conquer it.

The knock on the door. ''May I come in now, my dearest?'' The retreat to her dressing room, while he performed the discreet ritual—the snuffing of candles; the small, intimate preparations of cushions, bed-clothes, ointments, oils; the removal and careful folding of his own clothes. Then the pale, slim shape that dodged from door to folding screen and slipped between the embroidered bed curtains where he lay waiting as if for a stranger. The enveloping nightdress, impossible to remove altogether. It, too, he could only invade. The small cross set with pearls Charlotte had always made him unfasten—one could not, of course, engage in carnal converse with any religious object nearby. And the rosemary scent of her powder, shipped in fine enamelled boxes from London. A gift from her mother, to keep her forever a girl.

He caught a faint hint of the same scent now, as he sat on his own bed beside her. But in other ways his wife seemed oddly changed tonight, as though the fires had consumed some inhibiting mask she had worn all her life.

"Let me see," she said suddenly, and took his maimed hand in her own. She had always shuddered at the sight of the missing fingers, but now she drew off the leather glove and laid it aside. They had been severed just below the first joint and two blunt stumps were all that remained of them, with a faint webbing of scar tissue between.

Her eyes closed, Charlotte let her fingertips explore the damage.

"When you first met Mrs. Trevor," she said, "these scars were raw, were they not?"

"It was but a month or six weeks after Webb's Ford when I came here," he said. "I was raw then in more ways than one."

"And you howled in your sleep, as you do lately. And she held you and calmed you. I have heard you cry, but I have never come to you. I have never held you. I was afraid, and I left you alone."

"You are unwell, my dear."

"What do you see in your dreams, Daniel?" she asked him. Her voice was urgent, as though she knew he had meant to be long gone by now. "What makes you cry out so?"

"I have told you. The memories of war. The fighting—"

Her eyes opened, fixed calmly upon him. "Have you not seen me? Have you not seen me in my grave, and waked and wished me there?"

In fact, it was his own death that Daniel Josselyn so often dreamed. By drowning, by sword, by shot, by hanging. Every night different and every night the same.

"I have never wished you dead," he said truthfully.

"Then you are more a kindhearted fool than even I imagined," said Charlotte. "For I have wished it often enough myself, God knows." He was about to protest, but she smiled and put a finger on his lips. "As for the charge against your Mrs. Trevor, if she were to set about murdering anyone, it should surely have been myself, should it not? She has had ample opportunity with those everlasting potions and elixirs she sends me. And yet here I am. Alive.''

She looked down again at his maimed left hand. ''Did it fright her, when she saw it first? Did she weep for the pity of it?''

''She has seen far worse in her nursing,'' he told her. ''And tears do not come to her easily.''

''Ah, but a woman may weep with more than her eyes, my dear, and a man may not see it. She may bring forth tears and call them her children.''

Charlotte closed her eyes again and lay very still, and for a moment he thought she was sleeping. He folded the note he had written and laid it on the pillow beside her, but as he stood in the doorway she spoke to him again.

''Will you come back once she is safe?''

For a long moment, he could not bring himself to answer. To tell the truth, he still did not know.

James Trevor had found it easy enough to leave one woman he did not love and take another—or so it appeared. But Daniel Josselyn was not besotted with a romantic image of himself that overcame every objection of honor. If he clung to any definition, it was the one his grandfather, old Lord Robert, had taught him one bitter November afternoon of his boyhood, as they walked along a crumbling stone wall that bounded the far field of the estate.

The old gentleman pushed with his ancient walking stick at a stone in the wall and sent it tumbling down the hill on the other side, taking a small avalanche of rocks and gravel with it.

''See there?'' he had said, and handed his stick to the boy. ''Now you try. Go on, have at it!''

Daniel grinned and gave a mighty shove. Two more stones broke loose from the wall and went rolling down the steep earth of the hill.

''Right, then. What do you see? Name me the players.''

It was a game they had between them.

"Stick," said the boy. "Stone. Earth."

"And what else? Come now. Think!"

The boy spun round in a tight little circle of frustration.

"I know!" he cried at last. "Boy!"

"That's right! That's right! And of them all, which would you prefer to be?"

"The weak stone falls when it is pushed," Daniel had said, frowning. "I would not be weak, and fall from such a little push, and be nothing."

"Good! Excellent! And what of the stick! Would you be the stick?"

"The stick is strong," the boy replied thoughtfully. "I would like to be strong. But a stick may do nothing of itself. It must obey the hand that whacks with it."

"Even the hand of a fool." Lord Robert smiled. "And what of the earth? Would you be the earth, to have stones fall upon your back pushed by brainless sticks in the hands of idiots?"

"No, but see there, Grandfather," replied young Daniel. "The earth is still whole and the stone has rolled away into the brook, and carried down part of the loose stones and rubble with it. The earth can bear many such stones, and be strong and clean! I would be the earth, I think!"

"Ah, but you *are* the boy," said his grandfather. "Your hand pushed the brainless stick and struck the weak stone and battered the earth with it. You are the boy, and that boy did harm."

"But you *told* me to do it! I only obeyed you!"

"Ah, then you are a stick! You are brainless, if you do whatever you are told without thinking for yourself."

"No! I will be no stick!"

The old man had placed a hand, then, on Daniel's head. "A stick has no heart and no reason, and cares nothing for the harm it does to others or to itself. And therefore it has no honor—for that is what honor is, you know. Taking thought for the harm you do *before* you do it. Oh, the earth has a great heart beating, but you must not try to be the earth, either, and bear too much on your shoulders. Be but a thinking boy, my dear Daniel, and choose carefully before you strike on any poor, crumbling stone.''

"If I live, I will come back and be your friend," he said, looking down at the damaged body of his wife upon the bed.

I would not be a stick without a heart.

✖ THIRTY-FIVE ✖

PIECING THE EVIDENCE:
On the Nature of Rage

*I*n the thin, ungraceful body of the woman who killed because she was nothing, there lived a third woman, unstained and perfect. When she slept, she did not dream and God never raked His eyes across her when she woke.

Even before her birth, when she still swam in her mother's body, breathing through gills like a fish, this woman was beautiful. She was blessed also with perpetual innocence; men like Matthew Gwynn and Marcus Tapp and James Trevor, their minds muddled with false superiority and the guilt that is its bedfellow, could use her as they liked, reinvent her, claim to own and command her, even love her when they found she had left them no choice. But she would still be clean and free, tender and passionless, for her rage kept her pure.

By the night of Hannah's departure, Matthew Gwynn had grown huge in his own eyes; the shadow of his guilt overpowered the earth. All afternoon and evening, ever since the burials of Grace Stark and her children, he had been riding, riding. Up and down narrow lanes, along the dockside, up to the hill where they had buried Hannah's husband. He had ridden to Two Mills hoping to see her. But it was too late. The sheriff's men were already there in the yard. He came home to find Merriam—for so he had named her himself—in the small parsonage kitchen, packing some food and her few small possessions into a leather bag for her journey.

"Where are you going?" he said, and gripped her arm.

She glanced at him, suddenly furious, and her look struck him like the edge of a blade.

"You hate me," he whispered. "After all I have done."

She smiled. "Did you think I would not?"

"I have lied for you," he whispered. "I have condemned Hannah Trevor!"

"What you have done, you have done for yourself," she replied.

And of course it was true.

At first he had not realized or admitted his own intentions. For nearly a month after he bought her, Gwynn did not touch Merriam. She was too young for the appearance of respectability unless he passed her off as his sister, and so he began to do. "Oh, yes," he would say when the women of his congregation inquired. "My sister, Merriam. An excellent housekeeper. A fine singing voice for a hymn."

He had almost begun to believe it. But then, on the night before they were to leave one parish and go to another, when the scant household goods stood packed into crates and cases, he woke to find her beside him in the bed. She drew very close and began to touch him, gently and with great tenderness.

His breath quickened. "I have not asked this," he said.

"I give it freely." She stroked his chest and his belly, which was already paunchy with middle age.

"It is a sin," he cried, feeling himself clutch at her, his body's need already beyond his control. Soon his mind would follow it. His soul. "A great sin!"

She laughed in the darkness. "And have you never sinned before?"

He had, of course, many times, and thought little enough of it after. The difference was that, though his pride would not let him admit it, he had already begun to love her, to come home eager for her quiet movements around the hearth and her soft singing at the wheel, to find pleasure in the sight of her hair when she unpinned it by candlelight and to rest in her company. Around her, he need not think, need not pass judgment even upon himself. His spirit had wed her, but his pride still revolted at the notion.

Besides, she said she had somewhere a husband already. It was out of the question. Ludicrous for a man of his station. Utterly absurd.

"If you find yourself with child," he said on the night she first took him, "I cannot keep you. I shall have to turn you out or be ruined myself."

"There will be no child come from me," she told him.

She had proved to be right. No spark caught in her. No new life grew from his selfish seed.

Still he could not retreat from his pride. He paid her scrupulously, and if she saved enough money, in time she might buy what remained upon her bond. And Gwynn himself, should he find a woman he fancied, might make a respectable marriage of his own once the seven years of the bond was up. That was their bargain, and he had made it clear.

But then he had met Hannah Trevor, and seven years was a very long time indeed after that. He himself would be nearing sixty by then, and who knew but Mrs. Trevor might be past the age of childbearing? He saw life slipping away from him, but he did not yet realize that Merriam caught it and held it captive in the empty cup that was her soul.

On the night before the murders, he had sat with her beside the cold hearth in the kitchen.

"Tomorrow I mean to ask Mrs. Trevor to wed me," he said. "I will find you a decent master and a good place, and I will say you are a free woman and remit you the rest of your bond. Only you must go. I cannot bear this any longer. I can never be honorably married and have you near at hand."

"It does not matter," she said. "You will love me as much, once you are wed."

"I'm a clergyman, it is my livelihood! I should lose everything if it were known what you are— What you have been to me."

"And if I should tell them?"

"You must not! You will not!"

"No," she said softly "But I will not go. I will stay here. With you."

She began to make love to him, but he pushed her away and locked the door of his bedchamber against her. Outside the door he heard her moaning, a low, animal sound like the dying make in their last sleep, when the bones cry out of themselves.

All night he lay awake, listening, and all night he heard it. Near morning, he tried to open the door. Her body lay pressed against it, her eyes wide open. He lifted her up and took her to him and wept himself to sleep in her arms.

Next day came the murders. Mrs. Stark. Her three children. Trevor. The razor. The kerchief with Hannah's name. The gold piece in its pouch.

He knew what Merriam had done, but he could not stop her without destroying himself. He began to mourn, but not for Grace Stark and her children. "Why hast Thou abandoned me?" he cried, lying on his face before the altar of his church.

But after that first night, Matthew Gwynn could think no more of his principles. It was easy enough to give up all hope of Hannah, for what hope had he of anything now? Besides he had never really meant to betray her. Thinking only that he must be rid of the last bit of evidence to connect Merriam and himself with the crimes, he took the gold piece in its soft leather bag and gave it to the sheriff on the morning of George Anson's death.

"Where did you get this?" Hamilton Siwall had asked him. The magistrate prayed to excess, but he distrusted preachers by instinct; they cost him far more than they were worth. "Why do you bring it here now?"

"I found it near Two Mills," Gwynn had said. "When I visited Mrs. Trevor on the morning of— Of the crimes." Surely they would believe her story, now, that she had been working at home and was innocent. "The bag lay in the path by the pond," he went on, "and as I was late, I thought to return it at some other time. I was called to— To visit old Mrs. Beck."

That old lady had died in her sleep and could not dispute it. The minister continued. "If the murderer passed that way along the road, perhaps someone took note of it."

But then Marcus Tapp began to weave his web. Was Gwynn alone in the house with Hannah that morning? Had she not offered to lie with him while the rest were a-haying? Tried to purchase his silence with a promise of further joys once James Trevor was dead?

The minister sat silent, scarcely listening. He was an irrelevance. Whether he spoke the truth or perjured himself for their convenience mattered as little now as whether a leaf fell to the right or the left of a tree.

Whenever they seemed to desire him to answer yes, he did so. If he guessed incorrectly and they were displeased, they reshaped the question to suit his reply. They were a mechanism that manufactured guilt from the raw material of random circumstance, of sheer hazard; anyone could have been snared in their nets, and by the time they had finished even Gwynn half-believed in Hannah's guilt.

Tapp took the gold piece in its pouch and tucked it away in his jerkin. Siwall glanced at him and frowned. "I trust there will be no need to involve Mr. Gwynn in this matter any further, my dear Marcus?"

The sheriff smiled. "Indeed," he said, "it might reflect upon you, might it not, Mr. Siwall? As his patron?"

Gwynn waited, silent. So. They would save him, but not for his own sake. They spoke of him as though he were not in the room. He sat blind, useless, his hands twisting the corner of his coat.

"God help me," he had whispered as the men went on talking. But he might have been praying to dirt.

There was an ugly taste on his tongue, as though he had eaten tainted meat. He knew it at once and could feel it there, growing.

The gift Merriam left with him. The dark flavor of rage.

"Where will you go?" he said to her when he came home after the funerals.

She had finished packing, now, and was taking a kettle from the fire to make tea. Merriam poured some into a stoneware cup and offered it to him.

For nearly seven years she had lived inside the fragments of herself, like the jagged pieces of Hannah's crazy quilt, remembering now one scrap of her own history, now another, but never enough to be whole. Once she had killed Grace Stark and her family with the ax, they became vivid rags of guilt like the others, and James Trevor the same. Jarred by certain images, certain noises, children's cries, old songs, they made a clear pattern occasionally, something answerable to what was called reason.

Then they slipped away again, into the dark. She plodded on with her woman's work, still innocent of any harm. She went to the haying party and danced like the others. She went to the forest and helped find the bodies, and sat mourning the dead she had killed. She went to sew and sing with Bertha Pinch.

But now, in the small act of handing a cup of tea across a scrubbed-pine table, the pieces of Merriam Gwynn, of Mary Ann Stokely, and of the clean invisible self who was both and was neither, fell into place and were stitched firm. She remembered, with that terrible clarity of madness which is the other side of the coin of pure reason, every moment of her disregarded life.

"Why?" he said, in torment. He saw now with the eyes of the damned, with her eyes. "Tell me why you killed them. The woman and children."

She stared at him, wide-eyed. "Once I had seen him

and knew him, I could not live if they were still on the earth. She made me nothing. He put her in my place.''

''But the children! They were not to blame!''

''They were her children! Not mine! Nothing in the world is mine. You are not mine! God! Why should I want such a thing as *you* are?''

''You're mad,'' he said. ''Do you think I will let you go off and kill others?''

Then she went to the dresser and fetched the knife she used for butchering—a long, wide blade with an edge on both sides like a sword. She laid the hilt in his palm and closed his fingers around it.

''Slit my throat, then. Kill me.''

She unfastened her kerchief. Around her long neck was the necklace of dried raspberries she had strung for the child.

Matthew Gwynn stared at the blade. He had gone too far to go back. Even death was no use to him, hers or his own. He let the butcher knife fall to the floor.

Merriam picked it up and put it into the sack with the other things. Then she came and stood in front of him and kissed him, her tongue deep in his mouth and her body pressed hard against his sex.

''I love you,'' she said. She had never despised him so much. And yet, it was true that she loved him. ''You will say nothing, once I am gone. You will not follow me.''

Rage came up in his throat like vomit.

''Where will you go?'' he asked her.

''Why, down,'' she replied.

❊ THIRTY-SIX ❊

WAYFARERS

*T*he sky did not clear at morning as the moonset had promised. The air was cool, almost cold, but the clouds still hung like lead close over the river, and at midmorning a fog rolled in from the sea.

By that time, Hannah Trevor, crouched beside the ruins of Francis Ledyard's caravan, had made four unfortunate discoveries.

First, the knot she had tied in her petticoat to hold fast her twelve shillings' savings had come undone during the night's misadventures, and the money was gone. Search as she might, she could find not a single pence.

Second, Arthur the cat had gone off to answer some feline emergency, and no matter how much she called him, he would not come back.

Third, her spectacles, which she had carefully packed in her bundle so as not to risk losing them, were smashed beyond repair.

Fourth and most terrible, her daughter Jennet was nowhere to be found.

No oxcarts moved along the high road. No men on horseback with their wives riding pillion behind them passed her bound for the next of the fairs. It was a strange, smothering prison of quiet. Even the birds did not sing, nor the grasshoppers whirr nor the crickets chirp in the weeds by the roadside.

Across the Manitac, on the higher northern headlands, brownish smoke from the ruins of barns and haystacks mixed with the fog. Leaving Mr. Ledyard's body covered with his cloak, Hannah set off across the sodden flax field toward the little village of Oxford, which lay about three-fourths of a mile inland, on the southern bank of the river.

Nothing, it appeared, had been harmed there. The place proved little more than a hamlet—a half-dozen houses with a common well, a carefully oilskinned haystack near the smithy, and a ramshackle inn at the end of the muddy street. On the common land nearby, a flock of white geese pecked and waddled, and a few cows and sheep grazed peaceably. Near the inn stood an old brick beehive oven where already the wives were taking out their day's baking on a wooden peel, a flat board with a long handle that would lift three or four loaves at a time.

"Mind yourself, Becca!" cried a young woman. "Oh, what have you done now, love?"

A little girl clinging to her mother's skirts began to sob and her mother let the loaves fall with a clatter into the mud. She bent over the child, as Hannah ran the few steps between them.

"What's amiss?" she said. "Is she hurt?"

The other women stared at her. Hannah had forgotten that her clothing was covered with mud and her curls had not seen a hairbrush since yesterday morning and her face was bruised and cut. But she ignored the disapproving looks and forged on.

"Oh, she's burned herself!" said Hannah, looking around the yard. "Where's plantain? Ah! There!"

Against the wall of a nearby chicken house, Hannah spied a healthy clump of the shiny, broad, green leaves and pulled several. Then, crushing them up between her palms, she knelt down beside the howling little girl. She was no more than two years old, dark-eyed and sturdy.

"Come now, Becca dear," Hannah told her, taking the

child's hand in her own. "Oh, yes. It hurts, but it's only a little burn, where the fire kissed you. Hold still." She laid the crushed leaves on the small oval of already-blistering skin. "Hold that close, now, so the juice can find it, and let Mam take you home to the pump and then soak it in coltsfoot-water, cold as you can bear, to take out the rest of the sting."

She stood up and glanced at the muddy loaves near her feet. "They are not so badly spoilt, neither," she said, picking one up. "A little of the crust cut off and they will do for bread puddings well enough. Or stuffing one of those fine geese."

"Hunh! We need no beggarwomen to tell us our business!" said one old woman with a sneer. "Be off, now, or I'll set the dog on you!"

"Let her be!" said Becca's mother. She turned to Hannah. "How do you come here? Who are you?"

"I was traveling with my daughter," Hannah explained, "down the coast road to the fair at Bridgewater. The storm took us and our wagon overturned. When I came to myself by the roadside, she was gone. Wandered off and lost. Oh, please, have you not seen her, a fine girl of eight, with reddish hair in plaits? She cannot hear nor speak, and if any should try to misuse her—"

"I've heard of no lost children, but someone will find her if she be still about. Let me take you to the inn, my dear. Once you have slept—"

"I have no money for inns," said Hannah, and again the women looked from one to the other, drawing conclusions of their own. A runaway wife. A bond-servant escaped a hard master. A gypsy. "All my coin was lost from my bundle when the wagon broke apart," she went on. "And the driver—he is dead. Will someone here fetch in his body? He was—a very—good old man." She swayed slightly, as though she might fall. "I—I will do some work, if you have it. Cooking or sewing or carding. Only I have not eaten for near two days. Some bread and milk, or what porridge is left on your kettle."

"Well, now," said the sour old woman, her eyes narrowed and hard. "You may come home with me to help with the washing, and my son will see to the old man that's dead." She gave Hannah's shoulder a shove, and pain shot down the injured arm. "Well? Come along then, and don't dawdle so! I have no time to spare for a lazybones!"

The meal proved to be small ale and stale brown bread and strong yellow cheese that tasted of the smartweed they let their cows graze on. Across the table, Obed, the old woman's son, sat gazing at Hannah and smoking a cob pipe, tipping the ashes now and then onto the floor. He was a bachelor of fifty, red-faced and sullen.

He offered no insult, but his eyes focused too near the neck of Hannah's gown for her comfort; she slipped a small, sharp-tined cooking fork into her pocket from the old woman's table, just in case.

The minute the niggardly meal was over, her new mistress set Hannah to work.

"Upstairs with you, and strip the beds and bring what soiled linen you find to the wash house in the yard. Chop some wood and build a fire in the pit. There's a yoke and buckets in the barn yonder. The water must be brought from the well on the common. We are not so spoiled we must have our own well in the yard. Go and fetch it when you've done upstairs."

"Have you an old gown I may wear," Hannah asked her, "so that I may launder my own?"

"A servant, and wash your dirty rags with your master's linen? Why, I warrant you've lice in that mop of curls, and God-knows-what elsewhere about you! To work, and no more airs!"

Hannah stood up from the table and pushed in her chair.

"The airs are your own. I am a gentlewoman and no servant, neither yours nor anyone's. I will work what remains of the forenoon in payment for what you have fed me. For stale crusts and the rind of an ill-set cheese, it is quite pay enough."

*   *   *

The bedding stank of old sweat and unwashed bodies. The wood was full of knots and the ax had not been sharpened since Lent. The firepit in the wash house had to be shoveled out and the ashes taken away. The boilers were coated with scum from the last washing and had to be scoured before they were used.

But at last it was ready.

With a sigh, Hannah balanced the heavy wooden yoke on the back of her neck, settled her shoulders to the weight, and hitched the two leather buckets onto their lengths of chain at either side. When she set out for the well, the fog had grown thicker; without her spectacles, she could no longer make out the gleam of the river nor the farms on the opposite bank.

There was no sound on the common but the occasional honk of a goose. The women were gone home with their baking. No children ran and played in the yard.

She went to the well and let down the wooden bucket, and the scream of the ungreased winch rebounded from the closing wall of the fog.

Then all was silent again. Hannah poured the brackish water into her two buckets and set them with the yoke near the wellcurb. A task it would be, she thought, to get linen fine and white in such muck; a green scum of water plants was already settling over the surface of the pails.

But before she returned to her work, she was determined to ask at the inn for word of Jennet. She raked her fingers through her curls and dabbed some of the water onto the scrape on her face to make herself more presentable.

There were no voices from the inn, no horses tethered at the mounting block. Again the quiet closed round her, cool as the arms of the dead.

She walked a few steps toward the inn, then stopped. Did she not hear something? A soft jangling, surely. Chains, was it? The rigging of some mad ship whose ocean was fog?

Hannah's breath felt tight in her chest. The silence bore

down on her lungs and made her ribs ache. She peered into the fog and reached by habit to push up her missing spectacles for a better look.

And then, looming huge out of the drifting whiteness, they were upon her. A great black horse with a blaze on his nose, his harness brasses jangling. A man with dark curling hair and eyes that looked down at her like the clear glass eyes of the blind.

Marcus Tapp.

Two more rode behind him, and two more behind them. Seeing them, she turned and tried to run, but it was no use. Tapp spurred his horse and, leaning down, caught at her arm and pulled her up against the animal's side, her feet kicking and dangling, his hand smashed painfully down on her breast, her ribs banging hard against the horse's sides at every step.

She did not cry out, only hung there, her body no part of her.

The men were laughing, enjoying the triumph. Tapp pulled her higher, then slung her on her belly over the saddle before him. One arm was dangling over the side of the horse, but the other was trapped between the sheriff's body and her own. Hannah's fingers could just reach her pocket and the fork she had stolen from the old woman's table; her hand closed around it, waiting her chance.

She could feel Tapp's free hand fumble with her gown, then clutch the bare skin of her thigh under her petticoat. Rage filled her, its black wings folded softly around her.

He pulled up on the reins and the horse reared a bit, excited. Hannah's body rolled against Tapp's and she felt his hardness; when she fell back, his hand had slipped between her legs.

Now. If I wait another minute, he will finish it. Now.

With all the strength she could muster, Hannah plunged the sharp steel tines of the cooking fork into Marcus Tapp's crotch.

His scream was almost a woman's—high, shrill, terrible. She had done him damage—though not enough, to be sure.

But he let go his hold and she slid down from the horse and ran.

"Take her!" he roared, and his men spurred their horses toward her. "Alive! Do you hear?"

Hannah was running, running.

There was no world around her, neither built nor created. No sky, no river, no solid ground.

There was only the fog, and it was her last friend.

It opened before her and closed its soundless doors after her as she ran. It drove the frightened horses down upon each other before they knew it, and made them jostle each other and rear in confusion. Tapp was already up, furious and shouting. Hannah crashed into the corner of a building, found a narrow passage between it and its neighbor, and crept along it, flat against a rough log wall.

"Here," said a voice. The young woman, Becca's mother, stood in a low doorway. She was pale, like the fog, and when she spoke she had its soft, secret voice. "Come in here. Make haste!"

Hannah bent down and slipped inside and the woman closed the door silently after her.

"What have you done?" said the woman.

"Nothing. They say—"

"No. Do not tell me. I could see how it was. But they have other work here than you. They will search the barns and the houses. Our men are Regulators, and somehow Tapp has found it out. Obed has betrayed them, perhaps, or some other among them. They are all hiding, in the woods and the river islands."

She led Hannah into another room, took up a light cloak of a butternut color and put it around her. The little girl, Becca, was playing with a rag doll on the floor. The woman lit a candle. "Come, this way," she said.

They went down a rough, narrow stair to a cellar. The house was old, built with a great central chimney that heated four rooms, two upstairs and two down. Where its foundations were set into the dirt floor, there were small niches for the storage of root crops and pumpkins in winter. The young woman took a key from one of them and led the way to a heavy cupboard.

"Help me to shift it," she said, and between them, they inched it out from the wall. Behind it was another small door, nearly invisible, a kind of priesthole. The woman unlocked it and put the key into the neck of her gown. "My husband's father was a Tory," she said. "He dug this tunnel during the War, when the raids grew hottest. It leads out to the orchard, and from there to the river. A mile beyond is the ferry. An old man keeps it, and a boy to work the pole. The boy is my brother. Tell them Dorothy says you must go to Gull's Isle, to Mrs. Annable."

"How can I, with my daughter still lost? She is somewhere near, she must be!"

"When the men come back, I will tell them. They'll find her, if she is to be found." Dorothy kissed Hannah's cheek softly and smiled. "I saw what you did to him, bless you. You're a fury, surely. But Tapp will want you the worse now. Go quickly. Godspeed."

From upstairs there was a loud pounding on the door.

"God defend you," Hannah told the girl.

"I have a musket," said Dorothy, and she shoved the cupboard back against the door as Hannah slipped into the fugitive dark.

By the time the light came up and the fog began to roll up the Manitac, Daniel, riding his big sorrel gelding Yeoman, had reached the farmyard where they had tarred and feathered the tax-gatherer.

No one hung now from the huge old tree. There was a woman by the barn, gathering up the spoilt carcasses of a half dozen chickens whose necks had been wrung for their feathers. The wheat field beyond the house had been trampled by more than the rain, and in the small pasture beyond lay the carcasses of a half dozen cattle and a small flock of sheep. A boy was working over one of the sheep, shearing off what he could of the blood-soaked wool.

"Wolves?" Daniel asked the woman, knowing better.

She spat into the dirt and picked up a hayfork. "Get away!" she growled.

"What's happened here?" he said quietly. Yeoman danced a step, fearing her weapon. "Who killed your beasts?"

"Men," she said, and the word was a curse aimed at Daniel. "Men with a pot of tar came last night, dragging the taxman behind them on the end of a rope. They hung Gabriel Bent from my tree and killed my hens to feather him, and this morning other men came and said they must punish me for it, and they shot all my beasts in the field. Sheriff's men! Dogs and monkeys!"

"And Bent? Was he killed?"

"Him? He's living, with half his skin peeled off him and a bash on his head. They took him away with them this morning to be doctored."

"And your husband? Where is he?"

"Dead these five years, damn him. We owned this place once. It is Siwall's, now, and we rent the land that used to be ours. My boys and me, and the girls." She let one of the dead hens fall from her hands. "We shall have no eggs to sell, and no fleeces. No cheeses to make for the Michaelmas fair. No wheat to be ground." She looked up at him. "Is it true they have burnt down Markham's mill and killed all there?"

"No one is killed," he told her. "The mill suffered damage—a burnt roof. But the wheel was turning again when I left."

The woman's eyes went shut for a moment. "I am glad of it," she said softly. "Old Mistress Markham delivered three of my children when we lived nearer. She's a kind heart and a sound hand." She set down the hayfork and looked up at him where he sat on the horse. "Which side are you on, then?"

"No side. I have lost what is dear to me in the storm. Have you seen a woman pass by here, and a little girl with her, with hair the color of mine?"

"I saw no child," she replied. "But last night there

was a caravan passed through. An old man and a black sat the driver's box, but a woman came out of it and would have cut free Mr. Bent. They shot at her to warn her away, and the black man fetched her back to the wagon.''

"Which way did they go?"

"Downriver, toward the Hook, sir. She was darkish and had short curls, and no cap. What is she to you?"

"She is Hannah. My wife," he replied.

After that, he stopped at every farmyard to ask for them, and by the time he came upon the ruined caravan near the flax field, it was midafternoon. They had taken away Ledyard's body, but the old horse still lay dead in the broken shafts, the flies buzzing around him. On the ground, Mister Punch and Mistress Judy and the other puppets lay trampled in the mud.

It was easy enough to see what had happened. The broken wheel. The dead horse. The smashed box of the wagon.

But Hannah and Jennet were nowhere. Not a scrap of them, not a torn bit of skirt nor a hair ribbon nor a whisper of their soft scent upon the jagged boards of the caravan. The rain had washed them from the face of the earth and the fog hid even their bones.

Carefully, slowly, Daniel picked up every broken sliver, moved it aside, looked underneath it. He must have something, something.

He sat down on a pile of rubble, weary and empty, his head bent and his face in his hands. *So here,* he thought, *it ends.*

No one passed by. It was very silent, and he sat there a long time, not thinking, scarcely existing.

Then at last something brushed against his leg; Daniel dismissed it. A fog-borne delusion. It was almost dark now. He was very weary. Surely he had despaired and dreamed of her hands touching him.

But he felt it again, more clearly this time, and looked down. A cat was there, rubbing against his boot to mark him with the scent from its cheek-fur. An old yellow cat, with one ear.

At Daniel's feet lay a dead mole, a gift of welcome. The cat sat down and began to wash its face with a paw.

Oh, I know you, sir. Though you are foolish and human and don't know a mole from a muffin, I will put up with you for her sake.

Arthur the cat had finished hunting and come looking for his friends.

✖ THIRTY-SEVEN ✖

HOW HE DIED IN THE FOG

𝒟aniel took up the cat and put it inside his oilskin coat; it settled against him, purring softly, tired of prowling and willing to be tamed for a while into sleep.

When they reached the village of Oxford it was quiet, like the countryside. There were lights in the inn upstairs and down, and a woman scurried away from the well, carrying a heavy yoke and bucket on her shoulders. A dead dog lay in the middle of the street, trampled to death and unrecognizable except for its bush of a tail. Some windows had been broken out of a house across the common.

Somewhere a child cried. But it was not Jennet.

Daniel pushed back his long oilskin to put the hilt of his sword where he could reach for it quickly. Then he tethered Yeoman and went into the inn, his musket at rest on his elbow and the cat squirming inside his coat.

The inn parlor was small and dark, low-beamed and full of smoke from the hearthfire. A candle burned on the bar counter behind the tapster's grille, and another on a spike-stand by the flight of steps that led to the sleeping rooms above.

The tapster was a long, thin old man, and bald as an egg. "We've no rooms," he said sharply, "if that's what you're after. Not for such as you."

Daniel squinted, trying to see into the shadowy corners.

They were alone in the place, so it seemed. "You may keep your rooms," he said. "Bring me a pint of decent ale and a piece of that mutton I smell from your kitchen, and it'll do me well enough."

The food was brought without further argument and he ate quietly. The cat he set down on the floor with some of the mutton to keep him appeased.

"Here, now!" said the blowsy young girl who came to take the plate away and refill his mug from the ale pitcher. "Where'd *he* come from? He looks a right old rounder, with them lop-sided ears! Get away, Mog! Get away out, you scamp!"

Arthur, finding himself suddenly under attack, arched his back, fuzzed his tail, and gave a resounding hiss. Then he bounded away up the stairs.

"He's my daughter's," said Daniel. "Find me a cage to carry him, and there's a shilling for your pains. I'm in search of her, she and my wife were abroad last night in the storm. Have you seen them?"

The girl's smile faded and her eyes grew hard. "I seen nothing and no one."

"Five shillings, then."

"Piss on your silver," she said.

She started away, but he caught her wrist and kept her. "Who broke the windows yonder? Who rode down the dog in the street?"

"What dog? There is no dog."

"Who sleeps in the room above where there is a candle burning?"

"I'll tell you nothing!"

"Go to hell, then. I'll see for myself."

He stood up and pushed her aside, making for the stairs, but the girl followed him, clutching at his arm.

"Let her be!" she said. "She don't want you! She told me how she run off from you and took her child for to keep you away!'

"Hannah!" he shouted.

He took the steps three at a time. There was a door at

the top of the landing; he pushed at it, but it was barred from inside. ''Hannah!'' he cried again, and began to pound with both fists on the wood. ''Open the door, my heart! I will not take you back. Only let me see you are safe!''

And then, like the low breath of a wind blowing up from the sea or the forest, he heard it. That same strange, monotonous cry, half-moan and half-wail, with an edge of fear upon it, that had risen in the arbor of Mapleton Grange on the night of James Trevor's death.

''Annnnnhhhhhhh!'' screamed Jennet Trevor. ''Annnnnnhhhhhhhhhh!''

''Jenny!'' he shouted. ''Where are you? Christ!''

Daniel kicked at the door, but it would not give way. He fetched the iron candle-spike from the foot of the stairs and rammed the sharp end against the wood to weaken it, then kicked it again. The wood splintered and the door gave way, broken free of its hinges.

Jennet knelt on the bed, her hair unbraided and her face very pale in the candlelight. Around her neck was a chain of dried raspberries.

She saw him and stopped wailing, then jumped down from the bed. Forgetting all caution, Daniel stepped into the room. For a single instant, seeing Jennet, he felt happy and perfect, perfectly complete. He held out his arms for her, laughing.

But before he could reach his daughter, the blade of Merriam's butcher knife struck downward and plunged itself deep in his back.

The room grew very bright, blinding. The candle was a hundred candles, a thousand. They swam round him like the eyes of fishes around the drowned.

He screamed as the wide knife was dragged out of him, and he turned round, staggering, reeling, his sword almost in his hand and his back against the airing cupboard. She was very close and again she struck at him, not even aiming, once, twice, short quick stabs in his chest.

Daniel fell, soundless, and she pulled out the knife again

and snatched for Jennet's hand. The little girl's screams
had begun again and did not stop; he could hear them
where he lay and he tried to pull himself up, but it was
too far to reach her. He dragged himself a few inches,
then lay still, his back against the bedstead.

He could see the woman's face where the rim of the
candlelight struck it. Merriam Gwynn, the minister's sister.

She moved toward the splintered door, dragging Jennet
with her. The orange cat, Arthur, who had been hiding in
the hallway, streaked in through the door and tangled himself in the woman's skirts, clawing mightily to get himself
free. She screamed and kicked at him, furious, raising the
great knife to strike him.

It was the last straw. Jennet Trevor was her mother's
daughter and she had a mind of her own.

I will not be taken away again, thought the deaf child.
I will do what the soft one does when he is angry.

She turned suddenly and sank her small teeth as deep
as she could into Merriam's forearm.

The woman cried out and let go her hold, and Jennet
ran to where Daniel was lying and put her arms around
him, stroking him as she did the cat. "Aaannnhh-ahhhh!"
she said.

Merriam Gwynn's blue eyes seemed to see nothing for
a moment.

"*She* shall not have you. I am your mother," she whispered. "I am. I am. I am."

"Aannnhhh-ahhhhh!"

With both hands, the lost woman lifted the knife above
the child. With a great roar of pain, Daniel rolled sideways
across Jennet's body and landed a hard blow on Merriam's
forearm. He felt the bone crack and she dropped the knife
with a shrill cry.

"Murder! Help! Murder!" cried a voice from the
hallway.

The serving girl had fetched the old tapster and the
potboy to help her, and together they were too much for

Merriam. She rushed past them, knocking the wheezing old man halfway down the stairs as she went.

Daniel pulled himself up by the bedpost and Jennet's arms went round his neck. He rested his face against her warm shoulder and kissed her throat, her face, her eyes. At last he ran his hands over her, looking for damage. There seemed to be blood everywhere, and he thanked God that all of it was his.

"Lem!" cried the barmaid. "Send for the surgeon!"

"No," Daniel told her. "I have no time. Fetch water. And bring me my coat and my musket from below."

While she was gone, he took the pillow biers from the bed and made thick bandages of them. He put one against the deep wound on his back and others on the shallower ones on his chest. The thin old sheet he tore into strips to bind himself tight, so the pressure might stop some of the bleeding.

He knew, of course, that it would not be enough, that he might die. But there were many things that mattered more, and Hannah Trevor was one.

The wound in his back was a hollow ache that grew greater and greater with every minute. Around him the unwounded world drew away and grew smaller, as though he looked at it through his spyglass. The barmaid came, and helped him to wash away some of the blood and fasten the bandages, but when he reached for her arm, his own did not seem long enough to find her.

The shallower wounds in his chest were less urgent, more like the chewing of mice. He hardly noticed them at first.

"Where is my musket?" he said.

"Gone, sir," said the barmaid. "That harpy took it."

He drew a sharp breath of regret. So armed, there was nothing the mad woman could not do, and little defense from it. It was a good musket with a long range. She could strike from the woods and be gone before her victim reached the ground.

Daniel let the barmaid help him into the oilskin coat and then he made his way very slowly down the stairs, each step miles away from the last. His hand gripped the banister, fingers white and clutching, and Jennet kept close by his side with her hand in his.

Through his spyglass of pain he could see that there was another young woman waiting at the foot of the stairs with a dark-haired baby of two or three on her arm. She looked down at Jennet.

"She is your daughter, sir," she said. "That is plain. But which of the women is your wife?"

"She— Hannah is brown-haired, with cropped curls. She's alive? She has been here?"

The story was quickly told. Once the sheriff's men had ridden off, Dorothy said, this other one, this Merriam had come. They had recognized Jennet from Hannah's description. But this woman, too, seemed gentle and honest, and no sheriff was looking for her; she claimed Jennet as her own daughter, with a tale about an unfaithful husband and a runaway servant woman who had twice stolen the child by just such tricks. She asked their protection, and the townswomen, having only just got rid of Tapp, were unwilling to bring him down on them again. They said nothing, went home, and lay low.

"Do not fear for your lady, sir," said Dorothy. "She is safe by now at Gull's Isle, and Tapp will think twice before he affronts Mrs. Annable. She is much respected hereabouts. But—could you not wait until daylight? You are wounded and ill, and the fog is very thick."

Becca's sweet-faced young mother laid a hand on Daniel's arm and it seemed to reach him like the drafts that flickered the candle flames. His fingers were growing numb and his toes were very cold. If he slipped into shock, he might lie so for days. He must find Hannah as soon as he could; Merriam was armed now, and had nothing to lose.

"I beg you will keep Jennet's cat till we come again," he said, "and God protect you. But we must be gone."

*   *   *

Though the ferry was only a few miles downriver, they rode all that night, round and round in a fog so dense they might not have been any longer on the face of the daylight earth at all.

Only the great sorrel horse seemed to see through it clearly. Feeling his master's hand unsteady on the reins and his boots hanging limp in the stirrups, Yeoman chose his own paths. Sometimes they led into patches of woods, sometimes splashed through ponds and crossed sodden meadows. Now and then they arrived suddenly in farmyards where the burnt haystacks stood like ghosts of prehistory, black grave mounds against the fog.

It was everywhere. It lay thick on the ground and muffled the horse's hoofbeats and drifted cool and stinging against Daniel's feverish skin and made a pillow for Jennet where she lay in his arm. It smothered the senses. It erased time and guilt and fear, and the memory of pain and the hope of loving. It suspended thought, and in it he was selfless and free, for nothing mattered but the fog.

No profit, nor loss. No bondage, no freedom.

No marriage, nor giving in marriage.

No honor. No shame.

I am dead, he thought. *So, then. This is how it feels.*

Twice he fell, and somehow climbed back up again onto Yeoman, with Jenny in front of him in the saddle as before. He knew that if he fell a third time he would not get up, and they would find him and bury him where he lay. The wounds were bleeding steadily and the makeshift bandages were soaked with blood beneath the oilskin coat.

Using the edge of his sword, Daniel cut off the two long ends of the horse's reins and made the child tie his feet to the stirrups with the narrow leather thongs. Clumsy Jenny's knots were, that he knew, for her boots were forever untied. But when he bent down to make sure of them, a great pain roared up from inside him and he screamed into the dark.

The fog sent it back, very soft, like a whisper.

Not yet. Not yet.

The night went away, then, and in spite of the pain he knew he was dying. He drifted in and out of the world like a fever ship set adrift on the sea. It would be hours, yet, perhaps even a day. Daniel could do nothing but wait. He sat the horse without thinking or feeling, the warm, dense shape of Jennet against him, her hands gripping his arms.

"Ah, my Lily," he prayed, and kissed her hair.

"Lily-flower," whispered the fog in reply.

The old ferryman and his boy caught sight of them at daybreak. The fog was coming down in great drops like soft rain and the sun struck the Manitac and turned it to crimson and scarlet and gold, with a washing of silver from the sea that lay not a dozen miles downstream.

Gulls wheeled thick around the barge-ferry, mewing and swooping. On the small split-log dock, a second boy was gutting a salmon, and a young girl mending a net, a black-and-white collie beside her.

Daniel had been unconscious for the last quarter mile; Yeoman, proud of his newfound power and protective of his burden, picked his way delicately down to the water-side and stopped, and Jennet woke from her early morning doze and slid down.

Where is this place? she thought, frowning. *Where has he taken me?*

She had crossed with Hannah many times on Hosea Sly's ferry at home and she knew exactly what to do. It was one of her treats to take up Flash's reins and pat the old mare's nose and lead her on and off the flatboat.

Go, or not go? Jennet looked up at Daniel, but he could no longer speak nor even see what he looked at.

Across the narrow space of water lay a broad island midway in the stream. At the riverside, three women were spreading a long piece of new-woven linen to bleach in the sun on the rocks. Above them a narrow lane climbed sharply up through a grove of red spruce to a rock-faced

bluff topped with a wide sheep meadow dotted with larkspur and orange poppies, and several fields of flax, blooming blue and waving softly in the rising breeze. A house
was perched there at the back of a garden, and beyond it
rose the steeple of a church, where swallows swooped and
dived and played at tag.

Home, thought Jennet. She stiffened her small back and
took Yeoman's reins in her hand, and led him onto the
waiting barge.

"Well now, little miss," said the old man with a
chuckle. "Have you a ha'penny for passage?"

She only looked at him, sober and wide-eyed, her head
on one side and the end of one of her braids in her mouth.

"No penny, eh?" The bargee put a thick forefinger to
his lips and licked it, then held it up to catch the wind.
"Nor'wester, Bartley," he said to the boy. "Almanac says
the moon's full, too. No charge to red-headed lasses at
full moon when the wind's stiff from the northwest. Pole
off, Bartley, lad! Pole away!"

The boy grinned and pushed the great long pole down
into the water. The tackle-rope creaked. The windlass
ground into action. The barge began to move slowly along
its guy-rope, out into the stream.

When it bumped the dock on the island, Jennet led
Yeoman onto the shore. The three women looked up from
weighting their linen with stones; the older smiled at Jennet and dropped Daniel a curtsy, but he did not respond.
The bargee did not push off, only stood frowning, with a
hand on Bartley's shoulder.

"Dead, is he?" asked the boy.

"Dunno," said the old man.

Daniel's eyelids flickered open and he stared at the two,
seeing only two specks before him.

The boy looked up at the old man.

"Not yet," he said.

"Soon," said the man.

Jennet handed the reins back to Daniel, but he could
not close his hand upon them. The spyglass world was

very small, now, like something he had read of but never lived in, never seen. Suddenly, like another wound being made in him, memory returned, and he began to fall through a terrible white silence—past dead friends he had known in the War, past his grandfather and his father, past men he had himself killed, disembodied faces, hacked arms and legs. And past women. Children. Lily. Charlotte. Hannah. Nameless women he had buried on roadsides. All dead.

His body lurched crazily sideways and Yeoman, unnerved, turned aside from the road and started up a steep, rocky slope.

Daniel hung there, legs still tied to the stirrups. The weight of his body pulled one foot free and he slipped backwards, his coat falling open. Seeing the blood that soaked his shirt, the women ran to him. By the time they could reach him, the lashing on the other leg had pulled loose and he slid down into their arms. They laid him gently on the grass beside the path, hovering round him like the gulls.

"*Il est mort,*" he heard one of them say. "He is dead."

THIRTY-EIGHT

How He Rose from the Dead on Gull's Isle

That same early morning, Hannah Trevor, sitting at the quilting frame beside the open window of the large, bright upper room they had given her, heard the oxcart creak up the steep path and stop.

But she did not look out at first. The quilt on the frame was not the same as her pattern of red roses, but it set her mind to work in much the same way. Her journal lay open on the quilt top as she stitched, the drawing of angular blossoms and interwoven latticework borders within her view.

She could still quilt, even without her spectacles; once you followed the lines of the piecing, you did it as much by the way the needle pricked at your thumb when it came up and down as by sight, and her grandmother, half-blind at near eighty, had still done twenty stitches to the inch, keeping a true line of a quarter-inch precisely parallel to every seam of the piecing.

It was how she had been with this business of James—half-blind, groping her way along, feeling the needle bite her. But she had not kept the stitches true. She drew back and back, afraid of the pain. Running away as she had been ever since James left her. She had seen no pattern in the manner of his death because she looked too close, seeing only the separate scraps and the stitches she held an inch from her nose.

But now, when Hannah studied at the drawing on her journal page, blurred and made distant by her own weak eyesight, it took on another sort of shape.

Perhaps it was her separation from Rufford. Perhaps it was loneness, being far from Daniel and Jennet, from her uncle and aunt and the house at Two Mills.

Or perhaps it was Gull's Isle itself—a small independent kingdom of peace in the midst of upheaval. An island of women.

"Here you may cleanse your mind and think, and become yourself," Mrs. Annable had told her when she had trudged at last up the steep bluff, weary and exhausted, asking for some word of Jennet. "We all keep our secrets here, and all secrets are equal. If you have done any crime, leave us now and do not bring trouble upon the innocent. If not, you may stay here a month, no more."

"How if I am accused and am innocent?"

"Then you must answer our questions, if they be asked of you." Mrs. Annable studied the face of her guest. "The sheriff's men were here earlier, asking after a woman and child. Are you the woman?"

Hannah did not trouble to explain, only nodded. "I will stay but to rest for an hour," she said. "My daughter—"

"Folk are afraid of the sheriff's men, and they will say nothing if you go asking for the child yourself. Besides, one woman cannot search every copse and cove between the coast and the Outward. My brother Thomas has many friends and they have friends, too. It will be dark soon. Stay here with us till tomorrow midday, and let him do what he may to seek for—Jennet, is it?"

"I will welcome some food," Hannah had told her. "But I cannot stay comforted here while my girl is alone in the dark. I will go with your brother, if you will but lend me a pony."

"And how long will you ride before you tumble off?

Look in the mirror, child, and tell me what use you would be.''

The face that looked back at her was drawn and wild-eyed, and Hannah stared at her reflection as though she had never met herself before. Then her legs gave way and she sat down hard on the chair.

''Ann! Henriette!'' called Mrs. Annable, and two women came silently to see what was wanted. ''This lady is weary. Will you help her to a bed and bring food? She will stay until tomorrow midday.''

''But I have no money,'' Hannah protested. ''I cannot pay.''

''Never mind,'' said the older woman. ''When you are rested, we will find work for you while you collect yourself. The hand and the mind are all of a piece here, and a woman thinks best while she works.''

So Hannah had always found it, and so it proved as her fingers traced the seams of the framed quilt before her.

Triangle. Grace Stark, Hannah Trevor, and the other woman, their secret sister. *Think of me as of a sister, for whom you must pray.*

Triangle. Hamilton Siwall, Matthew Gwynn, Marcus Tapp. *My husband issued the warrant. I allowed James certain liberties. He danced his way onto your pillow at last.*

Square. Merriam Gwynn, Matthew Gwynn, Hannah Trevor, James Trevor. *The rightful station of a wife.*

Circle. Bertha Pinch. Single. Crooked, but oddly perfect in herself, blind-stitched down like the heart of a flower onto the finished design.

And James Trevor, the fourth side of the square, the acme of all the triangles, however you built them. Wherever you looked he was there, like the lattice in her drawing, like the brown-flecked unbleached muslin that was the background color of this simple album quilt in the frame.

Without a background, the pieces were nothing but jagged rags, a crazy quilt like *Maid of Bedlam*. With it, they fell into place and became reasonable.

But you must look at it squarely, and thus far Hannah had not been able to do as much with James. Oh, there were things she could not suppress; some she had told to Daniel and some to her aunt. Only the worst of it she kept, the last few months before her husband had left her—that she still had not faced down and fit into the pattern.

And one other piece, too, still would not come into focus. Isaiah Squeer. Why had he come back? What had he told Daniel?

The Prophet. Her forefinger traced the name onto the plain center of one of the album blocks. But like most people, her spelling was less than perfect.

Profit, she spelled it. She felt cold and pulled her shawl round her and her eyes closed shut upon tears.

"Hannah!" One of the women rushed into the room, a girl called Phillida. Except for the old woman, all here had only Christian names. "Mrs. Annable says you have skill in nursing, you must come! He can't die here! It would be terrible hard to explain to the sheriff!"

"What are you chattering about? Who can't die?"

"Look, down there!" Phillida pointed out of the window. "Henriette and Naomi found him, down by the rocks. He fell off his horse and he's all but gone already, and what will the little one do, his daughter, I expect she is, for she looks just like him, that red hair, but she won't speak, you know, and she can't seem to hear, and if he should die—"

Hannah stood up from the frame and her scissors and thimble clattered onto the floor. In her ears the blood beat hard, as if her head might burst apart at the temples. She shaded her eyes and squinted down into the sunshine, hands gripping the windowsill.

Mrs. Annable's brother, old Thomas, was unloading something from the oxcart, the bargee and his boy lending a hand. A man's body sprawled on its side in the cart, his chest and his back both soaked with blood where they had taken off his long coat.

His hat was gone and his hair was dark, matted with fever-sweat, but the sun caught it and drew out its natural color. A soft reddish brown it was.

And beside the cart, hand in hand with one of the women, another red-brown head. Two long braids. A gown of brown homespun. And one bootlace untied.

When they laid him in the bed, the two old men and the boy already believed him a corpse.

Daniel's breath was too shallow to measure and his heart beat wildly—very fast now and then, but for the most part impossible to feel even when Hannah put her ear against his chest. His lips and fingernails were cyanic, a greyish blue she knew well enough. It meant death could no longer be fought against. You must accept it, keep watch, give what comfort you could. Light candles. Pray for the ebbing soul. Give up. Give in.

"It's too late, my dear," said a woman called Ann. "God's will be done."

"If what lies there is a sample of His will," snapped Hannah, "then it had better be *un*done!"

So they cut off Daniel's clothes and washed the blood from him, and propped him on his left side with pillows to keep his weight off the wounds.

"Light a lantern and bring it," Hannah commanded, and the boy went running. He held it near the great hole in Daniel's back and she bent close, peering at it, then at the smaller wounds on his chest. "These will heal of themselves," she said. "But the back I must stitch. Bring me good linen thread, bleached and boiled. And the best needle you have. Strong, but fine, with a small eye. And lint for packing the wounds." She turned to the girl Phillida. "Have you comfrey in your garden? And calendula? Pick some and mash them. I will come down when I can and make the poultices."

The women went scurrying and while they were gone, Hannah poured water from the pitcher into the washstand basin and scrubbed her hands with the bar of strong lye soap.

When she turned back to the bed, she saw Mrs. Annable standing in the doorway, holding Jennet by the hand. Their reunion had been shortened by Daniel's wretched condition, and now the little girl pulled free and ran to her mother, holding up her face to be kissed.

Hannah bent and leaned a cheek against Jennet's and felt the small arms slip round her waist and the face bury itself in the skirt of her gown.

"Jenny," she said. "You must help me. Do you understand?"

The child let her go and looked up, solemn-eyed.

"Go and sit in the chair, there, by the quilt." Hannah looked in its direction and—without touching her scrubbed hands to it—laid her forefinger to her mouth and shook her head. "Be very quiet. Wait for me. Stay by me. I need your sweetness to look at. You are brave enough to stay, are you not?"

And Jennet, as though she had heard every word, marched straight to the chair and took up the needle and began to stitch upon the quilt, the tip of her tongue sticking out with concentration exactly as if she were at home in Aunt Julia's workroom.

Hannah went back to Daniel and began to sponge away the fresh blood that had oozed from his wounds.

"Your husband?" said Mrs. Annable.

"No. Let one of the boys take his horse and ride it upriver to Rufford. His wife is there, at Mapleton Grange. I think she must be told, in case he should die."

The older woman nodded.

"Surely there is no hope he will live. I heard what you said just now to Ann, when she spoke of it. But you must prepare yourself. You love him, that is plain."

Hannah drew a deep breath and did not answer. The French girl, Henriette, came in with the things she had asked for; some others came too and stood waiting, a half dozen nameless women, a few children, an old man.

"Go now. Leave me alone with it," Hannah told them.

"But surely—Thomas will help you to hold him still. Let Thomas stay, at least."

"No one. Only my daughter. The fight is ours, not yours."

Alone, then.

By the touch of her fingertips she threaded the needle, and by touch, by the habit of quilting in the faint light of candles and winter hearthfires, she alone stitched up the wound.

He lay very still, his cheek smashed down on the pillow. The terrible blue color remained upon his lips, but it had begun to recede from his fingernails and his toenails. She did not bandage the wounds at once. The air would seal them quicker than linen and lint. Once they were closed and the blood had stopped seeping, she would lay on the comfrey poultices and make an ointment from the calendula flowers to speed the healing.

But for now he lay naked on the bed. As she always did with the sick, Hannah put her hands on his body, stroked his arms and his legs and the lightly freckled skin of his shoulders, to make him feel life and know he might come back to it if he chose.

Seeing her, Jennet, too, came and touched him, laying her head against his arm.

What did he feel? At first, nothing. No nerve stirred. No muscle dragged itself free of the fog in which he still lay. In the somnolent prison-chamber of the brain, perhaps, some glimmer entered. But he was a prisoner still.

The little girl came and went from the room, and Hannah sat beside him, sponging the wounds with an extract of shave grass, touching him softly, putting brandy to his lips now and then. Once he reached out for her and gripped her arm painfully with his damaged left hand; it was strong, as the dying are sometimes, clinging to the wreckage as they sink.

The night came, and they brought her candles. There

was a second bed in the room, and they made it up with
clean linen and Hannah put the child to sleep there, facing
Daniel, where he might see his daughter if he woke.

By midnight, his lips were no longer blue, only greyish
white. Hannah went softly downstairs and made up the
poultice, brought it and laid it on the great stitched-up
wound on his back. There was no more bleeding.

"Have you prayed for him?" said a voice from the
doorway. It was the woman called Ann. She was narrow-
boned and there was anger under her piety.

Hannah barely glanced at her. "Here is my prayer,"
she replied, and shifted the poultice an inch.

One by one, the candles guttered. Only a single flame
was left when Daniel opened his eyes and saw her. She
was sitting on the small bed with Jennet and she had the
child in her arms, both of them sleeping. He closed his
eyes to keep them, and slipped down again into the dark.

In the first light of morning came the fever. He grew
wild, fighting and lashing, swearing such oaths as she had
never heard from him before. But Hannah would not let
them tie him down to the bed. She drew close, so that his
fists could find her and strike at her, and he hit out at her,
hard, at her breasts and her face and her arms. She did
not cry out or move away, only sat like a rock beside him,
taking the blows in silence, like a punishment she had
somehow deserved.

At last she caught his hands, held them to her face. He
lay still.

The strain made the wound in his back begin to seep
again. More sponging. More poultices. She made the ointment and applied it, then bandaged him with the help of
old Thomas, Mrs. Annable's brother, to hold him up from
the bed.

About noon, Daniel grew very quiet. Once she thought
he was dead and held a feather to his lips. But he opened
his eyes and stared at her.

Another hour, two. Late in the afternoon, he gave a great cry, so loud that the glass in the window rattled and the dog in the yard set up a howling.

And then, at last, he slept.

"He is much better," said Mrs. Annable, bending over the bed. "Two days since, I should not have believed it. Now you must lie down and rest yourself. Your Jenny will be well enough tonight in the common room down the hall, with the other children."

They brought her a meal of bread and fried bacon and greens, but Hannah was too weary to eat it. She lay down on Jennet's small bed and was asleep before the sun had even thought of going down.

When she wakened, it was dark. No candle was burning, but the moon streamed in at the open window. Daniel was sitting beside her on the edge of the narrow bed.

He bent and let his lips brush her eyes.

"Jenny?" he said.

"Safe. In the next room, sleeping."

He said nothing more. She felt him kiss her mouth, so softly at first that it might have been the wing of a moth that flew too near. Then quickly, again, still with the odd shyness that was always his way. And then urgently, hungrily, his breath in her mouth, his arms slipping round her.

But it was too much. Exhausted, he rested against her, shaggy head on her shoulder, two days' growth of beard scratching her face.

"Much more of this and I shall have to shave you, sir," she said, with a soft laugh that hung warm in the dark.

In another minute he would sleep again, and not wake till morning. Hannah drew his long legs up onto the bed and pulled the sheet over them both and held him.

"God's will be done," she said.

✳ THIRTY-NINE ✳

CAGE-BIRDS, AND HOW THEY FLY

"*W*hat is this place?"

Daniel woke a day later at midday to find himself surrounded by women. One or two, like the girl Phillida, were quite young. Ann was middle-aged, spinsterish. Several had the ripeness and the full breasts of much childbearing. Esther and Jerusha were very old, like delicate pieces of parchment close-written with the same stubby quill. Behind them in the doorway a few men lingered, dull-eyed in the shadows, and Josselyn could hear the voices of children beyond.

"It is my house," said a woman of about Julia Markham's age, with cool hazel eyes and iron-grey hair peeping out of her cap. "I am Harriet Annable. You are welcome here, Daniel. Like the others, you may stay until you are well enough to leave. But while you are here, you must respect our rules. Whatever we have been elsewhere, here we are all friends and equals—and men no more equal than the rest. When you are strong enough you must work as we all do. Are you good at anything?"

Somebody giggled. Daniel smiled.

"I will put my hand to any task, if you teach me," he said. "But who are you? Moravians? Shakers? Some order of holy women, surely?"

The women glanced at each other. One or two laid hands lightly upon whomever was beside them. Then they began to leave the room silently, clustering together in small groups or arm-in-arm, until only the lady of the house remained.

"Have I given them offense?" he said.

Mrs. Annable shook her head. "You spoke of them as holy and it made them shamed. In the War," she went on, "I myself wandered for six weeks in the Outward. What deeds I did—" She was silent for a moment, then continued. "These foreclosures are turning many from their homes. It is another kind of war."

"And you shelter them?"

Mrs. Annable shrugged. "I give them a dry bed. Work to do—we grow our own flax here, and make fine linen. For the most part, I offer them time to heal a bit." She smiled and bit her lip. "Well. You are a man, and wealthy. I do not expect you to understand."

"In the War, I was for a time assigned to the transport of prisoners. Many of their women followed them." Daniel spoke in a low monotone. "Most we left under stones by the roadside."

Mrs. Annable laid a hand on his arm. "But those you see here would not die—or death refused them. At times, they have wished for it. Some have attempted it." She glanced at Hannah, who had come in to sit at the quilt frame. "They are cage-birds, my dear. When you open the cage, they may sit on your shoulder and sing to you. Or they may fly straight at your eyes."

"That warning comes too late," he said, glancing down at his bandages. "Have you never had here a woman called Merriam?"

Hannah sat on the edge of his bed and took his hand in her own. "How is that, sir? Mr. Gwynn's sister, you mean?"

He studied Hannah's face. "She put the knife in me and ran away, and I could not pursue her. But surely she is guilty of the murders at Rufford."

"A dreadful business," said Mrs. Annable. "I have heard of it, of course."

Daniel sat up in the bed and pulled the sheet around him. "It was she who took our Jennet. If I hadn't heard the child cry, she might have her yet. And there's a little hunchbacked woman, Bertha Pinch. Merriam is dear to her, and she knows more than she'll speak of. And a man. Isaiah Squeer."

Hannah got up again and began to pace back and forth in the room. Daniel turned back to Mrs. Annable.

"If you know where Merriam is, if any here knows anything at all of her, I beg you to tell it. She may do more harm yet, if she's not prevented. She snatched up my musket when she ran. We must find her, and see she is stopped."

"Caged, you mean?"

Daniel looked at her steadily. "If she has done murder, she will likely hang. As a man would."

"Would he, indeed? With twelve men for his jury and a man in a wig upon the bench?" She turned to Hannah. "You are accused, and you say it is false. But if Tapp comes for you here, I cannot keep you from him. I can do nothing against the law, or we should all be taken."

"You can help me to find out the truth," Hannah replied. "That is all I ask."

The old woman frowned. "Rest now," she said. "I will consider."

Once he had told Hannah the rest of it, pouring out everything he had learned in the woods and from Mrs. Pinch and at Oxford, Daniel slept again, and Hannah went to be with Jennet for a time.

Then, having seen the little girl well-occupied snapping beans with the other children in the kitchen, she went with a gathering basket into the herb garden. Old Thomas, who kept it, had planted two thick beds of lavender, now in full fragrant bloom, with scarlet- and rose-colored bergamot to add its own spice, and beyond them rosemary, thyme, the hay scent of woodruff, anise, and a tangle of wild yellow clover at the back.

On three sides, lilac bushes no longer in flower hid the small open space from the house, but the river was there below, gleaming like rubbed pewter, and the gulls a dizzy cloud above the headland.

For a long time Hannah worked there alone on her knees, weeding, pruning, gathering the blossoms and laying them carefully into bunches for drying, the air washed clean and cool, the sun a warm hand on her hair, the bees bumping harmlessly against her bare arms.

When at last she realized that most of the light had gone, she stood up, arms loaded with lavender, and found Daniel sitting quietly on the split-log bench a few feet away. He had managed to put on his breeches, but he wore no boots and no stockings, and it had been too much to pull a borrowed shirt over his head. He held his long oilskin greatcoat round him instead, for it was growing cool.

"Idiot!" she cried and dropped the lavender. "How dare you? You'll split open the wound again. Turn round, let me see."

"Let it be," he said sternly, and she did not argue. "I have something I must say to you. Come here and sit down."

Her eyes evaded him. "I have work to do. You've made me spill out all my gathering."

"Come here. Please." He held out a hand to her. "Please."

Hannah sat down beside him, her own hands in her lap. "I am here, sir," she said.

"All these years, you've kept something back from me. What you said to me of James in the winter—your children, how he left you in Boston, how you tried to die there. It's not all. Is it? *Is it?*"

"No." The word was barely audible.

"It has to do with this Merriam?"

"It may. James had a woman before we left Boston. I never knew who she was. I didn't care."

"And Squeer? What has he to do with it? Why does he defame you?"

Now Hannah reached for his spoilt hand and found it and held it. It was dearer to her than the other that was whole.

"Let me keep but one thing to myself," she begged him. "Everything else I will give you freely."

"Tapp will not let you keep it, and I won't live to see him drag you to prison! I must know what it is."

"Help me, then," she whispered. "You are too far away."

He held open the worn old coat to her; Hannah slipped inside its folds, his arms close around her and his chest warm against her side.

"How shall I begin?"

"In Boston. The woman he had."

"Yes. He would go off for days at a time, sometimes weeks. She had some money, I think—he had used up most of my dowry by then, and she would buy him presents. A fine cut-velvet coat, he came home with. A new wig, very grand. We could not have afforded such things. His law practice was never more than a sham, but he fancied rich living. So he gambled, you see. He always lost at cards."

"Yes. I've been told."

"To make it up, he used people. Mostly women. But he had an uncle in the Royal Excise Office and James fawned on him until he got a post there, as an inspector of imported goods. He had represented an importer, a shady fellow called Baggett, and he knew something of the business. But he was dismissed from the Excise Office long before the Declaration."

"For what cause?"

"I was never told," she said. "James would never take counsel with me. But I heard whispers from friends. Embezzlement. Bribes to let in contraband."

Tea. Sugar. Bond-servants.

Ten pound for an ugly one. Thirty or more if she's handsome.

They are cage-birds, my dear. They may fly straight at your eyes.

"Do you think he was stealing goods from the Excise warehouse and selling it through this Baggett?" Daniel asked her.

It had been one of the abuses that had made Tories so hated in Boston—siphoning off British goods and selling them for two or three times their price through unscrupulous importers. Many British officials were appalled by it. But it went on all the same.

After war was declared, British imports were illegal and had to be smuggled in by longboat, through remote areas of the coastline.

Rivers, thought Daniel, *like the Manitac.* No wonder James had been suddenly willing to come up to Maine. "After he was dismissed," he said, "did James continue to work for this Baggett?"

"I believe so, yes. He and . . ."

"Isaiah Squeer?"

Hannah said nothing, but Daniel could feel her body shudder, and he drew her closer still, so that the wounds in his chest began to throb. He took another tack.

"So, James had a woman. Merriam, perhaps. Did you take him to task for it?"

"I? Had I known her name, I would have sent her a letter of thanks. Those days alone were the only peace I had."

"Who was Squeer? Where did he come from?"

"I don't know! For the love of God, Daniel. I cannot!"

"Shhh," he whispered. His body gave way a little under her, and he felt dizzy and weak again. But he couldn't let her go now. "Tell me slowly," he said, "how you lived when you came here."

"My— My aunt would have had me with her," she said. "But James would not hear of it."

"Surely he did not love you?"

''As a boy loves the sound of a breaking stick.''

She let her fingers brush very lightly over his features. It was growing dark in the garden and she needed to see him somehow.

''Besides,'' she went on, ''my uncle was well respected, and James feared what I might tell, I think. He came for me, prancing and snorting like a stallion in my aunt's dooryard. He had the law on his side. I had no choice, and I went with him—it was that or be summonsed and fined, or set in the stocks. He put me in that house by the dockside. It was damp. There were rats in the shingle and they used to run down the walls of my chamber in the night. I lived there for nearly two years. It was— unimaginable.''

Suddenly she drew away from him and stood up, her shape very straight in the darkness.

''One night, after I had gone to my bed, I heard them come in. James and the Prophet—Ike Squeer. They had one or two other men with them. They were drinking. I could smell the rum. Hear the dice rolling. For a while I slept. Then, I—''

Again she paused and he saw her shadow bend. She slipped down to her knees in the dew-soaked grass, her arms locked around her.

''I woke to the sound of my chamber door being opened. It was November, very cold. The bed curtains were closed. I could see a man's shape through the opening. Sometimes, if I pretended to sleep and James had had enough rum to make him sleepy, he would not—bother me. So I hunched on my side. I could hear him undressing. He climbed up the bed-ladder and came in behind the curtains and I— I knew it was not James. He stank of rum and stale sweat and some cheap pomade he greased his hair with. I knew that smell.''

She was sitting on the ground now, her knees pulled up under her chin and her arms hugged tight around them. Rocking, rocking.

"He said I surely must know what he'd come for. That any woman of Trevor's must have paid off his debts in her bed more than once."

"Squeer."

"Yes."

"Forced you?"

"Oh Daniel. Do you not see? He had no need of force. I did whatever he told me. What did I care? It was the only weapon James had left, and it broke me. As he knew it would. I had lived on my pride and he took it away. Next morning they were both gone. I never saw Squeer till he came back here in the spring. When I heard you had fought with him and dismissed him, I was sure he had told you." She hesitated. "He is right, you see. I *am* a Tory whore."

"Hannah." Daniel felt she was slipping away, and he went to where she sat on the grass and put his hands on her head, bent and laid his cheek against her hair. "My Hannah."

"What I had been as a girl, when I trusted the world— It was gone. That night I had no soul in me, Daniel. I was body only. And it could not bear to be forced again and hurt so deep, as it had been before."

Daniel took her hands and she got to her feet. He pulled his coat close around them both again. "Before? Who else? Who—"

She laid her head against his chest. "Why, James. My husband. James."

They spoke no more. Hannah left him there, alone in the garden. She went into the house and gave Jennet her supper of bacon and beans and new bread, then left her curled up like a sleepy squirrel on the trundle in the children's room.

Hannah sat for a long time in the dark of her own room, after that; Mrs. Annable came with candles and one of the other women, a motherly soul called Alice, fussing because Mrs. Trevor had eaten nothing, brought her a plate of summer apples and cheese.

But she did not touch the food, and she did not undress for bed. When Daniel came in at last, she sat quietly stitching at the quilt that was not hers.

He did not come at once into the room, only stood in the doorway. In his hand was a bunch of the lavender from the garden, and some rosemary and spikes of sweet yellow clover.

On the river, a pair of loons called to each other. In the garden, a hermit thrush sang in the lilac hedge.

"You are tired," she said, her eyes lowered upon the quilting. "Do you bleed?"

"Christ," he whispered. "How should I, if *you* do not?"

"Why, women will always bleed, sir," she murmured. "It is our common lot."

He came through the dark room towards her, the flowers still in his hand. The scent of them came with him, and the scent of his blood that was dried on the wounds. He stopped, still at arm's length from her, and let his hand lie in her hair.

"How rare you are to me, Mistress Trevor," he said. "My own heart is not so strong."

She lifted his hand from her. "One thing more I must say. I did not come to you until I was certain Squeer had not got me with child. She is yours, Daniel. I beg you not to doubt Jennet."

He laughed, very softly. "I have eyes, my love. I am not so much like my own father as she is like me." He paused, letting his hand lie on the quilting. "Besides, how could I not love her? She is yours."

"I wanted no other man than you. Even before James left, I had seen you. Heard you speak, so quiet. And your laugh, as it was a moment ago. Secret. Gentle. Afterward, when you had put Jennet inside me— When I sent you away, I said it was only the child I'd wanted of you, but that was a cruel lie. I— I needed your clean heart. That night I first came to you. How you washed the shame from me.''

"And you from me." He looked away from her. "Now I feel I have used you nearly as ill as Trevor."

"Be with me," she said softly. "It is your place, while I live."

Downstairs, someone was playing an accordion and singing, the old song they called "The Turtledove's Lament."

> *So fair thou art my bonny lass,*
> *So deep in love am I,*
> *But I never will prove false to the bonny lass I love,*
> *Till the stars fall from the sky, my dear,*
> *Till the stars fall from the sky.*

Hannah sat down on the bed and began to undo her laces, but her fingers would not obey her.

So he unfastened her bodice and untied the drawstring of her skirt and let it fall, and the petticoat with it. Then he knelt and took off her boots and her stockings. The lavender had fallen to the floor beside him and he broke some of it and rubbed his hands with the oil from the blossoms. He began to stroke her with it, slowly, moving the palms of his hands along her legs and feet, and upward, to her thighs, and the triangles and circles and ovals above them, the complex pattern he had memorized that first night and pulled over his emptiness for eight years, each time he lay down alone to sleep.

The candle flickered in the draft and went out.

Her shift drifted to the floor. Daniel lowered his eyes from her and touched his palms to her breasts, shyly, at arm's length, as though he had never touched any woman before. He bent to kiss her and she stood up to meet him, pale-skinned in the thin darkness of the whitewashed room. The scent rose up sweet and clean from her, like bride's linen kept in a chest.

When he came to her, it was in his own way—slowly,

intensely, with great concentration and no wasted motion, using every inch of himself in her behalf. The brush of his lips on her throat, the scrape of the unshaven stubble on his jaw against her belly, the delicate fingertips that stroked the great pounding vein in her thigh—every part of him was hers, and became her, so that when his sex slipped deep and unforced inside her at last Hannah felt he had been there all along, that he might have been born in her bones, grown with her, would die with her.

She drew in her breath and held it, as though if she breathed they would both disappear from the earth.

Daniel could see her eyes open wide in the dark.

"Wait," he said, and kissed them. "Be patient. Don't move."

"Please. Now."

"Shhh. What's your hurry? Wait for me."

His hands slipped under her buttocks and lifted her closer and she could bear it no longer. She clutched at him, forgetting the wound in his back, urging the warm sticky stuff of his life deep inside her, filling herself with him greedily, again and again. When he tired, she helped him, let him lean on her and rest, held him, laid him back on the bed and took him however she might.

She was bold and wild and fully herself, and yet Daniel had never known her so fragile. She was giving him the last precious inch of herself that James Trevor had worn almost to death.

She was breaking the cage she had called her freedom.

Towards morning they slept, but when it grew light the gulls began their mewing, a storm of them down in the yard.

"Old Thomas is cleaning his catch," said Hannah, with a yawn.

Daniel smiled. "Fine fishing hereabouts. I can witness to that."

"You are lewd, sir, I ought to smack your chops!"

She laughed, but then she grew suddenly sober.

"Daniel?" She lay a little apart from him, soldierlike. "What will you do to Squeer?"

"Kill him."

"For my honor? What honor have I?"

"Mine," he said, and buried himself in her again.

�֍ FORTY ✖

PIECING THE EVIDENCE:

Transcript of the Proceedings of the Common Court, Salisbury, Massachusetts, County of Fairfield, Against Mary Ann Ramsay, Born Stokely, for the Crime of Theft from a Rightful Master October 1783 Honorable Titus Dunham, Justice Presiding Zachariah Marsh, Prosecuting Counsel Edward Ivey, Clerk of the Court Testimony of the Defendant

*M*ARSH: What is your name and from what place do you come?

DEFENDANT: Mary Ann Ramsay, wife of Jacob Ramsay. I was born in Winslip. Just outside Boston.

M: Place your hand on the Testament, mistress, and swear that you—

D: But I cannot read, sir. How if I swear and cannot read what I swear upon?

M: It will be read to you! Make no more delays! Will you

swear to tell the truth, upon the Word of God and the health of your immortal soul?

D: I have no skill in lies. I will speak the truth. I swear it.

M: What man represents you here?

D: None, sir. I have no money for lawyers.

M: But you claim you are a married woman. You have no standing in court unless your husband is present! You cannot speak for yourself or give evidence unless some man is present to stand up with you in your husband's behalf.

Here a gentleman did rise and present himself to the Court, offering to stand up in place of the Accused's husband, who is not to be found.

M: What is your name, sir, and how are you connected to this woman?

WITNESS: My name is Matthew Gwynn. I was a friend of her late brother, Samuel Stokely. We attended Harvard College in the same year. Since she has been in prison here, I have prayed often with her and given her spiritual counsel. I am minister of a small congregation in this city of Salisbury.

M: Very well, Preacher. You will remain. She may answer for herself, but you are responsible that she be permitted to speak without counsel. Do you understand?

GWYNN: I do.

M: Now then, madam. You say you have a husband, Jacob Ramsay. But are you not in fact a spinster? An unmarried woman?

D: No, sir. I am fast married.

M: I remind you of your oath. No record of any marriage is recorded in the name of Mary Ann Stokely within the parish of Winslip or in all of Fairfield county.

D: I cannot sign my name. My brothers were taught the skill of it, but my mother did not consider it seemly for a woman. I was married in the Winslip congregation, to Jacob Ramsay, then of Rufford in the province of Maine. I made my mark in the book. If the clerk of the parish did not record me rightly, I cannot be held to blame.

M: Your husband, then. Where is he? In Maine?

D: No, sir. We settled at Carrington, which is near to Salem, on the coast. He was taken by raiders in the winter, three years since. I believe he is now dead, for I did hear his terrible screams.

M: By Patriot raiders? Or Tories?

D: I do not know, sir. Five men with muskets. They came in the night and dragged him from his bed, and myself with him. I was then eight months with child.

M: They shot this Ramsay? Bayonetted him? How?

D: They put the gun to his head and said he had robbed them, but that is a false lie! And then they beat him. And some other held a musket to my belly, which was then great, and said I must disrobe myself for their inspection, so that I be not concealing some stolen goods beneath my bedgown. And so I did as they said, for else I should surely have died. Then three of them put a rope round Jacob's neck and dragged him out into the yard. They had set fires there, and I heard him scream. I do not know what they did to him, for they left me there in the bedchamber, and the two other men with me, with their guns to my breast. One of them began to lay hands on me, but the other said if they used me there would be some taint of Tory left upon them. But the other said I was but a whore, and no Tory was fast married, for we did not keep the laws as we were told. And so they dragged me out into the yard and served me.

JUDGE DUNHAM: Mr. Prosecutor, I will not hear this! No affront was offered to women by any Patriot fighting in the great Cause of Liberty!

MARSH: Your Worship, many women are hesitant to speak of such. But when a woman is made to remove her attire, as many Tory women were—

J: Then the raiders were Tories themselves! Or else she is a whore, pure and simple! No complaints of such a kind have been filed in this county by any respectable woman!

M: But, Your Worship, my point is that if she filed such

a report, no woman would be counted respectable from that time forward. Many stories have circulated—

J: I am not here to sit in judgment upon stories, Mr. Marsh!

GWYNN: I beg you, sir! Let her conclude her history!

J: Master Preacher, sit down! This woman is accused of running away from her legal master, who purchased her bond for seven years in good faith. By running away, she defrauded him. That is theft, sir, doubly grievous since she made away with an unborn child whose bond this most generous master had also purchased, and which doubled her value. Those are the only points germane to this sitting of the Court.

M: With respect to Your Worship! The fate the child is yet to be proven, sir!

J: I say bosh, Mr. Marsh! We know well enough what these servant bitches are. Besides, most thieves have some pitiful history ready to hand in exculpation. Are you Prosecuting Counsel, man? Or do you brief yourself for the Defense?

M: I believe, Your Worship, that the remainder of her story has, indeed, some bearing on the circumstance of her indenture. If I may be allowed to continue—

J: Oh, very well. But be quick. I am engaged at the governor's table.

M: Now then, mistress. What of this Ramsay? Your lover, Jacob Ramsay?

D: He was my true husband, sir!

M: Very well, let us leave it so for the moment. What did they do with him?

D: They had torches burning in the yard, and I could see him there. They had tied his hands together and dragged him naked through the snow, back and forth in the yard, through the fire they had lit there. He fell and they came at him with an iron to brand him, and he screamed a great scream, so that my heart did crack apart. For I loved him greatly. I—cannot—

M: Clerk! Bring a chair! Is there a physician in the court?

GWYNN: Mary Ann? Take my arm. God will protect you.

J: Mr. Marsh, my gorge rises at these whinings! You are soft, sir! Soft and weak to encourage them!

M: Mistress, I think you must go on with it. What became of Jacob Ramsay?

D: I tried to go to my husband, but they pushed me away. I picked up the ax from the chopping block and struck at them, but they knocked me down to the ground with their fists so that I could struggle no more. They bent over Jacob, where he lay apart from me, and they talked in low voices. Then they marched him away to their boat they had left on the beach, and one set fire to my house. And so they left me.

M: What did you do then? Once they were gone?

D: I took snow between my legs and washed myself.

M: And what else?

D: The house was afire. I went inside, to my linen chest, and found the birth clothes I had made for my babe, and a gown for myself. The fire was falling around me, as though it was rain and the rain burning. And so I came out of the house. And I was then unwell and as I stood by the well-curb, the head of the child came out between my legs and I knew it was dead inside me. And when it was finished, I laid her on the fire, for the ground was hard-froze and I could dig no grave for her. A girl-child, dark haired. Judith, so I called her.

M: How did you come to indenture?

D: Next morning the men came back. They said my husband had betrayed them and owed them great debts and I must pay them. They took me down to the sea, to a boat. There were other women there, and some children. We were taken to Salem, and there sold into bond.

J: This story is the purest concoction, Mr. Marsh! We have laws in this country, sir! We are a nation of free men, not cutthroats and villains who make servants of respectable women! The king may no longer empty the dregs of his prisons into our best families by the indenture of criminals and trulls!

M: And yet, Your Worship, many among us are bond-servants. There is a law that allows it. There is a trade in them that supports thriving businesses. There is also a law that says a married woman may be held responsible for her husband's debts. There is another law that says he may indenture her to pay them, or the state may do so if she is otherwise a burden to the commonalty.

J: Oh, well, if you speak of debtors— Besides, if she has been wronged, she had recourse. She herself says her man was a Tory! Why did she not go to London, to the King's Commission for Redress, and get herself a pension? This is poppycock, Mr. Prosecutor, and I will hold you in contempt if you proceed with it! I shall myself ask her questions.

M: Very well, sir.

J: Now, girl. Stand up when you are spoke to! Remember you are in a court that may hang you for child-murder if you are found guilty.

Here the Defendant is raised from the chair earlier provided, and supported in the arms of Master Matthew Gwynn.

J: That is more seemly. Mary Ann Ramsay. When your bond was sold to Mr. Ashley Farragut, did you sign any paper giving consent?

D: I have said, sir. I cannot sign my name. I made no mark.

J: And yet I have here a contract of service in the name of Mary Ann Ramsay, clearly marked in consent.

D: I made no mark, sir! I gave no consent! I am a free woman, a gentleman's daughter! My father was—

J: We have looked into the estate of your father. His house also burned, it seems. Shortly after your mother's death by stroke, when your last brother's coffin yet lay in the parlor. You set that fire, did you not? As you set fire to your so-called husband's house!

D: No! I have told you—

J: You have told us the purest falsehoods! Jacob Ramsay does not exist! The man whose bastard you bore—if indeed you did not find some crone to root it out of you with the sharp end of a stick!—was James Ramsay

Trevor, a notable villain and smuggler, and a Tory wanted on warrant by the Province of Maine. Where he has, madam, a legal wife yet living. He took your inheritance and squandered it, no doubt, such as it was. Ran into debt to his confederates. And when they came to claim by night what he owed them, you signed yourself into service to buy back his life, fool that you were. Now, mistress. What do you say to that? Eh?

M: Sir! If this man Trevor signed for her, indeed—

J: She signed! She! I have a deposition to prove it, Mr. Marsh! Ha! There! I have taken you by surprise, I vow!

M: What man has deposed to her signing? One who bought her? One who sold her, and profited from it? If she was signed-for by a man not legally her husband, then no consent of hers was given to her bond. She is by law a free woman, and no charge of theft—

J: Are you her defense, you fool? You speak here for the Commonwealth, not for her!

M: I speak for the truth, sir, for God knows it needs some here to own to it!

J: You are in contempt, Mr. Prosecutor! Sit down and be quiet, or I will have you carried in bonds from my court!
    Here the Prosecutor, Mr. Zachariah Marsh, leaves the Court in great wrath.

J: Now, girl. Have you some other means of support than bond-service?

D: My inheritance was used, sir, to buy the small house where I lived with my husband, in Carrington. It is all burnt, and the property seized by the Committee. I may spin and do plain sewing and weave and quilt and wait upon table.

J: Have you a man willing to take you and pay what is owed upon your bond?

D: How can I wed, when I am wed already?

J: You do not comprehend. James Trevor has a living wife, Hannah Trevor, whom he married more than ten years ago. If he went through some sham of wedding you, it is no concern of this Court's. You are no man's wife. You were his whore, girl. That is all.

GWYNN: I will buy her! I will pay what is owed!

J: Hah! And give up your profession, Master Preacher, and turn bawd? At any rate, this Court does not trade in bondwomen. There are but two matters to settle, both plain and to the purpose. First, did this girl run away from the master who had paid a fair price for her bond? Well? Answer it, girl! Did you not run from Boston, from the house of your master, Mr. Farragut?

D: I did, sir. There was a traveling woman came to sew for my master's wife. She was kind to me and comforted me, and I had forgot there was such kindness and comfort in the world. We sang together of an evening, and when we slept we lay sweetly in each other's arms. Beauty, she would call me, and sing until I slept, and so I did not dream as I did before.

J: You? Beauty? She was a fanciful creature, by Gad! And was it she who incited you to run away? What is her name? A warrant shall be made for her!

D: When she had gone, I thought I could not bear it to be alone again. I was three months with child by one of the grooms, for my master said I should be double worth when I was sold, for they might sell the bond of the child with me, and so they would take me away to Canada and sell me to some other again. And so I ran away by night, into the woods. And did wander wide, many days, and there were soldiers, and muskets fired, and a great noise of guns. But I hid myself in the wood many weeks. And again I miscarried, and bore the child and dug out a grave for him in the wood with my two hands, for I had nothing else to dig with. A male child, it was, and I called him Jacob, for my husband who was taken from me. And I wrapped him in my apron and laid him small in the grave, and piled great rocks upon him, so that the wolves should not have him, nor the foxes eat his sweet eyes.

J: This grave was found, mistress! You did not miscarry.

The child was born living, and his throat was cut! You were yourself seen by the Patriot troops of the Portsmouth militia, which was training in those woods, running away from the grave!

D: There be many graves, sir. And many women running from them. Perhaps it was not I.

GWYNN: Sir, you cannot prove this same dead child was hers. She is innocent. I cannot allow—

J: Can you not? I— Oh, confound it! Master Clerk, what is the time?

CLERK: Half past four, sir.

J: I am bid to dine at the governor's at six! This business is a plague! Stand up straight, girl, and face me!

The Accused, supported by Mr. Gwynn, is helped before the Bench.

JUDGE: Mary Ann Stokely, you are found guilty of defrauding your master by stealing forth from his house. Ten stripes shall be laid upon you by the constable's lash. You are further fined the sum of twenty pounds, for which four years further shall be added to the term of your bond. As to the death of your child, who was the property of your said master, it does not suit the Court to prosecute the charge of murder against you. Neither does it suit the Court to encourage such disrespectful and wanton behavior in women of your class. For the child now lost to your master's service and the strain upon his purse of recovering you, you shall serve another five years or pay twenty pounds more, and bear five more stripes.

Here the Accused began to sing very soft and somewhat out of tune.

J: Be quiet, girl! Master Clerk! Put your question!

CLERK: Mistress Mary Ann Stokely, do you understand the sentence that has been handed down upon you?

D: *The cuckoo loves the summer,*
   The wild goose loves the fall.
   The lady loves the blood red rose
   That climbs upon the wall.

GWYNN: She is distracted! I beg the Court to suspend sentence against her.

J: We speak of the sacred rights of property, sir! We have thrown off the bonds of a king to protect them! I will not be induced to discard them for a foolish chit of a servant woman. Master Constable, take her down and deal with her. What is the time now? Good God, the governor! This Court is adjourned!

Deposition
Appended in Evidence

On the twenty-third day of January of the year 1779, Mistress Mary Ann Stokely, spinster, of Carrington, did present herself at my place of business to be indentured, for She was devoid of any other means of Income and sought a Good Master who would provide her Shelter and Board. She was offered a Legal Contract of Seven Years' Indenture, which was read out to her, and made her Mark before witnesses.

To the truth of which, I do Swear and Depose.

Isaiah Squeer, Merchant, Salem, Massachusetts, 1783
Factor, Baggett and Sons of Boston

✳ FORTY-ONE ✳

PIECING THE EVIDENCE:

Report on the Carrying out of Sentence
Commonwealth of Massachusetts vs.
Mary Ann Stokely, Servant
Town of Salisbury, County of Fairfield
Ezekiel Javet, Constable
Edward Ivey, Clerk of the Court
Mrs. Eliza Pattison,
Witness and Midwife
Reverend Matthew Gwynn, Witness
Mr. Ashley Farragut,
Witness and Complainant

On the morning of November 11, 1783, Accused having been found justly guilty of the Crime of Theft and Fraud against her Master, Mr. Farragut, She was brought from the cells and fastened up to the Whipping Post, and her Back bared in the presence of Witnesses of her own Sex. Fifteen Strokes were laid easy upon her, at the which She yet cried out aloud upon God and upon her Husband, that both had deceived her Innocence.

A Meditation upon her Great Sin was vouchsafed her, and a Prayer for her Repentance afterward offered by the Reverend Gwynn.

When Sentence had been carried out, and Mrs. Pattison had performed a Touching upon her to see that no Man had got her with Child in the Cells, Accused was washed and anointed with balm upon her strokes, and remanded to the custody of her Rightful Master, Mr. Farragut.

And She was then sold on the terms of the Court to the Reverend Master Matthew Gwynn, Bachelor, to be his Servant for the Sum of Seventy Pound, to which he gave his Surety and the half in hard Coin.

❈ FORTY-TWO ❈

THE PATTERN HALF-STITCHED

$\mathcal{M}$rs. Annable told them the story of Mary Ann Ramsay with quiet detachment, her own journal open on the table before her in the common room downstairs. When it was finished, Hannah sat silent, winding a hank of newspun linen thread from the spindle.

Daniel stood by the window, watching the women in their light gowns move in and out of the apricot trees in the orchard beyond, picking the first of the ripe fruit. Children darted among them, and he could see Jennet's long braids, flying as she ran.

"Merriam—so she is called now—and Bertha Pinch are like sisters," said Mrs. Annable. "Perhaps lovers; I am no arbiter of sins. We move in a great wilderness, do we not?"

The old woman looked at the pair of them; though they did not seem to look at one another, their awareness was vivid and constant, as if one took in breath and the other breathed it out again.

She went on.

"When the girl was caught and tried, Bertha learned of it. Nothing befell that she did not know of. She trusts very few, and she disliked Mr. Gwynn from the first. Perhaps she was jealous. Or perhaps she was right. He has not a strong nature, but to give him his due, it has cost him much. He was forced to leave parish after parish in order to keep her, once the gossip began. At last, no congregation would any longer employ him. He had resisted doing so before, knowing that this man Ramsay had connections in Maine. But at last he wrote to Rufford, to his cousin Mrs. Siwall, begging employment.''

Mrs. Annable consulted her journal, then went on. ''At the end of March—yes, the twenty-third of this year—he brought her here at Bertha's insistence and tried to free her and leave her with us. But the girl had no rest. It was scarcely a week before she set out for Rufford.''

''And so Gwynn took her back again, and called her his sister, come from Portsmouth to keep his house,'' said Daniel. It was a shabby and desperate deception. But had he not himself been driven to many such these last eight years?

''He was free to wed her decently,'' Hannah said, ''as he tried to wed me. And instead, he used her and called it Christian charity.''

''Ah, but Merriam still believes herself wed to your James. Let me not slander her. She can be most sweet and loving. Only she is brittle, and her wounds fester and do not heal. She does not merely love. She grips hard and in time she devours. She was too much for Gwynn, as she would be for most men. And most women, too. He probably thought a marriage to you would free him of her once and for all.''

''Then she is far gone in her madness,'' Daniel said.

''She is the weapon the world has made of her, and now it says she has too sharp an edge!'' Hannah cried. ''Was the lash mad that cut her?''

''Ah, Mrs. Trevor,'' said the older woman. ''Be careful! Do not pity her too much! You threaten the last illusion that sustains her. Even the memory of the touch of his fingers upon her belongs to you by rights. Unless you are dead, she cannot live to take your place.''

Mrs. Annable went quietly out, leaving them alone in the room.

Daniel stared into the fire. So Hannah must have felt of

his marriage to Charlotte, must feel now. *Even the memory of his touch belongs to you by rights.* And Charlotte—what had she felt, Charlotte who wanted the rights but never the touch? Was it this she had seen in him and feared from the beginning, this terrible power to use and discard?

I am not such a man, he thought, suddenly furious. *I will not carry Trevor's guilt, and Squeer's, and Tapp's, nor even that naughty puppy Jem Siwall's!*

And yet he could not erase Charlotte's face from his mind.

There are many kinds of murderers. Some kill for money, some for fear, some for jealousy. Very few see their crimes approaching and plan them carefully in advance. Most, like the woman called Merriam, are taken unawares by an unspecific fury, like sky in the landscape of their souls that is barely noticed except in the throes of a storm; they live quietly enough until chance springs it shut like a trap upon them, their heels kicking, their fists striking out at the sky.

On the night Merriam plunged the knife blade into Daniel Josselyn's back in the dark little inn at Oxford, she did not know him until he lay bleeding on the floor. On one level, she was conscious of everything, remembered everything, had reasons for everything. On another, she was the pale, naked shape that dived into the water of her mother's garden pond to look for her own empty soul.

At such times, she was long past plotting and planning. When the worst furies seized her, she struck in the dark and ran.

James Trevor—Jacob Ramsay, her husband, as she still thought of him—had appeared in the small town of Winslip, near Boston, about a year before he left Hannah in the Batchelder Street house and some six months before the day on which Merriam's mother sat by her last son's coffin, clutching the black-edged kerchief in her hand. He was clerk in a Boston lawyer's office, he said, in the village on business for his firm. In fact, he invented himself as he went along, believing the lies wholeheartedly, as most proficient liars do.

Merriam—then Mary Ann—had first met him as she stood before the window of the draper's shop, calculating the price of eight yards of a particularly fine sprigged muslin. Her mother refused to spend much on gowns for her plain daughter. Homespun, she insisted, was quite good enough.

"Shall you buy it, ma'am?" he asked her, very softly. "It suits you. You have the ideal coloring for flowers."

She could see his reflection in the cloudy window glass before her—bold, dark eyes; long brown-black hair that fell boyishly across his forehead and was caught with a ribbon at his nape; a wide mouth that smiled easily and laughed softly, his breath caressing the fair hairs on the back of her neck.

When she glimpsed her own reflection, her eyes glazed to avoid it: a plain oval face with wide cheekbones and a nose too long for it, a short upper lip that exposed the front teeth, and pale blond eyebrows that made her look faintly surprised and thoroughly innocent.

James let his finger drift over her reflection in the glass. "Would I be too bold, ma'am," he said, "if I begged the honor of your company tomorrow? I am alone in the town and I know no one. Bring a companion, by all means. Or a sister. I would not put your reputation at the slightest disadvantage."

What did reputation mean to her? She had never had a hope of any husband, any lover. So she came alone, telling her mother she was going to the village for the post as usual. Once, twice, three times they met, on his excursions from Boston. James hired a boat and rowed with her upon the Charles, bringing food and cushions and wine and a book of verse from which he read to her—some rather foolish poems by a Mrs. Seely, of London, the sort of thing ladies are expected to swoon for, especially in rowboats tied up among the willows, with the fragrance of lime-blossom in the air.

"Silly stuff, is it not?" he said, laughing, and closed the book with a snap.

"Yes," she agreed, smiling up at him.

And soon they found something much better to do.

Merriam was twenty-seven, a good ten years past the age when most girls married, and no man had ever kissed her mouth, touched her soft skin, even bothered to look twice at her, until James.

But did he never mean it? Not for even a single second, in the grip of his own myth, when he lay with her hands in his hair and her mouth suddenly eager and bold and irresistible upon his own?

Of course he did. No man can tell a credible lie with his body, and he was utterly convincing because he was himself, in that moment, convinced. Something in him loved her, just as he had loved Hannah when she lay splayed under him on the bedroom floor.

"I love you," he whispered. "I will never hurt you, Mary Ann. How beautiful you are to me."

But he loved himself far more. In six weeks, he began to ask questions. What was her dowry? Only one brother left? Who would inherit the old woman's fortune? Had she a trustee? Her father had been a Tory, had he not? Had the Whig raiders troubled them?

Then came her brother's death, and her mother's. The fire. Relieved to find she was not with child by Jacob as she had feared, Merriam bought a small house with what remained of her inheritance, at Carrington, near the sea, where she could wait for him to come to her.

But he went away instead, up to Maine. On business, he said. He was no soldier, he had no interest in the War, but a man had to put his politics where his fortune lay, and there was more money among Tories.

One year passed. Two years. Then at last he returned without warning, fatigued and excited—and frightened,

Merriam thought as she felt him lie tense in her arms. How soon might they be married, he begged her? He could no longer bear to be parted from her! No, he would not go back to Maine. He could do his business well enough here. What had she left of her inheritance?

They were married quietly, and he brought along only one man for a witness—a lean, sharp-faced man with sullen eyes. The Prophet Isaiah, Jacob called him. His business partner, Isaiah Squeer.

Within a month, she fell pregnant. She was happy, but Jacob seemed angry at first. He went away for a fortnight and when he came back, he had new clothes for himself and small presents for her—a lace, a china cup, a small wooden bird for the unborn child. He came to her sweetly, gently, as before. Read her more poems.

After that, he was often away, back and forth to the coast and inland, dodging the fighting, coming back when he could. The man Squeer she did not see again until he came back to take her away to Salem and sell her into bond. She thought him a friend and clung to him, poured out the story of Jacob's kidnap and capture and her own disgrace.

"You will help me, sure, sir. Will you not?" she cried, weeping softly.

He laughed and struck her hard in the face. "Did you think that great Tory puppy-dog doted upon you? A pale, scrawny, tight-arsed cow like you?"

Squeer told her the truth then. Why, the minister who had wed her to Jacob had been only a friend from the taverns, and no parson at all! They had all got drunk on her money that night and laughed, down in the inn parlor, while Ramsay and his unmarried bride lay upstairs in their bed. Besides, his name was not Ramsay. He was already wed to a wife—a bitch, he called her—in Maine. James Trevor was his name, and not Jacob Ramsay.

And so she was still what she always had been in her mother's house. A plain thing, to be used with disregard. No door had closed upon her, for none had ever opened.

The cup of her grief had no bottom, and God smiled down at her, mildly bemused.

How could her brain take it in and accept it? What defense had she left but to wash her mind of it as she took the snow between her legs and washed the men's dirt from her body?

"I am, I am, I am," she had murmured to herself as she laid her miscarried child on the same fire in which they had heated the brand for James Trevor's forehead, and later, when they made her a servant again and sold her to master after master. "I am. I am loved. I am."

And so she said still, when she swam the river by night and crawled up onto the beach at Gull's Isle. She had left the knife behind her at the inn. Now she had only Daniel's musket for a weapon, and it was useless; when he fought her off, he had broken the bone of her forearm, and she could not even raise the gun to her shoulder. She was sick and exhausted. Her clothes were soaked and ragged, her feet once again bare.

Two days she hid there, ranging the woods, picking wild berries, stealing fruit from the orchard at Spruce Cottage where she had once before taken refuge, and stuffing her mouth with it. With her good hand she scooped a new grave in the woods at the edge of the bluff overlooking the river, and lay down in it softly, and slept.

When she woke, she heard the jingle of bridles. Men were there, riding up the steep hill path toward the house.

She ran to the edge of the trees, the musket in her one good hand like a bludgeon, stock foremost. She could see them now. Five men on horseback. Marcus Tapp, the hard-eyed sheriff. A scrawny man with a squint and another, ale-bellied and mooselike. The Prophet, Ike Squeer. And Matthew Gwynn, ahead of them all, an acolyte in an Easter procession.

Behind them, their hands shackled, six men walked—or were dragged—up the hill. A long rope was tied to

Tapp's saddlehorn and run through the shackles. The men's faces were swollen and bloody from the rocks and branches. One had been slashed with a blade, his cheekbone laid open. Another hobbled with a crutch, his left leg broken and hanging at a mad angle from the hipbone.

She knew some of these, too. Freddy O'Neal. Rufus Penny. And the young one who had been constable at Rufford. Jonathan Markham, with one eye swollen shut and his mouth thick with blood where they had kicked his front teeth in.

Tapp set a fast pace for them, urging the horses uphill at a trot. The prisoners fell, dragged on the rope, pulled themselves up again, and ran on. Regulators, on their way to Wybrow Head to be tried.

They are poor and plain, thought Merriam, *and God mocks them.*

Where shall you lie tonight, Masters?
Why, sir, in Dog's Alley, where all the bread is stones.

And then she heard something from the meadow beyond her, not shackles nor men's groans nor the laughter of God.

"Jenny!" cried a woman's voice. "Stay close, Flower. Do not stray!"

If Jennet Trevor heard her mother, she gave no sign of it. The sun was bright and the larks were diving and dancing, and the high grass of the meadow was dotted with poppies and larkspur. The little girl pulled away from Hannah and ranged in circles around her, wider and wider, wading into grass that grew higher than her head.

Hannah went on alone, parting the tall grass before her, a shawl pulled close around her shoulders and a basket on her arm.

"You," Merriam whispered. She had forgotten the sheriff and his prisoners entirely, her hand gripping the barrel of the gun that was now her only defense against truth. "He is not dead. Once you are gone, he will come back to me. I am his wife. Not you. Not the other one. I am. I am. I am."

❊ FORTY-THREE ❊

THE ROSE AGAINST THE WALL

"*Oh*, ma'am!" cried Mrs. Twig, breathless and flapping, "here's a boy in the yard a-riding upon the major's horse, and John English would speak to you most urgently!"

At the command of Lady Sibylla, Charlotte had allowed herself to be "Hobbled" downstairs to Daniel's library. Now she took a backstitch and laid her work aside.

"Show him in, Twig," she told the housekeeper. "And bring us some tea."

It was two days since Daniel's leaving, and wild days they had been, indeed. Heavier rains upstream had raised the river and flooded the lower meadows, and bridges were out over most of the creeks that fed the Manitac. News had been at a standstill, and rumors rife. But of Daniel and Hannah there had been no word at all.

The steward stumped in, hat in hand and shaggy head drooping.

"What news, sir?" demanded Sibylla. "What of my nephew's horse?"

At the desk by the window, Andrew Tyrrell bent lower over his work.

"Boy rode Yeoman back home, ma'am," English said. "Major's cut up bad, he says. Set upon by a madwoman in some hole of an inn near Gull's Isle and stabbed, back and front. Ferryman found him."

"Dead?" Charlotte's voice set the prisms on the candleglasses swaying slightly.

"Boy says, if he lives yet, it cannot be for long."

For a moment none of them spoke.

"And the child?" Again the prisms danced. "My husband's daughter?"

The steward was startled; it had never been spoken of in Charlotte's presence. "Girl was with him, ma'am. Leading his horse, bless her heart."

"What has befallen Mrs. Trevor?" asked Sibylla. "I must send word to her aunt at once!"

English shook his head. "Boy didn't know. Storm was bad, and a wagon come smash near the Hook. Could be she were under it. Could be she weren't."

Another silence. John English bowed and took his leave. Tyrrell paced before the long windows, now, frowning and pale. The tea arrived, with a puffy-eyed Mrs. Twig to pour it out.

"Oh, my lady," she sniffled. "To think of poor Major Josselyn lying dead in some hovel—"

Charlotte's voice was quiet, but it had never been so loud.

"Go upstairs, Mrs. Twig. Tell Abby to lay out my riding costume."

"But my dear lady! You cannot!"

"And my boots. And we shall need some food for the journey. Pack a basket." She turned to Sibylla. "Your chair, Aunt—it can be borne between horses, can it not? Or set onto a flatboat barge?"

"Naturally." Sibylla did not try to dissuade her.

"Then if you will give me the use of it, I shall go to my husband," Charlotte said. "Mr. Tyrrell will perhaps accompany me, or Mr. English."

Over Charlotte's carefully-coiffed blond curls, Sibylla exchanged looks with Andrew Tyrrell. He excused himself and went out.

"What are you about, child?" asked the old woman sharply.

"I must go to him, Aunt."

"Why? For the sake of punishing him one last time before he expires? If you die in the doing, it will be triumph indeed." Sibylla looked at her steadily. "Or do you go for love?"

Charlotte did not answer. She knew only that she could not stay as she was. For more than four years, she had been a prisoner of her own slight body, kept here in this handsome, well-appointed cell she herself had designed and insisted upon.

Whether she loved or did not love Daniel was no longer very important. It was herself she went to claim.

When Twig bustled in and began to root about in the cupboard for Charlotte's green velvet riding costume with the gold buttons and braid, Bertha Pinch looked up from the new gown she was snipping and stitching.

"What's amiss, Pumpkin?" she cried, and slid down from the window seat. "Why, your piggy eyes have got tears in them from someplace! Have they beat you as you deserve, you silly old hoot?"

"My lady will go traveling and kill herself!" wailed Twig, and sank down on the chaise with the ends of her kerchief to her eyes. "Master is dead or dying, and to be sure it is the same woman killed him that set upon those in the woods."

"Stupid pumpkin! Where, where, where are they?" Bertha stamped both her feet on the floor and pitched the gown full of pins into the corner. "Tell me or I shall act upon my name and pinch you black and blue!"

"Why, Gull's Isle! He lies there, dying, and Mistress will go to him and she will die, too. And what shall become of me? Oh, Twig, when he lived, would have wept to see it. I am undone!"

Bertha left the housekeeper sniffling and wailing and thumped away, down the great stair one slow step at a time, dragging her uneven legs with her and her hump that weighed her one arm almost to the floor. She found

Charlotte at the foot of the stair in Tyrrell's arms, about to be carried up to her own room to change and collect herself before they set out.

"I am a queer creature, mistress," said the little seamstress, looking up at her with wide blue eyes. "My back has a hump and my hip has a lump and I cannot walk in the daylight but a dog barks at me and a ewe suffers a stillborn lamb. Yet I am human, you know, or something like it. My thumbs prick and my teeth bite. I ache in the winter and brown in the same sun that shines upon your counterpane." Her fair face crumpled upon itself. "I loved her. She saw nothing to laugh at in me. Nothing to scorn."

Charlotte looked at Sibylla, then at Tyrrell. "Whom does she speak of?" She let go of the secretary's shoulder and laid a hand gently on Bertha's hair. "What may I do for you, my dear?" she said.

"Take me with you, lady," replied Bertha Pinch, and took the hand and kissed it. "Take me where you are going. As far as to the grave."

They dared not risk the river; it was still very high and the eddies of current around fallen limbs and islands would have swamped any barge of less weight than a ferry. Instead, they slung Hobble between two draft horses, huge, plodding creatures too sure-footed to stumble on the rocky paths and too docile to rear and skitter at chance noises and strange scents. For Charlotte's sake, they traveled slowly and rested often, but always she was eager to go on. Sibylla rode inside with her, and Tyrrell walked by the lead horse, musket in hand, while Bertha Pinch, perched on the back of the rear horse, kept a close watch on the passersby. Sometimes she sang—hymn tunes and old riddle songs and catches—or mumbled children's rhymes.

Charlotte seemed scarcely wearied. But Lady Sibylla, her bright bird's eyes fixed on her nephew's wife without ceasing, could see a wrinkle of strain plow itself deeper and deeper on the pale forehead, and a line of weariness draw down one corner of the mouth.

"Have you any pain, Lottie?" she asked gently.

"None, Aunt," Charlotte replied, smiling. "Look how the sun strikes upon the river! Like the first day of the world! And the trees— We never had such trees at home in England, I am sure! What are those? Gulls?"

She might have been going on some May Day excursion, thought Sibylla, and not killing herself to visit a husband who lay, perhaps, already dead. What had seized the child?

Euphoria. Nerves. The strange, ecstatic release of not minding any longer what became of you, of having no future to protect. The old woman sat back in the cushions and closed her eyes.

Oddly pleasant, she thought. *Perhaps I shall not mind dying so much after all.*

They did not stop for the night. Charlotte would not have it. Tyrrell lighted a faggot of pine for a torch and walked on ahead of the horses, as Bertha Pinch dozed on horseback and Sibylla snored softly upon the cushions.

Did Charlotte sleep? Not a wink. The night was as new to her as the sunlight had been, and for the first time she was not afraid of the dark. She listened to the cries of owls and ovenbirds and hermit thrushes. When they passed through woods, she heard the whispering of the spruce boughs and the rustle of the ferns underfoot, and the cry of a kit fox to her mate in the translucent summer dark. She watched the Manitac, gleaming like a ribbon of glass beside them, a pair of moose come down to drink at the bank. This was what Daniel had wanted to give her, but she could not. Would not, until now.

She had left that old self behind in the house at the Grange. Charlotte smiled to herself as the sedan jounced and swung. Was there, perhaps, still the shape of a pale, prim, nervous lady in the upstairs chamber, bent over an embroidery frame? Did she still primp herself in the mirror

of a morning and sniff with disdain at the unruly sun and
the fragrance of roses?

She laughed in the dark to think of it. Charlotte thought
for a moment of waking Daniel's aunt to tell her the fancy,
but the old woman slept so peacefully that she could not.

Nor did she tell Sibylla her most precious secret. For
almost half an hour, she had felt it, warm and wet between
her legs under the traveling rug. Charlotte Josselyn had
begun to hemorrhage again. It was her last night on earth.

For the most part, Jennet Trevor had been happy since
they came to Gull's Isle. Daniel and Hannah were both
here, and she was allowed to run in and out of the house
with the other children, and all morning she had been
picking sweet orange apricots and stuffing them into her
mouth until the front of her gown was sticky and stained.

Only two things spoiled it. First, she had been foisted
off into a stupid old trundle bed in the children's room
for some nights now, instead of curling up next to her
mother where she belonged. And second, she missed her
soft friend, Arthur the cat.

He was an orange-striped tom, and the orange of the
apricots had reminded her of him. They had left him behind at the inn where the woman was, and the knife. She
had not seen Merriam's face that night and was not afraid
of her until she hurt Daniel. But when she remembered
the knife, it took her back to what she had seen, to the
white face and hands of the man, his white shirt, and the
shining blade in the arbor of roses.

Suddenly afraid again, Jenny hunched down onto her
heels and hugged her arms round her and stuffed her apron
into her mouth to keep from wailing.

"Jennet!"

Her mother's cry reached her as always, a sharp edge
on the dull muddle of half-sounds that made up her world.

I will not be taken and cuddled, thought Jennet, her
small lower lip pulled into a pout. *I know where the soft*

one is. I will go back for him, on the rope-boat. I will go now.

"Jenny, where are you? Come to me!"

Her mother glimpsed her through the long grass, ran toward her, but Jennet darted away again into the middle of the field where the grass was thicker and deeper, and flattened herself on her stomach to hide.

Hannah had wanted to be alone and think, to walk as she walked at home, with only Jennet beside her. Daniel had had to let them go, for he knew she was deciding whether or not to go back to Rufford and face out the charges, and part of her choice concerned him.

Instead, he had followed them, staying far enough behind to avoid being seen, keeping to a trodden footpath through the meadow that came out at the edge of the little fringe of spruces and oaks on the bluff. He could reach the two quickly enough to defend them, and he had his good sword by his side.

But Hannah walked too fast and took shortcuts. He should never have let her come out so far from the house and the gardens alone. They were too far apart, and the sun was in his eyes, and the grass too high, and Jennet never did quite what she was meant to. His hands were cold and his mouth was dry and there was a thin bead of fear-sweat on his forehead.

"Jenny! Where are you, Flower? Come out and let me see you."

Hannah's voice, too, had an edge of fear, and she was not staying far enough from the woods as she'd promised him. If the child had already wandered into the trees and Merriam should be there, waiting . . .

Daniel swore under his breath and began to run, the half-healed wounds throbbing.

It was then that he saw her, just at the edge of the trees. Tall, she was, and very pale, barelegged and shoeless. She wore only her shift, a thin linen, nearly transparent in the bright sun, so that her body shone through it like a torch.

Daniel could see her small, flat breasts as he had that night by the mill pond, with the nipples hard, now, from fear. Her cap was long gone and her dun-colored hair, still kinked from constant braiding, flew out behind her as she began to run toward the lone figure in the deep grass, the heavy gunstock held high in one slender hand.

"Hannah!" he roared. "Hannah! Run!"

She heard him, and turned, saw what confronted her.

There was not a breath of wind, and even the gulls were stifled. Merriam stopped, the musket still upraised. They were no more than five yards apart.

Hannah did not run. The shawl slipped from her shoulders and she lifted her hands slightly in front of her, the palms open, cupped to cradle the air.

"You are hurt," she said, very softly. "Your arm. It looks broken. Come to the house and let me see to it."

Merriam stared at her, blinking in the light. Her breath came too fast and her pale face was flushed bright rose on the throat and cheekbones. She was spent and sick and the rage that had driven her from childhood had all but seeped away. Daniel drew nearer, sword drawn. She ran a few steps and stopped short again, as though a chain held her.

"Where—where is the pretty child?" she said. "Have you lost her?"

Hannah's eyes were closed. "She plays at tag with me. Children have wills of their own."

"I— I took her from you. On the road. She is mine. I will have her."

"You kept her safe when I could not. You have been a kind sister to me, Merriam." She paused, took a step closer. "Grace was your sister, too."

"Grace?"

"The woman at the cabin."

"Ahhh."

The word came like air from a pierced lung.

"I remember," she said. "God wept."

"Did He weep for Jacob Ramsay?"

Merriam's lips opened slightly and she drew a jagged breath. "He loved me," she said in a fierce whisper.

She raised the stock of the musket and took a step toward Hannah. Daniel let his sword drop into the grass and caught the woman's thin arm, and she turned on him, wolf-eyed. For a single moment the heavy gun seemed to hang in the air between them.

"Jacob loved me," she said. "He was my husband. Not yours!"

"Indeed, to me he was nothing," said Hannah quietly. "My only husband stands here."

Then suddenly, the anger gone that had sustained it, Merriam's body crumpled and her legs bent crazily under her, the broken arm limp at her side. Daniel pried her fingers one by one from the barrel of the musket and Hannah bent over her, stroking and stroking the soft, braid-crinkled hair that tangled in the grass.

"We'll go to the cottage," he said, and began to help them up.

He turned to look for Jennet, then, and heard something—a jingling of harness, the steady thump of nearing horse's hooves. Above the heads of the ripe grass, a dark shape seemed to be floating, sailing on top of the grass, the head of the horse stretched before him.

Tapp was upon them before they could run or even breathe, riding straight at them. His men were behind him, dragging their prisoners with them. Squeer, black-eyed and laughing, riding behind them. Gwynn, pale and still upon his own grey horse.

Daniel tried to pull Hannah aside, but he fell with her, the sharp hooves struck at him and he felt the stitches give way in his wound. He lay still for a moment, unable to move, and heard Merriam scream, a high, shrill, animal sound. She fell unconscious and Tapp wheeled his horse at the edge of the clearing and spurred it, riding at Hannah again and again. He had a score to even with Midwife Trevor, and he meant to finish it here.

She ran one way, then the other, but from every direction the horsemen surrounded her, rode at her, boxed her in closer and closer, until she was smashed between them.

"Jennet!" she cried. "Jeeeeeennnnnnet!"

Leaning down from the saddle, Tapp smashed his gloved fist into her temple and she fell almost under the feet of Squeer's horse and lay still. Daniel dragged himself to his knees and managed to level the musket. The back of his shirt was soaked again with blood.

"Let her be!" he roared.

If he fired the gun, he would have to kill Tapp. And there would be no second shot. He would need to reprime the magazine with powder, put another ball into the bore. There was no line of infantry to support him. No cavalry at his flank. While he reloaded they would cut him down, and then do as they liked with Hannah.

"The day is mine, I think, Major," said Marcus Tapp with a sour laugh.

Helpless, Daniel lowered the gun. Two of the horsemen rode at him and one landed a boot square in his face. Hannah was on her feet now, stumbling toward him, blood streaming from a deep cut on her cheek.

Daniel looked up from where he lay on the ground and saw Squeer walk his horse towards her and reach a hand down to clutch at her hair. "A lock for remembrance, eh, mistress?" he taunted. "When I had you, you didn't fight so. Then you were sweet candy indeed."

A sound came from Daniel's lost boyhood, then, and from his grandfather's long lessons, and from all the dead in his dreams.

It began as a soft gasp for breath and grew to the growl of a wolf, and grew again to a great roar of pain, and yet again to the howl that had so long been torn loose from him in his sleep. Jennet's wild cry was in it, for her bones were his bones, but he heard it no louder than she.

No one could have stopped him. Catching up his forgotten sword from the long grass, he lunged up and sidewise, butting the horse with his head, and dragged Ike Squeer from the saddle. In another minute the point of the sword

was at Squeer's throat, the long sharp edge of the blade—
which had already cut through the jerkin and the homespun shirt—poised to lay open his chest.

Tapp's pistol was out and primed. "You, dog!" he said
to the big moose of a deputy. "Take up his bitch and
sling her over a horse and tie her. I've wasted enough
time on women today."

"No! He'll kill me!" croaked Squeer.

Tapp smiled. "Why, you ass. Look at their faces." He
nodded towards Jonathan and O'Neal and the other prisoners. "They won't hang before they say who Siwall paid
to betray them. And they have brothers. Uncles. Friends.
By Christ, if I were a kind-hearted fellow, I'd shoot you
myself. Well? Finish him, Major, and stand up. Or would
you die on your knees?"

Tapp raised the pistol and aimed it, pulled back the
hammer.

"I think not, sir," said the voice of Andrew Tyrrell.
His musket was pointed at the sheriff's back.

Bertha Pinch slid down from behind the secretary and
ran to where her friend still lay half-conscious. She bent
over the limp body and began to keen softly, her face
hidden in the madwoman's hair. They had just come off
the ferry when Merriam screamed, and the little seamstress
would have known the sound anywhere.

But Jennet Trevor heard no screams.

From where she lay hidden, she had heard only the
ripples of energy as the horses passed by. Her mother's
cry reached her, but she did not regard it. When they lost
sight of her, grown-ups always did ridiculous things, as
though she would go up in a puff of smoke when they
were not around. Jennet waited, her palms pressed to the
ground. She felt nothing. No footsteps. Nothing moving
at all.

But the game was no fun if they stopped looking for
her. She stood up and pushed her way through the tall
grass, invisible to those in the clearing at the edge of the
little wood. Even when she stepped out, nobody saw her.

There were horses and many people. Hannah's face was bleeding and Daniel's back was red and Johnnie looked like an oxcart had run over him.

What they said was not important. Jennet heard their looks and their angry gestures. She heard the gun in Tapp's hand and the sword point at Squeer's Adam's apple. She heard Bertha Pinch's cheeks wet with tears. She heard Merriam and was not afraid of her, for she had no knife in her hand now and was kind and sad again, as she had been by the side of the road. But most clearly, drowning out all the others, Jennet heard the goblin shape that had haunted her ever since the night of James Trevor's death.

"Lay down your weapons," Tyrrell urged them.

And Jennet Trevor saw him and began to wail.

"Annnnnhhhhhh!" she cried, and the sun came rattling down on them. "Annnnnnnnhhhhhhhhh! Annnnnnhhhhhhhhh!"

"Christ's wounds!" roared the sheriff, "clap the whelp in the head and shut her mouth!"

"You!" Hannah stared at Tyrrell. "It was you she saw in the arbor! *You* killed James?"

Tyrrell bent nearly double in the saddle and his feet slipped from the stirrups. "You are mistaken," he murmured.

But Jennet's cries did not stop. "The child saw you, man!" Daniel said. "Why else would she scream at the sight of you?"

Matthew Gwynn could not be silent. "Mrs. Trevor is innocent! She has done nothing!"

"Shut up, you fool!" commanded Tapp.

"No, I will speak! Madam Siwall sent me to meet with Trevor, to take him money and a horse. She had written him certain letters of a delicate nature— He— He already knew me. He said he would tell what Merriam was to me, that she was not my sister but my—my— I told him I would have the law on him for a Tory, but he said the law hereabouts would never touch him, that I must bring him more money. What money had I? I had given it all for her sake, all. It was for *her* sake I took the razor with me! If it had not been for her—''

''I shall scratch out your eyes in a minute, you sepulchre!'' cried Bertha Pinch. ''You prayed upon her pillow, a-moaning, 'God forgive me, I love you,' but when you would wed, you sought out another! You are not worth a farthing, and if God does not strike you with lightning this minute, I never shall credit Him more!''

She leaned against Merriam's body, weeping softly, her fists pounding the ground.

Gwynn slid down from the horse and went to them, his face against Merriam's shoulder. She was very quiet. Hope had left her, and she was empty and clean. But Gwynn's thoughts were not of her.

''Christ,'' he whispered. ''I am lost.''

Hannah smashed Jennet against her and held her close, rocking back and forth on her knees in the long, soft grass. At last the wailing stopped and a soft murmur replaced it, like the droning of bees. Overhead the gulls circled again, diving down now and then to explore.

''Merriam had seen James that morning in the woods,'' Hannah said. ''It made her wild, and she struck wildly at whatever was his. Perhaps she knew what she did and remembered it. Perhaps not. But that night she saw him again at the haying dance. When he went to meet you in the arbor, to get what money you had promised to bring him, she was waiting for him, too, and struck him down with the gardener's maul.''

''And Mr. Tyrrell was waiting, too,'' said Daniel. ''My aunt told me you left her for a quarter hour or so, near the time Trevor was killed. If he was already struck down, it was time enough.''

Tyrrell slid down from the horse and stood facing them, his musket still in his hands. It was not aimed now, and it might have been a tree branch or a walking stick as he stared down at it.

''I had waited all evening to speak to him again about

my sister-in-law, Grace Stark,'' he said. His voice was very calm and quiet. ''I spilled some wine on purpose and made an excuse of going into the house. But I went to the arbor instead, for I had seen him go there. There was very little light, only one small lantern, half-darkened to avoid notice from outside. Trevor was hunched on the bench against the lattice.

'' 'I am come for your answer, sir,' I said. 'Will you let Mrs. Trevor divorce you, and will you marry my sister-in-law in an honorable fashion?'

''He did not answer me. I took a step closer. Then I glimpsed her there, in the lantern light.''

''Merriam?''

''Yes. Trevor made a sound and I bent over him. When I looked up, she had gone.'' Tyrrell's eyes found Hannah's. ''He had been struck on the back of the head, very hard. The bone of the skull was splintered.''

''He could not have lived, sir. The dissection has shown so. There was a hemorrhage of the brain.''

''And yet—'' Tyrrell's eyes closed. ''And yet I killed him. I willed it and wanted it, more than my own salvation. I saw the razor on the floor and I bent over and slit his throat, and then I struck him again with the maul, in the chest. How can I explain it? I was four years buried for the likes of him. He was breathing the free air my brother should have been breathing! Using up the world with his greed! When I saw you kill the wolf in the square that afternoon, I already knew, I believe, what I must do. But I did not know when nor how. I laid no plan.'' His hands reached out and he looked down at Jennet. ''I saw her in the arbor, hiding there. But I would never have hurt her. I'm fond of children. How could I hurt such a child?''

Gwynn slipped down Merriam's body until his face was pressed against her bare feet. ''Christ,'' he said again. ''God.''

''What did you do with the maul?'' said Daniel, inexorable.

''I threw it into the river,'' Tyrrell said. ''Then I went

into the house and cleaned off the blood from me. There was a great deal of it.''

"And Mr. Gwynn went back to his patron, Madam Siwall, I suppose?'' said Tapp, eyes narrowed.

"I slipped out from the back of the arbor and went to the copse by the hayfield, where I had tethered the horse. I— I saw Mrs. Trevor there, alone in the field.'' The parson looked up at Hannah. "I wanted to be free, don't you see that? With you, I might have been free of her.''

"But then you found a better use for me than marriage,'' she said. She did not look at him, only kept Jennet close in her arms, her face hidden in the soft red hair. "Merriam would not have thought to put that kerchief into James's hand. Besides, she cannot read. She would not have known my name was on it.''

"How could I live?'' he cried, his face in his hands. "I had to live!''

Tapp's pale eyes took them all in, and his mouth grew hard. "This is no evidence. Mrs. Trevor is guilty and no one else. We found the gold sovereign among her things. Put on those shackles, and tie up my prisoners! She may go with her pig-headed cousin to jail!''

"*I* gave you that gold piece to put more guilt upon her and save myself!'' screamed the preacher.

"Ah, but that is no matter now, is it? For Siwall must have Hannah guilty and silenced. Now why is that, I wonder?'' Daniel turned his sword upon Tapp and Squeer scrambled to his feet, shaking and breathless. "This carrion and Trevor dabbled in smuggling during the War, and Siwall grew suddenly rich about that same time himself, I think. They were up to their old tricks again, in the Canada trade, and I doubt he's beneath a bit of black-market dealing, magistrate or not.''

"He was packed in it with us!'' cried Squeer. "And now he's lily-white, the old bastard, and praying over his money-bags!''

"For his wife's virtue, he sent Trevor away once on a Tory's warrant and had only to buy him off now to be rid of him. Squeer *you* had bought for him, as a spy on the Regulators. But he could never be sure of Hannah.''

The sheriff frowned, but his pistol was lowered. ''You can prove none of this.''

''I have no need.'' Daniel glanced at the prisoners. ''What was it you said just now to this rat's-piss Squeer? 'They have brothers. Uncles. Friends.' You and Siwall will play hell, Master Sheriff, pulling this fat from the fire. You may be rich. But they are many.''

Tapp's eyes closed. ''Enough!'' he said. ''Preacher Gwynn, you sour my guts, but I've nothing material against you. And you, Tyrrell—Trevor died of his blows before you cut him; so far as I'm concerned, you did no worse than let the gas out of a pig's bladder. But you're a pair of God-besotted idiots and if I smell the stink of you again, I'll put a pistol up you both!'' He turned to face Daniel. ''If you are a man, Squeer won't live past the edge of this meadow. Good morrow, sir. I think we are not finished yet awhile.''

He wheeled his horse and rode away through the meadow. Tapp's deputies began to tie Merriam's hands and she screamed when they touched her.

''You can't tie her so!'' Hannah cried. ''Her arm is broke!''

''She'd best get used to it,'' said the loutish one. ''In a week it'll be her neck.''

Merriam did not scream again. They fastened her between two ropes to their horses, laughing and jeering, pawing at her like dogs at a downed beast. At the back of the last horse, the battered prisoners hunched over their own rope, shackles jangling.

Hannah went to where Jonathan stood. ''Oh Johnnie,'' she said, and put her arms round him. ''What have you done, my lamb?''

''Tell Mam and Dada.'' His words came thick and blunted through the swollen, bloody mouth. ''Ask Sally. Forgive me. This is not done.''

The deputies nudged their horses forward into the grass.

Merriam was silent now, beyond pain, her arms out-stretched to the ropes and jerked from side to side as she ran, bare legs pale and thin body moving like a ghost through the shoulder-high blades. When she could not keep up their pace, they did not stop for her and her body dragged, swung from the ropes, then righted itself and ran on again. The deputies' laughter came back to them like the fierce, mad mewing of the gulls.

"Mr. Tyrrell," said Hannah very calmly. "Your musket, if you please."

His sober eyes studied her. "For the dogs, ma'am?" he said. "Or the wolf?"

She looked at him and his eyes turned away from her. But he handed her the gun.

Gwynn sat on the ground beside them, swaying back and forth and mumbling softly. If he knew they were there, he gave no sign, and at first Hannah thought it was still Merriam he spoke to.

"I love You," he said as his hands assumed the position of prayer. "I forgive You. Why do You always make me hurt You so?"

Seeing his chance, Squeer made a run for the woods; Daniel put Jenny down and would have gone after him.

"If you kill him, Tapp will come for you! It's what he wants!" Hannah caught at his arm.

He was growing weak again from the damage and strain. "How can I let him—go?" he whispered.

"He has none of my honor, nor yours! It is *there!*" She pointed to Merriam, where she half-ran, half-dragged herself between the deputies' horses. "You know what they will do with her tonight? Before ever she reaches Wybrow Jail?"

There was no time to consider. Squeer was out of sight among the trees. "Where is my gun?" Daniel said quietly. "It has a better range."

He began to run with it, on a slight ridge above the column of prisoners where the curve of the river let him make up the distance they had already gained. Hannah went with him, her boots slapping softly at his side. He could hear her breath, quick and sharp as the pain in his back.

When they reached a rise above the edge of the meadow, Daniel stopped and braced the barrel of the musket against the fork of a branch. In another minute, the deputies with their prisoner between them broke free of the long grass and came out onto the path.

Then they turned. Stopped to fondle the woman. Her face was bleeding and they had torn her shift at the neck to find her breasts.

The shot was clear. Another hundred yards and they would be out of range. Daniel pulled back the hammer and felt Hannah's fingers lie upon his own as he fired.

The musket ball took Merriam squarely in the back of her head. Her body jerked forward but the ropes did not let her fall, and she arched backwards again, a sweet, pure curve as though she dived up to catch the air. For a moment she stood very straight, as the knowledge of dying washed her clean. Then she caved in upon herself and fell, still jerked and pulled by the frightened horses.

And hung there. Equal. Free.

Dizzy and sick, Daniel let the musket fall and his body slid down the tree trunk. The gulls cried, their wings beating the sunlight, and Hannah took his head against her breast and let her own lie upon him.

"No one be mad, but she is sane as sweet bells in the grave," said the voice of Bertha Pinch behind them. "No one be crooked and lumpish, they say, but she dances with a delicate grace. Oh, Shadow. Kind Shadow. Has no one a knife-point for me?"

❊ FORTY-FOUR ❊

BLOOD AND ROSES

$\mathcal{M}$rs. Pinch told them of Charlotte, then, and by the time they reached her, Tyrrell was already beside her. They brought Hobble uphill to Spruce Cottage and Daniel carried his wife to a large, airy room at the top of the house. Her skirt and petticoats were soaked with blood, and Hannah could barely find the unsteady beat of the heart beneath the thin skin of wrist and throat.

"Bring some brandy at once!" Hannah commanded. "And I saw yarrow in the flowerbeds yonder. Pick some flowers. And senacle root, if you have it. Fresh-dug, and both well mashed." Ann and Phillida went scurrying, and she turned back to Daniel. "We must make her a bath of it, to stop the blood. Have the men fetch a tub and some cool water. Hot will only make the bleeding worse."

"I'll bring it myself," he said.

"You are bleeding too, boy," old Lady Sibylla told him sternly. She had been waiting for him in the hallway. "Be advised, and leave her to these good women here."

But he turned on her, cold-eyed. "Get away! This is your doing! She would never have done such a mad thing but for you and your lecturing!"

He went into Charlotte's chamber and shut the door, leaving the old woman in the passage outside. Hannah said nothing, only began to take off the blood-soaked clothing, and Daniel helped her, hands unsteady and fin-

377

gers fumbling. They put a thick linen towel between Charlotte's legs and wrapped strips of linen around her thighs as was done after childbirth, to stanch the bleeding.

"Let her rest till the bath is ready," she said, and set about repairing the torn wound on his back and bandaging it again.

They brought the hip-bath and the herbs and laid her into the cool water, but it was soon pink with her blood. Sometimes it seemed the hemorrhage had stopped, and Daniel lifted her out and wrapped her in clean linen. But always it began again.

He sat with his back against the head of the bed, a pillow on his knees and chest, and took her against him, his arms around her and his hands against her face. Charlotte's fine, soft hair lay tangled and matted, and Hannah brought a brush and smoothed it back.

When the bath failed, they tried poultices. Balm. Burnet. Tansy. Comfrey.

Another bath.

Another poultice.

Another blood-soaked towel and sheet.

It grew dark.

"She hates the dark," he said. "If she wakes, she'll be afraid."

"I'll bring candles," Hannah told him, and stumbled down to get them from the kitchen.

In the hall just outside Charlotte's door she found Sibylla, holding Jennet asleep in her arms.

"Will she live?" whispered the old woman.

Hannah bent to let her lips brush Jenny's forehead. "I think she cannot."

"Will she take him with her?"

Hannah took the slack-skinned hand of Daniel's favorite aunt and held it to her cheek for the barest flicker of a second, then let it go again. "I must fetch him a candle," she said, and was gone.

Mrs. Annable gave them large pillar candles, nearly a dozen, and they set them extravagantly all about the room.

Bertha Pinch came tiptoeing in and sat sewing at the end of the bed, and Daniel kept his vigil as before, his hands touching his wife's face, her shoulders, the unblemished skin of her forearms.

Once or twice, Charlotte woke.

"Is it morning?" she said.

"Indeed, my love," he replied—though it was not.

"What bird is that?"

Daniel heard nothing. Even the owls had gone to bed.

"That? A thrush, I believe. Yes. Thrush."

"No, sir. That. There, at the end of the room."

It was Bertha she meant, hunched over her stitching.

"Oh," he said. "That's a kind little bird."

"I think it is a bird of omen," she murmured, and drifted again into sleep.

It grew light, and they put out the candles. As though she had waited all night for that moment, Charlotte opened her eyes.

"Daniel?"

"Yes, my love?"

"Have you a book there?"

Of course he had none.

"When have you ever known me without one?" he said.

"Read to me."

"*The Pilgrim's Progress?* A psalm? A poem, perhaps, of Mr. Milton's?"

She smiled. "They are something too somber, sir. Find me a merry piece. Something of Shakespeare, now. Or Kit Marlowe."

He could not help laughing. "When last I read you any of that gentleman, you said he was a great barbarian, and called for a couplet of Pope's!"

She let her hand lie on his. "I am now in a humor for ruffians, sir. Have I not *you* once again in my bed?"

For a moment he could not speak, but she urged him again to read.

" 'Come live with me and be my love,' " he began, " 'And we will all the pleasures prove . . .' "

He broke off. Charlotte seemed to be asleep again. But she was not.

" 'That woods or steepy mountain yields.' There, sir. 'Steepy'? A foul, barbaric word. But pray go on."

" 'And I will make thee beds of roses . . .' " He leaned his head back on the bedstead, his eyes closed. " 'And a thousand fragrant posies.' "

"Ah, my dear," she whispered. "What—sort of foolish coupling was this?"

Daniel did not open his eyes, only sat holding her. " 'A cap of flowers,' " he went on, " 'and a kirtle.' " He waited for her to cap the line. " 'Embroidered all with leaves of—' Lottie?"

Hannah came softly into the room and bent over Charlotte. "She has gone, my heart," she said.

Two days later, they buried Charlotte Josselyn in the yard of the little abandoned church on the island. Daniel returned with the rest to Rufford, but he did not remain there long. As soon as Sibylla was settled once more at the Grange, he was off again. It was said that he had gone on a tour of his lumber camps, but Hannah had no word from him. In another day she must leave for Salcombe, to answer the summons of the Orphanmasters' Court.

"Niece! Niece!" hooted Julia Markham, and Hannah, who was tying up bunches of burnet and lavender in the stillroom, heard her aunt's sturdy legs come stamping through the workroom and in at the door. "Quickly, Hannah! That old dragon from the Grange is come! My kitchen is still in a muddle and God knows where Susan and Kitty have got to! Haste, child! Where's your kerchief? Can you *never* put a decent cap on those curls?"

For once, Hannah made shift to obey her. She tucked a demure bit of lawn in at her neck and shoved one of Julia's caps down on her mop of hair. It was too large and the ruffles flapped on her ears when she walked.

"Where is Jennet?" she said, removing her apron and smoothing her skirt.

"Why, the dragon's got her, and says she must not be Jennet anymore but Aramintha! I hope that cat of the child's nips the old biddy's nose, so I do!"

"Well, madam," said Sibylla. "There you are."

Hannah charged into the workroom like a northeast gale and found the old lady quite at home. They had put her in the best parlor, but it was dank and chilly and smelled of camphor. Besides, Sibylla had never been one to stay where she was put. She sat at her ease with Jennet at her feet, the pair of them winding up bobbins of linen thread for the loom.

"Not so tight," Hannah told her. "If you wind too tight, it will knot and tangle when it is put through the warp."

Lady Sibylla raised an eyebrow. "I am not used to be instructed, madam."

"Nor are you used to the work. *I* would not presume to teach *you* the fashion of society."

"A good thing, too, if that article upon your head is any sample of your taste! What is it, pray?"

Hannah bit her lip. "A cap, ma'am."

"By Harry, I supposed it a cure for the headache!" She put her head on one side and the bird's eyes sparkled. "Will you wear it to this Orphans' Court at Salcombe, to make the men think you modest? For I know you are nothing of the sort."

Hannah pulled off the cap and laid it aside. "Your nephew has spoken to you of the summons."

"*I* have spoken to *him*. He would lay no strictures upon you, and if you are silly enough to reject my proposition, it is your free choice to be a dunce."

Sibylla got up and began to wander about the room. Out in the yard, Jenks and Owen stood with Uncle Henry, passing a pipe amongst them.

"As you know," the old lady continued, "Daniel cannot adopt the child legally, even now that he is widowed.

It is a foolish law, made by foolish old fellows in musty wigs. But there it is.'' She shoved aside a basket of green corn that stood waiting for husking. ''My late brother, Major Josselyn's grandsire, left a sum of money to be used at my own discretion, for my nephew's benefit or that of his family. It is a large sum. Put out at interest, it will bring near three thousand a year. Robert had thought to make Charlotte independent and allow her to return to England and establish herself without Daniel if she chose. But when I arrived here and saw her condition, I knew that could not be.'' She turned and marched across the room again, stick scraping the sanded floorboards, and sat down beside Hannah on the settle. ''I propose to place the money with a Boston solicitor, a Mr. Thomas Petrie, in trust in the name of my nephew's daughter. He has written a letter to these busybodies at the Orphans' Court, and Petrie will appear for you.''

Hannah sat very still. ''I shall appear for myself, if you please. As you observe, I am not overmodest. Nor afraid of men in wigs. Where is Daniel?''

''Believe me, I comprehend you. I am stiffnecked myself, only it is Reason's part to know the time for bending the neck to circumstance. Will you agree to it, my dear?''

''Yes.'' She met Sibylla's look. ''I thank you kindly, for my daughter's sake. I do not mean to be ungracious. Only— Where is Daniel?''

''When he was young and someone had crossed him, he would go off alone. Once he was gone two full days, a boy of no more than ten, sleeping rough in the hills. His mother had vapors and his father beat him blue when he returned. Next time he was crossed, he did the same again.'' Sibylla took the midwife's hand in her own two that were cool and dry as worn silk. ''God has crossed him this time. It may take longer. But he left you this.''

She handed over a folded sheet, and once the old lady had gone off in her chair, Hannah opened it. It was the same note she had sent him by Jem Siwall when she left Rufford with Jennet in old Ledyard's caravan.

God protect you. I am gone, it said.

Underneath, in Daniel's sharp capitals, there was another message.

Wait for me.

" 'Soldier's Joy!' " cried Joshua Lamb, and put his fiddle to his chin. "Swing partners and ladies' chain!"

Jake Bull struck up his drum and Blind Patrick his pennywhistle. Lannie McGregor's pipes were silent tonight, but his plaid swung out and his boots thumped the floor of the Markhams' parlor and when Sarah Firth met him in the middle of the double line of dancers, bright-eyed and laughing, he kissed her as he danced.

The summons to the Orphanmasters' Court was long answered; Lammas fair, too, had gone by and most of the flax was pulled from the field. In another week it would be September, and still Daniel was gone.

Hannah danced one dance with John English, then left Jennet to cavort with the other children and slipped away to the workroom. Mr. Tyrrell was gone away to Halifax and Johnnie in prison and his father too worried to dance.

Besides, what with trying to replace the winter stores Tapp's men had ruined, there had been little leisure for quilting till now, and she preferred it to dancing with strangers. Hannah lighted a candle and set it near the frame, but it was not until she had begun to lay together the torn pieces of her red rose quilt that she noticed the dark shape that sat by the cold hearth.

My Daniel, she thought, and it came like a fresh breeze into the room.

"Have you had supper, sir?" she said aloud. "Or have you forsworn food as well as human company?"

"You do not dance with the rest," he replied. He stood up and bowed to her. "I'm a rough fellow, but I have a good enough foot for a reel. Will you partner me, mistress?"

She went to him, gave him a formal curtsy. "I am not

accustomed to prance with bearded pirates," she said. "But this once."

He took her hand and turned in a slow circle around her to the music of Josh's fiddle. "If you like, I'll go home and come back looking silken and powdered and handsome."

Hannah laughed. "Have you not heard, sir? The age of miracles is past."

They separated again, turned, moved together.

"What do we celebrate?" he said.

"Tomorrow they will raise a new roof on the mill. And this morning Sarah Firth and McGregor were wed."

"Ah, yes. Marriage." He stopped and caught her hand. "A fine old custom. As human institutions run."

There was applause from the parlor as the dance ended. " 'The White Cockade,' " shouted Josh above the chatter. "First couple down the center, back and cast off!"

Hannah raised her hand to begin the new dance, but Daniel drew her against him.

"You have been very long gone," she said, and leaned into him.

"I know. I had to beat up my nerve a bit."

"Am I so fierce, then?"

He found the candle flame and snuffed it with his fingers and kissed her. "Hannah. My dear. Would you dare it?" he said. "I know it's not what you wanted. But—"

"Let me not mistake. Do you ask me to wed you, sir?" she said very quietly.

"Would you risk it with me? Are you brave enough for it?"

"Whatever will Mrs. Twig say?"

"Damn Twig! My aunt may have her for breakfast. What do *you* say?"

She paused for a moment. "You know I can live without you."

"That is understood. And I without you. If you say no, I won't shrivel and wilt, I'm not a wilter. And it's not a threat, either. 'Marry me or I'll leave you to sleep cold for the rest of your days.' "

"Oh, I do love you." She found his mouth and kissed it again, and locked her hands around his waist. "But there are conditions. I will not be an ornament, and sit about playing the harp and sipping tea."

"*Can* you play the harp?"

"Of course not. I can't carry a tune, either. But work is my nature. I am needed by the women of this place, and I will work as I have always done."

"Excellent. You may plant the rose garden to comfrey root, and I shall learn to mow properly. And take up bee-keeping, I think."

"Idiot. But— Daniel? Your aunt thinks me immodest."

"Aren't you? I know *she* is, the most immodest woman alive. She makes a mission of it."

"But I would not have her think—"

"Hannah. Dearest heart. Must we always go on proving ourselves to each other and everyone else? Do we marry or do we not?"

She did not answer for another long space, as the music of Josh's fiddle grew faster and wilder.

"Why I suppose we must, sir," she said at last. "Your son, I believe, expects it."

He laughed in the darkness and she felt his palms lie low and warm upon her belly. "A son, is it? You're damn sure of yourself, girl. Or have you made your peace with God and got a promise of Him?"

"They do say, if a woman sleeps only on her left side in the first three months, it's sure to be a boy. Besides, I have made up my mind to it."

"And your freedom?" His voice was suddenly sober again, and a little afraid. "What will you do for your freedom?"

"Ah," said Hannah softly. "That my daughter expects. That I fight for, as men do. But be warned, my heart. I will fight even you."

He drew close and kissed her again, long and deep. "There's music now," he said. "And so long as it lasts, we will dance."

❋ FORTY-FIVE ❋

THE JOURNAL OF HANNAH TREVOR

12 September, the Year 1786

I write this upon the first day of my Cousin Jonathan's trial at Salcombe Courthouse, with five other men of the Regulators taken in charge for sedition and felony against the Government of these States. I have been with my Uncle to see him. My Johnnie is very ill.

The morning cool, with clouds in the southeast. The mill is new-roofed and the wheat flour at last grinding, and in another month the corn will be dry enough to meal. Major Josselyn and Mister English have helped my uncle to re-build the sluice-gate, and six rafts of cut timber lie at the foot of the race. Since the searching of his house and goods and the taking of Jonathan, my Uncle is sadly changed and takes little joy of his labor. He is grown most suddenly old, and sits watching the fire-ghosts fly up in the grate.

My Aunt will have Jonathan's Sally and young Peter Markham, their son of eighteen months, to stay here and work in the place of Parthenia Jenkinson, who has married and gone to housekeeping. God send Sally and Aunt do not wring one another's necks over how best to baste a meat pudding, for she is a spoiled, stubborn chit. But Aunt must be pleased with her, I am sure, for Sally wears ever a cap with lace ruffles, and smells of amber-water very strong.

She gives me the headache to hear her jabber, but even the headache will temper in time.

My daughter Jennet is much taken with Major Josselyn's Aunt, who will stay with him at Mapleton Grange till we be wed. Mr. Franklin has sent her information of a new invention of his, an ear-trumpet, that he says can make deaf folk to hear. He is, I warrant, a decent sort of old man, though political. But I have little faith in contraptions, for what we are is the hope of us, and not what we make and sell and buy.

If she hear, it will be with her heart and her hands, and if she speak, it will be from the strength of her mind.

But after all, I shall agree to the ear-trumpet. Her father will have her to read and write and cipher, and surely he is right.

For an Empty Vessel is soon Broken, and its Slivers may cut deep.

Matthew Gwynn is found hanged from the guy-rope of the Gull's Isle ferry.

How frail are the Spirits that breathe in us, and in what Mists do we stumble and fall. God pardon the torn Heart of the woman Merriam and Heal it at last in the Grave.

And they who used her to Breaking, may they be so used of God in their turn.

When I think of James Trevor, I see yet darkly and my memory burns.

Waste. Waste. Waste.

Mrs. Pinch is gone with Enoch Luckett to the singschool at Wybrow Head. My rose-colored wool gown is finished, tucked very fine in the bodice and ruched upon the outer skirt. She will make me a fine lace for my mar-

riage, and sew with me upon the bed linens and hangings and gowns. Though I have no dowry to take with me, I shall not shame myself and my daughter to go unprovided to my Husband, however much he says, he would wed me in my shift.

Have pulled the flax in the great field and the lesser, and dug the potatoes to store. Dipped this morning fifty dozen fine candles on the tow wicks of my daughter's spinning. Purchased from Hobart's the Chandlers thirty pound additional fine beef tallow at a cost of one shilling, nine pence, for if we dip no more candles before the snow come, we shall have a dark winter indeed. Uncle has killed the two red pigs and the old black sow that was barren. Forty pound fine pigs' lard. Tomorrow shall boil up the soap.

My Aunt's Receipt for Soap

In a common black Kettle of a Good Size, put to melt upon a Well-laid Fire in the open Air, your white Pig's Lard. To every five Pound of Grease, take from your Barrel a round Quart of Wood-Ash Lye, well-steeped. To this, put a Half or Third a Cup Sal Ammonium, Quarter Cup Soda Ash, and Three Round Soup-Spoons Borax, if it is to be had. When the fat be melted, swing the kettle from the fire and put in the Necessaries to it. Stir well, all in the one same Direction, with a sound wood Spirtle long-handled enough to keep back from the Fumes of the Lye, which may do great harm. When the whole be the thickness of a good pea soup or chowder, or the sauce for a custard, pour it into the soap-boxes, well-lined with muslin or cheesecloth. Score it when it is half-hard. It will set well in cool weather, and harden in a stillroom to keep through the winter.

Attended Mrs. Ann Whitney who delivered at six a.m. a fine Daughter, Elizabeth. Am owed for this six shillings. Received of Mrs. Prince a good white fleece and a pair of ducks, new killed, a present upon my Betrothal.

Molly Bacon is gone from Rufford and her son put to nurse with Mrs. Gately, whose child is dead this three weeks and her breasts very full and sore.

And where Polly, the wife of Mr. George Anson, is gone, I know not. Many are like to take to arms for the loss of her husband, but she may slip like a sad ghost among them and never be seen. A Man is a Candle that Burns on a Hilltop, but a Woman's Light is a Dark Lantern that Burneth underground.

The corpse of Isaiah Squeer found yesternight among the last rafting of logs floated down from the Outward, where my Love has been so long wandering. The body was pierced as though by a Sword. I shall say nothing and ask nothing.

No dissection is forward, the body being too much spoilt by the logs.

My Love has come to Supper, the first Meal I have cooked for him properly. A Salmon from my Uncle's stream, roast in Corn Husks. A fine Veal pie. A Sallad of the purple-spotted Lettuce and the Savory and Cress. A Dish of Beet Pickle and another of Onion. And an Apple pudding to follow. Spruce beer of my own brewing.

My Receipt for Apple Pudding, Baked

Take one pound ripe Apples, well grated or chopped fine with the Great Knife. To this, one cone White Sugar, 9 eggs, one Quarter Pound Butter, one Quart Sweet Cream, no older than the morning, one gill rosewater. A cinnamon. The grating of a lemon, if one is to be had, or if not add some juice of any tart fruit, or a mashing of gooseberry. Currants, raisins and citron to the Taste of the Cook. Cover this with good biscuit and bake in a deep dish in good coals well-raked from the hearth.

The landing horn heard this night as we sat to supper. Mr. Lamb is come from the Inn and says the brig Cincinnatus of Boston brings sad news indeed. Many are in arms against the courts and the government of Massachusetts, and some will march as rebels under Captain Shays to sue for an end to foreclosure. The men are suddenly away to a Town Meeting.

Very late in the night. My love has come to tell me. The town of Rufford has met to direct him to call up the Rufford Company into training and it may be they will march in arms on Salcombe Court. He fears Mr. Washington will send Continental troops to put down these risings and some will surely die.

Whether it be just or unjust, I know not. A soldier's child grows in my body, and we are again at War.

Have pieced together again my quilt of Red Roses and yesterday finished the quilting.

The wild geese are leaving. My mother used to say they were women's souls that had no hearth-place nor harbor. I heard their cries all the night.

Writ by Hannah Trevor, in her own poor hand.
1786

HISTORICAL NOTE

*T*he populist movement known as the Regulators was the vigilante arm of the mass of moderate and law-abiding farmers who tried to redress their grievances against the Equity Courts of Massachusetts in the autumn of 1786. The uprising known to history as Shays's Rebellion commenced when Captain Shays marched his militia upon the Northampton Court of Common Pleas. In this book, those events have been telescoped with others of a similar kind that took place in wilderness Maine nearly ten years later, long after the new Constitution was supposed to have put an end to the mass foreclosures and stabilized the inflated currency. It had not done so, and many sheriffs' sales were disrupted by vigilante groups and surveyors set upon by angry farmers, culminating in the Malta War of 1809.

"I hold it that a little rebellion now and then is a good thing," wrote Thomas Jefferson of Shays's Rebellion, "and as necessary in the political world as storms in the physical. . . . The tree of liberty must be refreshed from time to time with the blood of patriots and tyrants."

He did not say which side was which.

If you liked *Blood Red Roses* and *Hearts and Bones,* you'll love *The Burning Bride,* another unforgettable novel from award-winning author Margaret Lawrence.

The following is an excerpt from *The Burning Bride,* coming in November 1998 in hardcover from Avon Books.

The morning proved dense and grey and windless, but for Maine in November it was clement enough. Unless flood, tempest, or hellfire prevented them, the women of Two Mills Farm had always made the last of their winter candles on November Muster Day.

By Christmas Hannah Trevor would be mistress of Mapleton Grange, Dan Josselyn's fine manor, and rich folk burned candles of wax bought ten pound at a time from the chandler. Unless she had a craving for it, Hannah need never dip a tallow candle in her life again.

It seemed too much like a fairy tale to be credited and, like a stone in her boot heel, the voice of reason grumbled: *Madam Midwife, you are eight-and-thirty, and froward. He finds you pleasant enough in the darkness, no doubt. But willful Hannah Trevor, learn once again to keep a husband's daylight rules?*

She stamped her foot on the sanded kitchen floor and set her Aunt Julia's pewter to rattle in the dresser. *Bother the rules! Bother wax candles! Bother pewter! I am as I am, and he may like me or lump me!*

Her sense of herself thus restored, Hannah tied on her old brown sailcloth wrapper and set to work. It was clock-winding day, and she went out to the chilly front hall to pull up the chain weights, then locked once again the

395

door of the weight-box where the family's small savings was kept.

Finally she tied a woolen kerchief over her short, ash-brown curls, and glanced at herself in the hall mirror as she passed it. How Daniel would have laughed to see her, kerchiefed like a dairy maid!

I shall fail him, she thought suddenly, and it struck like a kick from the child in her belly. *I am not made for a gentleman's lady. I will wound him one day, deep, deep.*

Her first marriage had been like a shipwreck, and after James Trevor deserted her, Hannah swore never to marry again, not even for love. But that resolve had proved foolish delusion. Trevor was dead at last and in her heart she was married to Daniel already; if they might have gone to live on the moon, she would have felt nothing but joy.

But Rufford, Maine, was not the moon and even Daniel could not change the law. Once married, a woman was her husband's legal property until one of them died. Whenever Hannah Trevor let herself consider the risk of it, the blind folly of the laws and conventions that had bound her to a selfish, loveless rascal like Trevor and made her subject to every whim of his will, there was only one word for what she felt.

Surrender, she thought, and the clock ticked it back at her. Hannah sighed, picked up a bucket of tallow, and stepped out into the yard.

As soon as old Henry Markham finished his morning's milking, he and Ethan Berge, the new choreboy, had set up three fire-blackened oak poles in the doorway. Where they met, they were tightly lashed with rope, and under this tripod the women built their dipping fire, the great black iron melting kettle hung over it by a hook and trammel. It would hold just over forty pounds of melted beef tallow, with bayberry wax added for clean burning and fragrance, and it was wide enough to dip ten candles at once on wicks of homespun tow tied to willow sapling poles.

Aunt Julia's choice of a dipping day had earned her many a whisper of Toryism, for most women gladly forgot their household tasks on Muster Day and called it patriotic pride to cheer as the men marched and drilled. From the age of sixteen—though some boys added a year or two, unwilling to watch from the sidelines—to fifty or more, every able-bodied male was required to turn out for training just as they had done under the British governor, in readiness for their own defense. And every year their women trooped into town from the outlying farms and villages—matrons and grannies, old maids with ribbon cockades to their bonnets and a last faint hope of a husband, flirtatious young girls with a mind for mortal sin.

There were lesser company training days four or five times in the year, but this was the last and the greatest, a solsticial festival. *Before Muster,* they would say, as though the stars in their orbits turned round on it. *After Muster, the evenings draw in early. We shall wed before Muster. By Muster, he'll be in his grave.*

If midsummer haying was their summer feast, then Muster Day marked their penitential season. It was followed by a week of hectic preparation, as the women began their holiday baking and fussing: using up expensive cone sugar for pumpkin pie and mince tarts, sending the men out after wild turkies and deer, sprinkling clean new sand on their floors and sweeping it into painstaking patterns—a wheat sheaf border, a vine of grape leaves, or a chain of ivy and pine.

Then came three days of fasting and scanty meals of brown bread or Indian pudding and milk.

At last, with children and grandchildren, aunts, uncles, cousins, and old friends arriving from up and down the river, there was the annual day of Thanksgiving decreed by the Congress, the climacteric of their year. Families gathered at the Meeting House for five or six hours of preaching and singing, and for marriages and christenings that might otherwise have to be put off till spring. And on Thanksgiving night came the great annual ball in the assembly room at the back of Lamb's Inn.

But it was different this year. Because of the rebellion, Congress had set no fixed day for Thanksgiving. Though they still bit their lips to make them red and tucked tiny lavender pillows into their bodices, even the young girls were solemn and tense. Whatever they did, they must do despite troubles. Within the week, their men might be at war again.

The paper dollars Congress had issued to pay the Continental army were worthless and hard coin almost nonexistent, but the General Court in Boston levied more and more taxes to pay off the huge war debts, and though most men survived by barter, the law said that taxes could only be paid in hard coin. For the yeoman farmers and small craftsmen, it was a vicious circle that narrowed and narrowed; foreclosures were rampant and the debtors' jails filled to bursting.

Most men drew the line at armed rebellion and refused to act without a general popular vote. But at midsummer some of the hardest-pressed—Regulators, they called themselves—had exploded after a debt-ridden farmer was shot down in irons for defying the sheriff and the court.

A number of these hotheads were arrested and dragged back to Salcombe for trial, and three men selected at random to be hanged as examples. The last and the youngest of the three was Jonathan Markham, the miller's wild-hearted son.

But two nights before the hanging, a band of Regulators dressed in Indian feathers and masks made of grain sacks had burnt Salcombe jail and courthouse and set all the debtors and prisoners free. No one had seen Jonathan since, nor even had word of him.

From time to time, an emaciated, fever-ravaged corpse was found and brought into the village and each time old Henry Markham brushed his ancient tie-wig, hitched up his oxen, and went to see if this latest poor soul might be his youngest son. At dusk he would return, blank-eyed and stumbling, and find Julia waiting in the door of the stable.

"Husband?" would come her voice from the dark.

"Not yet, Mother," he would tell her, and trudge past her to unyoke the ox.

Hannah paused on the farmhouse doorstep and glanced down the hill at the high road. Though it was still barely light, a half-dozen mounted men were passing; at the head of them, his musket cradled in the crook of his arm with the bayonet already fixed, rode a tall man in a dun-colored greatcoat, with no hat on his head and curling brown hair tied back at his nape. He turned his black horse sharply up the path to Two Mills and Hannah knew him at once, not so much by sight as by a flood of nervous chills along her spine.

Marcus Tapp, High Sheriff of Sussex County, rode with a crew of rowdies and ruffians, most of them wanted for crimes that would be winked at so long as they did what they were bid. But today he left his men patrolling the high road and came on alone, very straight in the saddle, almost one with the horse.

Young Ethan Berge, red-haired, freckled, and not yet fifteen, threw down another bundle of willow saplings for the hired girls. "Oh ho, Kitty!" he cried. "Here's old Tapp, come to hang you and Susan for a-making of candles!"

"Hush! Mistress Sally will hear you!" whispered Kitty, peeping out from under her ruffled cap at a fair-haired young woman who sat idle on the wellcurb.

But if she heard, Jonathan Markham's wife did not mind. She stood up and walked to the edge of the yard, her grey cloak wrapped close around her and her blue eyes fixed upon the tall, lean figure of Marcus Tapp. Sally Jewell had been less than eighteen when Johnnie got her with child and was put-upon to marry her. Even now she was not twenty, and her mind was seldom on her work.

"He's a handsome creature, is he not?" Sally said as Susan passed her with a sapling of wicks.

"Oh how can you say so?" gasped the hired girl. "They do say he's a devil indeed!"

But Sally only laughed. "Why, I may admire even the Devil on horseback, if he keep so good a seat as that!"

Aunt Julia Markham came out of the barn with the large tin chest in which they would lay down the candles to ripen, too intent upon her task to notice the rider's approach. "Where, may I ask, is Black Tirzah this morning?" she demanded. "Sally, did I not send you a week since to bargain for her labor? I warrant you went gadding instead!"

The sheriff's horse wore many harness brasses that rang against each other like bells as he rode into the yard and dismounted. The old woman looked up at the sound, her gooseberry eyes staring and her long nose wrinkled as if she had smelt rotten meat.

"*You*, sir!" She dipped the end of her stirring stick into the fire. The tallow on it caught with a roar and blazed up, and she swung it like a weapon before her. "Run, boy, fetch Husband from the mill! Kitty! Susan! Into the house and bar my doors behind you!"

Hannah's favorite aunt was over sixty, horse-faced and dumpling-shaped, but she had a voice you could hear halfway to Halifax, and when she trumpeted an order, she was seldom ignored. The servant girls scurried and young Ethan took off running.

But Marcus Tapp only smiled. He stretched out an arm as the boy passed, and Ethan went down hard on his backside in the half-frozen mud. "No need to trouble the miller, old woman," the sheriff said. "You may pull in your horns."

Tapp's eyes scanned the yard, missing nothing—the fire, the pails of tallow and bayberry, the grey-cloaked girl. Strange eyes, they were, so pale they seemed in daylight to have no color at all, glass eyes that the world passed through without effect, to be recorded by the raw ends of his nerves.

Some would have called him a libertine, but in fact he was so selective as to be almost ascetic in his pleasures. Oh, he took a certain pride in successful and challenging bedding, as he did in the killing of equals; but Marcus Tapp did not love and he did not hate. At five-and-forty, he had carefully scraped himself clean of all passions, so that if he should die—it was bound to come suddenly and soon to a mercenary soldier—not a shred of him would be left behind to betray him, invested in any living thing.

And Sally was right. He *was* a handsome creature, sleek and bold and strong.

"Very well, sir." Julia doused the burning stick in the water bucket by the wellcurb. "Then state your business and be gone from my house."

But Tapp strode instead to where Hannah was working, calmly tying more wicks to the dipping saplings. "My business is with you, Mistress Gypsy." He smiled and made her a mocking half-bow. "Shall we go into the house?"

The midwife did not look up from her work. "You can have nothing to say that needs walls to conceal it."

"Indeed? Well, then. You attended some two days past an old woman named Esther Jory?"

"The mother of Mrs. Hewins? I did."

"For what ill did you medicine her?" Tapp's gaze was unnerving.

"Why, she'd broke her arm in a fall!" cried Julia, who had been Rufford's chief midwife herself before Hannah's time. "The whole village heard of it. Lady Jory's had fits this year past. With the last one, she tumbled from her basket chair and fell down on the turnspit. It's only God's mercy she kept from the fire!"

"His mercy has limits, it seems." Marcus Tapp smiled. "No doubt you heard the passing bell."

Hannah glanced at her aunt, then back at the sheriff.

"Then Lady Jory is dead," she said softly. 'I am sorry for it."

"You may soon be sorrier. Dr. Samuel Clinch has petitioned the Magistrate's Court to bring charges against you. Now that the old biddy's dead, they are of even greater—"

"What charges?" Julia's voice rang like a gong in the cold air. "If Clinch brings them, why does he not come here to speak them himself? Hah! I warrant his servant, Black Caesar, could not rouse him from whatever doxy he fell down with after last night's hunt!"

Tapp ignored the old lady, his pale eyes fixed on Hannah and a smile of mild amusement on his face. "Clinch vouches you interfere with his enlightened prescribing and dispense your own medicines instead," he told her.

Hannah raised an eyebrow, but no more. "And what else, sir?"

"He accuses you of drunkeness in your watchings."

"Drunkeness?" Julia exploded. "That old rumpot?"

"Aunt! Let him finish." Hannah turned back to Marcus Tapp. "And what else?"

"Lewd conduct."

"With old Lady Jory, sir? Or Mrs. Hewins?"

He looked her up and down. "Mrs. Hewins did not give you a belly that hikes up your petticoat a full two inches from your boots. I must say, it becomes you. Most breeding women look like drabs. His Lordship Josselyn consents to marry you this time, I hear."

Hannah bit her lip. "Is that why you came yourself instead of sending the constable? To offer your blessing on the banns?"

"I don't trust your constable, madam. McGregor's a thick-headed Scotchman." Tapp leaned a fraction of an inch toward her. "Besides, Gypsy, yours and mine is a sporting contest, though you did stick a toasting fork in me last summer. Pray, allow me to take some pleasure in setting eyes on you now and again."

"So long as your hands do not follow them." Hannah met his stare. "But surely Mr. Clinch's imagination is not satisfied with such paltry charges. Or had he some help in contriving better?''

Tapp drew a paper from inside his greatcoat, carefully folded and stamped with the seal of the Magistrate's Court. ''This letter charges you with wrongful prescribing,'' he said. ''Shall I read it out to you?''

''I need no letter to tell the intentions of Samuel Clinch. He has made such charges twice before. They have never been founded. I wonder Magistrate Siwall bothers to act upon them now, when he has so much else of import to concern him.'' Tapp's scrutiny was too much for her at last and Hannah pushed back her hair under the kerchief. ''What says Mrs. Hewins to all this? She was present and saw what occurred.''

''Oh, you women stick to one another, especially when you're broody. She won't hear a word against you. But the Coroner will cut open the guts at noon today, and then we shall see.''

Julia's cheeks were red, and not with the heat of the dipping fire. ''But Sam Clinch *is* the Coroner! What justice is that?''

''Justice or not, it is law. At noon today, in his surgery. Be there if you like.'' Tapp turned back to Hannah. ''Should evidence be found that your prescribings interfered with the efficacy of the—what's it called? This damned elixir Clinch swears by?''

''Laudanum, do you mean?''

''That's it, laudanum. Devil take it, let's have it in plain English. If your weeds and his potions crossed paths and the old woman died of it, you will be charged with murder-by-mischance.'' He smiled. ''It's not a hanging crime like your cousin's, but it'll keep you long enough in my jail to do your groaning there in what—six months? Five? I'd enjoy that—six good months of your company.''

Hannah did not reply and Marcus Tapp turned on his heel to be gone. But before he could mount his horse, Sally ran up to him. Her grey cloak was pushed back so as to show her fair hair to a better advantage, and her cheeks were flushed. "Oh, sir," she said, holding a fine linen handkerchief up to her eyes. "Have you no word if my husband is yet living?"

"You're the traitor's wife?"

The long blond lashes gave an enticing flutter. "I am that unhappy creature, sir," Sally said.

Hannah's eyes sought the patience of heaven. It was enough to make your back teeth grind!

The kerchief drifted down from Sally's hand exactly at Tapp's feet, and he took it up and sniffed it. For a moment he paused, his fingertips teasing her palm. "I've heard no word of your husband," he said, "but I make no doubt we shall find him. Whether he lives or not, it is nothing to me."

Marcus Tapp took up his reins and swung easily into the saddle, then urged his big black onto the steep downhill path.

Inside most things human, there lives a buried self that balances always on a narrow ledge between passion and mind and stubborn endurance. As Hannah Trevor watched Sheriff Tapp's horse skid down the steep slope of the hill, she felt that frail ledge start to crumble beneath her and the self that had so long sustained her begin a long, slow, strange descent.

"The Devil on horseback," she heard herself murmur.

Marcus Tapp looked back at her and laughed.